DOWN
INTO
DARKNESS

DETECTIVE STELLA MOONEY NOVELS
BY DAVID LAWRENCE

Cold Kill

Nothing Like the Night

The Dead Sit Round in a Ring
(published in paperback
as *Circle of the Dead*)

David
Lawrence

DOWN
INTO
DARKNESS

A DETECTIVE STELLA MOONEY NOVEL

THOMAS DUNNE BOOKS
ST. MARTIN'S MINOTAUR ✿ NEW YORK

THOMAS DUNNE BOOKS.
An imprint of St. Martin's Press.

DOWN INTO DARKNESS. Copyright © 2007 by David Lawrence. All rights reserved. Printed in the United States of America. No part of this book may be used or reproduced in any manner whatsoever without written permission except in the case of brief quotations embodied in critical articles or reviews. For information, address St. Martin's Press, 175 Fifth Avenue, New York, N.Y. 10010.

www.thomasdunnebooks.com
www.minotaurbooks.com

Library of Congress Cataloging-in-Publication Data

Lawrence, David.
  Down into darkness : a Detective Stella Mooney novel / David Lawrence. — 1st U.S. ed.
    p. cm.
  ISBN-13: 978-0-312-34742-0
  ISBN-10: 0-312-34742-1
  1. Mooney, Stella (Fictitious character)—Fiction. 2. Women detectives—England—London—Fiction. 3. London (England)—Fiction. I. Title.
  PR6112.A988D69 2007
  823'.92—dc22

                                                              2007024591

First published in Great Britain in 2007 by the Penguin Group

First U.S. Edition: November 2007

10 9 8 7 6 5 4 3 2 1

To Sean O'Brien

1

Someone looking up might have seen her hanging in the tree, but people don't look up unless something draws their attention, and she was almost completely hidden by broad green leaves. Now and then, a breeze caused the smaller boughs to shift and tremble, throwing on the body of the girl a dappled light that camouflaged her as effectively as the leaves.

Late spring in London and much too hot. It was shaping up to be a summer of drought. Newspapers carried long feature articles on global warming with artists' impressions of the deserts soon to take over the south. If you were in any doubt about those predictions, you could sniff the air for the unmistakable, scorchy smell of pollution hanging in the streets. The girls of London, leggy and stylish, had summer highlights in their hair; they wore crop-tops and micro-skirts and gold bangles that showed off their tans. The whores up on the Strip wore even less.

At eight in the evening it was still light and still hot. Couples strolled through the dusty streets arm in arm. There were people going home after a late shift at the office; people on their way to a bar or a restaurant; people with things on their minds. Bikers went by, and kids on Rollerblades; traffic went nose to tail.

A boy sat with his girl on the backseat of the top deck of a bus. They were new as a couple: everything fresh and exciting and slightly feverish. Even in public, they found it tough to keep their hands off each other. He kissed her and, just briefly, put his hand to her breast. The bus was slowing down, backed up in a line of vehicles waiting at a junction; as it came to a stop, its uppermost windows lightly brushed the leaves of a roadside tree. The girl smiled and touched the boy's cheek, then, for no good reason except that they had stopped, looked beyond him to the tree.

Sunlight glanced off the leaves, throwing jittery fragments of white light, and the girl saw what she thought, at first, was a fork in the tree trunk; the leaves rustled and shuffled, and the shape became a broken branch twisting gently in the breeze.

Then, as the breeze quickened, she saw the naked torso as it turned and, a moment later, the face staring across at her, dark as a ripe plum.

2

Stella Mooney and John Delaney were eating at Machado's, a restaurant in a small square just off Notting Hill Gate. Tables had been set up on the edge of the square, and strings of white lights sparkled in the branches of ornamental trees. Candles on the tables shuddered, throwing buttery pools of yellow light in the near-dusk, and swifts were flying wall-of-death circuits, shrieking as they skimmed the brickwork.

Stella said, "Well, fuck you, Delaney."

It was the end of a conversation that had gone like this: "Are you happy with us?"

"With us?" Stella had been eating langoustine, and when Delaney asked his question, she was holding the little creature between the forefinger and thumb of each hand and picking at it with her teeth. She wondered if the question had an edge to it. "Why wouldn't I be happy with us?"

"No reason."

"So . . . Are *you* happy with us?"

"Oh, yeah." Delaney nodded and smiled at her like a man with a secret to keep.

"Just a minute. You're not about to fetch a ring out of your pocket, are you?"

"No." And Delaney started to laugh. "A ring? Jesus Christ, no."

Which is when she said, "Well, fuck you, Delaney," then leaned across the table and stifled his laughter with a kiss.

He topped up their wineglasses and they ate in silence, his eyes on her. She said, "Then what—" in the same moment that her mobile phone rang.

Delaney said, "Don't answer it," more suggestion than instruction, but she had already taken the call. For the most part she listened, and when she spoke, spoke softly. Then she got up, kissed Delaney again, and walked across the square toward the side street where her car was parked.

One or two men at other tables paused to watch her go. Delaney noticed this and smiled, watching her also, making an inventory of his own. Stella was thirty-three: still young enough to use only a touch of makeup. Dark hair, blue eyes, tall and slim but not skinny; her mouth a little too broad, perhaps, and her nose a fraction long: little imperfections that made all the difference. Delaney stayed to finish his meal. He drank the rest of the wine, then ordered a single malt whiskey with his coffee as the cut of sky above the square darkened to lilac. He sat back in his chair and looked up, as few people do, because the swifts had caught his attention. They circled at madcap speeds, shrieking, shrieking, shrieking.

Detective Inspector Mike Sorley had called Stella because he'd worked with her before and reckoned her the best detective sergeant in Area Major Investigation Pool operations. He had already second-guessed Stella's own choices for the team and had checked the availability of DC Pete Harriman, DC Maxine Hewitt, DC Andy Greegan, and DC Sue Chapman. Sue wasn't a street cop; she was a systems coordinator with a tidy mind and an eagle eye.

AMIP-5 covered murder investigations over an area that included Notting Hill, Holland Park, the Kensals, and part of Paddington; it took in some multimillion-pound mansions, a high-rise, no-go, badass wasteland called the Harefield Estate, and pretty much everything in between. North of Notting Hill, as you get to Kensal Green, was the Strip: a blaze of lime and pink and purple neon, shebeens and shanty casinos, hookers working the curbs, deals going down in alleyways, music flooding from doors and windows with a beat so loud and deep that it shifted your viscera.

Stella drove the length of the Strip, then turned off into residential streets. The whole population was out, sitting on doorsteps, lounging in foldaway chairs, drinking beer; the smell of ganja drifted in through the open windows of Stella's car. Bust one, you bust the neighborhood.

The white glow in the sky four streets away was halogen.

Andy Greegan's job was to create an uncorrupted approach to the body, which wasn't easy when it was hanging sixteen feet above the ground. Sorley and Stella discussed a game plan.

"Portable scaffolding," Sorley said, "and drape the tree." They were staring straight up, like star-gazers. Pete Harriman joined them. "How did he get her up there?" he wondered.

"Yes," Stella said, "and when? There's traffic up and down this road all day. People are out and about, especially in this weather."

"He arrives with a body and a rope," Harriman said; "no one sees him, or if they do, they notice nothing unusual. He strings her up . . . How does he do that? Throw her over his shoulder and shin up the tree?"

"What makes you think he came with a body?" Stella asked.

Sorley's phone rang: a contractor with scaffolding and net-drape. He wandered off to take the call.

Harriman said, "You think he killed her at the scene?"

"Easier for him in some ways: he hasn't got a corpse to deal with—deadweight. If she's alive, she's more portable."

"Or else, easier if she's dead. The killing's done." They were still looking up. Stella's neck was paining her. Harriman added, "So—alive or dead, it must have been under cover of darkness, yes?"

"Seems that way."

"In which case, she's been up there since before dawn."

Stella lowered her head and massaged the nape of her neck. She was thinking of the way some birds of the air had with flesh.

3

Night had come in while they waited for the scaffolders. The tree was shrouded in green net, behind which lay a fretwork of steel scaffolding, and the area was lit like a film set. Men in white coveralls were walking the high platforms, taking samples from trunk and branch. They might have been botanists on a field trip. There were halogens at ground level; their harsh beams lit what they touched, leaving the rest of the interior dark and jungly. The warm breeze stirred a fetid smell.

Stella wasn't good with heights: the planking seemed to shift under her, like foreshore sand when the tide's out, and she felt a churning low in her gut. None of this was helped by the fact that she had started her period that morning. DC Greegan's photographers, one taking stills, one making a video record, were standing directly opposite the hanging girl. A couple of lights had been hoisted and roped to the steel in order to illuminate the body; they threw deep black shadows. The street was cordoned off, and the space around the tree held a cathedral quiet, so that the *clack-clack* of the shutter release and the whirr of the video camera seemed unnaturally loud. Stella didn't want to look at the girl.

Pete Harriman had made the climb with her, fast and nimble like a scaffolder. Stella's knuckles had whitened every time she shifted her grip, and she had climbed on her arches rather than on the balls of her feet. She and Harriman stood by the stills cameraman, who was shooting all angles. The girl was slim, and despite the pull of her own weight, her back still held a curve. Across her shoulders, just where a yoke might go, were two words written in black marker pen:

DIRTY GIRL

A small, warm gust shook the tree, and she made a lazy half turn that brought her full-face.

"Jesus Christ Almighty." It was Harriman's voice: all he had to say on the matter. Oddly, the sight cleared Stella's head; she forgot about the queasiness and the false sensation of movement in the planking. The girl seemed out of focus, her face blurred for being eyeless, the faint pubic smudge sketched in; the blood backed up in her veins gave her body a dark blush like spoiled fruit. Stella called down to Greegan, who was one level below them.

"How long now?"

"They've got what they can, boss. It's not easy, taking forensic traces from a tree."

"Can we bring her down?"

"Okay."

The rope holding the girl was tied off to a branch a little way below her feet. Stella watched as the forensic officers started to cut her down. One had attached a harness to the body; it fitted like a corset. He linked a winch hook to a steel ring set in the harness at the level of her shoulder blades, then held her round the waist, taking her weight, while another cut the original rope close to the branch, taking care to preserve the knot the killer had tied. People knot rope in different ways.

Stella stayed up on the gantry. She didn't want to be on the ground to witness that sad descent. She didn't want to see those white feet, blameless and bare, emerging from the leaf cover.

The police doctor pronounced the girl dead at the scene of crime, took rectal and vaginal temperatures, noted the lack of rigor mortis, and gave a thirty-six-hour time bracket for the moment of death. It was warm inside the SOC tent, and the girl was leaking fluids and odors. She lay heavy on the ground, as if she had fallen; her open mouth and the hollows of her eyes made a dark mask.

When the doctor had finished, paramedics moved in to lift her and take her to the morgue. Science hadn't finished with her yet. They each gripped a corner of the green plastic sheet she lay on and took her up tenderly, letting her body settle onto a collapsible gurney.

The doctor was a young man and hadn't long been seconded to police work. He stood close to Stella as the gurney was wheeled out. He said, "Who would do such a thing?"

Stella almost smiled. She said, "Someone. Anyone."

The AMIP-5 team would meet next morning: Mike Sorley had already requisitioned the basement of a police admin. building in Notting Dene. Stella left her car parked in the empty street and ducked under the blue-and-white police tape. Houses on one side, the railings of a children's play area on the other, the tree on the street side of the railings. She closed her eyes, the better to see how it might have happened.

Two, maybe three o'clock in the morning. But London was never still, never quiet, never dark. Streetlights, evenly spaced. A car draws up by the tree. Do other cars go past? Probably. Are people still on the streets at this hour? Of course, but not many and not often in a street like this. Is someone looking out of a window, someone unable to sleep, someone with a restless child, someone in love or in grief?

Is she alive or dead? Let's say she's alive. Has he stopped because he lives nearby? Or she lives nearby? Are they lovers—does she feel safe with him? Or has he picked her up? Did they meet at a party, in a bar, did he offer her a lift home?

Hey, I'm going that way. I could drop you off.

Is she a runaway, is she Ms. Ordinary, is she a woman with a career, a cheating wife, a mover and shaker, a minor celebrity, a hooker from the Strip looking for a quiet place to get the business done?

They get out of the car.

Is she still unafraid, or is he forcing her, threatening her with a gun or a knife? Is she laughing with him or pleading with him? Either way, somehow, he strips her, and he strings her up. Is she already dead when he does that, or does she hang in the tree, the night wind stroking her body as she writhes and chokes, a darkness descending on her that is deeper than the London half dark, a darkness filled with the howl of blood in her head and the hard rasp of her own torn-off cries?

Stella walked through the Strip. Dealers were trading openly, and the whores were strolling the curbside in their spandex and boob-tubes, their heels and halters, on offer to the needy and the woebegone. Their pimps watched the action from black SUVs with wraparound sound systems. The shebeens and casinos offered a three-day drunk or a five-day poker game. She knew the Strip, she knew some of the people, but no one paid her any attention; they were all too busy getting what they wanted: dope or sex or booze or fun. Or money.

Two streets away things were quieter, as if a truce had been called. She went into Nico's All-Nite and ordered a coffee. The owner was Turkish; he'd bought the place from whoever had bought it from Nico. He said, "It's too hot. For this time of year? Too hot."

The place was empty. Stella sat at a Formica table with cup stains and thought about the dead girl. What her name might be; who she was before she died.

She wondered what John Delaney had been going to say before her phone cut him off.

He was asleep when she got back: used to her sudden call-outs and erratic timekeeping. Sometimes she wouldn't go back to his flat but stayed, instead, at the place she had shared for five years with George Paterson; that was before she had met Delaney, and George had sniffed the air, getting the scent of betrayal.

She went to the freezer and took out a bottle of vodka. From the shelf, a shot glass; from the fridge, a single cube of ice. When she poured the vodka over the ice, covering it, a slight meniscus formed at the top of the glass, just this side of spillage.

Hey, I'm going that way. I could drop you off.

No, she probably knew him better than that. Most murder victims knew their killers; it was the fiercest type of intimacy. But how did he hoist her up like that?

And why?

She drank a couple. A couple or three. Then she took her clothes off in the hallway, so she wouldn't wake him. The bedroom was completely dark, the way he liked it, blackout curtains blanking the London nighttime glow. Delaney stirred as she got into bed and turned toward her; the heat from his body, and his earthy smell in the deep darkness, gave her a little erotic charge. Something to do with not being able to see him; something to do with anonymity. She let her hand slip across his belly, but he didn't wake.

The girl came to her in a dream. She was walking the Strip in lime-green Lycra and long diamanté earrings. A car drew up, and she went across, bending low to the window, showing the client the goods. They struck a deal, and she opened the car door. Stella could see, on the backseat, his killing apparatus: rope, winch, a metal ladder. She moved forward, wanting to stop the girl, but it was like wading through heavy surf. She called out, and her voice distorted, the words jumbling and shuffling.

The girl turned her head to look at Stella. Her mouth was open, almost a smile; her eye sockets were pools of darkness.

4

The constants in the AMIP-5 squad room were cigarettes, chocolate, crisps, coffee, and mild cynicism. The crisps were always salt-and-vinegar: squad-room rules. As for chocolate, Mars bars were making a comeback. Stella had quit smoking a while ago, though her secondary intake was the equivalent of a pack a week. DI Sorley was the squad's most dedicated smoker: his office, just down the hall from the main room, was under fog a lot of the time; the walls seemed to sweat nicotine. Sorley wasn't just a heavy smoker, he was world class, one of the all-time greats.

The squad white-board was decorated with a clutch of SOC photos: Tree Girl taken from the ground and from the scaffolding; all-angle shots of her as she lay on the green plastic sheet; images taken, later, at the morgue before she was put in a refrigerated unit and filed under "Female U-ID." Stella had brought her coffee in from Starbucks, an early-morning treat to herself: the squad-room coffee doubled as stain remover. The team listened as she ticked off a few facts and guesses.

"A dead Caucasian female, age uncertain at this point but young, found hanging from a roadside tree in the Kensals. Significant predator damage to the corpse. We think she died sometime between nightfall on Sunday and dawn on Monday. We think she died of strangulation. We think she was killed by a man, because hauling her up into the tree took strength. We think we don't know what else to think."

Maxine Hewitt said, "Dirty girl . . ."

Stella nodded acknowledgment. "Yes . . . Which makes you think what?"

"Woman-hater."

"Women, or just prostitutes?"

"It's an excuse. Remember the Yorkshire Ripper? 'I was cleaning up the streets.'" Maxine gave a sour laugh. "They're filth, so it's okay to kill them."

Harriman said, "Some guy who caught a dose, maybe. Classic Ripper motivation."

Sue Chapman asked, "Is there any reason to think she was on the game?"

"We don't know anything about her," Stella said. "Nothing. So first move: run a check on all missing-persons reports that fit her profile. Start with the most recent."

Mike Sorley was standing at the front of the room with Stella but a little way off, so that he didn't appear to be running the briefing. Like all DIs, he was a paper-pusher, not a street cop. He glanced over at the white-board photos and said, "Can we do something about her face?"

"Repair job?" Stella asked. When Sorley nodded, she looked over toward Andy Greegan.

"We can make a guess at the eye color—brown or green given the color of her hair—and we can do some retouching, sure. The shape of the eyes before the birds got at her . . . that's something else."

"Can we at least make her look human?" Sorley asked.

Stella thought the girl looked all too human: human and disfigured; human and dead. She said, "Let's think about this for a moment. He kills her;

we don't know why. Maybe he's a woman-hater, maybe he feels free to kill prostitutes—"

"We're back to the Ripper," Maxine said.

"Yes, sure, or maybe they were more closely connected than that, maybe she was a specific victim, and he killed her for a specific reason."

"And his chosen method was to hang her from a tree in a public place?" Harriman said. "Doesn't sound much like the average domestic murder, does it—bit of a falling-out over the washing-up?"

"Dirty girl," Maxine said, "there's the clue."

"Doesn't mean she's a prossie," Sue observed. "Cheating wife? Promiscuous daughter?"

"No," Harriman said, "the clue's in the method. It was premeditated: cold-blooded."

"People have been strangled to death in public places before," Andy Greegan said. "A guy was strung up to some park railings, remember that?"

"That was a race killing. They used his shoelaces. Idea was to make it look like suicide. Our killer went prepared: he had a rope, for Christ's sake."

"He also had a method." Stella turned to the white-board and indicated some of the shots taken of the rope where it was secured to a branch some way beneath the hanging girl's feet. "Once he'd hauled her up, he tied the rope off to this branch—"

"Belayed," Sorley said.

Stella turned to him. "What?"

"When you tie something off like that: it's called belaying. Nautical term." He looked oddly pleased with himself.

"Okay . . . So he knew he was going to be able to do that."

"He'd selected a tree," Maxine suggested.

"Preselected, yes. DC Harriman's right: it looks as if he'd prepared his ground."

Furls of smoke rolled low in the room like wave-break, or hung in midair streamers. Stella took a deep breath: why fight it? She said, "I'd be very surprised to discover this was a domestic, but let's not rule anything out."

The last time she had seen a hanging it was of two children who were dangling from a banister, four little white feet treading air. It was a revenge killing. Stella had kept the children's father in the lockup all night, believing he had murdered his wife. He hadn't. His sister had. His sister had also murdered the children.

Stella had found them, and the sight had stayed with her, awake and—worse—asleep, until it seemed to be permanently in her sight, like a projected image. A week or so later she got into her car and drove until driving became impossible, then holed up in a cheap hotel, not really knowing where she was, or how she got there, or what she might do next. George found her: the tirelessly patient, tirelessly loyal George Paterson. Very soon after that, she miscarried her own child. She sometimes wondered if that had been the real beginning of the end between herself and George.

"So forget the girl for a moment," Stella said, "and think about the man. Think about her killer." She sipped her coffee. "He kills her and takes her clothes off, and writes on her and—"

"Or takes her clothes off and writes on her and *then* kills her," said Maxine.

"Okay. We'll know more about that after the PM. It's the stripping and writing . . . that, and stringing her up. Why? What makes him do that?"

"A warning to others," Sue suggested.

Harriman said, "You mean . . . what . . . he's a pimp?"

"It did happen near the Strip," Maxine reminded him. "Some of those girls are slave imports."

"They run away," Harriman agreed, "or try to, and they get beaten, but a pimp wouldn't kill one of his girls—waste of resources."

"Not always true," Sue said. "Remember Trolley-Dolly?"

The lower half of a torso had been found in a supermarket trolley on the muddy foreshore of the Thames: a girl who had tried to run once too often. That sawn-off body, legs and pubis and butchered trunk, had been a plain message to the Bosnian and Romanian and African girls who were lured to London with the promise of jobs but found themselves raped and terrorized and put to work in massage parlors and suburban brothels. The message was keep your head down and your ass up and don't think tricky thoughts.

Maxine said, "If he killed her just because she was a hooker, there'll be more."

Sorley was lighting one cigarette from the butt of another. He said, "It's too early for that kind of thinking. Run a description through missing persons, take fingerprints, blood type, see if the PM gives us anything. Let's get an ID on her and take it from there."

Easily said, Stella thought. Her body naked, her face disfigured . . . She was anonymous but, thanks to the first editions of the tabloids, also famous. She was Body in Tree; she was Hanging Girl; she was Lynch Victim; she was Gruesome Find.

To the guys in the forensic team, who had been everywhere, seen everything, she was Dope on a Rope.

———

Stella stood at Tom Davison's desk in the forensic department and leafed through his report, while Davison looked over her shoulder. "Just the initial findings," he said. "To get more, we need to tie up with the pathologist, cross-reference, stack up some facts. It's a fair bet that there'll be a bewildering amount of DNA on the ground. On the tree: who knows? Difficult surfaces. The rope is likely to be our best bet. One thing we do know: he hauled her up from the ground; there was a lot of scarring on the branch caused by the rope running over."

"Which tells you what?"

"Strong guy. Also tells you she was probably dead when he did it."

"Go on."

"He dumps her by the tree, then climbs up to loop the rope over a branch, then climbs down and does the business. She was either dead or unconscious. Think about it: her hands weren't tied."

"Weren't tied when we got there," Stella said.

"Ask the pathologist—"

"Sam Burgess."

"Right, ask him, but I don't think there was any sign of a ligature on the wrists."

"What about the writing?"

"Dirty girl?" Stella nodded. "Black marker pen, so far as we can tell. We lifted a sample: soaked it, you know. It's gone to a specialist unit, but I think you'll find it's the kind of thing you can buy in any newsagent's or stationer's." He paused. "You'll be showing it to a handwriting expert? It's block capitals and written on a yielding surface, but there might be something."

"Okay," Stella said. Then: "How old was she?"

"Not very. Teens, early twenties. I can't be more accurate until we've had some material back from the autopsy."

"Material?"

"Hair samples; bone samples."

His office was little more than a cubicle, and he had been standing close to her as she read. Now she moved back a pace, though not just because he had invaded her body space; the uneasiness she felt went deeper than that. Stella had slept with Davison: a one-nighter, an impulse, a mistake; she had been angry with John Delaney, not sure about the relationship, and had given in to a whim.

Since then it hadn't been necessary for Stella to talk to Davison; nor had she answered his little flurry of e-mails. Now he stood close enough to kiss, and she remembered that he had been a good lover. The air was thick with things unsaid.

"Full report when?" Stella asked.

"We're backed up."

"You're always backed up."

"The world is full of nasty people doing nasty things, DS Mooney. Our workload is a sad reflection of a society in crisis."

She knew that addressing her by rank and surname was his method for pointing up the tension between them; calling her Stella would have been friendly and undemanding. *Forget it*, she thought; *it was something and nothing.*

"As soon as you can . . ."

He smiled. "Goes without saying."

She turned to leave, but he didn't step back. Her arm brushed his as she passed. She felt him watching her go out of the room and wondered whether she could have avoided that tiny contact if she'd really wanted to. She had promised herself that she would tell Delaney about that night, that one night, but she'd tell him when the time was right. Four months had passed, nearly five, and she hadn't found the moment.

She never would, and she knew it.

5

Up above the Strip, on the crest of the rise that looks down on the neon blaze, the whoring and the hustling, stood a long terrace of three-story houses. They were faced in dark red brick and had little stone porticoes over the windows; a hundred years ago they would have been the town houses of respectable merchants. Now they were apartments—mostly rentals, mostly short let—with shopfronts at street level.

The house at the center of the terrace had caught fire a year back. The owner had made some basic repairs and sold it to a company who needed a store for their product, which was safes of all strengths and sizes. The ground-floor window carried a display of their basic models. You could buy a safe that bolted to the cellar floor, thereby making it impossible for criminals to remove it. Instead, they would wait until you got home, then hold a knife to your child's eye to encourage you to reveal the combination. Or you could buy a small safe that looked exactly like a power socket. In this you could store your most precious items: jewelry, for instance, or the combination to the big safe in the cellar. This item was generally referred to by criminals as the "crap power-socket safe."

The first and second floors of the building were storage space, but the uppermost floor had been let through an agency. It wasn't much: a room with a living space, a sleeping space, a kitchen space, and a bathroom the size of a phone box. After the fire, the new owner had done little more than replace unsafe floorboards. Since the room was at the top of the house, it had four exposed rafter beams, and these showed the rough edges and fissures of fire damage. The walls had been stripped back to the bare plaster, which still bore scorch marks, and there was a persistent smell of charring that nothing could mask.

Unsurprisingly, the rent on the place was pretty low. It wouldn't have suited many people, but it suited Gideon Woolf. He hadn't signed the rental agreement in his own name, but he paid cash and he paid on time, so he could have signed Mickey Mouse and no one would have cared. As a child, "Gideon" wasn't a name that had done him many favors, but he knew that Gideon meant "great warrior," and it was a name that suited him now.

Gideon had been renting the burned room in the burned house for a few months. He lived alone, and he liked it that way. He liked being up high, being able to look down. He liked the simple life he led: fast food, canned food, packet food; a good supply of whiskey; his laptop and his computer games. He was crazy about his computer games. There was one called *Silent Wolf*; initially, he had bought it for the name—his name—but now he played it all the time.

Silent Wolf was a man with a narrow face, heavy sideburns, and a mane of coarse yellow hair that fell to his neck. The pupils of his eyes were yellow; his incisors were thick and took a slight curve. He wore a cloak like a pelt, beneath which he was all muscle and sinew. He wore a single glove to let people know that he carried a weapon; its fingers were cut short to just above the knuckle. He had a small arsenal at his disposal, but his weapon of choice was the knife.

Silent Wolf's history was what you might expect: abandoned as a child, brought up by *canis lupus*, lived in the wild until hunters spotted him, and his entire pack was killed in order that he might be rescued. That slaughter broke him, though he healed quickly, as an animal does. The problem was that he healed crooked. Attempts to tame him failed. Now Silent Wolf lived in the no-go areas of an unnamed city, the badlands and borderlands, where he stood for swift justice. His body, like his mind, bore scars, but he walked the city streets at night, alone and unafraid, ready to kill if there was killing to be done.

The game was aimed primarily at pre-teen boys, but twenty-six-year-old Gideon was both addict and aficionado. Like Silent Wolf, Gideon Woolf was on a mission.

6

In the postmortem room of the morgue, there was music in the air along with ethanol and a faint underlying whiff of decay. Sam Burgess liked easy listening in the autopsy room, because looking was often far from easy.

Steel tables, steel drains, steel instruments, blood on the slab, Grieg on the CD player. Sam had a monkish fringe of hair turning mottled gray, deft hands, and a soft voice with which to describe death in all its forms.

"People think that your neck breaks and you're gone," he said. "That's what the drop was for, or so they imagine. Those stories about the hangman secretly sizing up his victim, calculating height and weight, making the calculation . . . Truth is, no matter how you hang someone, they strangle. Death by strangulation. The effect of the drop is to sever the spinal cord and make things a bit more humane, that's all: breaking the neck renders the person unconscious, so the strangulation takes place without a lot of jerking and writhing. It's painless."

"Did her neck break?" Stella was looking at the body of Tree Girl lying on the dissecting table. There was a stillness about her that was unlike any other: not the stillness of something inert—a rock, a piece of furniture, something that had never moved—no, this was an unnatural stillness, a kind of absence.

"No."

"Was she dead when he hung her up there?"

Sam shook his head; his voice grew a little quieter. "No, she died of asphyxia. Clear evidence of that: facial congestion, swollen tongue, cyanosis as a result of constriction of the large blood vessels in the neck. The brain is gradually starved of oxygen; the technical term is anoxia."

"How long would she have taken to die?"

"Brain death or whole body death?"

It was a distinction that hadn't occurred to Stella. She said, "Both. Either . . ."

"A conscious person might take, say, two or three minutes before they start to close down. They'll struggle during that time: kick, squirm, you know . . ." Sam paused. "Is this need to know?"

"Well, it's not *want* to know."

"From that point to brain death . . . three minutes? Four? It depends. After that it's just a slow, natural process: asphyxiation or maybe cardiac arrest. Anything between five to fifteen minutes."

"Fifteen?"

"Could be. The person's deeply unconscious, though."

"Oh, well . . ." Stella looked again at Tree Girl's dark, distorted face. "Oh, well . . . that's okay, then."

"If it makes you feel any better," Sam said, "she probably didn't know a thing about it. Look."

He moved to the top of the table, and Stella followed. A patch of hair, close to the crown on the right side, had been shaved from Tree Girl's skull. Stella could see a cut, surrounded by a dark contusion.

"The head wound caused a hairline fracture of the skull; the bone is slightly depressed; I'm pretty sure we're going to find a subdural hematoma."

Sam worked with an assistant called Giovanni, a man of smiles and little speech. He brought to the table a trepanning saw and a bone saw and set them down with a conscientious deftness: tools of the trade. He and Sam had already examined Tree Girl's body, had combed her and swabbed her and touched her in places where even a lover would have hesitated to go. Now they would get to the heart of her—literally. As Sam prepared to make the great "Y" incision that would lay her body open from clavicle to pubis, Stella turned away.

Sam worked swiftly and surely as Giovanni sprung the rib cage to let him in among the delicate wet tubers and strange blooms: the lung-tree, the rich red pod of the heart that might, at some stage, have held all manner of secrets but now was empty and still. It was this that Stella turned from: the first long cut that made flesh meat and exposed the inner workings, the moving parts, the cogs and wheels, the plumbing. The human body as mere machine.

"There'll be some handwriting experts along; sometime this afternoon," Stella said.

"Yes." Sam nodded. "I saw the writing on her back. It's in capitals. Will they get much from that?"

Stella shrugged. "Who knows? Can you tell how old she is?"

"Forensics," Sam said. "Bone—"

"Sample, hair sample, I know. Take a guess?"

"From the musculature, physical development, elasticity of skin and so on—"

"I won't hold you to it."

"Twenty or younger."

After that, Sam didn't speak for a while: too absorbed in his work. He handed Giovanni the liver, which Giovanni took to a scale to be weighed, carrying the organ carefully, as if it were something rare. Finally, he said, "Okay. We'll have her looking presentable by the time the graphologists arrive."

Stella said, "A couple of questions." Sam waited. "Evidence of recent sexual activity?"

"Not sure; not unprotected, anyway."

"So, no semen."

"No semen."

"But she could have had sex—"

"The swabs might tell us. I'll get back to you."

"Okay," Stella said. Then: "The head wound . . . and how long before she died?"

"Not sure yet. More to do on that." Sam was bent over Tree Girl's body like a mechanic over a faulty engine. He paused and looked up. "You want to know whether he took her there conscious or unconscious."

"Might make a difference: potential witnesses, what they saw, what they didn't see. If she was conscious, people might have noticed a struggle, something of that sort."

"Someone seeing a struggle would have intervened, surely," Sam observed. "Gone to help."

Stella smiled. "Would you?"

Sam said nothing. Giovanni positioned a body block to elevate the head, and Sam made an incision at the back of the head and took the cut from behind the right ear across the forehead to the left ear; then he peeled back the scalp. Giovanni switched on the bone saw. A high, thin whine filled the room. He handed the implement to Sam, who made a cut line just where Tree Girl's hairline would have been.

Stella hadn't expected an answer. There was no aggression in Sam's world, no fear, no sudden cries for help, no moral dilemmas. When he cut the connection with the spinal cord and eased out the brain, Stella took a step forward, as if half expecting the face of Tree Girl's killer to be found there, like an image on a screen, her last sight of any living thing.

7

The Harefield Estate is a war zone: sometimes guerrilla war, sometimes all-out war, but always war. The timid noncombatants walk the battle lines with their heads down and their hands full of bags from Primark or ShopRite.

Between the land of civilians and the high-rise blocks of the estate was the DMZ, which, like all stretches of no-man's-land, bore the scars and detritus of conflict. Everything out there was ripped up or burned out: stoves, fridges, cars, sofas, a lone bed; and, topping all that, a strewage of condoms, syringes, fast-food boxes. An enterprising art dealer could have thrown a rope round the whole thing and claimed it as a vast installation.

Alongside the tiny, wind-buffeted apartments of the innocents who prayed for a few days' cease-fire were stills, casinos, armorers, whorehouses, drug factories, drug-distribution centers, and drug-wholesale facilities. The blocks surrounded a circular area that locals called the Bull Ring, but to reach it you would first have to negotiate the maze of pathways that only those who lived there had mapped. You would also have to risk the walk spaces under each stilt-lifted block.

On a day that was too warm, and in a way that was all too usual, drug deals were going down along the pathways, hookers were going down in doorways, and in the walk space under Block C, one man was killing another. The killer's name was Arthur Dorey, but no one called him that. He was Sekker: it was short for secateurs, because that particular garden tool was the method of persuasion he most often chose. Shake hands with

Sekker, people said, and then count your fingers: after which they would laugh. Well, some of them would laugh. Just at that moment, though, Sekker wasn't too interested in persuasion. He was getting a job done. It was a paid job, and Sekker needed the money because he was hoping to take his girl to Barbados before the hurricane season.

The job involved ending the life of a man whose name, Sekker thought, was Barry. Barry or Gary: that sort of a jerk-off name. Barry or Gary owed money to some people who didn't tolerate debt. The job wasn't proving difficult. Someone had pointed Barry or Gary out in the pub, and Sekker had followed him out into the street and across the DMZ until he took the shortcut under Block C. Sekker's method of execution was messy and somewhat gruesome, but Barry or Gary had upset some unforgiving people, and they were anxious that he should suffer before he died.

Sekker was wearing protective clothing for the job, and he sweated freely. When it was over, he shrugged out of the heavy cotton overalls and put them into a small rucksack along with the rest of his equipment. This left him in just his chinos and a polo shirt. He sauntered across the DMZ and walked on for half a mile or so—far enough from the job site—and found a bar, where he ordered a long, cold glass of export lager. It had been hot work, and he needed to slake his thirst.

The first mouthful went down without touching the sides. Sekker laughed at the thought. You couldn't say that of the drink he'd just given to Barry. Or Gary. Sekker still had to set up his alibi, but he didn't feel the need to get clear of the area. Even in warm weather there were too many competing odors on Harefield for the smell of a corpse to be distinguished from any other, and anyone going through that dank, dark space would take the dead man for a rough sleeper.

In fact, he had lain beneath Block C for a night and a morning when Stella and Pete Harriman parked in the Bull Ring. Or, rather, when their driver parked. No one who knew the place left a car unattended on Harefield.

Stella knew it well. She had grown up on the estate.

They were there because a missing-persons check had turned up a mug shot that could have been Tree Girl before someone had roped her and hauled her and left her for the birds. A picture of a girl taken at a party: she was looking into the camera and smiling a wide smile. The person in question was called Bryony Dean, and the place she was missing from was Apartment 1136, Block A, Harefield Estate.

8

Melanie Dean was a bird-boned woman with a worried look. Her daughter had gone missing, and that should have been enough to worry any mother, but her frown and the down-turned corners of her mouth had more to do with getting a visit from Stella and Harriman. Melanie was one of Harefield's non-combatants, but she thought in military terms: "collateral damage," "codes of conduct." One such code said don't speak to cops. This rule could be extended to mean don't speak to anyone. Or, simply, don't speak.

"I didn't report her," Melanie said. "That was Chris." She said it as if Stella might know Chris and his gabby ways.

"Can we talk to Chris?"

"He's gone."

"Gone where?"

"Who knows? I don't know. Gone."

"For how long?"

"Forever, I expect."

"No," Stella said, "how long since he left?"

"Couple of months?"

"Chris's last name is . . . ?"

"Fuller."

"And Chris wasn't her father?"

Melanie looked at her as if she'd spoken in Swahili; then she laughed, a sour cough. "*That* bastard."

"She hasn't been in touch with you?" Harriman asked.

"She's seventeen," Melanie said. "Got her own life to lead."

"Is that how you see it?"

"She'll be all right."

"So . . . why did he report her missing?"

"We got up one morning, she was gone. No letter or anything; no phone call. I suppose he was worried."

Harriman nodded. "And you?"

"She'll be all right."

Stella offered Melanie a retouched photo: Tree Girl with a cosmetic tweak, brown eyes wide. The woman studied it for a while. "Certainly looks like her, don't it?" She spoke as if Stella might know; as if she and Bryony had been friends.

"But it's not?" Harriman suggested.

Melanie shook her head. "Nah. It's got the look of her, though. Specially round the eyes."

They walked the sky-high concrete rat-run that led from the row of front doors to the stairwell.

"This is just a guess," Harriman said, "but I wonder whether Chris left at roughly the same time as Bryony."

"Not long afterward," Stella agreed, "and with as little warning."

"He reported her missing—"

"So that Melanie wouldn't think Bryony's disappearance had anything to do with his."

"But in truth—"

"Melanie has put one and one together and come up with a happy couple."

Some of the front-door windows of the apartments in the facing block still had glass in the frames; others were boarded up or had been replaced with steel shutters. The dealers liked steel; their doors were backed with it, and some had steel hatches fitted, so goods could be exchanged for cash hand to hand and no faces visible. Just now, the dealers were doing high-volume business in Nazi crank, drug of choice for the DIY enthusiast; you could cook it up out of ingredients from any hardware store and your local pharmacy.

A cloud moved away from the sun, and the light flashed like Morse on one of the windows, drawing Stella's eye. As she looked, a man and a woman were about to enter one of the apartments. The woman turned half profile to say something, then the man opened the door and they went inside.

Stella was looking down a long, black tunnel, and her legs were folding under her. Harriman had taken three or four steps before he realized she wasn't beside him. When he looked back, she was sitting on the walkway, eyes fixed and breathing hard. He went back and stooped to help her up, but without looking directly at him she lifted an arm to ward him off.

She said, "Wait."

After a moment, her breathing slowed and she got to her feet. Harriman said, "What was it?"

"Nothing." Stella shook her head.

"No," he said, "not nothing, boss."

She had started toward the stairwell, taking long strides, walking with her head down and her hands pushed into her jacket pockets. Harriman kept pace. He said, "Not nothing: something. What?"

Stella shook her head as if it were too trivial to mention. "I've got my period, I didn't eat breakfast, my body-sugar levels are probably round my ankles."

"Ah," Harriman said, "women's issues."

They clattered down the stairwell. You never left a car unattended, you never took the lift. The stairs carried graffiti tags and the dry stains of piss runnels. The smell was enough to ream your sinuses.

"It's a bastard," Harriman said, "all that monthly stuff . . ." Stella looked at him; he seemed to have more on the subject. Harriman shrugged. "For guys?" he said. "Very inconvenient."

It wasn't her, it just looked like her.

Round the eyes—like Bryony?

It looked like her, but it wasn't her.

How do you know?

It couldn't have been.

How do you know?

She lives in Manchester. She's hooked up with some guy.

Yes, the last you heard . . . How do you know where she is; who she's with? You haven't spoken to her in ten years.

She hasn't spoken to me.

Stella arguing with herself: one voice, two opinions, shared anger.

So you're saying it was her double . . .

Listen: ten years, right? She wouldn't even look like that anymore.

Her hair comes out of a bottle, her face is courtesy of Avon, why would she look any different?

Ten-year-old Stella sitting in her room high in the sky and watching the clouds roll by. Watching the lights of the planes as they drop into the Heathrow corridor. Watching the minutes tick by until the person social services liked to call "the sole responsible parent" comes back from wherever she is, whatever she's doing, whoever she's doing it with.

Little Stella Mooney: just like a motherless child.
It can't be her. She's gone.
Find out.
I don't need to.
Are you sure?
Sure.
Go back. Knock at the door.
No, she's gone. Gone for good.
Good.

Stella emerged from the stairwell into the Bull Ring and walked through a group of kids in hoodies drinking alcopops and smoking. The air was rich with the scent of dope. They were engaged in a stare-down with the driver of the car. It was an unmarked vehicle, but might just as well have carried a sign that said POLICE in strobe neon. Someone had finger-written FILTH in the dust on the rear window.

She dropped into the backseat and yanked the door closed. Harriman got in beside her. The driver was still eyeballing the kids as if he represented the long arm of the law, or some equally farcical notion.

Stella said, "Get me the fuck out of this place."

Giovanni brought Tree Girl out of the freezer on a whisper of rollers and peeled the sheet back to the small of her waist.

He had stowed her facedown so the handwriting experts wouldn't have to see the cobbled stitches that went from throat to groin, or the staples fastening her brow, or the eyeless face. The experts looked as if they had been handpicked for contrast: one tall, one short, the tall one pale with wild hair, the short one coffee-colored and bald. Tall and pale winced and swayed slightly as the sheet came off. After a moment they bent to their task, they made notes, they conferred, then they left, smiling and nodding at Giovanni as if that sort of thing was all in a day's work.

Giovanni turned Tree Girl right side up and slid her back into the dark.

9

John Delaney stood in the hallway of the Holland Park Avenue mansion and looked at the art on the walls: to one side, old masters; facing them, BritArt.

A pastoral scene in opposition to a lino-swatch. A haloed virgin facing up to a grainy black-and-white enlargement of a female nude. The nude made him laugh, once he'd worked out what it was: at first he'd mistaken it for a tunnel on a mountain road.

A secretary informed him that Mr. Bowman would be happy to see him now. Delaney wanted to say, "Would he? How happy? Happier than he was to keep me waiting for twenty minutes? Well, tell Mr. Bowman to go fuck himself." He didn't say it, because he needed the interview: one in a series he was writing on London's Rich List. Delaney was a journalist who had traded war-zone reporting for home-front features, and there were times, like this, when he missed the sound of shell burst and dust under the tongue. Just lately, he'd started to miss that a lot.

The secretary took him up to the second floor, leading the way. She was two steps above him, which brought her ass to his eye line; it was a good ass, and Delaney decided to think of this brief encounter with it as a form of compensation.

Stanley Bowman's office was the size of the average London apartment. He smiled at Delaney but didn't come out from behind his very large, very clear desk. He was a lean man in his late forties. He wore a little goatee and a mustache that trailed out toward the points of his jaw: gunslinger's trim. In the course of the interview he spoke of taking scalps and making dawn raids; of shooting from the hip, of robbing the bank, of the cavalry coming over the hill, his soft Scottish burr at odds with the shoot-'em-up terminology. He got up to pour a couple of drinks, and Delaney caught his profile: sharp and clean, just the merest hint of slack under the jaw.

Speaking of profit, Bowman said, "It's not about making money. It's about making money make money."

Speaking of bluff and holding your nerve, he said, "Not all trappers wear fur hats."

By the time the interview had ended, Delaney had started to like some-one he had previously decided to despise. As they parted, Bowman said, "I read some of your stuff before agreeing to see you. Sarajevo, Rwanda, First Gulf War: you were there for all that." Delaney nodded. "And now this." Bowman raised his eyebrows.

"I got scared," Delaney said.

Bowman laughed. "Good reason."

The AMIP-5 basement was hot, and no one could find a fan. DC Sue Chap-man had opened the window that let on to the street, but the down-draft of cadmium and cesium and carbon dioxide did nothing more than stir the room's thick haze of cigarette smoke.

Stella was reading through the preliminary report from Tall-Pale and Short-Bald.

We have been asked to provide, so far as possible, a psychological profile of the person who inscribed the words DIRTY GIRL on the back of a female murder victim. Accordingly, we made a visit to the morgue and viewed the exhibit.

The words are monolinear. They are in capital letters and appear on the upper/middle back, beginning and ending just clear of each upper arm and spanning the shoulder blades.

The implement used appears to have been the type of marker pen that is freely available from high street stores. We imagine that the forensic unit will take/will have taken a sample of this and would expect them to verify our finding.

Script written entirely in capitals is no less susceptible to graphological analysis than any other, though the specific significance of capitals where one capital might precede lowercase characters is compromised.

Also called into question, in this case, are both the comparative nar-rowness of individual characters and the graphic density, since the two words were formed to fit a specific area. There can be no certainty that this narrowness and graphic display are profile-specific.

A full breakdown of both general and particular aspects of the words is to follow. This summary report, bearing in mind the caveats already men-tioned, would suggest that the person who wrote these words has a tendency toward aggression, has a low anger threshold, and is emotionally restricted or covert, though with a high possibility of dynamic breakthrough.

These initial findings will be refined and modified in the full report and should not be taken as definitive. Our analysis was restricted by the lack of script characteristics such as upper and lower loops, baseline division of vertical structures, lowercase strokes, and so on. However, the stroke velocity in general, together with malformations, upper bars, enclosed bars, lines of intersection, and so forth, was indicator enough.

The report carried a rider that made the writers seem suddenly more human than expert:

Given that the words were written by someone who had just killed (or was about to kill) the victim, our findings might seem pretty obvious.

Maxine Hewitt walked through, fanning herself with a sheaf of missing-persons reports. She was wearing jeans and a white T-shirt that bore damp patches where it touched the slopes of her breasts. Pete Harriman watched her as she went by: pretty in a thin-lipped sort of way; heavy, dark hair that fell in a bob to her jawline. He tried to persuade himself that his interest was entirely academic, since Maxine was gay, but it wasn't.

Stella and Maxine exchanged reports. Maxine glanced at what Tall-Pale and Short-Bald had to say.

"So this man's aggressive and repressed. Hey, that'll lead us right to him."

"One in a million," Stella agreed. She was leafing through Maxine's documents: missing daughters, missing sons, missing husbands and wives and fathers. Missing mothers. "Are these up-to-date?"

"Pretty much. It's a nationwide selection, so coming in piecemeal."

"Any likely candidates?"

Maxine laughed. "Take a guess at how many slim, dark-haired girls in their teens run away from home each week." She handed Stella another file.

"What's this?"

"The house-to-house—so far. Silano's still out there with a uniformed WPC."

"Silano's joined us?"

"He was late getting secondment."

Frank Silano was a relatively new member of AMIP-5. He was soft-spoken and skinny and looked as if he didn't sleep nights. Stella liked him.

"The house-to-house so far," she prompted.

"No one saw or heard a thing . . . oh, except Mrs. Hallam, who lives five streets away. She was there when it happened, knows the victim, knows the killer, and has a photographic record of the whole event which she's prepared to hand over to us if we undertake to help establish her credentials as Anastasia Romanov."

"Tell me, has Mrs. Hallam ever been seen to bark at the moon?"

"It seems she has a reputation for it."

Stella took the missing-persons files, along with the scene-of-crime report, the graphology report, and the postmortem report, to Mike Sorley's office. Getting rid of paper was one of the subtle skills of police work. Every development, every piece of evidence, every interview, every squad meeting, and every phone call had to be papered. If there was an arrest, the paperwork trebled. The trick was to keep the paper moving. In a squad like AMIP-5, the DI was the last call for paper. When Stella walked through Sorley's door, he glanced up, saw the files, and reached for a cigarette.

"You've been through these." It wasn't a question, it was a plea.

"More or less."

"Which?"

"DC Hewitt was first stop. She'll have logged them. But—"

"I know." Sorley lit the cigarette like a man who was already eagerly anticipating the next. "Leave them with me."

Stella dropped the reports next to the pile that was next to the pile beside the pile in his in-tray. Which is where they would stay, with a file on Elizabeth Rose Connor about eight from the top.

Elizabeth Rose Connor aka Bryony Dean.

10

Stella's drive home was a dictionary of London traffic argot: *cut-up, rat-run, tailgate, red-light bandit.*

When her affair with Delaney had become unignorable, and George had left, she'd continued to occupy the Vigo Street flat she and George had shared, though as often as not she had stayed at Delaney's place in Notting Hill. To begin with, Vigo Street had always been "home." Then it had become the place she went to when things between herself and Delaney were uncertain: a refuge from rows and responsibilities. Now she wasn't sure where home was, or what it was, and the uncertainty troubled her.

When she walked in, he was pouring red wine into two glasses. He looked up at her and smiled his lopsided smile. She took the glass he offered and kissed him. The narrow planes of his face were dusted with dark stubble, and for some reason that roughness on her cheek made her want him.

"How did you know?" she asked.

"You blip the engine before you switch off."

"Hundreds of people do that."

"I know your blip." He was putting olives into a bowl. "The press are very excited by the mystery girl in the tree."

"They are, yes. Is there food?"

"Olives?"

"Other food."

"Some. They suspect you're holding information back. A few juicy details."

"They're right; we are. We usually do: it helps eliminate the crazies. Some what?"

"Some food. But not much. We could order in. What is it? And how juicy?"

Stella smiled. She walked over to him and kissed him, then bit him gently on the neck. "I'm not telling you, you're one of them." It sounded like a teasing joke, but there was more to it than that. Delaney's instincts as a journalist had caused trouble between them in the past.

He said, "I interviewed Stanley Bowman today."

She opened the fridge and peered inside. "Wheeler and dealer. Upper slopes of the Rich List."

"Yes. Holland Park Avenue mansion, houses in Courcheval and Tuscany, apartment in New York—"

"Money in Liechtenstein."

"It's a fair bet."

"When you say food, Delaney, do you mean this egg?"

She called him Delaney more often than she called him John: it was part of a fondness code. He reached for the stack of meal-delivery cards by the phone and handed them to her.

"These guys," he said, "these rich guys . . . They don't think of money the way we do. You know—we get some, we spend it, end of the month we get some more. To them, it's an abstract."

"Abstract . . . ? Like love or hate?"

"Yes." He paused. "It's not just having lots of money. It's a matter of degree. These guys aren't rich like moderately rich people are rich. It's something beyond that. Like they live in a different country with different customs and a language that only they speak."

"Chinese or Indian?"

"You choose."

She dialed a number and asked, "What do you want?"

He said, "You choose." Then: "Not hate, obviously, but not adoration either." He paused. "More like tough love."

The dream took her to the very center of the Bull Ring, the heart of the Harefield Estate. The place held special significance for her, because she had killed a man there.

When she was growing up on the estate, Stella knew the Bull Ring was a place to stay away from after dark. If she was sent down eighteen floors to buy a quarter of vodka, she would hurry round the perimeter to get to the booze store rather than walk across. Like all the estate kids who weren't gang members, she had mapped Harefield in her head, and the Bull Ring, like the walk spaces under the tower blocks, carried large diversion and no-entry signs.

She had been working on a case: asking questions that some people on the estate didn't want answered. She should have known what was coming when the cab took a shortcut through Harefield. The driver left her and the cab in the Bull Ring, where two guys were waiting. One was wearing new, white sneakers: Nike Man. She had reached back into the cab for a weapon and come up with a wheel-nut crank. When she swung it, the crank took Nike Man in the side of the neck. He went down like a dropped log, but she didn't know she'd killed him until a few days later when one of her informants gave her the news.

She should have told Mike Sorley, written a full report, cooperated fully with the SIO, and accepted suspension for the duration of the inquiry. In fact, she had told only Delaney.

Now the dream held her in that selfsame spot. Nike Man was propped up against the cab, where he'd fallen, eyes fixed on her and wearing an expression of infinite regret. Stella's mother walked toward her, wearing the farcical clothes that were fashionable in the late 1970s. She was smiling the tight little smile that meant trouble.

Stella began to cry, anticipating the slap that would rock her head sideways and leave her ears ringing, but then she was in her mother's arms, *It's all right, everything's all right,* and then she was standing by the big sash window in Delaney's apartment, fully awake and still crying.

A blush of light-pollution in the sky at 3:00 A.M., sirens over the low rumble of traffic. Stella stood in the darkened room, eyes closed, trying to recapture the feeling of being held, because in all her childhood that had never happened to her.

In his scorched room, high above the Strip, Gideon Woolf was also watching the night.

It was late for the whores, but there were a few still working the curbs, picking up small-hours punters from the casinos and shebeens who, for some reason, imagined that getting a high-speed blow job in a reeking alley would be the perfect end to a night of waste and loss.

Gideon liked the Strip: it was a place to come home to. In the *Silent Wolf* computer game there was a location called Gasoline Alley where all manner of bad guys hung out, where all manner of bad things went down. The girls of that place were hot and tough-talking, their short skirts and deep cleavages spoke of sex, but at a heavy cost. Some of the men had workout bodies and strong jawlines; others were ratty and mean and carried custom-built breechloaders.

The Strip and Gasoline Alley were the same place to Gideon. Like Silent Wolf, he would take a straight line through the dealers and the down-and-outs, the hookers and the hard men, imagining his eyes a pale yellow, his home-dyed yellow hair a spiky ruff across his shoulders.

Stella dropped a single ice cube into a shot glass and followed it with a big slug of vodka, taking the liquid all the way to the top. The vodka had come straight from the freezer, but the ice was part of a ritual. She drank it off in one, then repeated the dose. She would be a little sluggish in the morning, but it was a worthwhile price. She had learned that a clear head develops vivid dreams.

After the third shot, she felt an edge of weariness: her limbs heavy, her thoughts beginning to blur. She went back to bed. Delaney stirred and spoke a sentence in a jumbled sleep-alphabet.

Keep your dreams to yourself, she thought, then put her head on the pillow and fell asleep in the same moment.

Gideon Woolf lay on his bed under the charred beams.

His eyes were closed and he was dreaming, but he wasn't asleep.

11

Stella Mooney, images from the dream still floating in her head . . .

She parked her unmarked car a couple of streets back from one of the slip roads onto Harefield. Those two streets were a buffer. Any closer and she might come back to find the car up on blocks and the wheels gone. She was pretty sure she could get a fix on the apartment the man and woman had entered: go back to Apartment 1136, Block A, walk toward the stairwell for . . . oh, maybe a count of ten, then look across. She seemed to remember something yellow: a yellow blind in the window perhaps.

She walked the narrow strip of asphalt that lay across the wasteland of the DMZ, feeling she ought to be carrying a white flag.

I'll knock on the door, and if it's her—

If it's her . . . what?

It won't be her.

You saw her.

I saw someone who looked like her, that's all.

Sure of that? Then why are you going back?

As she got closer, Stella noticed activity round the blocks at ground level and on the high walkways: people moving in one direction, all of them seeming to have a purpose. Generally, people on Harefield either sauntered or ran; this was more a little procession of people with the same thing in mind.

When she reached the first of the blocks, Stella pushed in through the glass-and-chickenwire doors, took the bare stairwell to the first walkway, and went to the elbow of the building for a clear view. Strings of people were converging on the Bull Ring: a thin crowd but determined, like the die-hard supporters of a nonleague football club. She took out her mobile phone and dialed Harriman's number.

The first thing he said was, "DI Sorley's been looking for you, boss."

"Make an excuse. Before you do that—"

"What kind of an excuse?"

"A good one. Listen, call out the uniforms for an event on Harefield. Looks like a dogfight."

"You're down on Harefield?"

"Took a wrong turn. Make the call."

"You're looking for—"

"Make the call, DC Harriman. Advise them to request an ARV."

Stella had left the estate seventeen years before, but there were still a few people who remembered her. To many of them she was the bitch-cop, the one who'd gone over to the enemy. You didn't have to be a bad guy to think of cops that way: a "them-and-us reflex" worked for most of the people who were sometimes labeled as the underclass. If you were a member of that anti-elite, "Us" was anyone like you; "Them" was anyone else.

Underclass wasn't quite right, though; they were beyond class, class-free, just as they were beyond rules or conscience or sympathy. There were those among them who would knife you for your hamburger; if you looked at them the wrong way, they would jump on your face until you were dead.

Stella joined the procession. In her jeans and trainers and scuffed-leather blouson, she was as close to Harefield mufti as made no difference. They were heading for the Bull Ring.

The AMIP-5 team had worked the street three times; someone was always out, or else not answering the door. Maxine Hewitt and Frank Silano had decided to make another pass at the fifteen houses where they'd failed to get a response. This time every door opened; and of the twenty-eight people interviewed, three had something definite to report.

Gerald Arthur Montague. Victoria Mary Sansom. Susan Joanna Phipps. Gerry, Viki, and Susie.

"I saw them, it must have been them, she was leaning on his shoulder, like, you know, like someone in love."

"What I saw . . . it was a man and a woman. I thought she was drunk."

"Was it them? Was it her and him? Ohmigod, I saw them!"

They agreed to make statements there and then. Silano took notes while Maxine asked the questions.

Gerry had been walking through the park when he saw them. He thought it was them. It must have been them. The man was tall and broad, and the girl was a slip of a thing. No, he hadn't been close enough to be able to say what they looked like; they looked like lovers.

Viki had been walking down the road when she saw them in a car parked at the curb. She thought it was them. It must have been them. The man was tall, you could tell, even though he was sitting down; the girl, well, not so tall. The car was a red-blue-hatchback-saloon-jeep kind of thing. No, she hadn't been close enough to be able to say what they looked like; she looked drunk.

Susie had been walking home from her friend's house when she saw them sitting on the grass by the tree, just the other side of the park railings. The tree in question. She thought it was them. It must have been them. The man was average height for a man, the girl was average height for a girl. No, she hadn't been close enough to be able to say what they looked like. But it was her and him for sure, and ohmigod she saw them!

Maxine and Silano wrote reports suggesting that the man might be tall. It was more paper.

12

Apart from the bookie's, which was hallowed ground, there were only two operating stores in the Bull Ring: the booze store and the KFC. There had been seven in all, but calculated against the intermittent wreckage factor, profits didn't make the grade. The chain that owned the general store was still offering the premises for rent two years later. Now and again, an estate agent would check the property. While it remained more or less intact, nothing was said; and it remained that way because the place had a new purpose.

As soon as Stella saw the setup, she knew.

The cage was about sixteen feet square. The sides were a loose, mild steel mesh, and it had a flat webbing roof that would allow people in the high bleachers a bird's-eye view of the action. The place was about half full, but punters were pouring in. Stella went out and, careful not to backtrack against the flow of people, made a diversion that took her to the edge of the walk space beneath one of the blocks. Deep shadow, a warm breeze carrying a light payload of effluvium.

Harriman picked up on the third ring. He said, "They're on their way. ARV promised."

"Good. It's in what used to be Byrite—in the Bull Ring. They're dealing with a crowd of about eighty, maybe a hundred; some armed."

"How do you know?" Harriman asked, then checked himself. "Oh, right, Harefield . . ."

"It's a cage fight. Illegal betting, possibility of GBH charges."

"Jesus." A brief pause, then he thought to ask, "Where are you?"

"Outside. Just by Block C."

"Boss? Stay there."

"Sure; of course."

But she couldn't. There was a scent on the air stronger than the rankness brought by the breeze, a scent that was calling the crowd in, just as a whiff of fear calls the pack to a wounded deer. It was a complex scent, and fear was certainly a part of it, but there were strong overlays of excitement and an intense, black energy.

That scent was hot in Stella's nostrils as she climbed the pole-and-plank bleachers to sit eight rows back. A man with the face of a clapped-out angel was taking bets, clattering up and down between the rows of seats; his betting slips were cloakroom tickets, and his money bag was a battered school satchel. The fight handler was talking to the contestants, his voice low but urgent: pumping them up.

The cage fighters stood on each side of a wire-frame door, eyes locked in a stone-faced stare-out. They bounced on the balls of their feet and slapped one gloved fist against the other, but the stare never broke. The gloves were light and had individual fingers that stopped just below the middle knuckle. One of the fighters had a muddy tattoo of Christ crucified on his back; the other carried a scar that traveled from just under his left ear to his upper lip. It made Stella think of the scar Pete Harriman carried along the line of his jaw: the result of moving a fraction too slowly when a Harefield foot soldier came after him with a beer glass.

There were as many women in the place as men. When the fighters entered the cage, the men in the audience yelled advice and encouragement; the women whooped and screamed like mad birds. Something was added to that scent now: the pungent, thrilling smell of sex.

No rules, no quarter. As the fighters stepped through into the cage, Tattoo Man leaned sideways and kicked out hard, taking Scar Man in the thick of his waist and sending him back against the mesh. Tattoo Man moved in two-handed, but Scar Man was up, knocking his attacker's hands apart and leading with his head; he didn't make much contact, but it was enough to set Tattoo Man back on his heels. They circled awhile, feinting, trying to find an opening, then drove in at the same time, like stags locking.

They looked evenly matched; it was a fight that might have lasted; only cage-craft would make the difference, and Tattoo Man was the better equipped. He dropped low under Scar Man's guard and kicked the guy's legs out. There was a moment when Scar Man hit the ground, a moment of blankness, and in that moment Tattoo Man jumped on Scar Man's head.

Scar Man yelled in pain. He rolled and was fast getting to his feet, despite the damage. A second or two slower and he would have been straddled and beaten. He got in some hard licks as Tattoo Man came forward wanting to finish things: punches that snapped Tattoo Man's head back and brought gobbets of blood from his mouth. It was a good response, but the result was already there for all to see. Scar Man's face was lopsided where the cheekbone had caved in, and Tattoo Man was going for it with every swing. He connected with a tight hook to the head that put his opponent off balance, then kicked out stiff-legged, taking Scar Man just under the heart. Those close could see the light go out of his eyes; he took a step back, then another, hands high to block, but the punch got through anyway; then another; then another. He rattled the chain-link and sat down hard, one side of his face folded in like a fault line. Tattoo Man leaned down to follow up, to inflict the maximum, to be sure . . . then he paused and stepped back, his attention suddenly elsewhere.

Angel Face was on the move, his satchel tight under his arm. Maybe the bets had gone the wrong way, or maybe he had also heard the wail and whoop of sirens crossing the DMZ.

By the time Stella had got to her feet and was halfway to the door, the rest of the punters had heard it and were heading the same way. She had an edge, but people were funneling in from all directions. There was a shout of pain and fear as someone went underfoot, and a shoulder put her hard against the frame of the door, then she was clear and running toward the walk space under Block C, following Angel Face, because she had to pick on someone, and if he was the guy with the money, he was probably the guy with the connections.

From the corner of her eye she saw an ARV and a couple of people-carriers arriving. They fanned out, turning the crowd as a collie turns a flock, then rocked to a halt.

If you want to sneak up on the wrongdoer, she thought, *then head-banger sirens will do it every time.*

The walk space was half-light, litter, smells of fast food and putrefaction. She could see movement ahead and assumed it was Angel Face. He was running, though not flat-out—there were too many obstacles for that—but it was clear that he knew she was following, because he was taking a mazy path, going this way and that, zigging and zagging. Stella lost him for a moment, then heard a clatter and a curse and realized he must have fallen. She stood close to one of the concrete pillars that held up Block C, one dark shape melding with another, and looked left and right, waiting for his silhouette to show up against the dim light.

She thought that perhaps the money had spilled from his satchel, and she was right. No more than fifty feet away Angel Face was sitting on the ground scooping up the cash. It was a sack of garbage that had brought him down; he could tell as much from the stench of it. As he felt for stray notes, he looked about. Someone else was in the walkway, he knew that; someone under cover and under darkness, like himself, and he was holding a bag full of money. It was well on the way to being a lethal combination.

When he got to his feet, Stella saw him at once: he was much closer than she had imagined. He glanced back, then ran, this time taking a straight line toward the light.

Stella yelled, "Police officer. Stop!" and regretted it immediately; under these circumstances it was tantamount to shouting, "Shoot me!" She reckoned that if she could keep Angel Face heading toward the DMZ, she stood a chance of closing him down. If he managed to turn and get back to the Bull Ring, she'd lose him in the middle of whatever chaos was now going on there.

She was gaining. She was making good progress. He wasn't close enough to get a hand on, but he was losing the race. Then she hit the same sack of garbage and fell hard; the impact emptied her lungs, and she went down gagging for air. Angel Face clattered off through the walk-space detritus, while Stella lay on her back with her knees drawn up, mouth wide, making a raw gasping sound, like a woman urging a lover.

13

The sack of garbage was Barry or Gary; the stench told her as much. Given what lay round about him, others might not have made the distinction, but she'd smelled that smell before.

The first task force was still active in the Harefield warren when the second turned up: an AMIP squad fronted by a hardnut DS called Brian Collier. Stella had worked with him once in the past, and she didn't like him.

Collier had a bristly shadow of pepper-and-salt hair, a wrestler's neck, and a thick waist that pulled at his shirt. He and Stella sat on one of the low walls that formed the outer circle of the Bull Ring. Collier ducked his head to his cupped hands: lighting a cigarette.

He said, "You came because you thought she might have lived down here?" He was talking about Tree Girl.

"Missing-persons lead," Stella said. "Didn't go anywhere." Then: "He's likely to be off the estate." She was talking about Barry or Gary.

"Because no one would come down here if they didn't have to—"

"Exactly."

"Might have been on an errand."

"I suppose so. There's a lot of casual mugging; being a resident's no protection. Someone sees you leaving the bookie's with a smile on your face, or thinks you've just cashed your DHSS check—you're a target, no exceptions."

Collier laughed. "It wasn't that. Wasn't a mugging."

"No?"

"No." Collier took out his notebook and consulted it, as if giving evidence, his little joke. Stella remembered one of the many things she hadn't liked about him: he was a prick. "Initial report from the police doctor at the scene indicates that the victim's airway was occluded by a dense substance thought to be polyurethane, or a polyicynene and silicone mix." Collier looked at Stella and raised his eyebrows, then continued with the cod-official tone. "This substance expands freely when exposed to air and, in this case, flooded both larynx and thoracic cavity before quickly invading the trachea and lungs, causing death by suffocation." Collier looked up, grinning. "Someone jacked open the poor fucker's mouth and pumped him full of cavity-wall filler."

"I'll write you a report," Stella said, "unless you need me for anything else."

Collier shook his head. "Coroner's court, probably. I'll e-mail you the details." As she walked away, he said, "Weren't you from here?"

"That's right."

"I thought Harefield girls were all prossies."

"A missed opportunity," Stella said. "Better pay, less overtime, and you meet fewer pricks."

A yellow blind, something like that, something yellow anyway, and opposite Apartment 1136 on Block A.

Looked at from up on the walkway, Harefield was an ants' nest that someone had prodded with a stick. Arrests had been made, but there were crowds in the Bull Ring, young men mostly, and cops in Kevlar vests were walking through, never fewer than five officers together, more often ten. They would still be there when night fell, some up on the walkways, others drawn up round the place like herdsmen circling a corral. Nighttime riots were a Harefield speciality, not least after a police raid.

Stella thought, *Why did I call it in, for Christ's sake? Why not let them hammer each other shitless? Everyone was having fun.*

It wasn't a yellow blind; it was a magazine double-page photo-spread of a field of daffodils that had been pasted over a cracked window to hold it together. Apartment 1169, Block B. She rang the four-chime bell and waited, then rang again. People passed her on the walkway. Maybe she was recognized from the old days, because one of them put an elbow into her back, but she didn't turn: it would have been too much, too late.

There was a whiff of ganja on the wind; the sound of hip-hop from all directions; a splash of blood on the doorstep of 1169.

She walked back through the Bull Ring, heading for the DMZ, and DS Collier was there directing operations.

"Three fucking monkeys," he said, and did an eyes-ears-mouth routine with his hands, then laughed.

Stella said, "No kidding," but didn't stop. She knew he was watching her as she walked away.

She remembered one of the other things she didn't like about him: one evening, the job still in progress, the team in the pub for an after-work drink, and he'd hit on her, brash, insistent, and then sour-mouthed when she'd told him no. She pictured him with his arm against the wall, leaning to box her in, his whiskey breath in her face, saying, "I'm hung. I'm really hung."

She leaned against her car and took out her phone to make a call, but it rang before she could dial, Pete Harriman's name coming up on the LCD. She said, "I'm on my way," in the same moment that he said, "We've got another."

14

There was a light breeze off the river that rattled the sides of the scene-of-crime tent. Inside there was a smell of nettles and dogshit and blood. The tent enclosed a wooden riverside bench, slatted and bearing a little brass plaque that said:

IN LOVING MEMORY OF ARTHUR JAMES FITTS
(1933–2003)
WHO LOVED THE VIEW FROM THIS SPOT

The current occupant of the bench was unlikely to be enjoying the view, because he was dead, his head lowered, eyes staring at the ground where a sizable pool of his own blood had soaked into the dry ruts of the path. His chinos were stiff with it. His shirtfront carried a dark red bib. His shoes were crusted. The sleeves of his shirt were rolled back to the elbow, and his forearms carried what, at first, looked like tattoos. A closer look revealed that they were two words written in black marker pen:

FILTHY COWARD

"Two in one day," Stella said. She was talking about Barry or Gary.

"Only one of them yours," Harriman observed.

Stella looked at him. "It's not the paperwork, for Christ's sake, it's the body count. I'm not a pathologist—one's enough for me. Do we know who he is?"

"Leonard Pigeon."

"What?"

Harriman flapped his arms to simulate flight. "Pigeon. ID in his wallet: credit cards and so on."

"He still had his wallet—"

"He did; no cash in it, though."

Leonard Pigeon was leaning back, well down on the slats of the bench, knees out, as if he had been taking the sun and fallen asleep. Harriman walked behind the bench and pointed. A cord had been used to tie Leonard's belt to the lowest slat in the backrest; a second cord was round his neck to keep his head and torso in position, though the fact that his chin was on his chest made it impossible to see this from directly in front, and the rest was hidden by his shirt collar.

Forensic officers, dressed from head to toe in white, were active on all sides, gathering, assessing, bagging, some inside the tent, some operating in a wider area that had been taped off. Little bands of walkers gathered at the boundaries, asking when they could continue. It was just the Thames tow-path, but some wore hiking boots and carried rucksacks with rugged logos; uniformed officers pointed them back the way they'd come.

"Mobile phone?" Stella asked.

"Oh, yeah, sure."

"Use ICE?"

"Two entries: one a landline, no reply, no answer phone; the other a mobile, apparently switched off, no personal message. Sue Chapman's doing a trace. Shouldn't be long."

ICE had been established after 9/11, after the Tsunami, after the London bombings: *In Case of Emergency*, entered on to your mobile phone with a contact number; the whole world anticipating the worst.

There were flies feasting off the drying pool of Leonard Pigeon's blood and swarming round his chin; flies and a small contingent of wasps, those sharky little meat-eaters. The video man had been and gone, but the stills photographer was popping a few shots, sending flashgun glare off the walls of the tent. Stella stepped out, taking Harriman with her.

"Who called it in?"

"A couple . . . they were out for a walk. There's a small problem."

"Go on."

"He should have been at work, and she's married to someone else."

"They want us to be discreet."

"They do."

"Where are they?"

"Gave a statement, left contact numbers, went their separate ways."

"Have them come into the nick. It's none of our business. Called it in when?"

"Hour and a half ago? More like two hours."

"*What?*"

"The locals were doing it, boss. Then someone noticed they weren't tattoos on his arms and made the connection."

The scene-of-crime doctor was leaning up against a tree and making notes. Stella went across and asked him the one question he wouldn't want to answer.

"It would be a guess, you know that." He was a tall man in his early thirties, his long, thin face peppered with black stubble. His name was Larsen.

"A guess will do."

"The pathologist will give you an accurate reading: insect infestation, blood pooling, you know . . . I can only do rectal temperature minus ambient temperature blah-blah."

"So blah-blah."

"Somewhere between four and six hours don't," he added seamlessly, "quote me."

"He's been dead six hours?"

"Could be, I'm not prepared to . . . you know . . . outside limit."

"Is it possible that he was killed elsewhere and moved later?" She already knew the answer but wanted it from an expert.

"God, no. Once you're dead, the heart stops pumping: ergo, no blood loss." He flipped a hand toward the scene-of-crime tent. "You only have to look—blood all over the place."

"Okay," Stella said. "Cause of death . . ."

Larsen shrugged. "Asphyxiation, shock, either or both. Deep transverse incision severing the jugular vein and the carotid artery while also doing severe damage to the trachea and the thyroid cartilage."

Stella remembered Collier reading from the doctor's notes on Barry or Gary: death was all terminology in the end.

"Any thoughts about how?"

"Again, you'll get more from pathology—from forensics too, I expect. I think it's a fair bet that the killer approached him from behind, took him by surprise. It's a single cut, very deep, and the victim has no defensive wounds, so I'd say there was an element of surprise. Came up from behind, pulled the guy's head back, by his hair or with a hand under the chin, quick, hard swipe of the knife. Whoever cut this man's throat," Larsen observed, "made a good job of it."

"Can you make a *bad* job of it?"

"Certainly. I've seen a few tentative tracheotomies—a paramedic or junior A & E doctor who couldn't get up the nerve. This guy got it right." He shrugged. "If you see what I mean."

"Specialist knowledge?" Stella asked.

"I don't think he was particularly skilled," Larsen said. "Not necessarily, anyway. Just very vigorous."

"He was *vigorous*?" The word sounded strange to Stella—oddly inappropriate.

"Yeah." Larsen nodded. "Any more vigorous and he'd have taken the guy's head clean off."

A pleasure boat was chugging downstream, being paced by a pair of herons. The tourists were dressed for summer in spring and glad of the breeze. A PA system yapped at them, information overload from a bored girl who had seen it, and said it, hundreds of times before.

The sun was high and hot, the river flat, the towpath silent. A sudden rustle in the undergrowth close to the edge of the path was a rat, drawn by the scent of blood. Harriman stamped his foot at it.

"He might have been dead for six hours," Stella said, "and he died here. When was it called in—two hours ago?"

"Max."

"And no one noticed?"

They went back inside the scene-of-crime tent and looked again at Leonard Pigeon. His posture said "sleeping," but the blood was loud.

"The bench is set back," Harriman said. "Some are right on the edge overlooking the water, some are just a foot or two from the path, but others are well back under the trees and this is one of them."

Stella cast a glance to the brush at the back of the bench, all thick-leaved and in its summer green.

Came up from behind, pulled the guy's head back, by his hair . . .

"Even so . . . surely someone would have seen him."

"People walk without looking left or right," Harriman said. "They're locked up inside themselves." Then, as if to explain, "It's London."

"Yes, you're right." Stella nodded acknowledgment, a woman more locked up inside herself than most.

In fact, Harriman had been partly right. It was a weekday, the towpath wasn't busy, the bench was under the trees and in shade . . . A few people had passed Leonard Pigeon without noticing anything, lost in thought, or looking toward the river, or just keeping themselves to themselves. Several bikers had hammered past intent on speed averages, or too winded for peripheral vision to be a factor. But there must have been one or two . . . two or three . . . who had looked and seen and passed on quickly. A dog, eager for the blood, having to be called away or pulled away. Someone noticing the flies. Another drawn by the strange stillness of the man on the bench.

Three or four, perhaps. Maybe more.

It was London.

15

The towpath lovers were called Leah and Steve. They arrived at the AMIP-5 squad room together, though they had traveled there from different directions. Sue Chapman found some chairs and sited them in a corridor. The lovers sat there holding hands and waiting for a couple of interview rooms to fall vacant in the admin. building. Steve glanced at his watch from time to time, lifting his left hand; it was the hand Leah was holding and she didn't let go: when Steve checked the time, both their arms came up, as though they were acknowledging cheers from an audience.

Maxine sat down with Leah.

The interview room was basic pine furniture and off-white walls, everything pale just as Leah was pale. Her bottle-blond hair fell to her shoulders, and she wore a delicate pink lipstick.

She said, "Is this like the doctor or the priest?"

Maxine smiled, though not to reassure. "It's confidential, unless a reason is found for it not to be."

"I'm married. Steve isn't my husband."

"Yes, you mentioned it to the scene-of-crime officer."

"So, I tell you what happened, and then—"

"Possibility of coroner's court. We'll let you know."

"On my mobile."

"It comes as a summons from the coroner's office."

Leah was silent for a while: inventing tactics, perhaps. Finally, she said, "It was our bench."

"Sorry?"

"Our bench: the place where we usually sit. That's how we happened to see him. When I looked across, there was someone sitting on our bench. It was him."

"You realized he was dead—"

"After a second or two. The way he was sitting so still. Then I saw the blood; or Steve did."

That was Leah's story; all she had to tell. They went through the business of who had called the police (Steve), whether they had seen anything of significance (no), whether they had touched the body (no), what would happen if Leah's husband should learn of her relationship with Steve (mayhem).

Leah said, "It's complicated."

Maxine was reading through Leah's statement. Without looking up, she said, "I expect it is."

"It's a matter of timing."

Maxine said, "Look—"

"It's serious, me and Steve. A serious thing. He has to go abroad for a while. I could tell Nick, but then what would I do while Steve's away?" She spoke about Nick as if Maxine knew him.

Maxine said, "Look, it's none of my business. I just have to get a statement, you know?"

"I'm explaining—"

"You don't have to."

"When Steve gets back, things will happen then. It'll all be aboveboard. We've been to look at flats."

Maxine said, "We'll be in touch."

Leah stood up. She was tall and slim-hipped and pretty in an etiolated kind of way. She said, "If he hadn't been on our bench, we'd never have seen him. There might have been a dead body on every other bench we passed for all I know. Why did he have to be on our bench?"

Maxine countersigned the record of statement, then dated and timed it. More paper.

She said, "Yes. Selfish bastard."

Frank Silano sat down with Steve.

Someone had put a fan in the room, and it whirred very gently in the background while they spoke. Silano heard it as a flight of birds. Steve gave his age as thirty-two and his occupation as garden designer. He was unmarried, and his address wasn't permanent just now since he was about to go to America. Californian gardens, he told Silano, afforded a high cash yield. He spoke of sun and dollars and one hell of a lifestyle. When he'd finished with California, he told the same story as Leah: the walk, the bench they always sat on . . .

"She's married," he said, "which makes things a bit complicated, yeah? Just a bit tricky."

Silano didn't think for a moment that Leah and Steve had killed Leonard Pigeon, but he was a meticulous cop, and he liked to get everything down. He asked about the affair. Steve was all man-to-man on that; all fuck-and-tell. It had been going on for about four months and had started when Steve was landscaping Leah and Nick's garden: two-thirds of an acre, Richmond waterside, two-point-four million. Now they met during the day, when Leah's husband was at work: a couple of times a week at Steve's impermanent address. Leah lived for those two days, and Steve knew it, though he didn't say as much to Frank Silano.

"If you're freelance," Steve observed, "you can organize your time."

Silano passed the statement across for Steve to sign and mentioned the possibility of an appearance in the coroner's court.

"I go to the States in a couple of weeks."

Silano shrugged. "Leave an address—you might have to come back."

"You're kidding."

"But these things take time. Maybe you'll have finished the job over there by the time you're needed."

Steve shook his head. "No," he said, "look, I'm not planning to come back."

It went round the squad room as "story of the day."

16

John Delaney was getting a taste for it: the midmorning champagne, the big airy houses, the BritArt, the spare Maserati. It wasn't his lifestyle, of course, but it was definitely that of the people he was interviewing, and now and then, just for a few minutes, he was allowed to get a share.

If the champagne was being opened, he drank a glass. He strolled through libraries and snooker rooms while waiting for his interviewee. He climbed regal staircases. He noted those spot-paintings (everyone had them) and compared them one with another. If the interview transferred from town to country, he was naught to sixty in a blur.

Neil Morgan was an exception only in matters of taste: a Lowry, not a Hirst; a Lexus GS300, not a boy's toy. In all other respects, he measured up, with his house in Norland Square, his flawless wife, his directorships. Delaney sat in a large, elegant room, his back to the light, and listened to Morgan telling him about wealth and ambition. The essence of the story was you can't have one without the other. When Morgan started in on politics, Delaney held up a hand to interrupt, but only while he turned the cassette in his recorder.

"New Labor," Morgan said, "now New Conservatism. It's time for a change, you can feel it. Blair only found power and held it by parking his tanks on our lawn."

In addition to being a multimillionaire, Morgan was a Conservative MP: a backbench activist. He liked to think of himself as one of the coming men. This was because the press had labeled him "One of the Coming Men." Twice Morgan had turned down shadow cabinet posts; he was biding his time, waiting for the big one: Home Office, Foreign Office. Until that happened he would be a mover and shaker. Mover and shaker and lurker.

He talked about money: it was a key that unlocked doors.

He talked about the war in Iraq: it was a good thing.

He talked about a global economy: it was the one true way.

While Delaney sat, Morgan walked. He roamed the room, speaking in a low, passionate voice: a slight man in his early forties, formally dressed, his narrow, carefully shaven face glowing with conviction. His eyes had an odd, upward slant; they glittered.

"Remember Gordon Gecko?" he asked.

Delaney offered, "Greed is good."

"That's what people quote, that's their memory: greed is good, greed is right, greed works. They don't recall the rest of it." Delaney waited. "Greed in all its forms," Morgan said, "greed for life, for money, for love, knowledge—has marked the upward surge of mankind."

"You've got it by heart."

"By heart is right. By *heart*. And the country will feel that, and the people will respond, and they'll see that we're the future."

Delaney wanted to dim the light in Morgan's eyes. He turned his questions away from the future and asked, instead, about death. He asked about six hundred thousand dead Iraqis, he asked about Abu Ghraib, he asked about Guantánamo Bay and Extraordinary Rendition.

Acid leaked into Morgan's voice. "Everyone knows I voted in favor of that action. I would do the same again. Some unfortunate things have happened, but it's war, not a stroll in the park."

Off-the-shelf phrases, and old stock at that; Delaney allowed himself the ghost of a smile. He said, "A lot of people opposed it—ordinary people; there were marches, millions of people on the streets."

"This country isn't run by straw poll," Morgan informed him. "Governments govern, that's their job."

Morgan wasn't a daytime champagne man and, anyway, Delaney had taped enough. He stood up and got a firm, politician's handshake. As he hit the street, Stella and Harriman were just arriving to let Morgan know that his principal researcher had been found on a bench by the river, his throat cut back to the cervical vertebrae.

17

DI Mike Sorley was getting into his second pack of the day. Stella watched as he snapped his lighter, lit up, then allowed the flame to come dangerously close to the stacks of paper on his desk.

"It's one way," she observed.

Sorley laughed. "Don't think I'm not tempted." He pushed one set of files aside to accommodate those Stella had just brought in. The file on Elizabeth Rose Connor aka Bryony Dean had moved up a little but still lay five deep. He said, "We've got all manner of shit here. We've got a crazy person, we've got a multiple, and we've got a prominent MP. I know it's a multiple because I can count, I know it's a crazy because the press have it in page-high headlines, and I know the MP is prominent because the pompous bastard told me so."

He drew on his cigarette so the coal crackled: a lungful wasn't enough for Sorley.

"A crazy person, right? Has to be."

Stella knew Sorley was being wry—he was too good a copper to jump to easy conclusions. She said what was in his mind: "That, or it's what we're supposed to think."

"So either way we're looking for connections between the two."

"Would be if we had an ID for Tree Girl."

"What are we holding back?"

In every investigation, certain details would be kept from the press in order to eliminate the professional confessors who stood in line for their chance at fame, to be loathed and feared, to be up there with the best of the worst.

"The writing," Stella said. "Dirty girl; filthy coward."

"There's your link," Sorley observed. "There's your connection."

"I know. Except I don't know what I know. Whether it's a real connection or a connection the killer's making in his mind. I need to find out more about him."

"Talk to a profiler?"

"Yes."

"Stay in budget, Stella." There was enough of Sorley's cigarette left to light the next. He said, "This Morgan looks a problem."

Stella grimaced. "I thought he was pro-police: more money, more powers. Didn't he vote for ninety-day detention?"

"He did. But it seems we've let him down—a brutal and horrendous attack in broad daylight, an innocent man's life cut short, maniacs roaming the streets, a police force that seems unable to deal with the ever-increasing blah-fucking-blah."

"He has friends in the press," Stella guessed.

"Friends everywhere, flash fucker." After a moment Sorley said, "He likes public places, our maniac."

"He does."

"Big risk."

"Maybe that's what he likes."

The rest of the team were going different ways.

Sue Chapman was cross-referencing forensics.

Maxine Hewitt and Frank Silano were talking to Mrs. Pigeon.

Andy Greegan was reviewing the scene-of-crime material.

Pete Harriman was kissing a whore in a pub up by the Strip.

18

It was just a kiss hello, because Stacey didn't do professional mouth-to-mouth. She was a natural redhead with a neat body and the perfect lips for kissing, but you couldn't buy them. Stacey had a repertoire second to none: slow hand, good head, straight all ways up, dealer's choice, three-way humps, name your shame. She would look up for a facial, or stand in the rain, and if the money was right she might even stretch to anal, but kissing was off the list.

Harriman's lips brushed her hair, and he only got that because he'd known Stacey for five years and helped her out on a couple of occasions.

Occasion one: malicious wounding during an attempted fuck-and-run. Stacey had multiple abrasions and a cracked rib; the punter had crisscross knife lines on his buttocks. Harriman reported person or persons unknown.

Occasion two: a pimp takeover complete with death threats. Harriman pulled the pimp on suspicion and just happened to find, in the boot of the guy's Ferrari Modena, an attaché case full of street-ready crack.

Stacey was drinking Breezers because there were still some working hours left in the day. Harriman was on duty, so he'd decided on Scotch with a Becks chaser. He took out the retouched morgue photo of Tree Girl and pushed it across the table to Stacey. Underneath the ten-by-eight was the price of a blow job. That was their real relationship.

The trade-off for having a cop as a friend in times of need made Stacey Harriman's "chis." That's *c*overt *h*uman *i*ntelligence *s*ource. Stacey wasn't crazy about the arrangement, but some worked the curbs and cars, some worked the pubs and bars, and if you were an indoors girl, like Stacey, you needed good connections. She had an apartment in North Kensington, a client list, and an advertising network that brought the punters to her door. She was almost a class act and only hit the bars when the cash flow was low.

She palmed the money and held the photo to the light. "Is this the girl in the tree? Is this Tree Girl?"

"Yes."

Stacey looked closer; her mouth twisted in a little grimace. "What happened to her?"

"Someone hung her in—"

"Happened to her face."

Harriman tried to think of another way to say it, but gave up. "Birds took her eyes."

Stacey looked for a long time, and Harriman knew she wasn't running through a mental file index, she was thinking how all the girls on the Strip were just a step away from something like this. Just a step, a wrong word, a bad connection, a piece of lousy luck.

She said, "It's Lizzie."

19

That was all Stacey could offer: Lizzie. Lizzie Someone. Lizzie No Name. Though she did have more on Lizzie's connections and her way of life.

"She was freelance. The pimps tried to muscle in, add her to their list, but she wouldn't talk to them: she was like a guerrilla-whore, you know? Hit and run. She'd arrive out of nowhere, scoop a trick, go off in the guy's car, do the business, then turn up twenty minutes later in a boozer or some pizza-pasta place just off-limits looking for more."

"How did you know her?" Harriman asked.

"She worked the pubs sometimes, especially if the pimps were down on her: safety in numbers, though your hit ratio tends to be poor compared to working the curbs. Question of turnover." She laughed at the word "turnover"; she'd heard it before. "Lizzie tended to do pretty good business."

"She was special?"

"She was young. Fresh meat." Pimp terminology: Stacey said it with a sneer.

"Did you speak to her?"

"No. I heard her speak, though. To punters."

"What nationality was she?"

"You really don't know much about her, do you?"

"She was dead, she was naked. No, not a thing."

"Local. South London accent, Essex, whatever you call it."

"Tell me about the pimps."

"You know . . . they hate a bandit. She was picking up their business. They tried to kidnap her a couple of times, but pimps are lazy, and she was fast."

She finished her drink and looked for another. Harriman said, "Sure, in a minute. When did you last see her?"

"Who knows? A week ago, maybe. She'd picked up a cruiser . . . at least, he'd seen her and was pulling over. Trouble was, Costea saw her at the same time."

"Costea—?"

"Radu. Costea Radu. He runs ten or so from Romania: pays his street rental and doesn't take kindly to girls who stray in . . . or girls who stray out."

"He's violent . . ."

Stacey laughed. "He's a pimp."

"Where can I find him? What does he look like?"

Stacey held up her hands. "Pete, this only goes so far."

"I'm going to the bar to get us a refill," Harriman said. "You could spend the time looking at Lizzie's picture. Imagine what she looked like before they did the computer cosmetics."

When he got back, Stacey said, "Six three, carries some weight, long hair, looks like a roadie. He wears a big cross."

"Cross?"

"Crucifix, you know." She laughed. "He's from Transylvania, think about it."

"And can be found at—?"

"On the street sometimes. He drives a silver Jeep. Or there's a basement casino underneath a minicab company—Steadfast Cars. I'm going to need a smoke screen."

"We'll bust the casino: illegal gambling, nothing to do with Lizzie, nothing to do with you. Then some unnamed officer from Vice will let us know what Costea does for a living. After that, he'll be helping us with our inquiries."

"Okay . . ." She sounded unconvinced. "Don't come back to me for a while, Pete." Harriman nodded. Stacey picked up the ten-by-eight, looked at it, then shot it back across the table. "I used to work the Strip," she said. "It's a fucking treadmill."

"Meaning?"

"She might have turned twelve tricks a day; what's that a week?"

"Eighty-four."

"Right. How many a month?"

Harriman couldn't do the math. "A lot."

"In six months?"

"Your point is?"

"You only need one mad bastard, one crazy. Any one of them could have done her."

"You have to hate someone to do what he did to her." Harriman was thinking of the brand on her back: Dirty Girl.

"We're hookers," Stacey said. "The men who use us—they all hate us; it's just a matter of degree."

20

Maxine Hewitt, Frank Silano, Mrs. Pigeon, Mr. Pigeon. They sat in diamond formation in Mrs. Pigeon's drawing room. The apartment was on Chiswick Mall, and the room overlooked the river. Maxine calculated that the bench where Leonard Pigeon died must be only just out of sight.

Mr. Pigeon was Mrs. Pigeon's father-in-law. His name was Maurice, her name was Paula. The older Mrs. Pigeon had died five years before. Silano had all this down in his notebook. He wondered what Paula's name had been before she married and became Paula Pigeon; he wondered if she had stood at the altar and had second thoughts.

Do you, Paula, take this man . . .

Silano was distracting himself this way because he didn't think there was much to learn from the interview, but also because Maurice Pigeon was on a seamless law-and-order riff in which the police were looking pretty bad. Pretty inefficient. Pretty much willing to let throats be cut on towpaths, while teen creeps dealt dope, glassed each other, and threw up in city centers without let or hindrance. It was the same speech Neil Morgan, MP, had delivered to the tabloids.

Paula was completely in control of her emotions, apart from frequent swallowings and the occasional fractured syllable: techniques designed to kill the urge to cry. She looked like a woman full to the brim.

Maxine had already mentioned that they would be taking Leonard's computer away with them. That they would need to look through his papers. That they had already appropriated his BlackBerry. That they would like to have a good, clear photograph of Leonard. That none of these things meant they harbored any suspicions about Leonard's private life: it was routine practice in a crime of this nature.

Maurice Pigeon considered it outrageous and would be consulting his lawyer before they would be allowed to take anything, or look at anything, oh, and maybe they would like to tell him what progress, if any, had they made in finding his son's killer?

Silano explained, "We're gathering information."

"Oh, good, I'm pleased to hear that." Maurice's voice was tuned to a sneer. He added, "Have you the slightest idea of how we feel? How Paula and I feel?"

Silano looked at the floor. He said, "No, of course not"—barely audible, just holding his anger at bay.

Maxine stepped in. "Anything strange," she said, "anything out of the ordinary, any break in routine or change of plan—"

"It was his usual walk. He went at the usual time. He set off in the usual way." Paula's swallowings were punctuation.

"But he didn't come back," Maxine said.

"I assumed he'd gone straight to the office. He often did."

"Think further back," Maxine told her. "Anything in the last week . . . in the last month."

Paula shook her head. "We live a fairly well-ordered life," she said. "Straightforward."

Maurice said, "That business on the bridge." When Paula didn't respond, he said, "The bridge."

Paula said, "Yes." Her irritation was plain to see, but it was masking distress. To Maxine, she said, "Len was crossing Hammersmith Bridge . . . going for his walk. It was unusually early—about seven—he had a meeting with Neil at eight thirty. He got onto the bridge and noticed something was happening at the far end. Some young people—"

"Thugs," Maurice said. "Scum. Subhumans."

"Some boys . . . a couple of girls. They were threatening a woman. Mugging her, I suppose. It turned out they'd been taking things, drugs, all manner of drugs . . . they'd been up all night, it seems . . ."

Silano was writing. He asked, "This was—"

"A couple of weeks back."

"They threw her in," Maxine said. "It was on TV."

Maurice snorted. "Is that how you people keep up with the crime statistics—by watching television?"

"Len went toward them. He told me he shouted at them. 'Leave her alone' . . . something . . . Two of the boys came after him—"

"He ran away," Maxine said. It was more abrupt than she'd intended.

"He ran to get help. What else should he have done?"

"He ran," Maurice said, his voice trembling, "to phone for the police, who took fifteen minutes to arrive."

Maxine's mind went to the SOC video of the dead man on the bench: the buzzsaw noise of flies, the voice of the video operator describing what

he was filming, the hoot of a pleasure boat in the background. She saw
Leonard Pigeon's chin slumped on his chest, a little fan of severed flesh like
a ruff, blood dark on his shirtfront. She saw the marker-pen scrawl on his
forearms: FILTHY COWARD.

There was nothing else.

Silano put away his notebook and pen. He said they would be in touch.
He mentioned the forthcoming visit from a forensic team.

Maxine gave details of the postmortem, the inquest, the likely schedule
for release of the body for burial.

They got into their car and drove away. Silano said, "He bottled it."

"Most people would have."

"What happened to the woman?"

"She drowned."

"So . . . You made the connection," Silano said.

Maxine took avoiding action as a Vauxhall Vectra running a red light
on Hammersmith Broadway threatened a broadside. She leaned on her
horn, and Vectra Man popped a finger at her.

"Yes," she said, "I made the connection."

21

"Filthy coward," Stella said. "They mugged her; they threw her in; he ran; she
drowned. It was on local TV news, local press, even made the inside pages
of the tabloids. Anyone could have seen it."

"Is that what the press called him," Anne Beaumont asked, "a filthy
coward?"

"Not as extreme as that."

"But it was implied?"

Sue Chapman had trawled the cuttings and the news footage. A couple
of the tabloids had suggested that Leonard Pigeon wasn't the bravest of
men, and when Leonard had declined to be interviewed, readers and view-
ers had been left to reach their own conclusions. A radio show had run a
phone-in: "What would you have done?" Some listeners suggested that

Leonard had made a wise decision: the decision they themselves would have made. Most were not so kind. The question of whether Leonard had balls ran for a day or so, then faded and died.

"What do you think," Stella asked, "first impression?"

Anne smiled. She and Stella were sitting in the basement kitchen of Anne's house in Kensington Gore, just opposite Hyde Park. Anne was in her early forties but looked younger, an illusion that was helped by high cheekbones and strawberry-blond hair that needed only the merest help. She was a profiler but had also, once, been Stella's shrink: the only person who knew just how traumatic it had been for Stella to find those little bodies hanging in the stairwell.

Anne said, "First impressions are dangerous."

"Take a risk."

"Want some coffee?"

Stella said, "Okay," then sat in silence while Anne went through the coffee routine, a little frown on her face. Finally, she said, "I'm trying to think of something like it, and I can't, not really. Signature killings, yes. David Berkowitz—you know, Son of Sam—used to leave notes identifying himself that way. There have been killers who have left messages. The Washington Sniper's trademark was a note that read 'Policeman, I am God.' But this business of accusing the victim . . ." She stalled on her way to the table with the cafetière and cups, eyes closed for a moment, scanning an image. "It reminds me of those photos of wartime atrocities, women mostly, hanged by the Nazis: they often had a sign round their necks stating their so-called crime." She moved to the table and poured the coffee. "People put in the stocks were treated in the same way, weren't they? And the crucified—a list of their offenses displayed." She paused, then: "Maybe he's justifying what he does."

"To himself," Stella suggested.

"To himself . . . to you. Here's the reason. Here's why it had to happen."

"Don't blame me? Is that what he's saying?"

"Or just stating a fact: one that he expects you to agree with. Have you told Delaney you slept with the forensic guy? Harrison . . ." Anne was a left-field specialist.

"Davison. No."

"Will you?"

Stella laughed. "Do all shrinks like gossip?"

"Of course—it's just analysis with a bad reputation."

Stella said, "Delaney's planning something."

"What?"

"Not sure. Something up his sleeve."

"Tell me."

"He asked me if I was happy. Happy with us."

"What did you say?"

This wasn't therapy, this was serious girl stuff. "I was called away at the crucial moment," Stella said. "Body hanging in tree. Sorry."

"Of course, he might just be cataloguing."

Stella knew she didn't mean Delaney. "How so?"

"Maybe he's got a list—dirty girl, filthy coward—and he's ticking them off. Guilty people: guilty in his eyes, anyway."

"What, this guy sees himself as some sort of moral guardian?" Stella sounded indignant.

Anne shrugged. "It's a theory. Theories are all I've got."

"Can you describe him?"

"Oh, sure, roughly. He's almost certainly under forty, probably younger, low self-esteem, hence a need for power, strong fantasy life, history of violence, though possibly not known about, solitary by nature, though might well be good at faking regular-guy status, difficult childhood—"

"Textbook serial killer," Stella observed.

"The guy next to you on the tube, beside you in the street, behind you in the queue."

"And he'll do it again."

"As long as he can find people who have transgressed in some way or another—according to his rules, anyway."

"Sinners," Stella suggested.

"Good word."

"My God." Stella looked at Anne; the truth of it had just struck her. "And how many sinners in the world?"

"Well, there's us," said Anne, "to begin with."

Andy Greegan was sifting; sifting and screening.

He was a good scene-of-crime officer and had the habit of going back over the stills and videos; there was something about looking at an image, rather than the real thing, that permitted greater concentration. After ten years as a copper, he was still capable of being affected by violent death. They all were, though some pretended better than others.

There had been several keen pairs of eyes at the scene, and forensics had tweezered and scooped and bagged, but there was something else to find, and Andy found it. A matter of comparison. A matter of compare and combine. At Tree Girl's scene, it was at about shoulder height on the trunk. It wasn't surprising that no one had remarked on it, because the lower part of the trunk was scarred with initials, scratches and scrapes, blisters where the bark had been infested; mostly, though, it hadn't been spotted because until Leonard Pigeon's body had been found, there was no comparison to be made.

Andy had transferred the SOC images to computer and made a grid for both scenes of crime and then isolated each section. After that, he had laid a second grid over the individual sections and put them side by side: he was looking at fragments of a single image. Even with that kind of scrutiny, it took an odd accident to direct his eye. Leonard might have been sitting with one arm along the top slat of the bench when he was killed—that, or he had flung his arm out when the killer came up behind him and started his work. Either way, the arm ran through eight grid sections, ending in a loose fist with the index finger seeming to point, which drew Greegan's eye to a mark on the bench close to the finger in the final grid. Like the tree, the bench was defaced. A kid had tagged it with black spray-can paint, and the mark was within one loop of the tag, making it stand out.

Even then, Greegan might have passed over it; but something nagged at him. He went back to the first scene of crime and looked at the grids he'd made for the tree. There it was: a double "V" inverted over a single, upright "V."

$$\wedge \ \wedge$$
$$\mathsf{V}$$

Greegan isolated the grids, enlarged them, printed them off together with full images of both tree and bench to show their relative positions, sent the whole package to Stella's VDU, and then put the printouts on her desk, along with a Post-it note.

The note said, "What's this?"

22

Delaney was cooking one of the few things he knew how to cook; it involved eggs and onions and peppers; it involved shaking leaves out of a bag into a bowl. He'd made the dressing himself, because store dressings were sweet and he liked to be able to taste the vinegar. He looked sideways at the printout Stella had dropped onto the counter.

"No," he said, "you'll have to tell me."

"It's not a quiz. I don't know either."

He was using a fork to whip the eggs. "Do you ever do something, start to do something, and you're bored as soon as you begin?"

"Like?"

"Taking a shower, cleaning your teeth, shaving."

"I rarely shave."

"You know . . ."

"Those things bore you?"

"Shitless. And whipping eggs. What did Morgan say when you told him?"

"What people always say. There must be some mistake, it's someone else, no one would do that to . . . daughter, son, husband, wife, whoever. The only people who accept it straightaway are those who half expect it."

"Who are they?"

"Relatives of paramedics, firefighters, cops . . ."

"What did he say after that?"

"To me, nothing. He spent ten minutes on the phone rearranging schedules and finding a temporary replacement for the recently dead."

"Yep, sounds like the Morgan I met." He looked again at the printout. "Where's it from?"

"Scene of crime."

"What makes you think it means anything?"

"Both scenes of crime."

"Even so . . . You'd probably find the same graffiti tag nearby if you look. Hoodie boys are everywhere."

"You think this is a tag?"

"Sure. Why not?"

"How did Morgan come across to you?"

"Rich bastard. Open some wine. Rich pompous bastard."

"That's what Mike Sorley said. What are you making?"

Delaney gestured to the ingredients as if to indicate that they spoke for themselves.

Stella fetched a bottle of sauvignon blanc from the fridge and poured two glasses. "Spanish omelette, bag salad: the very outer reaches of your repertoire."

Delaney took a big slug of wine. "Not true, I can roast a chicken."

"I look forward to the day. There's something I need to tell you."

She hadn't meant to say it, but there it was, the words circling the room like little heat-seeking missiles. Maybe because Anne Beaumont had prompted the idea; maybe because she felt Delaney had intended to say something important to her at the restaurant, and she needed to get things straight between them.

He transferred the eggs to a pan and adjusted the heat. He didn't say anything; she wondered if he knew what was coming.

I slept with someone. It was stupid. It didn't mean anything. It wasn't to do with him, it was to do with us—a payback. And I'm sorry. I'm truly sorry.

But what she said was, "There's something else that connects them: the victims. He wrote on them."

"It's what you're holding back—to weed out the crazies."

"Yes."

"I thought you weren't going to tell me."

No, but I almost shot my mouth off, almost confessed; then my nerve broke and I needed some cover.

"It's privileged information. If I see it in the press, I'll arrest you."

"Writes what?"

"Insults."

"Yes, but what?"

"No. I *am* keeping that back." Something salvaged.

"Okay: appropriate insults?"

"More or less. Let's say they are."

"So he knows them."

"Or knows about them."

"Yes, or *knows* them. Has a connection."

"Is . . . what? . . . in their circle."

Delaney shrugged. "It's a theory."

"The girl was a hooker; Pigeon was a senior research assistant to a prominent Tory MP."

Delaney added the peppers and onion to the eggs. He laughed. "Circles come a lot wider than that."

When they were eating, she said, "I thought I saw my mother. I was on Harefield; she was going into a flat with some guy."

"Thought you saw her."

"She had her back to me. Well, a bit of profile, but only for a second."

"You told me she was in Birmingham."

"Manchester."

"And so . . ."

"So she's back. Could be back."

"You'd know your own mother."

Stella laughed without smiling. "I never knew her."

Delaney knew about this. Little Stella Mooney, address Apartment 1818, Block C, Harefield Gulag, watching the weather, following the flight of birds and wishing she could do that, wishing she could find a thermal, like the city gulls, and tilt, sliding down the wind until she reached somewhere that was somewhere else. Stella keeping quiet, keeping to herself, reading her own school reports, because her mother never would, looking for a way out, taking charge of her own life.

Her father was the man with no name. Stella wondered whether her mother actually knew it; could actually remember what he had looked like; could actually pick him out of the lineup of lovers and liggers and one-night stands.

"How long since you saw her?" Delaney asked.

"Ten years." She said it without thinking, as if she had been keeping a tally.

"What will you do . . . if it's her?" Stella shook her head. "If you meet her? If you go and see her?"

She forked up some omelette and raised her wineglass as if for a toast. "Good food, good wine, the evening lacks only one thing."

Their lovemaking still had a genuine hunger that, eventually, brought a sweet fatigue. They lay side by side, hands linked, half asleep.

Delaney said, "Maybe I'm right. The killer knew his victims. They knew each other. Leonard Pigeon had a secret life."

"Don't print it."

"I'm not a reporter anymore. I'm a features guy. The Rich List, the swells, their itch to be rich."

"Do you ever miss it, Delaney? Be honest."

Stella had never known him as a war reporter. He'd talked, sometimes, about the way he'd felt. Never about the things he'd seen. She remembered his descriptions of jeep rides taking him toward the smoke and the sound of gunfire; she'd heard something in his voice that was fear and excitement: a life lived on the edge.

"Never," he said.

She thought he was lying but was too sleepy to be sure. "What were you going to say—in Machado's? 'Are you happy with us?'"

"No," he said. "It'll keep. I'm sleeping."

Stella was drifting. She saw Tree Girl's pale body being lowered through the dark branches; Leonard Pigeon on the bench, head bowed as if to watch the river as it flowed.

He said, "I'll tell you tomorrow."

"I'll be late. Something I have to do."

"Okay." Then he said, "Take care," as if falling asleep were a leave-taking.

23

They were playing Texas Hold 'Em, and Costea Radu was looking for a queen or a spade on the flop. The dealer's name was Charleen, and even though the casino was only a shanty in old shantytown, she was dressed in a glitter dress of emerald-green, backless and cut deep at the front, so a full, plump cleavage appeared when she leaned forward to shoot the cards.

The basement was large and low, neon strips on the ceiling, bars on the windows, a throw-bolt on the door. Three poker tables, blackjack, roulette, fruit machines standing round the room. No pictures on the walls, no carpet on the floor; the roulette table was a bad hand-me-down, the blackjack shoes were scuffed, and the bar was a trestle table laden with bottles. In each corner of the room a standing fan stirred the soup of cigarette smoke.

Charleen burned one and turned one: the queen of spades, which gave Costea a pair and a possible straight. He made a careful raise: not so confident that he looked good, but enough to make people think he had hopes. Two hands folded, three stayed with him: check, check, check.

Charleen turned the river card. The nine of spades. Costea blinked. Two hands folded, but one stayed in: an Asian guy in a Redbear T-shirt and loose-fit Levi's. Redbear Man mantled his cards and lifted the tips. He seemed reassured: enough, anyway, to raise Costea five grand.

Costea smiled a smile that no one saw, because it never reached his lips. He flipped bundles of notes out onto the worn baize, everything he had.

He said, "Going all in."

Redbear shook his head. "You're full of shit."

"Yeah?" Costea laughed. "Find out."

Redbear was cash leader, but only just. He counted his stack and matched the bet. In the same moment the Notting Hill Clubs and Vice Squad came through the door, with Stella and Harriman keeping back and to the side. There was better than £23,000 on the table.

The CO14 squad members were wearing Kevlar vests and dome helmets with perspex eye masks. Some had holstered weapons, though two were carrying Heckler & Koch MP5 automatics. These men stood wide to get an angle of fire, but slightly in advance of the others to eliminate the risk of shooting their colleagues. In a confined space blue-on-blue was a real possibility. They had used a Hatton gun to take the door out, and the bang seemed to have paralyzed everyone. There was silence, apart from the fruit machines playing electronic scales.

Stella looked round the room and found him: tall guy, carrying weight, looked like a roadie, big crucifix on a silver chain. Maybe it was the fact that her gaze settled on him, though it was more likely that he acted from a mixture of panic and necessity. He hadn't got time to do time: he had girls to run, an investment to protect. He walked round the table and pulled Charleen to her feet. The neon threw a line of light from the open razor in his hand to the far wall, close to where Stella was standing.

There was a back door about twenty feet from where Costea was standing that led to a small, paved yard. He started to back off, and the CO14 squad leader gave a shout. A red laser dot from an MP5 raced across the thin nap of the poker table and fluttered over Charleen's glitter dress. Costea pulled her close, one arm round her waist, the other at her throat. She started to cry.

He said, "I'll kill her."

There was something in his voice: fear and anger, yes, but something more—almost a touch of regret.

He acted on instinct, Stella thought, *and now he doesn't know what in hell he's going to do.*

The squad leader said, "Let her go. Put down the weapon. It's the only way."

Costea risked a glance at the door and made a step or two toward it; Charleen shuffled with him. She was still crying, crying and panting; his arm was tight round her waist, but the shortness of breath was fear.

Now there were two red laser dots, and the other guns had come out of their holsters, officers using a two-handed grip, knees bent, eyes on the target. They could see all of Charleen and almost nothing of Costea.

He said, "They put down their guns."

"And you'll let her go . . ." This was the squad leader pretending he was prepared to strike a deal.

"No. They put down their guns, or I kill her."

"I can't do that."

"Okay." As he spoke, Costea cut Charleen under the jawline, pulling her tight as he did it. She screamed and leaped in his arms like a fish. The room was loud with noise for a moment: Charleen's scream, reactions from the gamblers, a yell—"No!"—from the squad leader and Costea's answering shout.

"Guns down—down now!"

Then silence; status quo. Stella could see the shake in Costea's legs, but no shake in the hand holding the razor. Blood was running freely from the point of Charleen's chin down onto her green dress; her eyes were rolling, but she was too terrified to faint.

If they push him, he'll kill her, because he doesn't know what else to do.

Stella looked across to Pete Harriman, who was leaning against the wall on the far side, as if he were enjoying the show, though Stella knew he was finding an angle that gave him a partial view of Costea's face, wanting to read the man's expression. Wanting to read his mind. The razor lay lightly on Charleen's throat close to the jugular vein.

Stella said, "Stay there; you're okay there. Stay put."

Costea was looking through the faces, trying to find hers. She raised a hand to pull focus.

"You're okay," she told him. "Stay where you are, and you'll be fine. I'm coming over. I'm coming over to talk to you." She didn't move.

Costea took a pace back. The blood soak on Charleen's dress had gone to the waist. He said, "I'll kill her. You hear me say that?"

"You don't have to. You don't have to kill her, and you don't have to get killed. I'm coming over there. Coming to talk to you." She didn't move; she said, "Okay?"

He said, "What?" meaning "What do you want?" It was the first time he hadn't spoken of killing.

The room was quiet. The squad leader's voice was barely audible.

"Not your operation."

"No." Stella wished he would shut the fuck up.

"You'll be putting yourself in the line of fire."

"I know." Then, to Costea: "Okay?" When he didn't answer, she took a couple of steps forward and stopped, then took a couple more. She said, "Okay?"

The squad leader moved to cut Stella off, then turned his back on the action to talk to her.

"He's not going through that door."

"He'll kill her. He'll cut her throat."

"I don't think so."

"He's scared. He wishes he'd never done this. All he knows now is: Don't back down; stay in control. He's not thinking clever thoughts. And she's bleeding."

"It's nonnegotiable."

"Negotiation is all you've got."

"One clear shot."

"See any chance of that?"

"You think he'll stand there all night?"

"No. And I don't think he'll give himself up either."

"So?"

"So he has to be persuaded."

"You think you can do that?"

"Yes." Stella didn't think that; she had another idea altogether.

The squad leader said, "If you like. But he's not going through that door."

Stella moved through the semicircle of guns. The punters had scattered when the CO14 squad first came in: they had gone to the walls. Costea and Charleen were out on their own. The door was ten feet back, maybe twelve. Stella walked toward them, moving slowly, stopping now and then, punctuating her progress with the same question.

"Okay? . . . Okay? . . . Okay?"

She could feel the red laser spots on her back and sweat starting up in her armpits and prickling her forehead. Just about everyone in the room was watching her, except Harriman, who was watching Costea, watching the way he made Charleen feel the blade, to remind Stella of the risk.

Stella stopped about six feet light of where Costea and Charleen were standing; she was close enough to speak softly and still be heard—by Costea at least. The girl stared straight ahead; she couldn't blink, and she couldn't stop crying, though now she was openmouthed, uttering a short syllable of pain with each sob.

"If you kill her, you're dead."

Costea said nothing.

"If you kill her, you'll die here tonight. You'll never get out of that door."

"So I go out of the door. She comes with me."

"The armed officers will shoot you if they can. It's their only thought."

"So they put their guns down."

"They won't do that. That's not going to happen."

"They put their guns down, or I kill her."

"You kill her, and they shoot you. See—it's a circle." Costea thought it through: thinking circular thoughts. Stella said, "Give her to me."

The razor moved. Charleen made a little sound: fear and pain. A laser dot played on the back wall.

Costea said, "You crazy bitch."

"Like this," Stella told him. "We'll do it like this. I come and stand close to her. Just in front of her, very close but to the side. That way you have two body shields, see that? Two people standing in front of you. Now you're no target at all. Now you've got cover. See that?"

Costea said nothing. Stella took a couple of steps forward, halving the distance between them.

"See that? Already, there's less for them to shoot at."

Costea moved the razor up, angling the edge to Charleen's throat. He said, "Where is your gun?"

Stella was wearing jeans, a T-shirt, a light jacket. She took the jacket off and dropped it on the floor behind her, then pulled the T-shirt out of her waistband and tweaked out the pocket linings of her jeans. Some loose change clattered onto the floor. Then she turned a circle to show the back pockets: flat and empty. She reached down and raised her jeans from the knee, revealing her ankles and calves, gun-free.

Costea said, "Lift up."

Stella lifted the T-shirt and turned another circle: nothing in the waistband of her jeans; facing him, she lifted it higher: nothing in her bra.

"When you stand by her—"

"You back off to the door. Then you give her to me. You go through the door. It's a chance."

"Why?"

"To save her life."

"And my life."

Stella said, "I don't care whether you live or die, you cocksucker. If you die, that's just fine by me. I couldn't give a flying fuck. Her life, that's why."

Costea could feel Charleen's blood dribbling over his arm. His eyes were fixed on Stella. He said, "When you stand, don't stand close enough to reach me."

Stella took another step forward. She reckoned she was screening him on the left side, the door side. When she'd stepped in, the laser dot had disappeared, and she wondered whether it was centered on her head or her heart.

"Go back," she said, "walk back now. Keep going."

He did just that, his eyes on hers, still expecting her to make a move on him. He was taking short steps, because Charleen was unsteady, the high heels of her casino shoes dragging the concrete. Stella wondered whether it was blood loss or terror. Costea's back hit the wall. He looked at Stella.

"You're there," she told him. "A yard to the left," and she made a compensatory movement to cover him. He matched the move, then kicked back with his heel to sound the surface behind him. Wood.

I know what she's going to do. Harriman glanced over at the squad leader, wondering whether he'd had the same thought.

"Okay." Stella could feel her own pulses, little registers of fear. "Okay, here's what you do. When I step in, let her go. I'll hold her. We'll still be in front of you. Open the door and go through. For a moment no one will know. You'll have some time. It's the best you're going to get."

Costea knew three things: the yard behind the casino had a wall he could climb, and there were other walls beyond; he knew the back streets and burrows behind the Strip as well as any of the whores who gave blow jobs there; and he knew that he'd made a colossal mistake.

Charleen slumped slightly in his arms. The laser dot skittered along the wall.

Stella said, "Use your right hand. They can't see."

Costea moved his razor hand, and Charleen sagged with relief. He leaned against the door, and she leaned with him, her eyes showing the whites. He turned the handle. The door opened an inch or two and stuck.

The squad leader realized what was happening. He said, "No!" Red dots crisscrossed but couldn't latch on.

Costea whacked the door with his heel. It opened. He let Charleen go, and she stood upright, swaying slightly, just this side of consciousness. Stella reached out, and the girl fell against her, trembling, making little cawing sounds. For a long moment that was all: Stella and Charleen standing in a one-sided embrace, the girl's head nodding on Stella's shoulder, Costea long gone. Then Harriman was there, passing them and going out of sight just a second or two before the CO14 squad cops barged across the room and through the door.

24

Harriman wasn't fast enough to find Costea still in the yard, but he heard the sound of garbage bins being scattered. He ran at the wall and leaped, getting a handhold, then levered himself up and over. The second yard was empty.

This'll be it, he thought. *One step behind until I finally lose him.*

He made the next wall and dropped down, landing lightly, and was running through when he heard the silence. He snapped round, expecting to find Costea coming at him, but there was no one. Then he looked toward the far wall and saw the fire escape.

He topped the wall and swung round to get his feet on the metal rungs. It was a long way up. The roof was one of a terrace, and Harriman could see Costea two houses away. There were low walls between each house— low but too high to hurdle. He started to run, unsteady at that height, conscious of the street noise below and the sheer drops on each side. His foot snagged a cable, and the trip took him staggering toward the edge. He recovered and ran, keeping his eyes on his quarry, trying to blank what was in his peripheral vision: TV aerials, neon signs, the landing lights of a plane as it banked, coming round toward Heathrow.

Costea half turned. Maybe he'd heard Harriman, maybe he'd felt a telltale coldness in the small of his back. Either way, it was a mistake. He was close to the next barrier between the houses and turned only in time to run into it, smacking his thigh against the brickwork. His leg went out from under him, and when he tried to get to his feet, let him down immediately. He pulled himself up as Harriman came close. The razor was back in his hand.

Harriman said, "Oh, for Christ's sake."

Costea edged along the wall, dragging the dead leg. He was heading for the edge, as if there were some way down from there, as if he might step off and somehow find himself in the street, looking up at Harriman, stranded amid cables and phone masts.

"Put it down," Harriman told him. "There's nowhere to go."

Costea beckoned him, crooking his finger to bring Harriman on. "Now you and me."

Harriman laughed. "Put it down, you stupid fuck, or I'll kick you off the roof."

"You and me—ready?"

A laser dot hit him on the chest and traveled up to his left eye. Harriman stretched out a hand and blocked the sightline. Without turning round, he shouted, "I need to talk to him. Okay? I need him." Then he lowered his hand. A second dot joined the first, shimmying about for a moment, then settling on Costea's right eye. CO14 with a sense of humor.

Costea closed the razor and tossed it across to Harriman. He said, "Jesus, man, it was just a game of poker."

Stella and Harriman sat down with Costea.

He said, "So, let's cut a deal." When Stella's hand went out to the tape button, he added, "Off the record."

She delayed but kept her hand close to the machine. "What did you have in mind?"

"You want money?" Silence from Stella; silence from Harriman. "Information—what? You people know how things are up there. That casino got guys from Clubs and Vice play blackjack regular. How many casinos you think they run on the Strip? Five? Ten? Sure, you're getting close."

"Gambling?" Harriman said. He shook his head. "Not interested."

"So?"

"We asked about you," Stella said. "Costea Radu. Stable of ten, all from Romania, all young. Some very young. That's what we hear."

"I need some way out of here, okay?"

"You've been arrested for malicious wounding and kidnap. Out of here is a long way off."

Costea sighed and looked down at his hands, folded and resting on the table: a man displaying patience, a man ready to talk. "You are not anti-gambling cops, right?"

"No, we're not."

"And you are not charging me with accident with the girl."

"Accident?" Harriman laughed.

Costea ignored him. "Okay, good, so you don't mind blackjack and you don't mind I cut the girl. You mind about other things."

"I mind," Stella said. "I mind that you cut her."

"But other things"—he looked for the word—"official."

"Yes."

"Some questions . . ."

"Yes."

"Good. So I ask you for deal. Maybe we can do some business. What questions?"

Stella took Lizzie's enhanced postmortem shot from an envelope and pushed it across the table. "First question: Did you kill her?"

Costea's body seemed to take a little jolt, as if he'd picked up a charge of static electricity. "You are murder cops?"

Stella hit the record button, then stated the date, time, and those present. She observed that Mr. Costea Radu had waived his right to have a solicitor present. She made it clear that she had passed him a photograph, mentioned its nature and the catalogue number given to it in the evidence room; then she repeated the question she had just asked.

"You fucking kid me?" Costea asked.

"Do you recognize the person in the photograph?"

"Never see her." He looked more closely. "She dead here?"

"Yes," Stella said, "she's dead. Violence against women—part of your stock in trade, Costea, that's what we heard."

"Stock in—"

"Something you do," Harriman said, "something you *like* to do."

"Not me."

"No?"

"Not me that killed her."

Stella said, "You knew her, though. You'd seen her."

"I don't know. A whore. How should I know?"

"She was on your turf. She was poaching, you tried to get to her."

Costea looked at the photo again. Little white face, big brown eyes. "Maybe. There was one like her. I never found her. I saw her, but never found her."

"You went looking."

"She was taking business. Fucking me around."

"Why your business especially?"

Costea pointed at the photo. "She's young, see? My girls are young. Some men want only this."

"What kind of men?" Stella asked.

"Men with wives." Costea shrugged. "Older men, of course. What happened to her?"

Stella weighed the risk and decided to take it. "She was found hanging in a tree a few streets—"

"Oh." Costea looked again. "That girl." He seemed curious: nothing in his face of things hidden or relived, no shadow of guilt. After a moment he said, "Guess what—I didn't do that. You want to take DNA? Take it, no problem."

"We intend to," Stella said, but she knew she wouldn't find a match; Costea Radu hadn't hauled Lizzie up into the tree. He had forgotten her already as he looked across the table, half smiling, eager to help, hoping for a deal that would put him back on the Strip before nightfall.

"Who would do this?" Stella asked. "Who was running her?"

"I never saw anyone," Costea said. "We can do something, okay? Do a deal."

Harriman asked, "No one putting her out there?"

"Okay, someone, what do I know? I never saw anyone. If she had someone looking after her, he never came up on the Strip. She was . . . what is it? Solo." He shrugged. "Or maybe her mother sends her out, maybe her husband."

"Do you know her name?"

"Her *what?*" Costea laughed. "Sure, I know her name. Bitch, that would be her *name.*" A pause, then: "So what kind deal we talking about?"

Stella switched off the tape. She said, "You can talk to the judge about a deal, you bastard."

A PC collected the prisoner from the interview room to take him down to the cells. Costea looked back at Stella. He mouthed the word "Bitch." Stella smiled a smile so wide it would almost have read on the interview tape.

The leg was still giving Costea trouble. As the door closed, Harriman flicked a glance at Stella.

"Pimp with a limp."

25

There was music, as usual, this time some slow jazz, and Sam Burgess was using a Stryker saw to open Leonard Pigeon's chest cavity. Then he cut through the ribs on each side and lifted the chest plate. The heart and lungs sat soft and inert.

Giovanni cut away some residual soft tissue from the chest cavity and made the cuts along the spinal column that would allow the principal organs to be lifted and removed. Open-coffin work: all done with care; all done with the skill and attention to detail that would allow the body to be seen by relatives without undue distress.

Once the organs had been examined, weighed, and tested; once the stomach contents had been sifted; once the heart and lungs, liver and lights, had been salami-sliced for the path lab; once the skull had been trepanned and the brain scooped out and scrutinized, Sam and Giovanni would put Leonard together again, his guts lumped back into the body cavity, his cranium sutured, the gash in his throat closed and tricked with cosmetics, the great "Y" incision that went from shoulder wings to breastbone to pubis cobbled together with blanket stitch.

"Overweight," Sam said, "and underexercised and on the road to a coronary occlusion."

"He was young."

Stella was standing some ten or fifteen feet back from the autopsy table. People reduced to their constituent parts had an unsettling effect on her. She could see the living person at the same time as seeing the skull beneath the skin.

Sam said, "I don't mean soon. Not next year, or the year after that; no. Soon enough, though."

"What can you tell me?"

"About the wound?"

"Yes."

"A sharp blade, obviously, but a heavy one, I think. Not a fish-gutting knife or a paring knife."

"Not a flexible blade."

"That's right."

"Hunting knife?"

"Sort of thing, yes. He didn't know it was coming."

"Sure?"

"No defensive cuts on the hands or arms, and the wound is clean and very deep. The killer could have avoided much of the blood."

"Of which there would have been lots?"

"Oh, God, yes. Arterial jet, like a hose pipe."

"But not all of it."

"What?"

"The killer's clothing would have been bloodstained."

"For sure."

Someone must have seen him, Stella thought. *Blood like a burst pipe.* Sue Chapman had organized yellow crime boards on the towpath twenty yards either side of the bench, but no one had come forward to say: Yes, I saw a man who . . . running in the direction of . . . acting in a strange . . .

Keep your head down, keep your mouth shut, don't make their problem your problem. London thinking.

"How much strength needed for the job?"

"Strength . . ." Sam considered. "Not so much strength as energy, I'd've thought. You come up behind someone, you're intending to cut his throat, you've equipped yourself with a really keen blade . . . You yank his head back, you slash." Sam made an appropriate gesture, then realized he was holding a scalpel in his hand and gave an apologetic laugh. "Not strength but determination." He went back to work: measuring, assessing. "Will the graphologists need him?"

"They will, yes." But Stella didn't expect them to say anything other than see our previous report.

Filthy coward.

Who are you to pass judgment? Stella thought. *Who are you to be judge and executioner?* She gave a little shudder and suddenly was filled with a just and intense loathing for this man, this lone vigilante, this angel of wrath or whatever he considered himself to be.

"Did you say he was a politician?" Sam asked.

"No. Worked for one."

"Ah . . ."

Stella took a step forward. "What made you ask?"

"I thought you said politician . . . and he would have been a very unusual specimen."

"Why?"

Sam was transferring something to the scales: he held it up for Stella to see. "He still had a heart."

26

Late in the day, and a storm was building in the Thames Basin, rolling up from Greenwich to the Isle of Dogs. Over West London the cloud cover bellied down and darkened. Lights went on in the AMIP-5 squad room, and in Mike Sorley's office eddies of tobacco smoke wafted around the desk lamp: one cigarette burning forgotten in the ashtray, another clipped in Sorley's fingers. He took a long toke, then scratched his head. Ash dropped into his hair. He picked up a sheet of paper that lay atop the other sheets, files, memoranda, faxes, e-mails, reports, reminders, draft budgets, schedules, minutes, FYEO documents, and interdepartmental bullshit.

"I have to answer this," he said. "I have to make some kind of a fucking comment."

"I know." Stella was sitting in a chair on the other side of the desk; she only sat down in Sorley's office when there was a problem. As it happened, there was a problem, and she was it.

"So what do you suggest I say? You were along for the ride. They were doing you a favor. They raided the casino so you could nab this guy"—he glanced at the memo—"Radu. The whole thing was headed up by a CO14 inspector. He's looking at a situation, he's handling it, you come jumping in through all the fucking windows."

"Except he wasn't handling it. As I've explained. He was likely to wind up with the girl dead and Radu dead."

"So I should say my sergeant quickly appraised the situation, took note of your gross incompetence, and decided to save your ass."

"That would do it."

The lights dimmed a moment and there was a far-off crackle of thunder. Sorley took the last of his cigarette in a long pull, crushed it into the ashtray, and reached for his ever-open pack.

"This is just between us and CO14 at present: unofficial. My unofficial reply will be that you acted foolishly, but things turned out for the best . . . that sort of bollocks. It will include an apology from you."

"He was getting it wrong."

"Okay, I believe you. At the moment this is just bitching, rank to rank. I can't get caught up in some sort of fucking inquiry, DS Mooney. It's not going to happen."

That "DS Mooney" made matters clear.

Sorley gestured at the piles on his desk. "If kiss-ass is the way to avoid that, kiss-ass is what will happen." Stella was tight-lipped. He added: "Jesus Christ, a line will do."

"Do I have an option?"

"No." Sorley glanced at his watch and started to stack papers into an attaché case. "Have we got a DNA match for the killer?"

"You mean DNA found at both crime scenes?"

"Yes."

"We're waiting for the lab. But, listen, it's the same guy: has to be." Sorley looked at her. She said, "You're not thinking copycat?"

He shrugged. "It's unlikely, given that we haven't released anything about the victims being written on. Depends who might have seen the bodies before we did." Then: "What have you got?"

"Nothing. No motive, no link between the victims . . . and if it's serial, then the likelihood is that any connection lies in the mind of the killer, and logic isn't going to help us much. Basically, we need more evidence; need to see more of the pattern."

"Would another body help?" His weary tone leached all humor out of the question.

DI Mike Sorley had left his wife because whenever they had a row she would hit him, and he'd been frightened: not of her but of himself. Frightened he would forget to tolerate it; frightened that he would hit back, one time, and find he couldn't stop. He'd lived in the office for a while, bringing pizza and Thai takeaways back, sleeping between two chairs, using the AMIP-5 bathroom for a strip-wash and a shave before the team arrived.

Stella had known about Sorley's problem. She'd been working late in those days too; returning to the squad room after downing a couple of vodkas at the pub, trying to displace a problem of her own: a problem called John Delaney. She'd lived with George Paterson for five years, and George loved her in the way people want to be loved, which wasn't enough to save him, because to make an even match Stella would have needed to love George in the same way. Her love for him was a different thing, had *become* a different thing: fondness and tenderness and admiration. Admiration—that was the killer.

Delaney had come into her life at just the right time. Just the wrong time.

Sorley had lived in the office not because he couldn't think of anywhere else to be, but to avoid that final, that conclusive, move; Stella was staying late because she couldn't—or wouldn't—make a decision. They would sit together in the AMIP-5 squad room—green curry and Tiger beer, cigarettes and sympathy—with Sorley doing most of the talking. He was a man lost; he needed advice, and he needed reassurance, and Stella had done what she could. It had created a bond of friendship between them, which is why when he called her DS Mooney, she knew she had to listen. Eventually Mike Sorley found a new wife. Karen was almost pretty and liked to laugh and was generous in bed.

The storm was circling in the middle distance as he put his key in the lock of his own front door and felt, as he always had since they'd started to live together, as if nothing bad would happen under that roof. They had their first-of-the-evening drink together, as always, and talked and made a few unimportant plans.

While Karen cooked, Sorley spread his papers out on the kitchen table and lit a cigarette. Karen sighed, and he said, "I know." It was her habit to underline the health warnings on the packs in red pen and put Nicorette in the pockets of his jackets. It was evidence of the way she felt about him, and he had vowed to give up smoking to make her happy. In fact, he was going to give up tomorrow; or the day after that, for sure.

He thought being happy was a knack and wondered why it had eluded him for quite so long.

27

Storm-light over London: yellow, blue-white, dirty pinks in the cloud-wrack, and the rain still holding off like bad news delayed.

Arthur Dorey, aka Sekker, was standing in the hallway of a grand house admiring the paintings. He didn't know much about art, but he decoded the female nude pretty quickly. It made him laugh, just as it had made Delaney laugh. After a short while he was shown into a large room where a man with a goatee and a gunslinger's mustache sat behind a broad desk. It was a straightforward deal, the terms already agreed, the job already done.

Sekker pocketed a white envelope that was reassuringly bulky. He said, "It was slow coming."

Stanley Bowman nodded. "It was on its way."

"Yes. Slowly."

Bowman pressed an intercom button on the phone, and the man who'd brought Sekker up to the room took him back downstairs, to a side door. The first few fat raindrops hit as Sekker emerged onto a side road close to the park, and a wind was shaking the trees. It was two hours before sunset, and already the streetlights were flickering into life.

Bowman made a phone call. His voice was even, but it carried a cold edge. "He came to the house."

The answering voice was looking for a similar, calm tone, though failing to find it. "No, he shouldn't have done that."

"He came to the house to collect."

"Did you pay him?"

"Yes."

"I'll have the money refunded to you."

"Why wasn't he paid?"

"After he'd . . . completed . . . he left town for a couple of days. It's usual. We didn't know where he was. He thought we did." The voice had a faint burr to it: maybe Irish, maybe American.

"Make it clear to him that he doesn't come to the house."

"Of course."

"Make it clear." A pause; then Bowman said, "I hear there's a trader on Harefield."

"Small time."

"They always start small."

"You want it fixed?"

"Keep an eye on him."

"We can fix it for you."

"That's good to know. No, just keep an eye on him. As long as it's low activity, low yield."

"Anytime you say."

"I know."

"And I'm sorry he came to the house. He shouldn't have come to the house."

"Tell him. And listen, keep the money."

"Keep it?"

"For the time being. In case this other guy . . . In case we need to move on him."

The thunder was like sheet metal, tearing.

Bowman poured himself a Scotch, cupping a handful of ice into the glass, and sighed. He went to the window to watch the storm as it hit.

28

Thunder-rain moved down the Strip in solid squalls, bright in the streetlights or shot through with red-and-blue neon where it sluiced the shopfronts. The storm was overhead, thunder slamming rooftops and ringing in cornerstones.

The television in Gideon Woolf's room fizzed and popped. He never turned it off, night or day. Just now it was showing what looked like a news broadcast: houses and vehicles burning, men in tricolor DCU combat fatigues running in a fast crouch from cover to cover, holding a line on each side of a dusty street. Bodies lay out in the open. He picked up the remote control and zapped through a few stations. Men in jungle-greens were running in a fast crouch from cover to cover as incoming ripped into the tree line. Either this was a movie and the first scenes had been real, or the other way round. He zapped a few more and got back to the men in DCUs. Or men a lot like them.

Gideon was dressing to go out. He favored an ankle-length black leather coat he'd found in a charity shop: that went over a cotton roll-neck and combat pants together with calf-high lace-up boots. He felt the part. Last, he pulled on the single glove, left hand, that was street code for *I'm carrying.*

He went to the window and peered out at the downpour, at branch lightning glittering against a plum-colored sky. He liked the look of it. He had no particular intent; this wasn't a mission; but this was the kind of weather that often took Silent Wolf to the streets. Gideon carried an image of the man in his mind, the skirt of his coat turned back by the wind, leaning into the slant of the rain as he walked the canyons and gulches of the city.

Who would be out in such weather? Only wrongdoers and their Nemesis. Only those who had nothing to lose.

He was saying those lines to himself and smiling: they were lines from the *Silent Wolf* game. As he watched, a broken-backed column of lightning hissed and crackled, arcing up through the rain. The smell of scorch in the sky was the smell of scorch in his room.

He pushed a sheathed, broad-bladed knife into the top of his right boot and opened the door. He had nothing particular in mind, no one to seek out; the knife was *in case*; it was *who knows?*

He dimmed the lights and locked the door as he left. The TV flickered in the half-light: men flanking an APC, coming under fire, fanning out to find cover.

The body count rose: dead men or actors playing dead, who could tell?

He was down on the Strip when he saw her, a woman hurrying home, shoulders hunched against the storm, dark hair hanging in wet tails over the collar of her coat. She was a civilian, that much was clear, because even the toughest pimps had let their girls take to the doorways, the cafés, the bars, to look for work.

Mostly, innocents stayed off the Strip as evening fell, but for those in a hurry it was a shortcut; you walked quickly past the dens and dives to the main road, then took the path through the churchyard that would bring you out four blocks away. In weather like this, it was tempting to save five minutes or more.

He saw her, and he saw the two followers, blurred by the downfall, their dark hoodies gray like the light, their faces cowled, though Gideon could see that one man's hair had a bad blond dye. Gideon knew she would risk the churchyard, even though a woman had been killed there last year, because taking that path was the reason for using the Strip: it was all part of the same shortcut. And he knew that the followers knew that. The woman had looped the strap of her shoulder bag across her body, and that frail gesture—that pointless precaution—moved him strangely.

The followers had been tracking her from the far side of the street. Now, as she came off the Strip and headed for the church, they crossed over and closed the gap, walking twenty, maybe thirty feet back.

Gideon kept pace, but they didn't see him, a dim shape in hanging rails of rain.

29

The weather looked wilder from the twenty-first floor. The man Stella had identified as Angel Face, the man she'd been chasing when she fell over Barry or Gary, was sitting close to the window of a Block A apartment and thinking it was a little like being out at sea: rain, wind, a flowing sky, no sight of land. He was in the room with three other men who were passing a hefty spliff back and forth with a slow grace. It was an interview of sorts.

One of the three was doing most of the talking. His name was Jonah, a squat man with heavy dreadlocks and a workout torso that was freighted with bling: heavy bracelets, rings to every finger, a gold torque necklace; when he raised his hand to lift the spliff to his lips, his biceps popped and the room glittered.

Angel Face had given the name he most often used: Ricardo Jones. He'd used it for so long that no one knew him by any other, though sometimes he would invent another for a one-off job and people he wouldn't be going back to: people he ripped off. His real name was on prison and police computers, so he never used that. It was a simple-enough alias: his given name was Richard and Ricardo was a nickname. Even friends had forgotten his real surname.

He said, "I'm a matchmaker, okay? I'm just here to let you know. Here to offer my services. They said you were the man to see."

"Who said?"

"People I asked."

"Matchmaker . . ." Jonah smiled. "Maybe you can find me a nice wife."

Ricardo smiled back. "So, I'm in 1169 B, you know that." He gave a mobile number. "I'm, like, everything: white goods, electrical, small items"—casting a glance at Jonah's laden arms and fingers—"cars, you know."

A matchmaker puts buyers and sellers together; he scams stolen goods; he shifts high-risk items. He's not a fence; they tend to be specialists. A matchmaker will deal anything to anyone. He'll have a talent for finding the right people on each side of the buy/sell divide and he'll be a great organizer. Matchmakers are tidy-minded people.

Jonah said, "What are we talking here?"

Ricardo shrugged as if money talk was the least of it. "I take ten percent off the top."

Jonah laughed. "I take ten percent off the top of your fucking head, man."

Ricardo held Jonah's hard-man stare. "You're paying twenty on a job-by-job basis, and you have to set things up before anything comes your way. A car man for cars, white-goods man for white goods. I do everything. Reliable contacts, fast work, quick return. Why am I only ten percent? Because I expect to get all of your business. I make ten, you save ten." He paused. "Except money. Money costs."

"I already got someone for money."

"Yeah? Well, like I said, money's expensive. With money, you lose money. Am I right?"

Jonah stayed silent, because Ricardo was right. Money was high risk, and not just for the handlers. He said, "This guy isn't like you. He only does money." He could have added: *And the last person who tried to edge his business wound up with plastic lungs.* He didn't say it because he was interested in Ricardo's blanket ten percent.

"So he only does money—?"

"Special, you know? Exclusive. He expects loyalty."

"He expects thirty-five percent, am I right?" Ricardo was quick to scan Jonah's expression; reading people's faces was a necessary skill. "No, he expects fifty."

"I dealt with this guy a year or more. No problems."

"Except you're taking heavy losses." Ricardo pretended to consider the matter. "With money, I take twenty-five; just between you and me."

Rain battered the glass. Jonah reached round to scratch his neck, and his bracelets clattered.

"Next coupla weeks," he said, "some class gear coming in. I'll let you know in advance. Not money, though. I can't let you handle money."

But Ricardo knew he would; it was there in the man's face.

30

They were going to take her before she reached the churchyard. The man with the blond dye crossed the road and quickened his pace to get beyond her. It was standard: Gideon had seen it before. The lead guy would gain a few yards—ten, maybe twenty—recross the road in a long diagonal, then slow his pace so she caught up with him. The other follower would have been gaining on her. It would be quick. As the man in front turned, the man following would be close enough to hold her. They would take the bag, and they would put her down, hard, to give them lots of time. A sap, perhaps, or a knife, it didn't matter how badly they hurt her, so long as they could get clear.

Once he'd crossed the road, Blondie didn't look back; he knew that the other follower was moving up on her. Gideon glanced around. There were cars on the Strip, their lights on, their wipers working hard, but no one walking; the rain was wind-driven, the sky dark and low. He paced the second man, matching him stride for stride, looking for an opportunity and all the time chuckling to himself.

Wrongdoers and their Nemesis.

They passed a shebeen and Steadfast Cars and started along the side of a blind wall that had once fronted a car lot. Gideon came up behind the follower and put him in an armlock, fast and hard, wrenching the arm high so the man doubled up to compensate for the stress put on his shoulder joint. The rain doused his cry. Gideon rushed the man at the wall, up on his toes and moving at speed, as if he expected to break through. It was head-on, like a battering ram; Gideon felt the impact in his wrists. He released his grip and the follower hit the pavement, limbs loose like something partly dismantled.

It took a few seconds. Gideon only had to quicken his pace a little to catch up with the woman as she, in turn, caught up with Blondie. When he turned, she wasn't sure, for a moment, what was wrong; the rain blurred her vision; then she saw the knife and stepped back and said, "No!" as if that might make a difference.

Gideon moved forward, and Blondie saw him for the first time. He looked round for the other man and saw no one. He shouted but got no answer. Gideon wagged a finger at him as if to say, *He's gone; it's you and me.* Blondie lifted the knife to eye level, but backed off and to the side. The woman saw the gap and ran past him, going toward the churchyard, and in the same moment, Blondie moved in the opposite direction. Gideon had expected it. He swung his leg, taking the man just below the knees and bringing him down with a clatter, then he stepped in and stamped down on the man's head: a double blow because the boot made contact on one side a moment before the pavement on the other.

A little flush of blood appeared and was swilled by the rain, then another, longer streak of red feathered off toward the gutter. Blondie got up and turned away, like one man giving another the cold shoulder. He walked a pace or two and sat down, his back to the wall. His feet moved, sporadically, like a man working a treadle, then he lifted himself onto a knee and stayed like that awhile before making it to his feet. He took two steps, three, then sat down again, almost wearily, his legs out in front of him, his hands in his lap.

After a moment his head nodded down onto his chest.

She was standing on the church porch and that took him by surprise.

She said, "I'm sorry."

He had taken the direction she took only because he didn't want to walk back toward the first guy; the Strip was thinly populated, but someone would find him pretty soon—would find both of them.

She said, "Has he gone?" not realizing there had been two.

"Gone, yes. Why are you sorry?"

"I ran away. I was frightened. And I was frightened to come back."

"Why would you do that?"

"To make sure you were all right." She took her hand out of her rain-coat pocket and showed him a mobile phone. "I should have called the police. I forgot. I wasn't thinking." She shivered. "He had a knife."

He nodded, thinking fast. *Can't leave alone; can't leave her here to call the cops and tell the tale; can't wait with her.* For a moment, he considered that the easiest thing to do would be to kill her. He took her arm, moving her out of the porch.

"Come on."

She stood her ground. "The police—"

"No, look . . . it's just more trouble—more trouble for you. It goes to court, he gets a good lawyer, he tells a good story, whatever happens he knows your name and where you live." She looked at him, worried now, and pulled back a little.

"We should call them."

They stood in the rain, his hand on her arm, her face turned to his, water running off the tips of her hair.

He said, "Trust me."

He walked her to a tube station and bought a ticket so that he could wait on the platform until her train came. She had a narrow, pretty face, good cheekbones, her eyes green, her lips rising in a slight curve.

She said, "You don't have to."

"No, it's fine. I want to." Was this what Silent Wolf would do? "You've had a bad experience." He was making up the lines as he went along.

"Do you live here?" He made up a street name. She added, "I don't live here, I work here." Then, as if he'd asked, "I'm a dental nurse. Park Clinic."

He was looking down the track, willing the train to come. He felt edgy standing there like one of a couple. "What's it like?"

She laughed. "All right, if you don't mind watching people in pain."

"I don't mind."

She looked at him as if expecting more, then laughed again, acknowledging the joke and the deadpan way he delivered it.

When the train came, he handed her aboard, then stayed on the platform to watch it draw away. She stood by the doors and looked back. She raised her hand and he raised his in reply.

She had thanked him a dozen times. She had told him that her name was Aimée. She hadn't told him that she was married.

31

Men in combat fatigues were running up a wooded slope, a chain-stitch of mortar fire dogging them. Delaney heard the blasts a fraction of a second after he saw the explosions. It was a fine day, and a blue sky bore the puffy white tracks of shellfire. He felt good. He was riding in a UN jeep, heading for the smoke and the sound of gunfire.

Or he was hunkered down behind a shell-scarred wall at a crossroads with twenty, thirty, fifty civilians, second-guessing the right time to cross. Second-guessing the sniper. When they came out of cover and ran, himself in the thick of it, he felt the jolt of adrenaline like a backhander to the gut.

He was with a line of combat troops as they walked the scarred and smoking remnant of a village. He was speeding in Crossfire Alley. He was in the marketplace five minutes after the mortar cluster hit.

The dream scenes shifted, but he could always smell the smoke.

The storm had struck and left, making the streets cool for a while, cool and clean. Now it was rumbling somewhere off toward the south, threatening to roll back in. Stella found him stretched out on the sofa with a predawn whiskey. She sat down and lifted his feet into her lap.

He said, "Did I wake you?"

"Not you. Your absence. It's unlike you to have a disturbed night."

"Dreams woke me."

"Bad dreams . . . ?"

"Eventful dreams."

She didn't ask him for more and he didn't offer it. Didn't tell her that this wasn't the first time, recently, that sleep had returned him to a war zone; didn't tell her how strongly that mixture of fear and exhilaration came back to him; didn't tell her that, last week, he'd had a meeting with Martin Turner, the editor who had first sent him to Africa, to Palestine, to Kosovo.

Turner had swilled the ice in his glass and smiled. "I never had you down as a features man, John. What is it just now?"

"The Rich List."

Turner laughed. "You must be thrilled." Then: "You want to go back?"

"No," Delaney said, "not really."

"Front-line stuff. Cutting edge. There's always a war zone somewhere."

"I don't think so; never go back, isn't that what they say?"

"Then why are we having this drink?"

"Old times' sake."

"Yes," Turner said. "Exactly."

"He kills them, and he writes on them, to let us know . . ."

"Let us know what?" Delaney asked.

"The reason, I suppose. The reason why they had to die. She fucks for money: Dirty Girl. He ran the wrong way: Filthy Coward. What I'm trying to do," she said, "is think less about the victims than about him."

"Think what?"

"Whether his victims were random sinners or specific targets."

"On the one hand, any hooker, any coward; on the other, that particular hooker, that particular coward?"

"Yes."

"Meaning did he know them?"

"Yes. And if he did, then Leonard Pigeon becomes my focus."

"Because anyone could be a client of the hooker, but Leonard Pigeon's friends and acquaintances are fewer and easier to find. Do you want one of these?" He waggled his glass.

"No." She got up and went to the kitchen. "Coffee."

"In fact," Delaney observed, "whichever way you look at things, Leonard Pigeon is a particular case, isn't he? It wouldn't be difficult for your killer to choose a whore at random, but he had to know about Leonard's ignoble retreat from the bridge."

"It was reported pretty widely."

"Sure, yes; but he would have had to be looking for some such act; trying to find a coward."

Stella opened a cupboard and took out coffee beans, a grinder, and a cafetière. She started to load the beans into the grinder, then said, "The hell with it," and found a jar of instant.

"I sometimes forget," Delaney told her, "that you're off the estate."

Stella said, "A mind's-eye picture of him . . . not his face, not a photo-fit, just a notion about him. He's almost certainly white, young, strong—"

"You got this from what's-her-name."

"Anne Beaumont. From her and from Sam Burgess."

"Who?"

"Pathologist. Psychological typing from Anne—white, young, the serial-killer clichés; physical type from Sam—strong enough to haul her into the tree, and to cut Leonard Pigeon's throat to the neck bone."

"Who's your forensic man?"

Stella was spooning coffee into her cup. Delaney's question jogged her, as if he had nudged her elbow, and coffee granules arced over the counter. She tore off some kitchen paper.

"Tom Davison."

"You must be hoping for something from him."

"DNA match." She felt a little blush come to her throat and turned away.

"He's a man on his own . . ."

"What?" For a moment she wasn't sure who he meant. Then: "Not necessarily. There have been killers who were happily married, an apparently normal home life, the wife in ignorance, the kids well cared for."

"Secret lives," Delaney said. "Who could ever know everything about anyone?"

Dawn came in, cool pastels, blue and pink, a clear sky above shreds of mist that the sun would soon burn off.

Woolf stood on the street outside the Park Clinic. He wanted to know where she worked. He wanted to know where he could find her again. He wanted to know what the place looked like and how quickly he could get there from where he lived and what route he might take.

He didn't know why he wanted to know these things. He felt uneasy, like a man in a locked room who hears a voice not his own.

32

Each new day began with mopping up from the night before: break-ins, muggings, domestics, bar fights, street fights, casualties in the drug war, casualties in the turf war. Up on the Strip, police tape sketched the area in which the followers had met Gideon Woolf. The statistic was one dead, one comatose. The local cops had already put it down to a territorial issue.

It was Blondie who was in the coma: the guy Woolf had stamped on. The other man had suffered impacted vertebrae, a fractured skull, and a cranial bleed that had left his eyes looking like cherry tomatoes. His death had occurred fifteen minutes after Woolf had run him on to the wall; for the moment Blondie's death seemed to be on hold.

A new day also brought the usual piles of paper, some of which Stella was reading before shipping the lot down to Mike Sorley. The door-to-door had expanded to take in an area five streets deep on each side of the scene of crime, but to no effect; the yellow-board request had resulted only in the theft of the yellow-board; a cross-reference computer search for lookalike crimes had drawn a blank.

Stella fished out an e-mail from Anne Beaumont:

I've been thinking about him. Easy to assume he's an avenger, bringing rough justice to the unworthy. That way, he's tracking down anyone who's offended his dubious moral standards. But what if there's a pattern?

She e-mailed back:

I wondered about that too. But what sort of pattern?

Maxine Hewitt stopped at Stella's desk to report on the number of confessors so far: nine, mostly anonymous letters, though none had made mention of the fact that the victims had been written on. Of the confessors, three were angels of death sent by the Almighty to rid the world of prostitutes, two slept each night in coffins filled with the soil of their country, and the others were just standard-issue deranged souls with lively imaginations and a limited vocabulary. They all had to be investigated just in case one of them was a killer with a bleak sense of humor, though the chance of finding any of them was pretty remote. Stella added photocopies of their letters to the pile she would soon deliver to Sorley.

Maxine said, "Everyone's talking to a chis."

Stella nodded. "And they're all saying that this is obviously the work of a serial killer, so why ask someone who only knows career criminals."

"That's right." Maxine had poured herself a plastic cup of squad-room coffee and grimaced as she sipped. "The girl's still a complete mystery: she's anonymous; no one knows her."

"Or no one wants to know her. Keep asking." Stella picked the top letter from the pile.

I kiled her becose she was slut all wimon like her shood die.

"Given that it's computer-generated," she said, "you'd think the prick would have used spell-check."

She was still going through paper, sorting paper, hating paper, when she picked up a return e-mail from Anne Beaumont.

Who knows?

33

Frank Silano was in a riverside bar, buying a lunchtime drink for a man called Derek Crane. Crane was his real name and one he sometimes used, though, in his time, he'd carried credit cards, driving licenses, and passports that provided him with a dozen other identities. Just now, or so Derek claimed, he wasn't impersonating anyone: after his last conviction he'd turned the corner; he'd straightened out; he'd found a job.

"Job?" Silano said. It wasn't a question, it was an expression of disbelief.

Derek smiled. He was a dapper type with thinning sandy hair and freckles that were beginning to look like liver spots. His dark suit and gray Oxfords were dressy without being tasteful.

"Self-employed."

"Please don't tell me," Silano said. "Then I won't have to inform Customs and Excise."

Crane laughed, but not at Silano's cynicism: he was looking at a couple sitting on the far side of the bar, the man leaning close and talking softly, the woman looking at him wide-eyed with love.

"He's promising her the earth," Derek said, "but I don't think he can live up to it."

Silano always liked to see a craftsman at work. Derek had made his living as a con-man and one of the con-man's desirable skills was lip-reading. You hang out in local bars, you sip your drink, you read your paper, and you watch people talking about themselves, because when you know about their lives you know how best to con them.

"You think he's lying to her?"

"I know he is. When she went to the ladies' room just now, he was on the phone to his wife. The woman he's with doesn't know he has a wife. That's why she's agreed to the weekend in Paris."

Silano thought it was quaint of Derek to use the term "ladies' room," but then a certain dated charm was part of the man's technique. "Paris," Silano said. "He's a romantic anyway."

"I don't think so. He'll be there on business, and she's joining him. He's flying her budget from Stansted. I know who he was," Derek said, as if it were all part of the same train of thought, "and I know a little about him, but nothing of interest; not really." He was talking about Leonard Pigeon.

"Tell me."

Derek hesitated. "I wasn't working, Mr. Silano. It's just force of habit: watching people, filing secrets."

"Of course you were working." Silano shrugged. "But I'm assuming you didn't use what you learned, because if you had you'd be denying you ever knew him."

"There wasn't much I *could* have used. He was relatively clean—for someone involved in politics anyway. I wasn't really . . ."

". . . interested in him so much as in his boss," Silano said, finishing the indiscretion.

"Yes."

"And?"

"Certain possibilities. Morgan is ambitious and playing both ends against the middle. He plans to be party leader and doesn't much care what he has to do to get there: kiss ass or bust ass." Derek shrugged. "He's a politician."

The couple at the far end of the bar got up to leave. The man put a guiding arm round the woman's shoulders, ushering her out.

"He's got a train to catch," Derek said. "Newcastle on business."

"Has he?"

"Not from what he said to his wife on the phone." Derek laughed. "Perhaps he's got another one lined up." Still laughing, he went to the bar, then came back with refills. Silano looked surprised.

"You buying, Derek?"

"Are you serious? They're running a tab for you." He sipped his white-wine spritzer: con-men don't drink: it clouds the memory, and memory is all important. "He has a few directorships that might not be quite kosher"—he was back to Morgan now—"and a few contacts in the Middle East that his party might frown on, but mostly his business interests are just the right side of legal." Derek laughed. "Pigeon took a few meetings for him: with an American manufacturer, I think it was."

"Took meetings for him?"

"Did the business. Cut the deal."

"You mean he pretended to be his own boss?"

"That's right. Either Morgan had to be somewhere else, or the business was sensitive and he needed to be able to say he'd never met them. I expect they make jump-leads for Abu Ghraib, or something similar. Look"—he spread his hands in a gesture of innocence—"I pick these things up from lip-reading conversations. I get fragments. I remember everything, but most of it doesn't help me."

"The business interests would have helped."

Derek lifted his spritzer, dampened his lips, and put it down. "Only if I'd been planning a con."

"You were planning a con," Silano said, "but someone got murdered, so you backed out fast."

Derek shook his head. "You can't know that."

"Where were you, when you got all this?" Silano was trying to picture the scene. Morgan and Pigeon on one side of a room, like the cheating husband and his lover who had just left, Derek Crane on the other.

"Sometimes the local Conservative Club, sometimes a House of Commons bar; or there's a club Morgan likes to go to in Orchard Street."

Silano looked at him. "How did you get in?"

"Anyone can join a club."

"No, the House of Commons."

Derek smiled. "All you need is a pass in a plastic holder and a confident tone of voice. Years of practice give you the voice."

"The pass?"

"*Please.*" Derek looked affronted. "A computer, a passport snap."

Silano went to the bar and paid the tab. When he turned, Derek was standing beside him.

"You put the word out, and I said I could help. I didn't say it would come free."

Silano reached into his pocket and took out an envelope. It looked disappointingly thin, and Derek sighed.

"I didn't get much," Silano said. "It cuts both ways." He smiled ruefully. "I thought at least there might have been a shag on the side."

"Pigeon? No, not Pigeon."

Something in Derek's voice alerted Silano. "Not Pigeon, but—"

"Morgan."

"I'm pulling teeth," Silano said.

Derek waited until Silano had dipped into his wallet. "She's either a natural blonde or her hairdresser's a genius. Late twenties. Named Abigail."

"Where does he meet her?"

"I said: a club in Orchard Street."

"You were saving the best till last."

"Well," Derek said, "I didn't know we were going to be talking about Morgan."

Silano walked out of the bar into bright sunlight.

Couples were walking by the river, arm in arm, hand in hand. He wondered how many of them were married to someone else.

34

By day, business on the Strip slowed down. There were even a few shops, a dingy café, a pawnbroker, a gimcrack arcade. Harriman walked past the police tape and a scene-of-crime tent, where a forensic team was still brushing and tweezering. He didn't look twice. SOC teams weren't that rare on the Strip.

Harriman was there to rattle a few cages. He knew that Costea Radu's arrest would have caused problems: problems and opportunities. Radu's girls would have to be managed, his turf covered, his profit redirected. It took Harriman two hours to work the street on a drop-in basis; during that time he spoke to pimps, dealers, gamblers, and other assorted lowlifes, but got no nearer to Lizzie the Tree Girl. She was freelance, she was taking risks; she made tricks, she made money, but she made no friends.

He came up from a basement club, all stained velvet and stale air, and started to walk down toward the church. On the other side of the road, Gideon Woolf was walking uphill, looking neither left nor right, a little movie running in his head: scenes of violence and vengeance, in which he himself played the dark hero.

John Delaney was sitting in Martin Turner's Canary Wharf office watching a garbage scow push against the tide; gulls were tracking it, wheeling on the breeze. From inside the room, with its air-con and its Plexiglas, the whole thing looked contrived: a world at one remove.

Delaney and Turner were having a lunchtime beer and a sandwich and talking in carefully constructed circles. The editor was wearing a blue shirt with red braces, like a man who believed in his role. He said, "Why did you go in the first place? I mean, why did you ever go?"

"Well, it was no accident. I asked to go."

"Where was that?"

"Northern Ireland."

"Then we sent you"—Turner tried to remember—"the First Gulf War, and . . ."

"Rwanda, Bosnia, Kosovo . . ."

"Five years, wasn't it?"

"More."

"Then no more."

"That's right."

"Why?"

"There's a point at which death becomes personal."

"Isn't it always?"

"You know what I mean."

An intercom voice told Turner he was needed: a five-minute problem. He took a gulp of beer and got up. "And now?" he asked, then left before he could get an answer.

Delaney walked to the window and looked out at the silent world. He remembered the smell of smoke and the juices flowing. He remembered nights in some bar or another, journos in combat gear, booze and laughter and the sound of incoming mortars. All of that. He also remembered skeletal men in camps, sitting still, hollow-eyed, dead inside their heads. He remembered women from the rape camps unable to speak of what had been done to them. He remembered the bodies being flung onto trucks like cordwood, some without legs, without arms, without heads. He remembered his fingers stalling over the keyboard, because nothing he could write, nothing, would even come close.

Turner came back, bringing with him two more bottles of beer. He said, "And now?" as if he'd never been away.

"I think," Delaney said, "I'm trying to work out where I really belong."

Turner laughed. "Don't get all fucking philosophical with me, John. Look, there's Palestine, there's Iraq, there's Chechnya, there's Somalia, there's the Congo. Last time I looked, about ninety small wars going on round the globe. Take your pick; I'll have you on a plane tomorrow."

Delaney said, "I'm contracted to do this Rich List thing."

"Sure," Turner said. "Sure, of course you are."

Stella piled up the files and photocopies and reports and carried them up to Mike Sorley's office. The door was partly open, and a little fog of cigarette smoke was seeping into the corridor. When she went in, Sorley was staring thoughtfully at two cigarettes smoldering in the ashtray, one down to the tip, one freshly lit. His desk was six inches deep in files and photocopies and reports.

Stella said nothing. She put her pile on the floor near his chair. She said, "Today's load. Sorry, boss."

Sorley looked at her. He said, "You know what? I think I'm having a heart attack."

Stella looked at his desk. She gave a brief laugh. "I'm not surprised."

Sorley said, "No, call an ambulance. I think I'm having a heart attack."

35

In a scene from the movie running in Gideon Woolf's head, a man left his office and took the lift to a basement car park. No one was there apart from the man and Woolf. When the man used his key to blip the lock on his car, Woolf stepped out of hiding. He said, "You lying bastard."

He liked it: the gloom of underground, the concrete pillars, neon strips reflecting hard, white rods of light back off the rows of cars. He liked the sudden surprise, the way he appeared from behind a pillar or from between two high-sided vehicles. He liked the startled look in the man's eyes and the way it quickly turned to fear.

There was a problem, though. The car park was a "restricted access facility"; only employees went there, and singly unless they were part of the company's share-a-ride scheme. Woolf needed a more public place: where the man would be seen; exposed, like the others; held up to shame. He constructed other scenes that allowed for this. The man at his office, at his club, at his home . . . yes, that had possibilities.

The expensive suburb, the detached house screened by a line of silver birches, the radio-controlled gate of black iron railings, the long, broad driveway. The man uses his remote control to roll the gate back, but then sees that there's something in the driveway: it might be the green recycling bin that's kept close to the gate but to one side; it might be a child's bike. He sighs, he gets out of the car . . .

Yes, that one looked promising.

———

Woolf's room contained a desk, an operator's chair, a bed, a low table made from ply and veneer. He sat in the operator's chair with his feet on the desk, watching the television that was never switched off. On screen was either a newscast of police action in some unnamed city or a shoot-'em-shitless TV drama, he couldn't tell which.

That night, he had dreamed of Aimée, the pair of them far out to sea in a small boat and waves breaking across the bow. He had told her everything about his life while the storm raged. It was clear to him that she was afraid of the darkness and the running sea, so he'd put his arm round her, and she had folded against his chest, her body supple and warm. Now, in his recollection of the dream, she told him she loved him, swore she would never leave him, though he wasn't really sure whether the dream had offered that moment or not.

He crossed to the bed and lay down. Woolf lived a life that took no account of when people normally slept or woke. He hoped that the dream might return, and the moment come round again when Aimée talked about love, but although sleep arrived almost at once, his dreaming was a series of random images that melted as he woke.

Traffic buildup outside the window and lengthening shadows in the room told him it was late afternoon. He checked the clock on his laptop and saw that it was just after five. The sun had moved round, but the room held that warm, sharp odor of charred wood. He drank water straight from the tap, then went out and walked to the Park Clinic. It was a storefront façade: two pavement-to-lintel plate-glass windows and the name in blue neon script. Venetian blinds guarded the privacy of waiting patients, though some before-and-after blowups on each side of the glass door were distressingly intimate. Woolf walked to the top of the street, then back, as if that was what he'd always intended. He went into a fast-food place almost opposite, ordered beer, and moved to one of the stools by the window.

He looked for her, and sure enough, after a while, she appeared. She wasn't quite as he remembered her from the dream—not as slender, not as pretty, not as dark—but he still liked the look of her. He could see that her hair, now it wasn't wet, had a soft curl to it. He had thought he might follow her, but when he stepped out into the street, she saw him at once, and he realized that he'd wanted her to. Her face changed when she smiled—softer, warmer—and she crossed the street to him as if they had done this before.

They walked for a while until they found a pub with a garden, then ordered some drinks and sat in a thin rectangle of sunlight and told each other lies.

Aimée reached home an hour later than usual, though Peter barely noticed. Not that he was indifferent or even hostile—far from it—but it would never have occurred to him to be curious about Aimée's activities. Or about Aimée. He was a good husband, and that was a large part of the problem. He wasn't much good at being a lover or a friend, but he was a top-notch husband.

It must have seemed a pretty likable setup: likable Aimée and likable Peter with their likable ten-year-old son, Ben. Aimée had grown tired of being told how lucky she was. Just recently she had started to believe that there were different brands of luck, and that the brand she'd been given led to the sort of quiet, uneventful life many people sought.

Aimée wanted a different kind of luck. The kind that had to do with risk, with chance, with a throw of the dice.

36

A scrum of doctors and Mike Sorley in the thick of it. He'd died twice, and they'd dragged him back. Now someone was using the defibrillator paddles again. Sorley hopped and flopped, and his heartbeat flickered on the monitor.

In the relatives' room Karen sat with her hands on her knees, then got up and went to the door, then took a turn round the room, then went out and walked down the corridor and back, then sat down with her hands on her knees.

When Stella came in with two cartons of coffee, Karen said, "No one's saying anything. No one's saying a word."

"Then they're not saying he's dead."

Stella had made a triple-nine call for the first time in her life. While she was on the phone, Sorley had got up and walked out of the office as if he were on his way to meet the paramedics; or maybe he thought he stood a better chance in the open air. He got as far as the squad room, Stella hard on his heels, when he went down, clattering into a white-board pinned with SOC shots of Tree Girl and Leonard Pigeon. His face was the color of dishwater and he was breathing in stop-start gulps.

Traffic was backed up in Holland Park Avenue and in gridlock round Shepherd's Bush roundabout. They could hear the whoop of the siren, but the ambulance wasn't getting any closer. Stella got on to her knees, laced her fingers, and leaned on Sorley's chest. She counted as she pumped.

A hospital, in the small hours, echoes and ticks. The corridors are empty, but you'll hear cries or the sound of running feet. There are deaths like sudden silences. In a side room, under white neon, people sit and wait for bad news to walk in the door.

At 2:00 A.M. a doctor in green scrubs told Karen Sorley that her husband was in ITC playing pitch and toss with death, but looking the likely winner. He said it would be okay for Karen to go and sit with Sorley. To Stella, he said, "It was you who found him."

"I was with him when it happened."

"You gave him CPR."

"The ambulance was backed up in traffic."

"It was a bad occlusion. You saved his life." The doctor sighed and pulled off his skullcap; it was the end of his endless shift. He turned to Karen and smiled. "He's not a smoker at all, is he?"

Stella waited until dawn, when Karen came back to the relatives' room to say that Sorley had made it through the night.

"It was you," she said. "You saved him."

She took Stella's hands and held them tightly, the sort of intimacy that only fear and deliverance can provoke.

"Anyone would have done it," Stella told her.

"Yes, but it was you."

A London dawn can be bright and fresh for ten minutes or more.

Harriman had driven her to the hospital, ambulance-chasing through the back streets and rat-runs, his blue light clamped to the roof-arch. Now she walked back toward the Kensals, birdsong over the low drum of engines, the morning sky crisscrossed with jet trails.

When she reached the park railings, she realized that she'd been heading there all along. The tree cast a long morning shadow. Stella stood in its shade and looked at the trunk; it was about shoulder height, just where Andy Greegan said it would be.

∧ ∧
∨

Who are you, you bastard, and why did you do that to her? What were you thinking when you hauled her up into the tree? Dirty Girl. Is that why she died? Do you think she deserved what she got?

Suddenly she was seized by a wild anger.

Who are you to be judge and executioner? I'm going to find you, you piece of shit. You shithead. You bag of shit, you're mine.

She went home and showered and sat by the window with a coffee. Delaney came out of the bedroom and looked at her. She said, "Not dead." She drank more coffee while he made eggs.

When she got to the squad room, Sue Chapman handed her the day's reports and cocked a thumb toward Sorley's office. Stella walked down the corridor and looked in. DS Brian Collier was sitting at Sorley's desk; it was nearly clear of paper. He grinned winningly.

"Acting DI, AMIP-5, and trying to get a handle on all this crap." He indicated two files, side by side in front of him. "Bryony Dean, know her?"

"Missing-persons possibility. When did this happen?"

"Last night. I got a call from the SIO. Oh," he said, remembering the etiquette, "how is he?"

"Good. Doing well. Be back at his desk pretty soon, I should think. Sorry about that."

"Stella . . . you turned down three promotion boards. And this is *Acting* DI—they're not making me up."

"It's fine. It's fine with me, Brian."

"Okay. So, I've read the case papers, but I'll need to be brought up to speed."

"Sure."

"Good. And look . . . it's Brian in here; in this office; it's Boss in the squad room. You understand." He pushed the two files forward an inch or two. "Bryony Dean, missing-persons file, follow-up by yourself and DC Harriman, your conclusion: that the girl had run off with her mother's boyfriend, have I got that right?"

"We think the mother knew. The boyfriend reported her missing to put himself in the clear."

"Okay, well . . ." Collier paused for effect. "Her file's here. And there's another—it was about three deep—on someone called Elizabeth Rose Connor." He flipped open the file covers to show the photos provided for the MPB. One had been taken at a party, the girl looking into the camera and smiling a wide smile.

Bryony.

The other was less clear: taken in a club, perhaps. The girl had a cigarette in her hand, and her gaze was beyond the camera, as if she had just spotted someone coming in.

Stella leaned over to get a better look. The same girl. There was no doubt about it. She looked at the MPB form, and the name leaped out at her.

Elizabeth.

Lizzie.

37

Melanie Dean said, "So it was her, then." She hadn't even bothered to look at the Elizabeth Rose Connor mug shot Harriman held out to her. "It looked like her, I said so."

"You said it looked like her. You also said it wasn't her."

"I didn't know. Only that she'd gone."

"You thought it might be her, but you didn't say."

"No, it just looked like her. I could see it looked like her, but I never thought it was, not until now." She half turned away. "I mean, I looked at the picture, and I could see something of Bryony in it . . ." She was trying to find an excuse for herself. "I didn't like to think about it."

Stella said, "I'm sorry."

Another flawless day apart from the carbon emissions, the jet-fuel off-loads, the ozone factor. From 1136, Block A, all you could see was blue sky. Melanie went to the window and opened it; at that height there was a faint breeze.

Stella looked at the woman, searching for some trace of sorrow. She said, "Why would she be calling herself Elizabeth Connor?"

"That was her nan's name. She loved her nan."

"Why would she use it?"

Melanie sighed, as if anyone ought to know the answer. "She had to live."

"Benefit fraud," Harriman said.

"She was on the Social already. I expect he put her on again. He always claimed twice. Most round here do."

"Your boyfriend," Stella said. "Chris Fuller."

Melanie laughed. It sounded like someone shaking pebbles in a box. "Yeah, bloody Chris."

Harriman asked, "And would it be Chris that was sending her out whoring?"

Melanie didn't blink. "Yeah, that sounds right."

"And when he was living here," Stella said, "did he send you out too?"

"Yeah."

"And Bryony?"

"Yeah." There was a pause before Melanie added, "Course, we did think of being famous film stars or marrying royalty, but it seemed like a lot of bother."

Stella asked for a photo of Chris, and Melanie found an away-day threesome, Chris in the middle looking solemn. She handed it over. "It rained that day. Day out to the sea, it was. Day wasted."

Harriman said, "If you wanted to find Chris, where would you look?"

"I don't know. How would I fucking know?" No one spoke for a while, then Melanie said, "He'll still be claiming for her. Saying she's sick . . ."

Stella looked round the room: chipboard furniture, bare floor, bare walls, a lick of grime over everything. Little Stella Mooney's home from home. She said, "I'm afraid we can't release the body to you, just yet. There'll be an inquest."

Melanie said, "I can't afford no funeral."

A squad-car siren started faint and grew, stopping somewhere eleven floors below. The Bull Ring, Stella guessed. Just the one vehicle, so not a major op: the dealers could go on cutting and wrapping, the whores whoring, the fixers fixing.

As they were leaving, she asked, "What do you think? Was it Chris? Did Chris kill Bryony?"

For the first time, there was genuine surprise in Melanie's expression. "Chris? No, course not."

"Why?"

"He loved her, didn't he? That's why they went off together. First off, he loved me; then it was her." She gave a shaky little smile. "He was always selfish like that."

Cuts of sky between the blocks, a shimmer of heat haze rising and bringing with it smells of fast food, dope, decay, and a subtle admix of bad luck. Little Stella sitting all alone in a room on the eighteenth floor, watching birds drift by, hearing the slam of music, the blatter of TVs, the yells of pain and hatred filtering up the stairwell.

Harriman shrugged out of his leather jacket as they emerged onto the walkway. He said, "Shit, it's hot." He started to walk away, then realized Stella wasn't with him. He turned and saw her standing utterly still just outside the door of 1136, Block A, staring across the gap to the door of 1169, Block B. A woman was standing there, arm raised.

Across that short distance, that limitless distance, almost near enough to touch, almost lost in planes of blue, standing on the concrete walkway, Stella's mother waved like an excited passenger on the deck of a ship coming gently in to dock.

She said, "Hello, Stell. I thought that was you."

38

Gideon Woolf was off territory. In a scabrous pub by London Fields, he sat with a beer and waited to be approached. He would have been noticed before he got to the bar to order his drink; being noticed was easy; being approached constituted a commitment. He was easy in his mind, though that area of London was a risk for the unwary. While he waited, he ran the movie scene again.

The car, the gate sliding back, the man getting out. Since devising the scene, Woolf had been on location: he'd scouted the venue, he had been the eye of the camera. To the left of the gate was a tall hedge and then a narrow path between the hedge and a screen of four skinny silver birches. The car is running, the gate is back, Woolf and the man are in that screened space. He acknowledged the need to be quick—the car is on the drive-up from the road, still ticking over, the gate is open, the man is nowhere to be seen.

That necessary speed was one of the reasons that had brought him to London Fields. A knife isn't always fast, isn't always fatal, and it can be hard work. But speed wasn't the only reason; a single gunshot was part of Gideon Woolf's story.

He drank his beer and bought another. It was early afternoon, and the pub was filling up, but no one sat at his table.

Bryony . . . Lizzie . . . down from the tree and laid out on a slab.

Stella was looking at the postmortem blad when Maxine Hewitt perched on a chair at her side. Chocolate bar of the day was Tim Tam. Maxine was carrying one for each of them. She looked over Stella's shoulder at the evidence of Sam Burgess's delicate butchery: Bryony laid open, her ribs sprung, the heart-lung system gone.

"Do you think he killed her—the boyfriend?"

"Her mother doesn't." Stella shrugged. "It wouldn't be unusual, would it? But then, did he also kill Leonard Pigeon?"

"You don't think so?"

"Not really. We'd better find him, though." She let go a little hiss of annoyance. "DI Collier's insisting."

"DI Collier's fairly loud on the issue."

"DI Collier thinks boyfriend Chris is our man."

Maxine tossed her wrapper toward a waste bin and missed by a mile. She said, "Surveillance, then: if he's still picking up her benefit."

"And his own," Stella guessed. "Fancy it?"

"Sitting in a car with a Tango, a cheeseburger, and a sweaty cop, how could I resist?"

"Ask Collier to get some local help, but coordinate it yourself."

It was Maxine's cue to leave, but she didn't take it. After a minute she said, "When I came out to my mother, she slammed the door and locked it."

Stella continued to turn the pages of the PM blad: Bryony at various stages of lack and loss. Eventually, she said, "It's not like that—a disagreement, a feud . . ."

"No? What, then?"

"I hate her. I always have."

"Always?"

"So far as I can remember."

"Oh . . ." Maxine didn't know where to go from there.

Stella said, "Take Frank Silano with you. Tell him not to sweat."

She leafed through the blad as if the sight of Bryony's body, broken down to spare parts, might cause a clue to spring out at her—an answer, a *reason*—but her mind wandered.

She remembered standing at the door of 1169, Block B, and ringing the bell; she remembered the splash of blood on the doorstep.

Harriman passed her desk and glanced sideways at the blad. "That's us in the end, isn't it?" he said. "Meat and bone and hair."

Stella's reply was too soft to be heard. "Yes," she said. "That's us."

A tall man with razored sideburns and laughable aviator shades sat down at Woolf's table. He seemed a little vague, which might have been anything from coke to cool. After a few checks and trade-offs, he made some offers. He offered coke, crack, Billy, rophie, blow, scag, Nazi crank, skunk, rush, coco snow, black Russian, Texas red, and acid.

Woolf said no thanks.

The man offered girls, boys, trans, black, white, Asian, Oriental, straight, bent, blow, hand, skin, anal, facial, pain, rain, rubber, and leather.

Woolf said no thanks.

The man offered a Merc C180, a Porsche Boxster, a Lamborghini Gallardo, a BMW Z4, a Ferrari 360, a Jag XK8, a Maserati Spyder.

Woolf said no thanks.

The man offered a straight choice: a Swiss SIG Sauer P220 or a Czech CZ75.

Woolf took the SIG Sauer.

Melanie Dean sat on the floor and looked at the photographs. There weren't many; she kept them in a shoe box. They were baby photographs and class photographs and photo-booth foursomes; some had been taken on disposables and were mostly from hen parties or a girls' night out. There was one taken when Bryony was six, a school photo, in which she was looking straight at the camera and giving a toothy grin. She looked so happy you could almost believe it.

Melanie had arranged the photos in a semicircular spread, so she could look at them all in turn. She had been down eleven floors and across the DMZ to a liquor store for a bottle of vodka, which was now almost gone, and she looked at the photos, which seemed a little blurred, a touch out of focus, which in fact some of them truly were.

She closed her eyes and, for a moment or two, slept. A little dream was gifted to her in which she could hear Bryony's voice but couldn't see her daughter, so she assumed she must be somewhere in the flat. She went from room to room, but the place was empty and, when she woke, just a few seconds later, it was with the realization that "empty" was the word for it, "empty" was the best possible description, and if she hadn't been able to find a word before to describe the way things were now and had almost always been, "empty" was it, "empty" was spot on, "empty" was right on the money.

She picked up Bryony with the toothy grin and slipped her into a pocket, stepped out of her front door onto the walkway, then hopped up onto the concrete balustrade and spread her arms. For a moment she was still, then she tilted an inch, then another, and then she was gone.

39

When Tom Davison's call came through, Stella was on her own in the squad room reading reports.

He said, "I used to enjoy these phone calls."

"Tom, it was a one-night stand, though I know you don't want to think of it that way, and there were things I should have told you, and it was my fault and I'm sorry."

"Sorry about?"

"Misleading you. Disappointing you. I don't know . . ."

"I wasn't disappointed. Not at the time, only later." She didn't speak. He added, "You're with someone, I know."

"That's right."

"So what was I?"

"You were lovely."

She hoped it was what he wanted to hear, but she also knew it to be the truth. Her night with him had been strange: strangely exciting, strangely intimate. Stranger still was the fact that she felt uncomfortable using his given name.

He said, "Yeah, okay." Then: "So, you've got a DNA match, and you've got a letdown. The match is in all twenty-six CODIS sites; that definitely gives you the same man at the two scenes of crime you nominated: Leonard Pigeon and unidentified female."

"Bryony Dean."

"Oh, okay."

"The same man in what role?"

"Well, he killed them, I think we can safely say that."

"The letdown being?"

"He's not on any database, so apart from being able to put him at both scenes, I can't be much use to you."

"Well, we know it's not copycat. That was always a possibility."

"Okay, so . . ." Davison paused. "That's about all I have to say."

Stella said, "I'm glad we're not doing this face-to-face."

"We already did it face-to-face." Then he laughed: "Sorry. My mouth takes off sometimes."

"I'm glad because I should have spoken a long time ago, and I didn't, and that was weak of me, and I'm sorry."

"Don't be."

"Sorry if I . . ." She was going to say "hurt you" but that felt too intimate, and too likely. "If I made things difficult for you."

Davison gave a little laugh; a neutral laugh. "Don't worry, Stella. That wasn't me; it was someone who looked like me."

She drove home through an early-evening mist of petrol fumes, the sun filtering through, gold and orange, in-car sound systems feuding with each other, the sky a high, pale blue fretted with white vapor trails, as one-a-minute planes bellied down into the Heathrow flight path.

There was something nagging at her, something someone had said, like a tune almost remembered or a name on the tip of the tongue, but she couldn't call it up.

Delaney was closing off his piece on a very wealthy man with a gunslinger's mustache and a wry sense of humor.

She sat down with him and told him about the encounter on Harefield, she and her mother looking at each other across an unbridgeable gap. It was the first thing she said: not "Hi," or "Fancy a drink?" or "How was your day?"

"I saw my mother today. She came back. She's living on Harefield."

Delaney knew the story of Stella and Stella's mother. He said, "What happened?"

"Who knows. Maybe something fouled up in Manchester; maybe she got homesick."

"No—what happened?"

It seemed he did fancy a drink, because he went to the fridge for wine.

"Nothing happened. Our eyes met across a crowded slum. She said hello, I said good-bye. Lyrics by Paul McCartney."

He handed Stella her drink. "That was it?"

"More or less. Not entirely. She'd seen me go in, I think—flat across from hers on another block. She must have been waiting for me to come out. We said a couple of words to each other; I did this . . ." She held a fist up to the side of her head, thumb and little finger extended, the universal sign for a telephone.

"And will you do that?"

"Sure, of course. Yes. Obviously."

Delaney laughed. "So you have her number, then . . ."

Stella was silent on that one. "She's living with some guy. Must have brought him with her."

"He was there?"

"Standing back, just inside the hall."

"So . . ." Delaney closed his laptop and settled into his drink. He expected Stella's mother to lead to a long evening and more drinks. ". . . how did she look?"

"The way she used to look. Hair from a bottle, lardy makeup, clothes from the seventies." She laughed. "The time-warp mother."

And that, to Delaney's surprise, was all she had to say on the matter. Sure, they had a few more drinks and, sure, he kept expecting Stella's mother to reappear, but that didn't happen. They ate, they watched the news, they went to bed, and that was where he got a hint of what she was really feeling, because she made love to him like someone trying to displace a memory.

He didn't hear her get up at 3:00 A.M. He didn't hear her pour a drink, ice cracking as the vodka drenched it. He didn't hear her say, "Bitch, you *bitch,* get the *fuck* out of my life."

40

On Harefield, 3:00 A.M. is the beginning of the end of the day for those with business to contract.

Ricardo Jones was still sharp, though Jonah and the two who sat with him looked a little heavy-lidded, which was less to do with the lateness of the hour than with the top-ups they'd been enjoying throughout the evening. You can do booze and dope on a rota basis, but there's a risk of nodding off. For the inexperienced, there's a risk of nodding off forever.

Jonah said, "Twenty-five, that right?"

"Twenty-five percent," Ricardo agreed.

"No extras, no supplements, I got that right?"

"Twenty-five is a net figure."

A silence. Jonah was thinking this through, calculating the risk. On Harefield, he was a big man, but he knew Harefield wasn't the world. He also knew that someone called Gary . . . maybe it was Barry . . . had been pumped full of cavity-wall filler and thought this might be considered a warning to others.

On the other hand, Jonah had his own rules and didn't like to be told what to do. What the *fuck* to do. And twenty-five percent was one hell of a good deal, whichever way you cut it.

"You off-loaded the other gear," he said; "that was a good job. That was fast, and it was clean."

A pair of class cars lifted to order in Mayfair, Ricardo given the type, the registration, the color, the add-ons, a week in advance; customers located;

shipping and customizing arranged; a deal done that had three-way approval.

"Yeah," Jonah said, "that was sweet."

"Twenty-five percent," Ricardo assured him, "no surprises."

"How much can you handle?"

"Try me."

"Two-fifty."

They were talking in hundred thousands.

"Is this ongoing?"

Jonah hesitated. "Just now it's—"

"Can I get a rollover on this?"

"Man, don't press me here."

"Twenty-five percent, think of that."

Ricardo knew that there was always a rollover with drugs. The money kept coming in, because the gear kept going out; there was a need involved, there was a *craving*.

Jonah was smoking a Havana-Havana. He took a pull, and for a second or two his face was shrouded in smoke. "Do this one," he said, "impress me. Everything's a maybe, know what I mean. But listen: you do a good job. I can see that. I'm gonna put a lotta things your way."

"Including money?"

Jonah laughed. He said, "You're hungry. I like that." The laugh died. "Just stay out of my face."

Day is night, and night is day. The tower blocks lit up, music like hammers, deals going down, hookers hard at it. Only the civilians were in their beds, the noncoms, deaf, blind, and dumb.

One of the two men who had sat with Jonah was taking a walk on the littered wasteland of the DMZ and making a call to a mobile number known only to a few.

He said, "They're cutting a deal."

"For?"

"Two-fifty."

"Okay."

That was all. Jonah's friend, who was also his enemy, walked off the DMZ to find an all-night bar. He didn't want to be seen going back into Harefield as if he'd been on some sort of a mission.

Stanley Bowman snapped his phone shut. The girl in bed with him said, "What?"

"Nothing," he said. "Business. Shut up."

He closed his eyes, but his mind was busy. After a few moments he got up and took his phone through to the room where he'd had his meeting with John Delaney. The first call went to message, so he called three times more, each time hanging up before the divert could cut in. Finally, he got an answer. A voice with a burr: Irish maybe; maybe American.

Bowman said, "There's a problem."

"Same problem?"

"The same."

"Same solution?"

Bowman paused. "Listen, see if a warning will do it. Let's try a warning."

"Your choice."

"The other guy, the first guy, he wouldn't listen. I had to make a decision."

"Will this guy listen?"

"Let's try it. Let's see."

"Okay." The voice was apologetic but concerned. "Only, a warning can have repercussions, you know. For me, for the operative. There can be a kickback. People have friends, you know? They have *business* friends."

"Yeah. What are you saying?"

"How well connected is this guy?"

"He's an asshole. He's freelance: a nobody."

"No status . . ."

"That's it: no status."

"One warning."

"You know about this stuff."

"Just one, either that's enough or it's not."

"Yes, okay." Bowman sighed. "Jesus, everyone's a dealer, everyone's a fucking *entrepreneur*. I blame Richard Branson."

Aimée was roaming the house, looking for somewhere to settle, but nowhere felt right: not the kitchen table, where family meals were taken, not the living room sofa, where everyone gathered to watch TV. Least of all the bed, where she would lie alongside her top-notch husband, her caring husband, the husband about whom no one could find a bad word to say.

She was making plans. She knew that plans and action are not the same thing. She knew that plans are hopes, and hopes are fragile. She also knew that falling in love is an easy task for the loveless, but there were some things, she felt, that just couldn't be set aside or ignored. One of them was your last chance.

They would be fine together: Peter and Ben; after the shock, after the brief sense of loss. People changed their lives—it happened every day—and those they left recovered; they became happy in different ways. Everyone knew this; it was a commonplace; and it allowed her to advance her plans to the point where, in her mind's eye, she left the house for the last time.

Then, in the midst of that imagined moment, she thought: *I can't do this. I can't leave them, husband and son, can't abandon them, can't bear the thought of their sorrow. It's beyond me, this new life, it's out of my reach.* As if intending to convince herself, she spoke the words out loud, but it was the voice of some former self speaking, someone trapped by repetition; the words were a mere echo, hollow and fading fast.

Aimée closed her eyes, and there she was, stepping out into sunlight.

The sky was cloudless. Her future was laid out like a map of dreams.

41

Climate change: the ozone layer peels back, a chunk of Arctic ice the size of Ireland falls into the sea, London overheats and kids cruise all night, some of them packed into a supertuned Imola-red BMW on Stella's street at 8 A.M., gaining ground on the inside and clipping the wing mirrors off parked cars.

Stella called Notting Dene nick and gave them the Beamer's registration number more in hope than expectation. Getting into her own car produced a moment of déjà vu: whatever had been nagging at her as she'd driven home the night before was still there, like a trapped fly buzzing on the windscreen.

Something someone said . . . something she had read.

She was slowing for a set of lights when Harriman came through on her mobile. As she picked up, a black Freelander just behind her made a three-lane switch and caught a corresponding three-way horn blast.

"You're driving."

"No," she said, "I'm queuing."

"Okay, well, it took a little while for the cross-referencing to bring up AMIP-5, but I got a call to say that Melanie Dean topped herself."

Red went to amber, and everything moved. Stella trapped her phone with her shoulder and shifted gear. The Freelander cross-cut to claim her lane, and she tapped her brake.

"Tell me."

"She jumped off the walkway outside her flat."

"When?"

"Not long after we interviewed her."

"Jesus Christ."

"You didn't say anything, boss. I didn't say anything."

"No."

A long pause. He asked, "Boss? Are you there?"

"Send a global e-mail to the squad. Send the crime report to Collier."

And send my apologies to the late Melanie Dean.

"I've applied for a search warrant . . ."

She must have loved seeing that picture. Tree Girl with the eyes patched in.

". . . maybe there's some trace of the boyfriend, Chris, who knows?"

She must have been really pleased to see us when we dropped in with the positive ID.

"No reason to go to the postmortem, not that I can see."

Yes, it's your daughter. Your daughter, Bryony. We found her hanging from a tree.

"She was drunk when she jumped."

He hung her up naked for everyone to see. And when we showed you the picture, it looked like her, but it didn't look like her.

"Apparently, she'd done most of a bottle of vodka."

It's odd. It's strange. Relatives often don't recognize the dead. They go to the morgue, and someone pulls out the body tray, and the relative, the mother, the father, whoever, they stare, they say, "No, I don't think that's her."

"Are you there, boss? I think I'm losing you."

Little Stella Mooney out on the walkway, eighteenth floor, too hot to be inside . . . Stella with her book and her drink, kids running past but she's invisible, adults going past but she's invisible . . . and even there, even in that miserable place, the sun is catching glass and metal and sending lines of light across walls blotchy with pollution, livid with graffiti.

Then the book is snatched from her hands and flung high and wide, pages being turned by the breeze, fluttering, catching the sun, her mother's laugh, the man's laugh. Little Stella Mooney standing at the walkway's balustrade and lifting herself up and looking down, the book still airborne, rocking to and fro as it falls, so you could imagine how dreamy its descent, how soft its landing . . . and Stella wondering how it would feel to follow, to climb up, to let herself go, drifting down, flying almost, the mother's laugh fading in air until there is just the whicker of the wind in her ears.

It feels likable to her. It feels possible.

The Freelander slipped her on the inside, thought about running a red, then decided against it and shimmied to a stop. Stella beat the light without intending to, clearing the box scant seconds before the lead vehicles from the cross street arrived.

Not me, she thought. *Little Stella Mooney. Not me, but someone who looked like me.*

And suddenly she had it.

Tom Davison saying, "Don't worry, Stella. That wasn't me, it was someone who looked like me."

Relatives not recognizing the dead.

Not him. Someone who looked like him.

She turned into the AMIP-5 car park, another vehicle close behind. It parked alongside—the black Freelander. And there was Collier getting out, giving her a sideways look.

"Passing a signal at red while simultaneously talking on a mobile phone . . ."

She shook her head. "Someone who looked like me."

42

Silano said, "It was an American company, that's what I got from my chis. Pigeon took the meetings, because Morgan either couldn't be there or didn't want to be there. Chance of some sensitive content, apparently."

"How was it possible?"

Silano considered. "Maybe they'd never met Morgan?"

"Yes, right, so let's say they've never met him. Have you met him?"

"Morgan? No."

"But you know what he looks like?"

"I've seen him on TV, I think. In the papers."

"Did you look closely?"

"No, I don't expect I did."

"A photo, a screen image, it's not the same, is it? Ever meet someone famous?"

"A couple of times. News presenter doing an after-dinner speech; a model whose boyfriend had overdosed."

"Did they look like their pictures? The way they looked on screen?"

Silano thought about it. "They did, yes, but . . . more so. Or maybe I mean less so. What? It's a two-dimensional, three-dimensional thing? People seem smaller in life; TV makes you look fatter . . ."

"I don't know what it is," Stella said. "Now think about this. Could you stand in for DC Harriman?"

Silano laughed. "Totally different types. Physical types, I mean. No resemblance."

"So, if I wanted someone to stand in for Harriman and fool people who had only seen his picture, I wouldn't choose you. Who would I choose?"

"Someone who did actually look like Harriman."

"Yes. So, think about Morgan and Pigeon. Does he?"

"What?"

"Does Leonard Pigeon look like Neil Morgan—enough to fool people who'd only seen him on TV or seen his picture in the papers?"

Silano found the photograph of Pigeon that his widow had handed over. Stella googled a mug shot of Neil Morgan. They propped the photo next to the screen.

Dark, thirties, clean-shaven, neat hair, fleshy, eyes pretty much, nose more or less, mouth very close.

Silano looked at the two images, then at Stella. "You think he meant to kill Morgan?"

"I think it's possible, yes."

"But the writing on Pigeon's arms: 'Filthy coward.' He ran when he saw the incident on the bridge."

"And we know that because . . . ?"

"It was in the papers, on TV."

"Was it? The incident was reported, we know that."

Silano looked at the two images, then glanced up to the white-board and another picture of Leonard Pigeon, a man sitting on a bench, his head fallen forward, a flabby spread round the jowls where the jaw was unsupported by the slashed throat.

Leonard in life, Leonard in death. Not looking himself.

Open windows were letting cigarette smoke out and exhaust gases in. Texan Bars had taken over from Mars and Tim Tam, and people were drinking Highland Spring, except Sue Chapman, who claimed that she knew full well London water was full of estrogen, but she needed the boost.

Maxine Hewitt said, "It's where he got the information from—the killer. Newspapers and TV."

"You sure? Did the stories include a full account of Pigeon seeing the attack on the woman and instantly legging it in the other direction? Did you read the reports? Did you check them out?" Maxine shrugged. "No, okay, let's do it. DC Harriman and I will go back to see Morgan."

"Why?"

This was Collier, leaning against a desk, center-front and right under Stella's nose. It had always been Sorley's practice to stand just inside the door, observing but allowing Stella to run the briefing. Collier wasn't the unobtrusive type.

"If he was the target," Stella said, "we need to know more. 'Filthy coward'—if that wasn't meant for Pigeon, it was meant for Morgan. Why?"

"It's just a theory," Collier said. "You could be wrong. Probably are."

"But it ought to be looked at."

"He's an MP and a high-profile one, at that. Tread carefully."

There was a tiny silence in the squad room, like an indrawn breath. A touch of color sprang up on Stella's throat. She turned back to the squad members. "There's a link between Bryony Dean and either Leonard Pigeon or Neil Morgan. They might have known one another. Or it might be something that connects them only in the mind of the killer. We have to find that link. Whatever the common factor is, it will point back to our man." She paused. "Okay, that's it."

"No, wait." Collier stepped forward. He motioned to Stella to sit down at a nearby desk, then stood where she had been standing. "You might have heard that the mother of Bryony Dean committed suicide yesterday, not long after being interviewed by DS Mooney and DC Harriman. Questions are being asked, mostly by the SIO, but also by the press. The official response from this squad—that means all of you—is 'no comment.' I'll require written reports on the incident from the officers in question. That's separate reports, not one account signed by both of you." The briefest of pauses before he said, "DS Mooney, my office, just a catch-up, okay?"

He left. Stella left. Collier went to his office. Stella went to Coffee Republic and bought a two-shot American. She didn't want a coffee, but she needed to put some air between herself and Collier. No one thought it was a catch-up. Everyone knew that Collier shouldn't have butted in that way, or given the needless warning about treading carefully around Neil Morgan, or mentioned Melanie Dean's death without making it plain that there was no blame attached to anyone on that score. Pete Harriman second-guessed her destination, got himself a double espresso, and walked her back.

"You know him from—?"

"Fulham Cross."

"And the problem is?"

"He's an asshole."

"Yes, that's plain to see. You think so, I think so, I bet everyone thinks so. But something else."

"He hit on me, I knocked him back. But, listen, that's not it. Not really. It didn't help. But mostly the problem is as stated—asshole, grade-A."

"How's DI Sorley?"

"Out of ITC, but only just. We're not expecting him back for a while."

"A while?"

Stella shrugged. "God knows . . . months . . ."

They crossed the street between vehicles and homicidal cyclists. Harriman said, "Well, lucky us."

Collier had been involved in some interior design: Sorley's desk set crosswise, to make an isosceles triangle with the corner of the room, some steel shelving to hold the files and reports, trays for current work, a color-coded progress chart on the wall. Or maybe, Stella thought, it was a form of feng shui that specified all assholes had to be triangulated.

He said, "Melanie Dean's death . . . She topped herself, we're sure of that?"

"I haven't seen the report. Have you?"

"Yes. It assumes suicide. Who knows?" Stella said nothing. "No possibility of a robbery, rude boys off the estate, some wiggy bastard out of his head on crank lobbing her over the side?"

"Is that what we're hoping for?"

"On Harefield it's got to be a possibility. Look for it."

"I don't think it's there."

Collier lit a cigarette and coughed. "You know how the red tops love a police brutality story."

"They couldn't possibly try that."

"Did you think of suggesting counseling to her? You went round there and told her that her daughter was dead—for sure, dead. No mistakes. Up in a tree with her fucking eyes pecked out."

"Read my report. You'll see just such a recommendation." She smiled sweetly. "Your job—admin."

"If we could give this to some madass crackhead, it would be simpler." He thought for a moment. "She was pissed, right? Could it have been an accident? Could we go that route?"

"Anyone who goes over those walkways either climbs up or is shoved over; you can't fall off; and, anyway, I'm sure she jumped."

"Are you? Why?"

"Under the circumstances, it's what I would have done."

43

The boys in the Imola-red Beamer cruised the Strip. Their sound system would have reversed a pacemaker. The whores were doing deals for the lunchtime trade. They could probably have sold all-fruit smoothies and tuna-mayo wraps on the side.

Aimée was checking the kitchen in a North Kensington apartment: what estate agents like to call "Notting Hill borders." She opened cupboards and drawers and took stock. After that, she went into the bathroom and left some gels and creams, makeup, a toothbrush and toothpaste. She had brought some CDs and books from home to help her think of the place as hers. As theirs.

The friend who had loaned it to her would be working abroad for six months. She needed an apartment-sitter; Aimée needed a place to be with Woolf. They had met several times after she'd left work; they'd met in her lunch break; they had kissed on parting and pretty soon those kisses had become more than a peck.

She had waited for him to invite her to his place, and he hadn't done that. It made her wonder whether there were entanglements in his life too. She didn't care if there were. The last time they had kissed, she had stepped closer and put her arms round him; his hand in the small of her back pulled her in, and she could feel the hard, flat planes of his body. The apartment would be their world. She hadn't told him about her husband and son, and she didn't intend to.

It was a first-floor apartment in a Victorian four-story house, just four rooms, but the ceilings were high and the rooms light and airy. She went into the bedroom and lay down; she imagined herself lying down with him, and her nipples hardened.

A butterfly, too early for the time of year, was trapped between the window and the pale blue chiffon drape her friend had hung to diffuse the light. Aimée watched the creature's shadow seeming to dance as its wings fluttered at the glass. After a moment her eyes closed and she slept.

Gideon Woolf sat in his operator's chair, his back to the TV, the laptop, and the window. He was thinking about Aimée and whether he would have to kill her.

Frank Silano knew that Maxine Hewitt was gay; she knew that he was divorced. Apart from this information, which seemed, to each of them, largely irrelevant, they knew they worked well together. Silano tended to take a backseat. This was technique, not deference; it was the opposite of what people expected to happen, and it put them off guard.

Paula Pigeon was on the receiving end of this tactic: Silano sat back and made notes, while Maxine asked a few questions that Paula could easily answer. She asked how long Leonard had worked for Neil Morgan, where he'd worked before that, whether the job entailed long hours. Did he, Maxine wondered, always take his walk at the same time each morning, and did he drive to work or take public transport, and how many times, exactly, had he impersonated his boss?

Paula said, "Three, I think."

There was a little silence in the room, a drawn breath, a panicked look. She didn't try to backtrack: she said, "Does it matter?"

Maxine said, "I don't want to appear callous, but how could it?"

"No." Paula gave a sharp little laugh. "Of course . . ."

"Why did he do it?"

"Sensitive issues, I think. Neil was on several boards. I imagine he had to be careful not to compromise himself: clash of interests, you know."

Maxine nodded. "So rather than back off from a deal he shouldn't have been involved in, he sent your husband along."

"I suppose if questions were asked, he could truthfully claim not to have been at the meeting, not to have a connection with the company."

"But your husband could pass information on to Morgan, who could then pass it on to whichever board of directors was cutting the deal."

"The idea was for Neil to impress the Americans, make them believe that if an MP was backing the company, it must be safe to invest . . . that sort of thing."

"But in fact it was your husband who was making the impression."

"Not always. Not most times. Just those three occasions, so far as I know."

"Do you know what the clash of interests involved?"

"I'm not sure. Just business Neil didn't want to be publicly involved with, I imagine."

Silano remembered something Derek Crane had said. "Jump-leads for Abu Ghraib . . ."

Paula turned on him. "Len would never have gone along with such a deal."

"How would he know?" Silano asked. "They wouldn't call themselves Instruments of Torture, Inc."

"Where did the meetings take place?" Maxine asked.

"At a hotel. The Royal Lancaster."

"And how did Mr. Pigeon get there?"

Paula nodded, as if to acknowledge a point. "Yes . . . In Neil's car, with Neil's driver. It was part of the subterfuge."

"Where did he leave from?"

"Sorry?"

"Did he go to the meetings from here or from Mr. Morgan's house?"

"From Neil's house, obviously. It was—"

"Part of the subterfuge," Silano offered.

Maxine followed up fast. "And where would Morgan be when this was taking place?"

"I think he arranged the meetings for a time when there was a vote in the House. He'd be surrounded by colleagues. Organized a chat with the prime minister, for all I know."

Silano picked up on the tightness in her voice. "You didn't approve—"

"I did wonder what would happen to Len if things went wrong. He was loyal, that was Len's problem. If he'd backstabbed and ass-licked like the rest, he'd have been better off and higher up the ladder."

Maxine asked, "Did you think they looked alike?"

"Superficially, I suppose. No one ever accused them of being brothers."

"But you could see how one could be mistaken for the other by someone who'd never met either?"

"The Americans, you mean . . . Well, yes, I suppose so."

Silano put away his notebook. Maxine answered a few tricky queries about funerals and inquests, then Paula showed them to the door. She had smiled her thin, buttoned-up smile and was turning the latch when she said, "Oh," and stopped and looked at Maxine wide-eyed. A flush came to her throat. She leaned against the wall, then slipped down to sit on the hall floor. She was breathing hard, like a runner, head bowed.

Without looking up, she said, "You think it should have been Neil. You think he wanted Neil. You think Len was a mistake."

Silano let himself out. Maxine sat on the floor with Paula Pigeon. She said, "It's just a theory."

"He should be alive."

"It's a possibility, that's all; we don't know."

Paula said, "Could you go now? Please go. Please." Maxine got up and went to the door. She thought the burden of sorrow Paula was holding back must weigh on her heart like a stone.

When Aimée woke, the butterfly was still making shadow patterns on the blue chiffon, its wings a ghost-percussion against the glass.

She took a shower and made coffee and ate a sandwich she had bought on her way to the apartment. She felt at home. She wanted him to be there with her and wondered how she was going to be able to go home that evening. He had her phone number at the clinic and her mobile number. He hadn't offered his, and she hadn't asked. She liked it that most evenings she left the clinic, and there he was—his choice, no pressure, no calls, no expectations. Most evenings, but not all.

She liked it that she could recognize him from a distance: his hair falling to the nape of his neck, the duster-coat he liked to wear over a T-shirt and cotton combats tucked into high-lace boots. He wasn't like anyone she'd ever known. Dressed like that, he looked ready for anything; ready for her.

Little by little, she would get to know him. For now, she loved him and that was enough.

44

There were two clubs in Orchard Street, and it was a tough call. One was a dining club where the waitresses wore French maids' uniforms and bent low over the tables to serve the food. The other was a high-class drinking club with a backroom poker table and a two hundred percent markup. Stella chose booze and bets over butts and tits and got checked in at the entrance desk by a blond ball-breaker in an Armani suit. She showed her warrant card, and the girl said, "I'm not sure that will do."

Stella leaned on the desk and smiled a winning smile. She said, "This is a top people's club, so it'll be full of top people. If Clubs and Vice turn up here and find those very same people gambling, or doing a line in the men's room, or coming on to high-class whores, they'll be obliged to make arrests. And I expect word will get round. You're lucky, because I'm not here to make any of that happen, I'm here for reasons your bosses need never know about. Now"—the smile disappeared—"is Abigail in tonight?" The girl tried a shrug. "This would be the Abigail," Stella told her, "who has a special friend called Neil Morgan, MP. And please don't tell me that the private lives of the members are none of your concern, because inside knowledge requires discretion, and discretion buys Armani."

"She's in."

"Her friend?"

"Expected."

Stella climbed a flight of polished mahogany stairs to the bar, which was about the size of a football pitch. It was the kind of place where everything smelled of money except the money, which smelled of nothing at all: an electronic connection, a deduction made in the stratosphere somewhere between dusk and dawn. She asked for a glass of champagne and started a tab that she had no intention of paying, then sat in a leather club chair by the door so that people entering wouldn't see her unless they looked back.

The clientele was smooth-rich or rough-rich or wannabe-rich. The blonde on the far side of the bar was a wannabe: the Donna Karan dress and the ragged highlights just overstated her case, and the Fendi bag wouldn't have been charged to her own card. She was toying with a cigarette that she was struggling not to light. Morgan came in twenty minutes later, when Stella was on her second drink and the blonde had got through three unlit cigarettes. Stella watched them together for a while; watched them *being* together. The body language was interesting: the way she leaned in toward him, touched his hand with her fingertips; the way he smiled and chuckled at whatever she was telling him, then fixed her with a look that was solemn with desire. It was difficult to see where need merged with greed.

When Stella came up to them, having made a wide circle to approach from behind, Morgan was talking about a fact-finding trip he had to make soon. They couldn't go together, of course; couldn't travel together; but they could certainly find each other once they were there.

Stella said, "Mr. Morgan?"

His shoulders tightened as he turned, and she said, "I'm not a journalist." She waited a beat, just a beat or two, before adding, "Though I do know a few."

The blonde said, "Neil—"

"It's all right," Morgan told her. "She's the police."

They sat at a corner table by a window, their reflections at their sides. Morgan looked out to the street. It was dusk, and London was lighting up against the night.

Morgan said, "So you think he meant to kill me?"

Stella had a fresh drink in front of her and could feel the merest hint of blurriness. "I think it's a possibility."

"Why me?"

"Why Leonard Pigeon?"

"The cowardice thing, wasn't it? I mean, this guy's crazy, isn't that it? He killed a prostitute, hung her in a tree, and wrote on her, filthy bitch, then the same with Len, but with him it was the incident on the bridge, the woman they threw in . . ."

Stella's hand was stalled over her drink. The blonde appeared in the middle of the room and stood there a moment, as if waiting for a decision, her reflection merging with theirs. Morgan looked at her, then away. She waited another second or two, then made for the door, walking briskly.

Stella said, "Dirty girl." Morgan laughed, but made no comment. Stella shook her head. "Not her. Not Abigail. The prostitute. He wrote dirty girl, not filthy bitch."

"Oh."

"Filthy bitch is your thinking."

"I knew it was something like that."

"Filthy bitch is what you might have said."

Morgan's face darkened. "What do you want?"

"A few things," Stella told him. "To begin with, I'd like to know who told you about the girl in the tree and the writing. For instance, was it the same person who told you about the writing on Leonard Pigeon and the possible connection with the incident on the bridge? I ask because none of this has been released to the press—the writing, the bridge—so no one has connected the two deaths."

Morgan said, "I'm a member of Parliament."

"Yes, I know that. Who told you?"

"I think that's covered by privilege."

"No, it's not, and you're coming dangerously close to obstructing—"

"It was common knowledge. People saw the girl in the tree; people saw Len on the bench by the river."

Stella sighed with annoyance. "No. Very few people saw the girl, and when we brought her down, it was dark. People walked past Leonard Pigeon without noticing he was dead—or else they didn't want to notice. The couple who found him thought the writing was a tattoo . . . and, in any case, weren't all that eager to go public on the fact that they were together at the time. If it was common knowledge, it would have been in the papers. Try again."

He tried. "Paula Pigeon told me."

Stella smiled. "She knew about the writing on her husband, sure; she knew nothing about the girl in the tree." Morgan turned to the window, and his own reflection confronted him with a stern look. "You were expecting me," Stella said. "You knew that I was a police officer."

"Not here. I wasn't expecting you to come—"

"Someone got in touch. Someone who thought you ought to know."

"Yes, you're right," Morgan said, suddenly combative, "one of yours, yes, to give me a bit of background. So you'd better sort it out yourself, hadn't you?"

Stella wanted to hit him; it was a strong impulse. She said, "Let's assume it was you he wanted—that the killer got the wrong man, that it was your throat he wanted to slit."

"All right, assume it. Now tell me why."

"No, you tell me. Filthy coward, that was what he wrote. Now, why would that have fitted you better than it fitted Leonard Pigeon?"

"Some lads on a bridge, a woman being attacked . . . Would I have made a better showing than Len? Run toward them instead of away? Taken them on? Well, I don't know. I've never been in a situation like that, so I've never had to make the choice."

"No reason why anyone should think of you as a coward?"

"Honestly? No." He was turning a drinks coaster in his fingers: *flip-flip*. He said, "If you were coming here to talk to me about this, you must have intended to tell me yourself—about the writing on Len's arms and so on."

"But not about the girl in the tree, not about the connection between the killings, so listen: if I hear it's being talked about or it appears in the press, I'll be looking for you with a warrant."

Morgan allowed her to see his smile. "Yes, sure . . ."

Stella laughed. "Try me . . ." The smile disappeared. After a moment she said, "You don't think much of my theory, do you?"

"Not much."

"So no protection, then."

The question startled him. "Sorry?"

"If we'd agreed that it was a possibility you were the target, that someone somewhere might think of you as a filthy coward who deserves to die, then I would have suggested surveillance-and-protection cover for you and your family. After all, two murders, both in public places, people around, but no one seems to see or hear anything—this guy is good at what he does." She finished her drink. "Still, if you're not worried, I'm not worried."

They sat in silence for a full minute, Morgan with his head lowered. Finally, he looked up and said, "I can't think of anything. I can't think of a single thing. Some act of cowardice . . ." He shook his head, as if trying to remember and failing. "But this man, whoever killed them, he's not sane, is he? He could pick on anything, anything I might have done, anything he decided he didn't approve of."

"Anything he thought cowardly."

"Yes, that's what I'm saying. It won't necessarily be rational."

"You mean it won't necessarily have been cowardly."

"Exactly."

"You're opting for protection."

"It seems the sensible thing to do."

"For you and your family."

"Yes."

"What about Abigail?"

Morgan looked startled. "How do you know her name?"

"I'm not at liberty to say." Stella almost smiled: those snippets of official bullshit that keep civilians at bay. "So . . . Abigail . . ."

"Even in the best marriages," Morgan said, and offered what he hoped might be a conspiratorial grin.

Stella nodded as if to say: *Why tell me?* She said, "I'll need to speak to her."

"There's nothing she can tell you."

"I bet you're right. I still need to speak to her."

Morgan took out a business card, wrote a name and number on the back, and handed it to Stella. In the same moment that she took it, she saw the sudden panic in his eyes: *My business card; her name on the back; how stupid is that?*

She said, "Don't worry, I'm a cop, not a counselor."

Morgan was still flipping the coaster. As Stella got up to leave, he said, "By the way . . . Len wasn't impersonating me; he wasn't even standing in for me. He had some sort of business with an American company, I know that. Nothing to do with me."

"That's not the way I heard it."

"Then you heard wrong. Why would I lie?"

"I don't know," Stella told him. "No idea." She paused. "Unless your involvement with the American company in question involved passing on privileged information of some sort, and you wanted to be able to say that you knew of no such company, had never met its representatives, there was no paper trail from you to them, and you had evidence to prove you were somewhere else entirely on the dates in question." She shrugged. "Just a guess."

The coaster speeded up. Morgan said, "You're on dangerous ground, DS Mooney. Len's business was his own affair."

"His wife claims he attended those meetings with the express purpose of pretending to be you."

"I wonder why Len would tell her that. I imagine he had something to hide. Still, he's dead now and beyond recrimination."

"She's pretty clear on the matter."

"If that's what he told her, I suppose she would be."

The place had filled up: older men and younger women; older men and younger men; business deals going down in quiet corners; lone gamblers at the bar waiting for a place at the backroom table. Eyes followed Stella as she walked out, as if she had "Police" in large white letters across the back of her much-older-than-last-year's jacket from T. J. Maxx.

45

Even in the best marriages . . .

Stella drove down to the Embankment, parked, and took a walk. She thought about her conversation with Tom Davison and the way she had felt when he'd stood close to her; she thought back to the evening at Machado's, strings of lights round the square, swifts circling, Delaney asking, "Are you happy with us?"

He was restless, she knew that, but she didn't know why.

The Imola-red Beamer went by. Someone had fitted blue sill-lights that shed a glow on the tarmac—car-bling. The sound system slammed off the Embankment wall and the boys were hanging out of the windows, laughing, yelling, cruising for girls.

They saw Stella and ran through their repertoire.

Hey, bitch . . .

Aimée lay in the arms of her lover, tucked into him, holding on. His chest, slowly rising and falling, was hard; his stomach carried little ridges of muscle; she could feel his bicep, bunched against her shoulder. She had made him a meal, they had drunk some wine, they had made love in a way that was new to her for its intensity and pleasure, new to her for its touch of pain, and it was what she wanted, what she now craved, even as she lay beside him, still damp between her thighs, still hot from his touch.

Gideon, Gideon . . .

Love had taken her by surprise, but she had adapted quickly to its demands. She had a mother in Oxford who was mostly deaf, somewhat infirm, and a good alibi. If her daughterly trips became more frequent, if she had to spend the night down there, or the weekend, who could possibly complain?

Over dinner they had talked about themselves, lies going back and forth, each of them open to believe.

Aimée had lived in this flat for a year or so. She had been engaged, once, a long time ago; since then there hadn't been anyone, really. No one special, anyway. She worked as a dental nurse, he knew that. There wasn't much else to tell.

Woolf had worked as an engineer. He chose "engineer," because it was vague and sounded complicated. He'd been made redundant and got a really handy payoff. He was looking for a job but wasn't in any hurry. There wasn't much else to tell.

She had suggested a weekend away together. He'd told her it sounded fine.

She thought he was sleeping, and maybe he was, but when her hand trailed down over his belly, he turned to her at once, scooping her up, and she cried out, shivering, knowing she could never get enough of him. Afterward, it was Aimée who slept while Woolf lay awake.

He thought, *If we go away somewhere, not a city, somewhere wild, no people, woods and sea and open land, I could kill her there.*

Mike Sorley was sitting up against his pillows and seemed to be looking at a football match on the TV angled out over the bed, but in fact he was looking at the wall opposite. The wall was blank, the usual hospital magnolia, but he could see something there, something from a dream. The dream had come when he was dead.

He knew he'd died, and he knew when, because Karen had told him how they had used CPR and defibrillation, working hard to haul him back. The dream wasn't tunnels of white light or sweet meadows in the peaceable kingdom; it was a series of dark alleys and dimly lit dead ends, himself running through, going this way and that, every turn a wrong one, every wall a blank, unable to find a way in, unable to find a way out.

In the end, he stopped and sat down on the ground. He knew the alleys and pathways went on forever, and his heart shrank at the thought. He felt bereft in a way that was so great it was almost beyond pain: everything he had ever loved lost to him, everything he'd ever cared for come to a black negative. He sat on the ground and cried. Then they had brought him back, but he couldn't remember how: just that there had been glare and voices and pain and anxiety and relief.

Karen came in and sat beside him and continued to sit for a minute or two. Someone scored in the match, and the crowd went wild, but Sorley didn't seem to notice. Finally, she pushed the TV aside and said, "Are you there?"

Sorley turned, startled, then laughed. She had brought him some fruit and a book and a TV guide but not the Tree Girl/Leonard Pigeon case reports he'd asked for. She kissed him, and he held on to her, so she got up on the bed and he lay with his head on her shoulder, her arm round him as if to guard and protect.

He said, "You know what being dead is? It's being afraid and alone. I used to think it was nothing, you know, like being switched off. It's not. It's being on your own forever."

Karen gave a little shudder. She said, "You're not dead."

"No." Then he said, "You know what's totally fucking outrageous about this place? They won't let you smoke."

Stella watched the nighttime river craft and the black waves lapping the stone wall.

Dirty girl. Filthy coward.

Who are you to say, you arrogant bastard? You murdering bastard. She had a picture of him in her mind's eye: young, white, strong; the body was easy to imagine, but the face stayed blank. She thought of Bryony Dean, her eyes plucked out. She thought of Leonard Pigeon, his head sunk on his chest, his features fallen and out of true. Killer and victims, none of them looking themselves.

She felt a chill at her back, something more than the wind off the river, and turned fast to see him coming toward her, one of the city's haggard desperadoes, clothes stained and torn, face dark with grime, one hand held low and in that hand something that caught a glint from the riverside lights.

Hit him with anything that will stop him, anything that cuts.

She reached for her keys, sidestepping at the same time, and held them in her clenched fist, the serrated car key protruding through her knuckles, but he turned, eyes wide and vacant, and set off down the street at a fast shuffle. She realized that he hadn't even been looking at her; might not have known she was there, able to see only the vision inside his own head.

The glint had been from the soda can that doubled as a crack pipe. But another time, it wouldn't be that. Another time it would be a knife.

London at night. Expect the worst.

46

Pete Harriman was a man who liked women. He liked them so much, he tried not to be exclusive: why deny himself or them? At present he had three relationships in progress, and schedules were a part of his life, but one woman took precedence. Her name was Gloria, and she was dangerously close to stealing the show. She walked naked into her bathroom where Harriman was shaving and held his mobile phone up to his ear, but a fraction away from the foam on his cheek.

He said, "Hello?" then, "No kidding," then, "On my way."

He watched Gloria as she walked out of the bathroom. She had the clear skin and firm lines of youth. The way her back curved out to her ass, the way her ass curved in to her thigh, was enough to leave any man breathless, and he wished she hadn't picked up the phone, because under other circumstances he wouldn't have been on the road for another thirty minutes.

Stella was in the local Coffee Republic with an espresso and a Danish that carried a sky-high calorie count. She had chosen the smoking area as a concession to Harriman, who came in looking a touch surly and sat down without placing an order. Stella told him about her moment with Neil Morgan: that someone had put Morgan ahead of the game, that she was pretty sure the person in question—the *asshole* in question—was Brian Collier.

She said, "I want you to know, because, just for the present, I'm saying nothing."

"And you want a witness to that fact. Also a witness to confirm, if necessary, that you *did* suspect that Acting DI Collier might have overstepped the mark."

"That's right."

"Because you ought to be sending a report to the SIO."

"I'm unsure of my ground."

"Not enough to go on."

"Just a feeling."

"And it would be wrong to make an accusation against a brother offi-cer on the basis of a feeling."

"Highly irresponsible. Also bad tactics."

"Because you'd sooner wait until you *have* got some evidence and then nail the bastard."

"Long pointy nails."

"Which evidence might well be forthcoming, if you bide your time."

"My fervent hope."

"Why would he do that?" Harriman wondered. "Tell Morgan to ex-pect you, let him know that we had information about the blonde?"

"He's career-building. Names in high places, favors to be done in the hope of eventual payback, putting himself on a name-check list . . ."

The raw contempt in her voice was plain to hear, a rankle from the past. Harriman asked, "When he hit on you—what did he say?"

"He told me he was hung."

Harriman was caught in the act of bringing a match to his cigarette. "He what?"

"Told me he had a big dick."

Harriman smiled a slow, broad smile. "A prince among men," he said.

The prince had left a message for Stella with Maxine Hewitt. Maxine de-livered it along with the morning's paperwork: *My office now.*

Stella looked through the reports and e-mails, sorting the wheat from the chaff. There was a letter marked "Personal." She dropped it in the bin, then took a moment to read the opening paragraph of an article on serial killings that Anne Beaumont had sent as an attachment. There was a high-lighted passage:

One notable characteristic of serial killers is their tendency to recklessness. They proceed with a plan and part of the plan is, of necessity, repetition. There might be a rationale to their actions—some sort of spurious reason for these killers to act as they do—but studies suggest this is less important to the killer (though no less important to the investigator) than the simple need to kill. This irresistible impulse is more important to the perpetrator than the need for preparation or caution and is more likely to lead to an arrest than the discovery of any motive, not least because motive is often irrational or obscure.

Anne's accompanying e-mail message said:

> In other words, serial killers get a taste for it; already <u>have</u> a taste for it. This
> is right, though it underplays the business of motive, especially in this case,
> since the writings on the bodies indicate some specific (and therefore
> traceable) reason for their deaths. But, yes, he might slip up. Is there
> something you can do to get ahead of him?

Stella was aware of being watched and knew it must be Collier. Resisting
the impulse to look toward the door, she put Anne's e-mail down on her
desk, turned her back, and made for the corridor and then the exhibitions
room. She had nothing to do in there, but she took her time doing it. When
she came out, it was just Maxine and Sue Chapman, eyes down over key-
boards.

As Stella walked through, Sue said, "He doesn't look pleased."

Collier was smoking, but he was a dilettante compared to Sorley: he
smoked his cigarettes one at a time. He was working on some papers and
didn't look up when Stella came in, a technique so worn round the edges
that she almost laughed out loud. *Acting* DI.

He said, "I told you to tread carefully: my exact words, I think."

"Sorry?"

"You know what I'm talking about."

"Neil Morgan?" Collier didn't reply. "I called on him to offer the
theory that he might have been the killer's real target. We'd agreed that I
should."

"You harassed him."

Stella's laugh almost took her by surprise. "I offered him protection."

"Don't bullshit me, Stella. You could have gone to his home, instead
you nobbled him at a club in Orchard Street. You embarrassed him."

"There was a blonde with him—she wasn't his wife. He embarrassed
himself. Here's another thing: it's very likely that he's using his position as
an MP to some advantage in business."

"We're a murder squad. And he's not a suspect. In fact, he's a potential
victim. So in future—"

"How did he know about the connection with Bryony Dean?" Her
wait-and-nail-him tactics shot in one flush of anger.

Collier started to speak, stopped, started again. "Did he?"

"About the link between her and Pigeon, about the writing on both of them." Collier shrugged, as if that would do the job. "He wasn't supposed to talk about that, was he? Okay to mark his card; okay to give him the drop on me; okay to fill him in on confidential details . . . he'd know what was coming, and he'd know the background; but he forgot to keep his mouth shut." She let a silence develop, then: "Something you forgot—politicians and journalists, they think they stand outside the normal conventions, think they have some kind of license; and the word 'loyalty' doesn't exist in their vocabulary."

"He's a man with contacts," Collier observed. "Anyone could have—"

"Who?" Stella asked. "Who would be looking for an advantage? Who'd want to impress the great and good? Who'd want to jeopardize this investigation just to have the opportunity to kiss ass? The SIO? Sam Burgess? One of my squad? Me?" She waited. "You?"

Collier colored up. His hand moved reflexively, raking the desk—a blow redirected—and papers spilled onto the floor. He said, "Get the fuck out of my office."

Stella walked to the door. She said, "Now I know it was you."

Harriman saw her walk into the squad room and through to the restroom. He followed her and went in. She was bending over to wash her face at a sink and spoke through the water.

"It's probably sexual harassment."

"What is?"

"Your being in here."

"How did you know it was me?"

"Heavy breathing." Harriman laughed. "You want to know what happened."

"Well, you did look pissed off, so . . . yes."

Stella pulled a handful of paper towels and dried her face. "With myself. He knows I know."

"How?"

"He prodded me; I prodded back."

"Harder."

"Yes."

"So now what?"

"He'll be covering his ass, and I'll have to watch my back."

"All sounds a bit"—he searched—"anatomical."

Stella laughed: a genuine, hearty, out-front laugh. "You do cheer me up, Pete."

"What are you going to do?"

"About Collier? Nothing, for the time being. Try to find out what else Morgan might be involved in. If he was the intended victim, there'll be more to find in his life than in Bryony Dean's."

"They're still an odd pairing."

"As are Bryony and Leonard Pigeon."

"Do you want me to take a closer look at Morgan?"

"Maybe . . ." Stella nodded. "Leave it awhile . . . I've got a bit of inside track with our MP."

A little silence fell between them, and Harriman raised his eyebrows: *What?*

"Well, if you wouldn't mind leaving," Stella said, "I'd quite like to take a piss."

47

Woolf was bench-pressing two hundred, staring up at patterns of reflected sunlight on the ceiling. At two in the afternoon the gym was almost empty. The brokers, the bankers, the traders, the headhunters, the sidesteppers, and the second-guessers were back at their desks; the leotard-and-Botox sisterhood had left for lunch in their shiny SUVs. Woolf got through his reps, plus five, turned to bicep curls for a while, then made three circuits of the weight machines before getting onto the treadmill. He liked running. When he ran, he blanked.

He set a gradient and worked steadily for half an hour, barely thinking a single thought, then stepped off and went back to the weights section and loaded the bar. The patterns on the ceiling had changed. Somewhere, outside, a tree was filtering the sunlight before it struck up off the chrome weight bars, and when he stretched out on the bench and looked up, there were forms shifting and shimmering, human forms, seeming to walk forward as the light fluctuated.

He remembered the day; he remembered the heat haze on the dusty road and the sudden silence like a vacuum that had to be filled.

He lay on the bench, his breathing short and quick, his mouth twisted in something like pain, something like grief, and tears ran from the corners of his eyes across his cheeks and into his hair. He cuffed the tears away. He bench-pressed two-twenty, his teeth grinding, the veins cording on his neck and arms.

He took a cool shower and walked out into the afternoon sunlight. He was ready. He was pumped up and ready to pop.

Stella had stopped off before going home; it was a while since she'd done that, but Collier was a problem that needed some thought, and Delaney worked alone, so was often eager to talk when she got back.

The pub was close to the squad room and she was known there: well enough known for the barman to reach for a shot glass as she approached the bar. A single ice cube in a shot glass, vodka poured over and taken to the brim. She carried it to a booth at the back of the bar.

Collier: keep tabs, keep quiet. On the other hand, does it matter? Well, if Morgan shot his mouth off and the business of the writing became common knowledge, they'd have round-the-clock loonies walking in the door to confess: then it would matter. She'd look pretty silly making a retrospective report that fingered Collier; but if she went to the SIO with it now, she'd need something more than a long-standing resentment and doubts about the size of Collier's dick.

Leave it. Let it lie.

Her mind went to Delaney, the Rich List, her man on the inside. She laughed at the notion. She wondered what question he was going to put that night before she had left to look at Bryony's body strung up and naked.

She wondered why he hadn't asked it since.

When she got back, he was asleep in a chair by an open window, his hair ruffled by the breeze. She kissed him awake and took him to bed.

For Stella, sex displaced doubt; with most people it was doubt's double agent. She felt a rush of desire and took him in hand, drawing him on so he covered her, then looked past him to where sunlight smudged shapes and patterns on the wall. She felt good when he touched her: good in a way like no other.

The breeze rippled the curtains. The shapes on the wall shifted, like watchers jostling for position.

48

Turner walked away from his desk, leaving the computer on screen-save. Like all computers in all London offices, it was doing its bit to accelerate climate change.

It was late, nearly eight thirty, and he'd had enough. He walked through a deserted outer office, using his mobile to make a call to a well-paid mole in the Cabinet Office, who told him that things were quiet—nothing duplicitous, scandalous, or globally significant was likely to happen within the next twenty-four hours. He lost the signal when he got into the lift, but the call was effectively over anyway.

Turner leaned against the lift wall. He was forty, overweight, and truculent; he was also tired of bad news, and that was all the news there was these days. At one time bad news was all he'd thrived on; now he thought the world was going to hell in a handcart and he worried for his children, two boys, one six, one four, growing up amid bad things happening with warnings of worse to come. He wondered whether he would have grand-children: whether there would be time. Put like that, he hoped not.

His worry, though, somehow didn't extend to switching off his com-puter or driving something more eco-friendly than a Mercedes SL. The lift let him out into the underground car park, false neon daylight on rough concrete. An alarm was sounding somewhere on the other side of the space, and, for some reason, it made Turner more edgy than annoyed. Then it oc-curred to him to wonder who had set it off.

He imagined someone coming at him through the lines of cars, one hand slapping the bodywork, eyes locked on and wide with fury, one of London's army of crazy people, the ones who lived on the edge of things, lived in the fissures and cracks, the city's fault lines. The mind-picture lasted only a moment, but was so vivid that he caught his breath and quick-ened his pace, taking his key from his pocket and blipping his car doors from thirty feet away.

He got into the car and grinned at his own foolishness, then pulled out and drove to the mesh portcullis that closed off the exit. His radio fizzed and buzzed, unable to get a signal underground. He lowered his window and slipped a user's card into the exit pillar.

As he pulled out onto the road, the radio came clear, a news broadcast, the trivial caught up with the catastrophic. Turner thought he badly needed a drink.

Woolf walked past the house, taking a quick glance sideways to make sure that everything was as it should be. The front garden wasn't the sort of place where children might play or people gather; the birch trees were there to screen the house from the road, and the space between the trees and the house was given over to the driveway and parking spaces for three cars. On the left-hand side of the driveway, just by the gate, was a concrete trash bunker over which someone had grown creeper. A wheelie-bin for green waste stood just to one side.

He knew what to expect. Turner was usually home between eight and nine. Woolf had made three or four dry runs and things had gone according to plan. Then he'd picked a night, arrived prepared, walked the street just as he was doing now, and Turner had never shown up. Woolf had scouted early the next morning, and Turner's car wasn't in the driveway, so an overnight trip, perhaps. That was all right. There was no time scale on things. The next time Woolf had intended to set things up was when Aimée had taken him to the flat in North Kensington. That had been more frustrating;

he didn't want to keep running the moment in his head like a dream from which he would have to wake.

It was dusk. The sky was clear and the moon, almost full, was showing just above rooftops. The suburb where Turner lived was close to the river, and Woolf could hear the chug of a pleasure vessel making the last leg of the last round-trip of the day. There was music playing and a crosshatch of voices and little plumes of smoke from backyard barbecues. He reached the end of the street and turned round. When he got to Turner's house, he vaulted the iron gate and slipped into the tree cover. The gate was high, but he'd cleared it with little more than a three-step run-up.

The grass between the trees and the hedge had been recently mown and gave off a warm, sweet smell. He sat down cross-legged. The SIG Sauer was pushed into the waistband of his jeans by the small of his back and hidden by his jacket; when he brought his legs round, he could feel the gun, hard against his lower spine.

He heard the door of the house open, and light from the hall spilled out over the drive. He moved sideways, taking cover behind one of the birch-tree boles. A woman came into view by the gate; she was carrying a full bin liner and stood in profile to him while she opened the bunker lid and dropped the garbage in. She was wearing linen trousers with a designer T-shirt, and Woolf liked the look of her full figure, liked the way her hair fell to her shoulders in a thick sweep, liked her bare arms and the way the linen molded to her when she bent over to catch the lid and close it. She turned to go back to the house but paused, just a moment, to look up—at the moon, he guessed; and he liked that about her too.

He knew that some sadness would soon come into her life, but he thought she would get through that and, eventually, find happiness again. He could hear his thoughts as a voice-over as Silent Wolf walked back through the empty streets under a rising moon, his work done.

It was ten to nine. Woolf got up and walked out of cover, thinking of himself as a shadow against shadows. He lifted the green waste bin and laid it sideways across the drive and just inside the gate.

49

When the Merc whispered up to the gate, Turner already had the remote in his hand. The iron bars rolled back, and the car inched forward, then stopped. Woolf heard the ratchet of the handbrake going on before the driver's door opened and Turner stepped out.

He said, "Oh, for Christ's sake."

As he reached the bin and stooped, Woolf caught him by the throat, one-handed, his fingers closing hard. Turner made a noise like water in a drain as he was dragged sideways into the tree cover. Woolf kicked the man's legs out from under him, and he fell on his face; the flat of the gun barrel took him on the side of the head, and he bucked, then lay still. Woolf stripped Turner of his jacket and shirt, made a bundle of them, pushed the SIG Sauer into the cloth, and placed it against the back of the man's head. The shot sounded like a door being slammed. It had taken a minute; a minute or two.

The clothing had caught the blood spurt, just a splash or two landing on Woolf's gunhand and forearm. He stepped over Turner's body, walked quickly to the Merc, found the remote, closed the gate, and drove the car to the end of the street. Voices, still; music, still; but no one walking the dog or arriving for dinner. He walked back feeling light and powerful, no need to run, no need to worry.

He hopped the gate as before and walked into the tree-lined space. A dark stain on the clipped grass was seeping and growing, though it was a couple of feet clear of the body, a thin track seeming to connect it to Turner's head. The man had moved. It brought Woolf up short. He tried to imagine the moment: Turner shot through the head, bone and brain matter and blood a pulpy mulch on the grass, his life drawing off like vapor into the dark air, and somehow he finds the strength, somehow he finds the last jot of instinct that allows him to dig at the grass with his nails, pull himself an inch or two, then an inch or two more. He wished he could see that moment preserved on a *Silent Wolf* game: the last moment, the agonizing hope against hope.

He took some twine and a marker from his pocket. The moon was higher now, its light silvering the boles of the trees as he worked.

50

In the days before Stella, Delaney's fridge had been for wine, milk, bacon, and eggs. Even now, it was never stocked for two. Sometimes, Stella went back—she never now thought *back home*—to the flat in West Kensington that she had shared with George Paterson. There was even less in that fridge. The place was to be sold and the money divided, but she was slow moving on the matter and realized it might be a bridge she was reluctant to burn.

There was always pasta, of course. Delaney emptied a carton of carbonara sauce into a saucepan, while Stella opened the wine. They had fallen asleep after lovemaking and Delaney had woken first; Stella had come to find him, walking naked into the living space, and now she stood at the counter, still naked, drawing the cork from a bottle of chilled Sancerre, her breasts drooping slightly as she bent to her task.

She poured two glasses, then disappeared briefly and came back wearing a pink and gold silk robe that Delaney had bought her. It wasn't her sort of thing at all and she suspected he knew as much and had bought it as a challenge; she wore it because it made her look like someone else.

He was putting pasta into a pan of boiling water, and she let him finish and get clear before asking, "Why do you want to know if I'm happy with us?" as if he'd asked the question just a moment ago.

"Did I?"

"At dinner, last week."

"Oh. Okay."

"So why?"

"I'm trying to remember."

"I asked you if you were about to fetch a ring out of your pocket."

"That's right." He smiled. "Did you think I was about to propose?"

"Not really."

"What would you have said?"

She could hear him edging her away from the question. "I'd've said yes, church wedding, white-silk meringue, reception for two hundred, honeymoon in the Maldives." She knew him better than to push. Instead she asked, "Neil Morgan's on your Rich List, isn't he?"

"Yes. Why?"

She told him why, because, if she wanted his help, there was no avoiding it.

"You think he has things to hide—beyond the blonde and the usual undeclared this and that."

"I think it's possible."

"Things that would make him a target for this killer?"

"Who knows? At present, I haven't got a thing to connect the girl and Pigeon or the girl and Morgan. All I've got is the fact that Morgan seems to have been using Pigeon to cover his tracks."

"The company?" Delaney asked. "The Americans?"

"Pigeon knew who they were. He's dead. Morgan's denying he ever had any involvement."

"I did some superficial research on him," Delaney said. "It's a superficial article." He heaped the pasta onto two plates and poured on the sauce. "I could go a little deeper: would that help?"

"It might. This is all classified information, Delaney."

He smiled sweetly at her. "I know that."

The moon was thick and yellow and sat four square in the center of the windowpane as they ate.

Delaney said, "Suppose it should have been Morgan. A teenage hooker and a millionaire MP with ambition. I can only think of one connection."

"He has slightly classier taste," Stella said. Then: "Well, maybe not."

"But sex aside—"

"Dirty Girl. Filthy Coward. There's a logic somewhere."

"Mad logic. He's mad—whoever did it."

"There are those"—Stella was thinking of Anne Beaumont—"who would tell you that mad is a term so broad as to be meaningless."

"Yeah? What term would you use?"

"No. Mad is okay with me. He's mad, all right. Totally fucking mental."

51

He ran the sequence in his head. Silent Wolf walking the city streets, the job done, the world a better place. Too smart to hail a cab or take a train, because who could fail to notice a man like that: his narrow face, the mane of coarse hair, the yellow pupils. He wore the cutoff glove on his left hand to show that he was armed and ready. It was a long way back to the Strip, but he wanted the trip, a chance to walk off the surplus energy, a chance to make more plans.

Good—yes, he felt good, he felt fine. He crossed a bridge to the north side of the river and walked east along the towpath.

Moonlight danced on the water.

Valerie Turner listened to the voice-mail message on his mobile once more, then topped up her gin. It was a sticky night and she'd taken a shower, putting back on the linen trousers she'd worn earlier and a fresh T-shirt. The kitchen floor was cool to her bare feet.

He was late, though he'd been later. She could hear the kids in the living room fighting over which computer game to play. They had eaten, but she hadn't, so she put some olives in a dish and broke open a pack of breadsticks. There was a TV in the kitchen, and she was half watching a rerun of a comedy classic.

After ten minutes or so, she would notice that the kids were unusually quiet. She would glance at her watch and think, *Really late*. She would try his mobile again and hear his voice saying, "Can't take your call . . . leave a message . . ." as she walked through to the living room and saw her sons kneeling up on the sofa by the window that looked out to the front garden.

She would cross the room to see what they were looking at, catching sight, suddenly, of their open mouths, their frozen expressions, and look out of the window herself, at the drive in moonlight, the figure splayed against the railings of the gate, body slumped, arms spread wide.

She would leave the house at a run, calling, already knowing it was him the way a wife knows her husband, her bare feet cutting up on the driveway concrete, and fall on her knees in front of him, calling his name, shaking him, crying, fizzing with shock, not knowing what or how or why, holding his head up to try to make him see her, see who she was, the thickness of congealed blood clinging to her fingers like glue, calling for help, *screaming* for help, barely noticing the fact that he was half naked or that there was something scrawled across his belly, as she held him and rocked him and called his name and howled and howled and howled.

LYING BASTARD

52

In another life Ricardo Jones would have been a Tony Ryan or an Alan Sugar; a Donald Trump or a Howard Schultz. Ricardo had an instinct for second-guessing market movements and for predicting a trend, but he knew that those skills—those talents—were nothing without a network of contacts. He had only been able to guarantee the kinds of discounts he'd offered to Jonah the bling king because he knew he could off-load fast at a fixed price.

To Ricardo, everything was merchandise, and that included money. Money that had to be laundered wasn't money that could be spent, so it was a commodity, its market value nothing to do with its face value. In fact, nothing, Ricardo had discovered, was worth its face value: not when it came into his hands, anyway. Precious stones, cars, booze, cigarettes, guns, electrical goods—everything was priced minus its risk value and the dealer's cut. Only two kinds of merchandise Ricardo didn't touch: drugs and girls. It wasn't so much a moral issue, just that these were specialist items, and the risk factor was proportionately high.

Another aspect of Ricardo's success was that he worked alone. It meant he worked long and hard, but it also meant there was no one to foul up, no one to get greedy, and no one who could lift his methods or his contacts. The downside to this was that Ricardo had no backup. On a few, rare occasions he'd hired some muscle, but those guys were just attack dogs. Because he didn't want a partner or permanent protection, Ricardo's method was to stay in the shadows as much as possible. He wasn't showy, he wasn't flash, he didn't hang out with the guys, he drove a midrange Peugeot, dressed in off-the-peg casuals, and because he never took any extras off the top, his clients had no cause for complaint.

He thought now that it had been a mistake to run a book at the cage fight; it was too visible, too exposed; but it was a fast way to make money and shifting operations from Manchester had involved cash-flow problems. Ricardo had done so well in the north that he'd attracted attention, and people had begun to crowd him out. He'd had offers to join bigger outfits, bigger setups, and his refusals hadn't met with universal approval. All in all, it was time to move on. London was the obvious option. Business was good in cities all over the country, but London was wide open. London was one big market.

When Tina had told him that her daughter was a police officer, Ricardo had said, "Get in touch. Ask her round for a drink. I could use a laugh."

The sky was deep blue, the moon high, dabs of cumulus backlit by a hard, blue light.

Ricardo slipped along the walkways to Jonah's apartment. He had just received a text that told him an offshore money transfer had been made, and Jonah would be happy about that: happy enough, perhaps, to put some more business Ricardo's way. A rough calculation told Ricardo that he could get rich on something like three percent of the Harefield throughput, and Jonah was a fair percentage of the percentage.

Music from all directions, shock-wave bass and the seamless, angry monotone of rap. People on the walkways were whores and punters, gam-blers and boozers, druggies and dealers. Ricardo slipped through it all, head down, a man minding his own business. The doors of the righteous were barred against the night.

When he got to Jonah's apartment, he stood outside and made a phone call. No one ever knocked. Knocks were anonymous. Jonah didn't take the call, Ricardo hadn't expected he would, but a voice said, "Yeah, okay, wait." After a moment a man appeared at the door. He stepped outside and looked around. He said, "Just you?"

"Ricardo Jones. He's expecting me."

"Yeah, sure."

The man stood aside and Ricardo went past him, hearing the lock fall.

He walked into the room they'd been in before, the room where the deal was struck. Jonah was sitting in an armchair and smiling at him. Ricardo smiled back: for just the merest moment, he smiled back. Then he noticed that Jonah's posture was odd—strangely formal in the way his back was so stiffly upright, and the precise manner in which his hands extended along the arms of the chair. And he wasn't smiling.

Jonah's head was up because his dreadlocks had been tied to the chair-back. His hands had been nailed to the arms of the chair, and his posture was odd because he was in considerable pain. The smile was a rictus of pain. Pain was all Jonah could think about.

Ricardo noticed that there was something about those nailed hands, something odd and unaccountable; then he saw that neither had a thumb. He registered all this in about as much time as it took for him to give a little heave and let go a gob of vomit onto his shirtfront. When he turned, the man who had let him in was leaning on the door frame.

He said, "Hello, Ricardo." And his smile was genuine.

Delaney shuffled through some interview notes. He said, "Rich people: what are they good for?"

"How many more do you have to see?" Stella was watching TV: the news. So far as she could tell, the weather had turned on the human race: in one country a famine, in another a hurricane, in a third mud slides had buried a village. These, it seemed, were acts of God.

"Five."

"Do you hate them all?"

"All, yes."

On TV, refugees crowded a mud-slick road, carrying what they could, rendered silent by misery. "When they say act of God," Stella asked, "do they mean our God or someone else's?"

Delaney laughed. He watched her for a moment as she sat cross-legged on the sofa, her face in profile to him, her expression serious and occupied. He knew he loved her, and that she loved him, but wasn't sure what the love would bear.

He said, "The question I asked—if you were happy with us—has another question attached."

"Which depends on the answer I give?"

"Exactly."

"Okay." She switched the TV off. "Yes, I'm happy with us."

"Me too." He grinned at her. "So I thought maybe we should move in together."

A little silence, then she said, "We have, haven't we?"

"Sort of. You still have the flat in Vigo Street."

"Which I'm selling."

"Sure."

"I'm here all the time."

"Sure. I don't mean live here."

"Buy somewhere together?"

"That's right. Somewhere a bit bigger perhaps."

She nodded, speechless. When her phone rang, she crossed the room to get it, looking at him all the time, still nodding. He'd only given her half the reason for the question, of course.

If you're happy with us, we could buy a place together.

And if you're happy with us, maybe you'll let me go away for a while, and ditch armchair journalism like the fucking Rich List, and do the kind of thing I'm really good at, and run the risk of getting killed in some war zone halfway round the globe.

So the look of guilt on his face was plain to see when she flip-closed her mobile phone and said, "Do you know a man called Martin Turner?"

53

They had police-taped both ends of the road, but Andy Greegan had called in help from the locals to keep the neighbors at bay. Now he was establishing an uncontaminated area, which took in the ground between the trees and the hedge as well as the gate, the driveway, and the pavement. The tent was a jerry-rigged affair, because Turner was still tied to the rails of the gate, and the screen had to be on each side. One of the uniformed men had gone from house to house asking for a Stanley knife, and Harriman had slit the thick plastic so it slotted over the rails.

Halogens fizzed. The video man and the stills photographer took turns.

The police doctor gave an accurate account of how and when. A forensic team were covering the ground inch by inch. Turner's coat and shirt were already in an evidence bag. A tightly controlled crime scene was a method for bringing order out of chaos.

Stella and Harriman stood just outside the circle of light. She said, "I want the whole team down here. Better to be at the scene than look at snaps on a white-board."

"They're on their way," Harriman said. "Except DI Collier."

"No, I said the team. Fuck Collier."

Harriman looked up and down the street. "No cameras," he observed. "Same with the other two scenes—a street by a park, the towpath; no CCTV." A thought occurred to him. "You don't think that's a factor?"

"In his choice of killing ground, perhaps. Not in his choice of victims."

A night wind rustled the leaves on the silver birches. There was a smell of charcoal smoke in the air, mixed with the whiff of early decay coming off the body of Martin Turner.

"Dirty girl," Harriman said, "filthy coward. Now we've got lying bastard."

Stella asked, "Where's the wife?"

"Local A and E. She went into shock."

"Children?"

"Two boys—one six, one younger. They're with a neighbor." He hesitated. "They saw it."

"Saw what?"

"That's just it. We don't know. Neighbors heard her screaming. When they arrived on the scene, the kids were up at the window."

"And who knows how long they'd been there or what they'd witnessed—"

"Yes, that's the issue."

"How many neighbors?"

"We think a dozen or so. The uniforms are doing a house-to-house."

"We need to be careful with the children."

"I know."

Stella was watching Maxine Hewitt walking down the empty street toward them. "Isn't DC Hewitt one of our ABE staff?"

"She is."

"Okay, put her on to it." Then: "The neighbors—how many of the dozen or so saw the writing?"

"All of them. It was dusk, but the street lighting's pretty good."

Maxine ducked into the scene-of-crime tent, shepherded by Andy

Greegan. There were places she could stand and places that were out of bounds: areas that the forensic team had marked off and would come back to. She looked down at the body of Martin Turner, arms out in a wide cruciform, half his face blown away, the inscription scrawled across his bare midriff, and thought how like waxworks the dead seem, how very far from life.

The low, persistent hum in the tent, like a running dynamo, was flies. They formed a black crust on Turner's face and were swarming over gobbets of blood and matter on his chest. She made mental notes: the bruising round his throat, the lack of blood for a wound that gross, the grass stains on the knees of his trousers. She held her breath against the smell.

When she emerged, Frank Silano was talking to Greegan. He looked at her but didn't say a word. The halogen lights would make anyone look pale, the smell make anyone grimace. He went in, brushing through the slit in the plastic.

Stella and Harriman sat with Mark and Carrie Phipps, who had heard the screams, been first to reach Valerie Turner, had pulled her off her husband's body and also had the foresight—in Carrie's case, at least—to throw up a fair way off from the crime scene. It was Carrie who had finally looked up, perspiring, trembling, to see the two little faces pressed to the windowpane. She had entered the house through the wide-open front door and gone into the living room. When she spoke, the boys made no response, nor did they move; they stared out, eyes wide and fixed, tiny dabs of breath misting the window.

She went to them, talking softly, trying to coax them away, though it was impossible for her to keep the ragged edge out of her voice. Finally, the younger had turned to her, dry-eyed, and asked, "Who is it?"

Stella asked questions that brought no useful answer. "Did you see anyone, anything? Did you hear anyone, anything? His car had been driven to the end of the street, so did you—? A shot was fired, so did you—?"

Carrie shook her head. A fine evening, she explained, barbecues were lit, all the activity was in back gardens, people talking over the fence, music playing, children running about—

"Did the children say anything to you?" Stella asked.

"The little boy—James—wanted to know who it was."

"What did he mean?"

"He was asking about the dead person—asking who it was."

"Are you sure?" Stella worked to keep the note of challenge out of her voice.

"What else could he have meant?" Mark asked.

Stella looked at Carrie. "What were his exact words?"

"He said, 'Who is it?' "

"Meaning?"

"Well, he must have meant . . . Their father, mustn't he? Who was it they could see lying . . ." She stopped, then picked up again. "Who was it tied to the gate, who was it dead?"

"What else *could* he have meant?" A touch of irritation in Mark's voice, shock emerging as anger: anger he had already dampened down with whiskey—the bottle was open on a side table, and he had a full glass in his hand.

Carrie was looking at Stella but spoke to her husband. "She thinks they might have seen it happen."

"It's possible," Stella said.

Suddenly tears were running down Carrie's cheeks. She said, "You think he was saying who is it that killed my daddy."

Collier arrived fifteen minutes after the press, which was lousy timing, because several journos had managed to bypass the police cordon by knocking on doors in a neighboring street and infiltrating the back-garden gossip. Put the right questions in the right way and people will talk; they've just witnessed something terrible; they *need* to talk. The journos are good at this; suddenly they're counselors, they know how to prompt, but, more, they know how to listen.

Collier stepped into the camera lights. He knew what to do: talk to the interviewer but glance at the camera from time to time; don't lean into the microphone; don't elaborate or you'll grope for words.

It was a particularly brutal murder.

Inquiries were in progress.

Anyone with information should come forward.

He couldn't be more specific at this point in time.

The interviewer's technique was second to none. He drew Collier on with the easy ones, making his interviewee look good, a man in control.

Then he named the victim, and Collier hesitated a second before saying that details would be released later.

Then he mentioned the fact that Martin Turner was the editor of a national newspaper, and Collier repeated his earlier remark, though he didn't seem to know enough to cut the interview short.

Then the interviewer asked about the words that had, apparently, been scrawled across Turner's body: LYING BASTARD.

This stopped Collier dead, so the interviewer took the opportunity to mention that many people now believed that a serial killer was at work, given the city's other recent killings, given the public and gruesome nature of their deaths.

Collier had the wit to say, "No comment," though a denial would have been the better option. In journo terms, "No comment" means "Yes, but I'm not prepared to confirm just now."

As he backed off beyond the police tape, voices called after him; he turned and walked away, and the voices stilled as the journalists frantically hit the speed-dial buttons on their mobile phones.

Collier emerged from the tent as Stella and Harriman were leaving Mark and Carrie Phipps. He gave Harriman a look and took Stella by the arm, steering her to the far side of the road.

"Why wasn't I called?"

"I thought you had been. Sorry."

"I just walked into a press trap." He was speaking quietly, but the tremor of anger in his voice was unmissable. "I got this call as part of an up-date bundle from Notting Dene. You were named as investigating officer."

"I'll send an e-mail."

"You're the DS. It's your job to notify me."

"Look . . ." Stella wondered how long he would spend on bitching with a dead man roped to the gates and a scene-of-crime team waiting to be told what next. "Look, I got the call because one of the triple-nine guys re-ported the writing on the body; that was picked up on the computer and cross-referenced, and my name was on the Bryony Dean crime sheet. Aren't you listed as team leader on those entries?"

Collier looked back at the lights and activity by the SOC tent. After a moment he said, "I don't know. I should be."

Admin. Stella thought. *Paperwork. It can bury you.* For a brief mo-ment, she felt sorry for him.

Collier went into the tent and came out again a couple of minutes later. Stella was organizing the ambulance and the police doctor, putting in a call to Sam Burgess. Collier signaled to her, and she handed over to Harriman.

"The press asked about the possibility of it being serial. They're tying it in with the other two."

"Are they? Why?"

"Three in the space of a week, apparently random, out in the open, it doesn't take all that much imagination."

"Did they mention any of the details we're holding back?"

"Yes, but for this case, not the others. They seem to know that this one had writing on him." Collier suddenly saw an opportunity for a fight-back. "They can only have got that from people at the scene. How many neighbors showed up before we did?"

"We're not sure. Maybe twelve."

"There you are, then. So the press managed to get to some of those people and question them. Your job is to stop that happening. That sort of leak is just another form of crime-scene contamination."

"There are sixty or so houses on this street," Stella said, "with the same number backing on to them either side. A hundred eighty houses, each with an average of . . . what . . . three occupants?"

Collier nodded. "High risk. You didn't cover it."

He walked away. Stella couldn't see his smile, but there was a trace of it in the set of his shoulders. She thought it took someone like Brian Collier to make capital out of a man with his face shot off.

Andy Greegan was still patrolling the crime scene, watching for any danger of contamination. Stella walked the path by the hedge, dressed in the white coverall and shoe covers that Greegan had given her. She had been back into the SOC tent with a torch. The halogen lights threw a hard glare, but they also threw strong shadows, and she had used the torch to illuminate the undersides of the railings and certain patches of ground. What she was looking for wasn't there. Now she was checking the boles of the trees, each in turn, the entire circumference to head height and beyond. She'd expected to find it there, but so far she'd had no luck. Forensic officers were still searching the far end of the walkway, each carrying a halogen baton. They were looking for it too.

She gave up on the trees and walked to the garbage bunker, though she knew that the forensic team had been over it, that it had been dusted for fingerprints, that DNA sweepings had been taken.

It's the one thing no one knows about. Morgan heard about the writing from Collier, Delaney heard about it from me, that sort of thing spreads like a stain. But this is the one thing that lets me know there isn't a copycat at work. A sign, a signature. It's yours, isn't it, you bastard; yours alone? It's here. It's got to be here.

Harriman found her on her hands and knees at the curbside. He said, "Tomorrow, boss. It's hopeless in this light."

"You're right."

Stella stood up and switched off her torch. Everyone would be back to-morrow for a second look in daylight. She dusted herself down and walked along the street toward her car. Three uniformed men were winching Turner's Mercedes onto a low-loader, getting ready to cover it; the interior had already been hoovered and tweezered. Stella stepped sideways to skirt the trailer as the car tilted. A little river of light from the halogens ran down the wing, and there it was, finger-drawn into the film of London grime:

^ ^
V

A smudge of red on the outline; a sticky drop of red in the cut of the lower V.

Forensic officers in white were eerie figures between the silver birches. Camera flashes bounced off the Merc's paintwork. The moon was high, a clean-cut white disc in a midnight-blue sky.

Two paramedics came out of the tent wheeling a body bag on a col-lapsible gurney; the scene-of-crime team, the photographers, the AMIP-5 squad, went about their business, all of them throwing hard, clear shadows.

I'm being followed by a moon shadow, moon shadow, moon shadow.

The tune would run through her head all the next day.

54

Ricardo Jones was sitting in the front passenger seat of a car, his hands resting quietly in his lap, his back straight. He wanted to blot the drop of sweat that had sprung up alongside his left eye, but he left it alone. Not that he was unable to reach it; he just felt it was better to remain still.

The driver was the same man he'd encountered in Jonah's flat. Some-where just off Notting Hill Gate, they had stopped to pick up another man, who said, "Don't turn round." He didn't speak again until they had driven up to Wormwood Scrubs and parked. "You're Ricardo Jones."

Ricardo wasn't sure whether it was a question or a statement. In the end he said, "Okay."

"Don't speak," the man said. "You don't have to speak at all."

They sat for a while in silence, apart from the *tick-tick* of the engine as it cooled. Ricardo could hear himself breathing; he could smell his own sweat, rank and hot. They were parked in a side street close to the Scrubs. Moonlight frosted the rough ground. Ricardo could see himself lying out there, dead and done with.

The man said, "You've been providing a service on Harefield, Ricardo. You've been offering premium rates, which is all well and good, except you've been offering them to my clients. You've been undercutting me. You've been poaching. Don't speak; there's no need for you to say a single fucking word. Now, you did a very nice deal for a man called Jonah, and as I think you know by now, it was not to his advantage. He thought it would be, but it wasn't. The thing about hands with no thumbs, Ricardo, is they're not much use for anything. You can't count money with them, for a start."

A soft Scottish burr, not so much angry as chiding.

"Of course, that could have been you, Ricardo. The man sitting beside you would have been happy to perform the same sort of operation on you—a bit of a warning, a way of letting you know you'd overstepped the mark. In fact, that was my intention, at first. I was pissed off, *really* pissed off, and I wasn't thinking straight. Well"—he chuckled—"I could still change my mind. Not the thumbs but . . . I don't know . . . the little fingers of both hands . . . just a reminder . . . but don't worry about that now; just listen to what I have to say, because it's a way you could keep all your fingers and make a little profit into the bargain. Not the kind of profit you've been making, of course; no, a *little* profit. It's simple. You turn your contacts over to me, and you act as go-between. As gofer. For a small percentage. Why am I bothering to use you at all? Well, I'm buying your goodwill, Ricardo. Your goodwill and your good reputation with your clients, and I'm sure they'll feel happier—to begin with, anyway—if they're still dealing with someone they know and trust. As for the future . . . we'll have to see how things go, won't we?"

There was a faint buzzing: a mobile switched to vibrate, and the man rummaged in his pocket, rising slightly to get purchase; Ricardo caught a glimpse, in the rearview mirror, of a narrow face, a goatee, a gunslinger's mustache.

"Call you back." After that there was a long silence. Finally, the man said, "Well, you can talk now. Just say yes or no."

Ricardo said, "Yes."

They drove back to Notting Hill, Ricardo next to the driver, neither saying a word, the man in the back looking out at the crowded streets and humming an almost inaudible tune. Ricardo thought it was "Lord of the Dance." The driver pulled over in Pembridge Road. He said, "Get out, walk away, don't turn round, we'll be in touch."

Ricardo walked across the hill to Hammersmith Road, then down North End Road, his legs jittery, his lips dry. When he got back to 1169, Block B, he was badly in need of a piss. Tina Mooney looked up as he went through and noticed the set of his mouth. He came back carrying their stash and did a couple of lines without looking up.

When he told her, she said, "Who is he?"

Ricardo described him: the face hair, the soft, Scottish brogue. "I don't know his name. The guy that drove—Sekker, that's what they call him."

"Is the black guy dead?"

"I don't know."

"What will you do?"

"Play along. I'll have to." He sounded apologetic. "I'm admin., Tina, you know? I'm deals and percentages. They cut the poor bastard's thumbs off and nailed his hands to a chair."

"What, then?"

"I'll have to give him something—lose a few good contacts by the look of it. Bastard! I'll keep most of it back, though. Christ, it took me years to get my fucking list together."

"He'll expect the lot."

"He will, yes. Scotch cunt."

"So we're on the move again."

"After a bit. After I've given up a few names."

"I like London. I've missed London. I had good times here."

"Why?" Delaney asked.

Stella had just got out of the shower; she'd run it hot, but now stood by the window to let her skin cool in the night air.

"If I knew that, I'd know everything."

"I saw him just the other day," Delaney said.

"Did you? What for?"

"Just a drink . . . I used to work for him: freelance, mostly; on the staff for a short while. I didn't know him well, but I liked him. And he was a good editor."

"What did you talk about?"

She had her back half turned to him; he tried to read her expression, but the light put her face in shadow. "Nothing special . . . Why?"

"In case he said something that might—"

"Oh . . . No, just old times, you know. Want some coffee?"

"Okay."

"Lying bastard," he said. "It must be the paper, don't you think—something he published?"

"It's possible. How many lies in the average paper in the average week?"

"None. Sometimes there are disputable facts."

"I'm keeping a straight face. All right, how many disputable facts?"

"Hundreds."

"Over a year?"

"It's exponential."

"Exactly. Here's another thing: this guy, whoever's killing these people, has an agenda of his own. His reasons aren't going to be what we would call rational. So who knows what he considers to be a lie?"

"It was pretty straightforward with the other two," Delaney observed. "Dirty girl was a hooker, filthy coward ran away."

"*If* Leonard Pigeon was the intended victim." She turned to confront him. "This stuff I'm telling you: it's not for publication."

"I thought you said the serial-killer thing was breaking now."

"It is . . ."

"And they know that the killer wrote on him."

"They don't know about the other two cases—that they were written on, or what the writing said."

Delaney laughed. "Stella, it's just a matter of time."

"We need to hold things back, things only the killer could know. We're already getting half a dozen confessions a week."

"Look," he said, "I'm doing the Rich List. Color-supplement trivia. I'm not in the front line anymore."

Her head came up, but he was spooning coffee into a cafetière and didn't see it. Something about the way he'd said it, something hidden.

No, you're not. But you'd like to be.

55

ABE—*Achieving Best Evidence*, which is what Maxine Hewitt was hoping to do. She sat in the video suite with James and Stevie Turner, who seemed oddly at ease, if a little detached. James was looking round the room, seeming to take it in piece by piece, his head moving once every few seconds; Stevie was hunched over his Game Boy.

There was a discreet camera, and there were wall-mounted directional microphones; there were games and dolls and drawing materials, designed to help stir memories. Under normal circumstances, Maxine would have had an ABE colleague with her—a member of the squad who had also been given specialist training; on this occasion, and at Stella's request, the other person was Anne Beaumont.

The trick was to start the boys talking and then just listen for a way in. It took a while. Finally, Anne asked about the house, the house they lived in, trying to steer them toward the front room and the front-room window with its view of the drive.

Stevie looked up. He said, "We don't live there now."

James said, "It's not good there."

And they started to talk about themselves and their mother and the new life they were, apparently, going to live. About their father, they said not a word.

When Stella walked into Chintamani she was wearing the only substitute she possessed for the T. J. Maxx jacket, which was Jigsaw, last year, Gap jeans, a touch too much makeup, and fuck *you*. She could have pulled Abigail into the AMIP-5 interview room, but she wanted her at her ease, on her own territory.

She was defensively late and had barely sat down before two waiters arrived with a bottle of white wine and eight separate dishes.

"The meze," Abigail told her. "Their speciality, okay?"

Stella said yes, it was okay, the meze was fine. She realized that she hadn't been able to take a close look at Abigail during that evening at the Orchard Street club, and saw that the woman was not quite the stereotypical blonde she'd been carrying in her mind. The looks were classy and intelligent, the clothes expensive but unshowy, the voice low with no identifiable accent. Abigail tore off a piece of flat bread and scooped some tahini. She said, "I'm not a whore."

"I didn't think you were."

"It crossed your mind."

"How do you know?" Stella asked.

"Because it crossed mine."

Stella laughed out loud. She said, "So what's the deal?"

"I'm not sure I know. We met at a party. I guessed he was married, but there was no wife in tow, he was attractive . . . power, mostly—I think I might have a thing for powerful men—we left the party, had dinner, he's quite funny, you know, witty, mostly at the expense of the world's movers and shakers. He's old money; that makes a difference. He sees politics as a rather simpleminded game with everyone trying to win by whatever means they can; something that excludes the population at large completely."

"Has he spoken to you since he and I met?"

"Oh, God, of course."

"What did he tell you?"

"Pretty much everything, I expect. You think Len Pigeon might have died in Neil's place."

"There's a possibility."

"How much of one?"

"I might have a better idea of that if I knew why Leonard Pigeon was impersonating him."

"Neil says he was just doing a job."

"I know he does. The Americans—what sort of business are they in?"

Abigail shook her head, smiling. "You think I ask Neil about business?"

"Why wouldn't you? You're not stupid."

"Exactly."

Stella was trying each dish in turn. Everything was good. The wine was terrific. She said, "I never saw Len Pigeon in life. People look different in pictures . . . they look different when they're dead. It seems to be generally accepted that he could be mistaken for Morgan."

"They looked alike, yes; same build too"—she paused—"though I never saw Len with his clothes off. People remarked on it, you know; joked about it—did Neil send his researcher through the lobby when he couldn't be bothered to vote?"

"Did he?"

"Yes."

"Convenient alibi, apart from anything else," Stella observed.

"You're right. Len seeing out a late-night sitting, me and Neil taking a couple of days in Paris."

Stella almost smiled. "Does his wife know?"

"I don't ask."

"Have you met her?"

"Oh, yes. Another party—I was someone he'd met somewhere; she gave me a funny little damp handshake."

"And?"

"I think she knows, yes."

"The handshake—"

"More the fact that she smiled without looking at me. What else do you want to know?"

"Whether you can think of a reason why Neil Morgan might be considered a coward."

"Ah, yes, he told me about that." She gave a little shudder. "Jesus, who *is* this guy? He must be running round the streets foaming at the mouth."

"You might think so. It's not like that. He's not like that."

"How do you know?"

"Profiling." Stella was quoting Anne Beaumont: "The chances are he won't look crazy, won't dress crazy, won't act crazy." She looked round. "The man in the pin-striped suit over there, for instance. Him, anyone; it's what makes sociopaths so difficult to catch: we mistake them for one of us."

"I can't," Abigail said. "Can't think of any reason why Neil might be thought a coward. In fact, in some ways he's a risk-taker, certainly at a career level."

"Domestic level too," Stella observed.

Abigail smiled. "Not really. If she does know, she's not going to do anything about it."

"Meaning she would have by now . . . because you're not the first."

"Nor the last."

"So what's in it for you?"

"I mentioned that he's old money. Well, there's quite a *lot* of old money, and Neil's generous. He buys me nice things; we stay in nice hotels; I have a nice time." She smiled. "You see, I am a bit of a whore, aren't I? Also, he's fun."

Stella paused, her wineglass at her lip. "Is he?"

"Oh, yes." Abigail smiled. "I don't think you've seen him at his best. And by the way," she said, grinning, "the guy in the pin-striped suit? He's a hedge-fund manager; he invests in the high millions. And he *is* crazy."

John Delaney was reading through his piece on Stanley Bowman and watching TV at the same time. A battle zone; a crowd; gunfire; military vehicles on a dusty road; burning cars; a line of troops edging down an empty street.

He remembered having been on a satellite phone to Turner from the Holiday Inn in Sarajevo. Turner had said, "Good copy, John. It sounds like hell."

Delaney had been looking at a homemade cocktail being poured for him by a very pretty woman who was doing the to-camera work for a Canadian broadcaster.

"It's hell," he'd confirmed. The hotel had been hit a couple of times that night. There had been a rank smell of high explosives in his nostrils, and the girl's faux-military shirt was showing just enough of her breasts to let him know what she was thinking.

Martin Turner, a civilian casualty.

The boys hadn't said much, but they'd said enough to let Maxine and Anne know that whatever they had seen would remain locked away for a while. Perhaps forever. The women left Stevie and James in the care of Sue Chapman and took five minutes out with coffee.

"It's enough," Anne said. "You can try again if you like, but this is as far as it'll go today."

Maxine nodded. "I think they saw him," she said. "What do you think?"

"The same. But they don't know what they saw, not really. They've no way of decoding it."

"It's like a snapshot that hasn't developed."

"Good description."

"No," Maxine said. "I mean, it's like that for me. Those images exist somewhere in their minds; I just can't get at them." She sipped her coffee and grimaced: AMIP-5 brew. "They saw him . . . Did they see everything? Did they see what he did?"

"If they did," Anne said, "it's a lifetime of recovery."

The boys came out of the video suite and said good-bye. James smiled at the women, but Stevie was concentrating on his Game Boy. He manipulated the controls, bringing the superhero into frame.

Silent Wolf, out on the city streets, bringing swift justice to the evildoer.

56

This time Tom Davison was a voice on the phone, and Stella realized she was glad of the distance. Her next thought was: Why? Is he *such* a danger? She remembered how things had started: his calls on police business becoming less and less official, his jokes, his flirting.

Last Christmas. Herself and Delaney at loggerheads. Taking up Davison's oh so obvious offer, in order to see how it would feel. The sex too good to ignore. Then leaving abruptly . . . the startled look in his eyes . . . and finding herself out on Chiswick High Road, pavements glittering with frost, on the phone to Delaney with her sense of guilt building, image by remembered image.

"The forensic team dug a nine-millimeter parabellum bullet out of the ground, exactly where the major bloodstain lay . . . as if we needed that confirmation."

"Does it tell you anything?" Stella asked.

"Tells me he was shot with a gun that takes a nine-millimeter load. They're not unusual. Find me the gun and I'll tell you a lot more."

"What about DNA traces?"

"Well, the site was swamped with them. It'll take a while."

"How long?"

"I'll do my best. Look"—Davison laughed—"we'll find a match; it's going to be the same guy."

"I believe you." The SOC photo of the killer's signature was on the desk in front of her. She didn't mention it to Davison; she wanted the forensic tests to be meticulous and impartial.

"It'll be him." A pause. "Stella, the other day, I wasn't blaming you; I don't think blame comes into it. So—"

"No, I should have been more honest. I was having problems with someone. It was selfish of me." She stopped, but he knew there was more. "You . . . unsettled me. It felt good with you, so it also felt like one hell of a risk. Does that make sense?"

Davison laughed. He said, "Oh, yes. Because fucking leads to kissing."

The boys in the Beamer were cruising the West End, taking it slow because the traffic was backed up, as always, solid metal wherever you looked, but also taking it slow because they were stoned, even the driver was stoned, and things were brighter, louder, funnier.

They were sharing their music with everyone in the street and with people in a few streets beyond. One of them sat in the backseat with his feet out of the open window. He was examining his new toy: a converted Brocock ME38. He didn't need it for anything special, just street cred. He aimed it at one of the crew and fired off an imaginary round.

The boy grabbed his heart and grimaced and died an imaginary death. They laughed. They all laughed until they hurt.

Since Bryony's boyfriend, previously her mother's boyfriend, had been on the must-see list, Maxine Hewitt had been making an on/off stakeout of the local benefit offices, a duty that involved sitting in an unmarked car, pretending to be there for no particular reason, eating unwise food and trying not to notice her partner's body odor. Her current partner was Andy Greegan. Andy had noticed the early arrival of summer, the unaccustomed heat and the city's humidity levels, and his concession to all this was to wear a deodorant called Chill.

Greegan had been on sandwich duty. The best he'd been able to do was cheese on white and two cartons of regular coffee. He lodged his paper carton on the dashboard, next to the enhanced away-day photo of the elusive Chris Fuller. Maxine set her sandwich aside and drank the coffee, which was already cool.

She said, "No offense, Andy, but your deodorant smells like machine oil."

For a moment, Greegan didn't register the remark; then he did. "No *offense*?"

"Absolutely not, no. I'm sure it seemed like a must-buy at the time, but it's clearing my sinuses. Machine oil or else drain-devil."

"It's advertised on TV by a godlike young man with a workout body. A girl wearing three handkerchiefs slithers all over him."

"Maybe it's an open-air deodorant. I've seen that ad. The young man in question is backed up to a waterfall."

Greegan looked mournful. "Or it smells better on guys that look like him."

"Or it smells the same, but girls just don't notice when it's a guy who looks like him."

"You think?"

"I don't know," Maxine told him. "I was looking at the girl."

"I could open a window."

"On Kilburn High Road?"

"That guy," Greegan said, "the guy in the ad. He's not so good-looking. It's just gym time: abs and pecs."

"The girl was hot, though."

"That's what I was going to say."

Maxine laughed and took a bite of her sandwich. She said, "Hey, it's him."

Greegan looked up, not sure, for a moment, what she meant. Then he saw a face he knew coming out of the post office on the other side of the road.

The face on the dashboard.

A cop's relationship with a chis is strictly business before pleasure. In fact, pleasure doesn't come into it.

Frank Silano had spoken to three people, and from those conversations came the names of five likely contacts. It was a work-intensive business. He chased down the five and got rerouted to a further four. Of these, two deflected him with the same name, a matching description, and the name of a pub in London Fields—which is where Silano now sat drinking a beer and asking awkward questions.

Eventually, the man with the razored sideburns and the dated shades turned up and stood in the doorway. He looked unhappy. Silano nodded, but didn't make a move. Sideburns left. Silano knew that his presence in the pub was making people nervous, but he also knew that Sideburns would be under instruction to solve the problem, so he let the man wait while he finished his beer.

They went for a walk through Hackney's blue haze. Silano said, "I'm told you're the armorer. You're the man to see."

Sideburns gave a little cough-laugh. "Yeah? Who tell you that?"

"Everyone told me that."

"Everyone knows jack shit."

"You sell someone a nine-millimeter weapon recently?"

"You talking to the wrong man."

"I hear you sell most things. I hear this from what I consider reliable sources."

"This is people talking crap. This is people don't know me."

"They seemed to know you pretty well."

"Got their names?"

"Look," Silano said, "you can either help me out here or I could turn up at your address with a full squad, a Hatton gun, and some dogs with a keen sense of smell. It's up to you."

"I don't know, man. I sell stuff, everyone does. Cars, mostly. TVs sometimes. I'm legal."

"Of course you are. What did he look like?"

"I saw a man in that pub back there. Few days ago. He was looking for something. I told him I couldn't help him, you know?"

"Sure. What did he look like?"

"People come up here, they want all kinds of stuff. Do I know them? Do I know who the fuck they are? No."

"I believe you. What did he look like?"

"White man, it seem to me."

Silano sighed. "We're running out of time," he said, "or you are."

They had turned off the street into a shopping mall. Sideburns stopped and leaned up against the window of a media store. Fifteen plasma screens were showing an afternoon movie in which John Wayne was taking on a regiment of gooks. Gooks died. Gooks were mowed down and blown up and plowed under.

"For fuck's sake, man, does it matter to me? What do you think? I'd give him up, no problem."

Silano said, "So go ahead."

"I think he had long hair." Sideburns shrugged.

"It was that long ago?"

Sideburns laughed. "I was stoned. Okay? That's all there is. I was off my fucking face."

"What did he sound like?" Sideburns shook his head. "Young or old?"

"You want a guess? Young."

Silano wiped a hand across his eyes. "Was it a nine millimeter?"

Sideburns said, "Whoever this man was, he's fuck-nothing to me. If I knew, I'd tell you. Like I need this shit from you." He spread his hands. "I was wrecked, you know? I was nailed." He pushed himself off the window.

"Don't come with me, man. Don't come any farther." As he walked away, he looked over his shoulder. "What kind of gun?"

"Nine millimeter."

A faint smile. "Yeah . . ."

TV images flickered at the corner of Silano's eye. John Wayne shooting from the hip. John Wayne winning the war.

57

Collier was running the briefing. Stella sat on a desk, to one side, head down, saying nothing. Collier, on the other hand, was saying everything from "We're going nowhere" to "Make it happen." "Get results" was also high on his list, though if he had a method for doing this, he wasn't sharing it. The whiteboards were covered with the front pages of national tabloids, all of which, one way or another, said MAD DOG SERIAL KILLER AT LARGE—COPS WORSE THAN USELESS—EXPECT MORE DEATHS—IT COULD BE YOU AND YOUR LOVED ONES NEXT.

The squad room was littered with crisp packets and chocolate-bar wrappers and water bottles. Bar of the day was Galaxy. Stella waited until Collier had run through his list of grievances before stepping up to say that DCs Hewitt and Greegan had arrested Chris Fuller.

"As I remember," she said, "you considered him our prime suspect."

It was clear from the expression on Collier's face that he didn't appreciate Stella's timing. He said, "And I wasn't told about this because—"

"Sorry, boss." Stella gave the perfect imitation of a little, helpless shrug. "I thought I'd be giving this briefing. It was top of my agenda."

Stella and Harriman sat down with Chris. The air in the interview room was stale and tepid. Harriman switched on a freestanding fan that pushed the air round without releasing it. The enhanced postmortem photograph of Bryony Dean was on the table between them. Chris had looked at it, then replaced it, facedown.

"You knew it was Bryony," Stella said, "the girl in the tree."

"Not at first. She just didn't come back."

"Which is why you reported her missing."

"Yeah."

"As Elizabeth Rose Connor."

"She changed her name."

"No," Harriman said, "she didn't change it, she used both. I expect you're doing the same—four identities, four social-security payments."

Chris had nothing to say on the subject.

"How did you find out that it was Bryony?" Stella asked.

"She had some friends over at the Kensals, I—"

"No, no . . ." Harriman shook his head. "Don't bother with all that. We know she was on the game, we know that you were pimping her, we know that she used to work the Strip."

Chris's hand jerked on the table, as if he'd been stung. "I went up there looking for her. It had gone round that she was dead, that she was the one in the papers." He massaged his eyes with finger and thumb and didn't speak again for a full minute. Finally, he said, "I didn't like her doing that. I didn't ask her to."

Harriman snorted. "Sure. You pimped for her, you pimped for her mother."

"Think it was simple as that?" Chris's voice was sharp with indignation. "You don't know. What do you know? Fuck all."

He turned away and stared down at the floor. Stella gave Harriman a look. To Chris, she said, "So why did she do it? Why did she go whoring?"

"She wanted things, you know, the usual."

"What?"

"The stuff they advertise. The stuff everybody wants."

"So it was just down to her."

"We needed money. She had something she could sell."

"Bryony was reported missing once before," Stella observed.

"I know."

"But she wasn't really missing on that occasion, was she?"

"We wanted to be together, you know how it is . . ."

Harriman said, "I know you were shagging both the mother and the daughter."

Chris sighed. "It wasn't like that."

"No? According to Melanie Dean, it was exactly like that." Harriman paused. "Why didn't you just tell her that you and Bryony were going away together? Why piss about?"

Chris looked at him as if he ought to know the answer. "I didn't want the fuss."

"Did you kill Bryony?" Stella asked him.

He had been expecting the question. "She was stripped naked and hung up in a tree"—he turned the photo over—"she lost her eyes. Those aren't her eyes. What happened to her eyes?"

"Birds," Stella spoke softly.

Chris stared at her a moment, then looked away. "Why would I do that to her? Why would I do anything to her? We were together, you know? We'd decided on that." He was doing everything but use the word "love." "I'm not violent, all right? Ask anyone. Ask Melanie."

Stella and Harriman exchanged a glance. Chris said, "What?"

"Melanie killed herself," Stella said.

The tape rolled. Chris sat with his head down, his shoulders up, his arms folded, as if a chill had suddenly come over the room.

He said, "Both. Both dead." After a moment, he said, "You don't know. You know fuck all."

Aimée lay spread-eagled and heavy. Woolf had made love to her long and hard, and she had taken it as evidence of his passion, evidence of his love. Now he was unloading items from the fridge and making a cold platter. She had bought beer and wine and food they might, she thought, cook together while they talked about the future.

She heard the raised voices and rapid-volley gunfire of a TV show and got off the bed to walk naked into the kitchen. Being naked in front of him was a particular luxury. He was sitting at the table watching the show, and she leaned over him, her breasts grazing his back, to roll a slice of ham. On the screen were burning cars and civilians yelling and soldiers looking edgy. It might have been the news. She ate the ham; it was cold from the fridge; she took a swallow of his beer.

He said, "I thought we could go away somewhere, take a break . . . Could you do that?"

She said yes without thinking; then, "How long for?"

"A couple of days; three, maybe."

She turned his face to hers and kissed him. "Of course; of course I can do that."

She went back to the bedroom and found a light robe. When she returned he was staring at the screen, his beer halfway to his mouth, a look on his face that was something like outrage. A man was talking politics, his subject war and the pity of war; also its inevitability. A caption brought up his name: Neil Morgan, MP.

Aimée said, "Are you okay?"

"What?" Woolf turned toward her quickly, his reverie broken.

"Just the way you were looking at him."

"Who?"

She gestured at the screen, though Morgan had now been replaced by a newscaster. "That guy."

"No." Woolf shook his head, thinking fast. "What guy?"

"You looked upset."

He smiled at her. "I was thinking."

"Unpleasant thoughts . . ."

"Just something I remembered I have to do."

He got up and put his arms round her, the smile still in place. "So it's okay—you can get away? A couple of days."

She nodded. Already she wanted him again. That hunger, that fierceness of need, had never happened to her before. "Whenever you say."

"Soon," Woolf promised, "a week or so. Soon."

It was 3:30 A.M. when Sorley called. London was still awake, and so was he. Stella, on the other hand, had been asleep and caught up in a dream in which Delaney was on the deck of a ship throwing streamers while she stood on the dock, waving. The streamers were blue-and-white police tape and printed with the words DO NOT CROSS THIS LINE. As she watched, the ship started to move. This happened in freeze-frame moments. Each time the ship was a little farther off from the dock, and Delaney's face a little less clear. Then it was night, and the moon was up; shadows danced on the water and Delaney stood beside her, looking at the ship, a dot on the horizon.

He said, "Where are you sending me?"

Sorley sounded as if he had surprised himself. He said, "I just realized what time it is."

Delaney half woke and said something. Stella got out of bed and walked through to the living space. She said, "Me too."

"I'm sorry, Stella. I sleep when I sleep and I wake when I wake; everything's a bit fucked up."

"How are you?"

"Home, laid up, bed downstairs, Karen's my night nurse and someone called Patricia is my day nurse."

"What's she like?"

"Blond, nice tits, gives good head."

"It's pleasing to hear that you've emerged a new man."

Sorley laughed. "Well," he said, "I was just curious to know what's happening."

Stella gave him a short update. "I could send you copies of the crime reports."

"I'm supposed to be taking it easy: Karen's on the case. A little light exercise, a little light reading."

"The reports are light reading, you know that."

"This third one—"

"Martin Turner."

"It's the same guy, is it?"

"Definitely."

"So we're in trouble."

"It looks that way, yes. The tabloids certainly think so. We're getting City Under Siege headlines: the New Ripper, that brand of shit."

"She won't let me see the papers."

"She cares about you; she's a good woman."

"Send me the reports," Sorley said.

"Karen will intercept them."

"Use a courier. The day nurse is more respectful."

There was a little pause; Sorley sounded breathy. Stella said, "What was that?"

"Nothing."

"Jesus Christ, boss. Are you smoking?"

"No, I'm not smoking." A snap in his voice. Then: "It was oxygen."

"Oh . . . Sorry, it sounded like—"

"Oxygen," Sorley said. "DI Collier—they say he's a good man."

"Have you met him?"

"No."

"He's a prick," Stella said. "Get well soon."

Stanley Bowman was making money, something he did well, and something he did all the time. If anyone were ever to devise a way of making money in his sleep, it would be Bowman. Just now he wasn't sleeping because it was

3:30 A.M. in London, which meant it was 7:30 in the evening on the West Coast of America, and there was business to be done.

Bowman was on the phone to someone who needed high-level contacts in Britain but couldn't be seen to make them. Someone who needed friends in smoke-filled rooms, friends who had the right friends. Bowman was a trader. Sometimes he traded money, sometimes he traded goods, sometimes he traded information. About eighty percent of his business was legitimate financial services and created a very effective shield for the other twenty percent, which returned eighty percent of his income. The math was irresistible. He was an international version of Ricardo Jones, which was precisely why Ricardo's activities on Harefield so pissed him off. If you use your perfectly respectable shop-window businesses to collar a certain market, cut-price competition from trade minnows is a big irritation. It's like the corner shop getting into a price war with Wal-Mart.

The man Bowman was talking to sounded a little edgy. "We're not sure things are proceeding as we would have liked."

"Wrong direction," Bowman asked, "or not fast enough?"

"Well, we need a procurement guarantee by a certain point in time to make our quote viable."

Bowman laughed. "It'll be viable. Listen, Britain manufactured its own Apache helicopters at a cost of forty million pounds a unit. Israel bought theirs ready-made from you guys for . . . what?"

"Twelve."

"Right. It's win-win. You just need someone to see sense."

"See sense?" The American's voice took on a sour edge. "The British military has a fleet of Mark 3 Chinook helicopters that still aren't operational; they've got tanks with communications systems that are thirty years out-of-date; they issue their troops with the SA80 rifle, which doesn't like sandy conditions, for Christ's sake; our problem is that the people we need to deal with have shit for brains."

"Did you speak to Neil Morgan?"

"And paid him a hell of a lot of money."

"He's the guy to plead your case."

"We had a couple of meetings, but not much was said. Now he's avoiding us. We need you to talk to him—get things speeded up."

"I don't really know him," Bowman explained. "I know *about* him. I know he's a coming guy, and I know he likes money. Politics is a game to him, is what I hear; he doesn't care about who builds what or how much it costs. Also, he has friends on the Defense Select Committee. They like to look after their own."

"Yeah, well, listen, I think we need you to talk to him. We need to see progress."

"I'm not happy about that," Bowman said. "I don't think I can do that."

"Too much exposure?" The American sounded amused.

"If you like."

"If I *like*? I don't fucking like. We have an investment here, you know?"

"I gave you a name," Bowman said, "and I made a few connections. I talked to people who talked to people who talk to him."

"Yeah. Well, it's time to cut out the middle men."

"Look . . ." It was Bowman's turn to sound edgy. "I've done my job."

"And taken our money."

"Sure. For doing the job, like I said." A pause on the line. "For fuck's sake, you can sell arms anywhere in the world. There are wars all over—what can I tell you?—people like killing each other. Helicopters, armored cars, tanks, small arms, mines; it's a growth industry. War is the new rock and roll."

The American sighed, as if he wasn't getting his point across. "The big thing about the global economy? New markets. Expansion. Growth. The UK is prime for us. Go talk to Neil Morgan."

Bowman said, "I can't do that."

"I'm sure there's a way."

Suddenly Bowman caught the smell of money on the air, heady, intoxicating. "There might be," he said. "Let's talk about that."

58

There were theories that tied the early summer to icefall, to carbon footprints, to mud slips and hurricanes on the far side of the world. Maybe that's why London dawns and London dusks suddenly looked much the same: dusks were salmon-pink striation on gray-blue going to blue-black; dawns were the same pinks on deep blues fading to eggshell. It was as if the weather couldn't tell day from night. The first cool dawn wind—arriving before most London drivers cranked their engines and made their nose-to-tail cross-city trips—still carried a faint trace of cherry blossom.

Outside, the pink and blue, that fragile scent; inside, four people grouped round a hospital bed. Since his meeting with Woolf on the day of the storm, Blondie had been dead to the world. Impossible to know, doctors said, the real truth about coma. Could Blondie have caught that whiff of blossom? Could he have been aware of these people at his bedside—mother, brother, girlfriend, best friend? The consultant had a little descriptive image he liked to use: he told them that Blondie had been going steadily downhill, a step at a time. For a man who is already *deep,* already *down,* those steps could only lead to the underworld. This was the picture the consultant wanted to convey.

As the day brightened, as London picked up, Blondie descended farther and grew fainter. There was an issue for the people at the bedside, and it involved life-support systems and switches. Images of dark descents gave way to hard-edged talk of brain-stem death and vegetation. Tears were shed. Feelings ran high. Finally, farewells were said, the switch was thrown, and organs were harvested.

Blondie was said to have been the best son who ever—the best mate who ever—the most loving man who ever— It was agreed that he had a heart of gold, the same heart that was put on ice and sent by courier to an operating theater where a woman waited who would put it to better use than Blondie ever had.

The AMIP-5 squad who had caught the call to the Strip on the day of the storm registered Blondie's death as an unwelcome statistic: Unsolved Murder No. 27. It was a page-nine paragraph in papers that were carrying banner headlines that featured a mad-dog killer at work in the city.

Stella was walking into the squad room with an Americano and a chocolate muffin when she picked up a call on her mobile and heard her mother's voice.

There had been more than one letter marked "Personal," and they had all gone the way of the first: dumped unopened. The voice wasn't so easy to dump: not because it had authority, but because of the tremor it carried, the note of anxiety.

Tina said, "Stell . . . it's me."

Yes, it's you. It's you, all right. It's you, the absentee bitch. The tart. The drunk.

"Did you see me that day? I waved at you." Stella was silent. "Stell?"

"I'm here."

"I wrote you some letters. I didn't know the address, so I just put—"

"Yes. I got the letters."

Stella had walked straight through to the women's room. Both Sue Chapman and Pete Harriman had noticed her expression: ice under glass.

"The thing is, Stell, I won't be here much longer. We're moving. We're moving on." Stella was silent. "It's weird being back on the estate, Stell, you can imagine."

"What do you want?"

"Weird being back after all this time. What were you doing?"

"Doing?"

"At that woman's place. She killed herself."

Stella tried not to think of it as an accusation; however, this was her mother speaking, and memory compelled her.

"I know she did."

"She threw herself over the—"

"Is there something you want?" Stella asked.

"It was seeing you. Seeing you made me think." Stella was silent. "I don't know where we're going, that's up to him. It won't be back to Manchester, but it could be somewhere like that."

"*Is* there something you want?"

"Why don't you come over, Stella? Before we go. Or I could pay you a visit, couldn't I?" Tina hesitated. "Where do you live?"

"The point being?"

"I know I haven't been in touch, Stell. Oh, listen—it's not money, or anything. Not money. It was just seeing you—"

"What's his name?"

"Who?"

"The man you're with."

Her mother gave a laugh of surprise. "It's Ricardo. Still Ricardo. You know Ricardo."

"Never met him," Stella told her.

But I'd like to: oh, yes. Angel Face . . .

"I've missed you, Stell."

"You haven't seen me in ten years."

"That's what I mean."

"When are you there?"

"All the time. All the time, Stella. Come whenever you want."

Stella flipped her phone closed and leaned against the edge of a sink.

After a moment she put down her coffee and muffin, ran the cold tap, and sluiced her face, reaching round to get a wet hand to the nape of her neck.

I wish I didn't know you. I wish I didn't know your name.

Maxine Hewitt and Anne Beaumont were in the video suite with James and Stevie Turner. It was called "secondary coverage." People often remembered more about an incident after a short time had passed, after the trauma had lessened. A jumble became a pattern; someone half hidden stepped into the light.

In this case the pattern refused to emerge; the shadowy figure stepped farther into the dark. The boys seemed to have withdrawn into the strange, unsettling life they were now living: their mother sedated and always in need of the help of friends, they themselves living with grandparents who had long since lost the knack of child care.

Maxine and Anne made remarks, asked questions, offered suggestions that they hoped might unlock a memory. The boys listened, answered, smiled agreement, but had nothing else to offer. After half an hour of this, the women left the room, the VTR still running, in the hope that the boys might say something to each other that they wouldn't say to someone else.

Later they watched the tape. Maxine said, "Perhaps we're wrong. They weren't looking out of the window when their father was attacked. Or else they saw something but didn't know what it was."

"And still can't decode it, you mean?"

"Yes."

Anne shook her head. "I think they saw everything. That's why they're not talking. Significantly, there's no denial. They're not saying they saw nothing. If they're asked leading questions about looking out of the window, about their father returning home, they're silent. Here's something else: they were looking out of the window, we know that. But they won't even talk about that in a general sense. Did you see the cars going past? Was it dark? That sort of thing."

"They're too traumatized to talk about it."

"That's my guess."

The women watched the rest of the tape in case there was something they'd missed, some hint, some inflection, a stray word. The section of the tape when the boys had been left alone seemed to yield nothing. Stevie went back to his Game Boy. After a moment he showed the screen to James, who sat next to his brother to watch the game play out: two blond heads bowed in concentration.

Silent Wolf moving through the city streets, a man in shadow, his rough justice a way of life, his methods falling to a pattern that even the boys could understand.

Silent Wolf descending on the godless. James nudged his brother, Stevie nodded: tiny gestures that barely registered with Maxine and Anne. Two boys of the screen generation getting their daily dose of violence, balletic and bloody, and nothing new because they'd seen it all before.

59

Tina Mooney must have seen Stella's car crossing the DMZ because she opened the door as soon as the bell rang. She put her arms round her daughter; she left a leaf-shaped lipstick blot on Stella's cheek. Stella remembered such moments: they had come when her mother was drunk, or else was apologizing for what drink could do. She stood with her arms at her side and suffered the kiss.

Tina went to the kitchen to make coffee. And here was Ricardo—Angel Face—his hand out for a shake, his smile broad and genuine. They sat down and talked about the fact that summer had come too soon. Tina brought the coffee in on a tray, her smile no less cheery than his. She sat down with them and talked about old times.

Did Stella remember the flat on the eighteenth floor?

Stella remembered.

They'd had some good times there, hadn't they?

Stella laughed.

Life had been far from easy, but they'd muddled through.

Stella agreed that life had been far from easy.

Tina recalled Stella at the kitchen table with her homework; Stella out on the walkway with a book.

Stella recalled the slap, the book turning and floating, its pages riffling in a breeze of its own making.

On the tray was a plate of the tea cakes Stella had liked as a child, thin chocolate covering marshmallow with a biscuit base. She stared at them. Her hands trembled.

Tina explained that Ricardo was a businessman. A man in business. People trusted him, she said. The essence of good business practice was to be trustworthy. To be the kind of man people remembered as reliable. Ricardo nodded along to this. He echoed the odd word for emphasis: "Good business, yeah . . . Reliable, yeah . . ."

Tina remarked how good it was to be back after all this time. How sad it was that they had to leave, but . . . that's life. Ricardo's business came first, and they had to get away. It seemed an odd thing to say: We have to get away.

Stella took a tea cake and bit into it. A flood of memories washed over her. Memories like a shock wave, like drowning. The periphery of the room grew dim and cloudy, an old photograph, and her mother's voice came from a place as far away as childhood.

She went to the bathroom and rinsed her face. Then she retched into the sink. A cry came from somewhere, and she thought the voice might be hers, until it came again, urgent and pained, from some other flat, some other life.

Stella set her mobile phone alarm clock to ring in five minutes, and laughed out loud at the cowardice that took. When she went back into the room, Tina was still talking and Ricardo was still smiling.

The alarm rang and she took a fake call. On the way out she shook Ricardo's hand again, damp and soft; she took her mother's kiss on the face, unflinching; she noticed the piles of homemade DVDs in the hallway—CAGE FIGHTS UNCENSORED; she remembered the splash of blood on the doorstep when she had called that day and got no answer.

On the walkway, heading for the stairs, she passed a man she recognized, someone from the old days. She only knew his nickname, Sekker, and why people called him that. She turned a corner, then turned back to see him ringing the bell of 1169, Block B.

Now she remembered something in the area reports: that a man had been found with his hands nailed to the arms of a chair, his thumbs neatly clipped off, a clean cut through the bone. A call from a pay phone had sent the local cops to the address. She remembered Ricardo's damp handshake and his pinned-on smile, her mother's nervous chatter, the fond farewell.

Sekker at the door.

We have to get away.

60

The day was warming up.

Two drivers went nose to nose in a side street north of Notting Hill. They flashed their lights, they leaned on their horns, they got out and hammered away at each other, their cars ticking over. Ripe scents of blood and diesel fumes.

A man walked into a convenience store and showed the owner a gun. He yelled instructions, but the owner was too scared to understand, so the gunman tagged him with a shot that took him in the belly, left-side low. Piss and cordite.

A woman walking her dog on the towpath was raped by two men who laughed at the dog as it stood a few feet off, barking rhythmically. River mud and hawthorn blossom.

The boys in the Beamer were cruising enemy territory, the first drugs of the day seeping through. A car they recognized was coming the other way: a tuned Toyota with smoked glass and a fuck-off sound system. As it floated toward them, the boy with the Brocock leaned out and waggled the gun.

The Toyota was impassive behind its black, blank windows. The Toyota was cool. The Toyota, it seemed, didn't give a shit.

The Beamer boy took loose aim and pulled off a quick shot that went through the Toyota's bodywork with a flat *thap!* followed by a high-pitched ring.

The Toyota pulled over and stopped. The Beamer weaved and laid some rubber. Shouts and laughter.

Delaney was sitting in a bar near the House of Commons drinking a lunchtime beer with a man he had once punched in the mouth. It was a while ago. He and Nathan Prior had been stopped on a country road by a couple of

Serb checkpoint guards who had started the day on Slivovitz and were looking for some action. Being a checkpoint guard isn't glamorous; in fact, it's de-
meaning; and in a long day's checkpoint guard duty, the most fun you can
have is shooting a bastard journalist, especially if you're getting bad press in
the bastard journalist's country of origin.

Delaney had seen it coming. When they were ordered out of the car and
he saw one of the farm boys in uniform unsling his gun, he started ranting
at Prior as if the scab had just come off an old argument. Prior understood;
he ranted right back. The guards stood off and laughed, but it was still
fifty-fifty until Delaney threw the punch. Prior's lip split, and he sat down
heavily. Delaney got back into the car and drove off, Prior running behind,
the guards laughing harder and longer now. In some obscure way, honor
was satisfied.

Delaney had stopped fifty yards down the road. When Prior got into the
car, he said: "Next time, it'll be my turn to save your life," and spat blood
onto the floor of the car.

While Prior went to the bar, Delaney watched the traffic of journos and
spin doctors, turncoats and lobby fodder. The bar was called the Agenda,
so clearly the owner had a sense of humor. Prior came back with their
drinks and sat with his back to the room, as if declaring himself temporar-
ily off the case.

He said, "So far as I know, Neil Morgan's pretty straight. Why do you
want to know?"

"It's nothing hot."

"Is there a story?" Prior asked.

"I don't think so," Delaney said, "but if I find one, it's yours."

Prior believed him. He knew that Delaney had never had a taste for the
backstabbing and smoking guns of politics.

"You're just curious about Neil Morgan but for no particular reason?"
Prior laughed as he asked the question.

"Pretend it's that."

Prior shrugged. "He's considered a coming man, of course; he's ambitious; he's got a raft of directorships, nothing new there; it's rumored that
he's got an offshore bank account; nothing much new there either. He's
thought of as a bit of a dilettante by some of his own people. You know—
party politics as insider's game. Which probably means he's in line to be
party leader: he's not issue-led."

"No?"

"Well, only when it pays to make the right noises: hard line on the war,
soft on Europe, tough on crime, liberal-right, looks for specific advantage

in domestic issues. They all need a cause, and he seems to have decided on social justice, which has the dual advantage of sounding virtuous and being largely meaningless."

"The offshore bank account," Delaney said. "Suspect money?"

"Could be, I suppose. Why?"

Delaney took a small risk. "He might have had clandestine meetings with an American company, name and nature of business unknown."

"Really?" Prior's interest sparked. "Well, could be anything. The Americans are all over us just at the moment; they're using the WTO as a can opener: closing down fair-trade organizations, promoting GM foods, you name it. The multinationals have more lobbyists in the WTO corridors than dogs have fleas. You think Morgan's getting his hands dirty?"

"I don't know," Delaney said. "I'm whistling in the dark."

"Is it personal?" Prior asked. "You're obviously not coming at this from a professional point of view, are you?"

"No. I mean, no, it's not personal."

"I'll tell you one thing," Prior said. "He's fucking rich."

Delaney laughed. "Yes. That much I do know."

Gideon Woolf was prepping. He didn't think of it that way, but it's what he was doing. He'd already decided on his killing ground, and he'd devised a method. A tactic. Now he was sitting cross-legged in his room, eyes closed, running through the event in his head. As if he could see it on a screen.

You observe and you plan. You watch and you wait. You have a couple of dry runs in the hope that they will alert you to the unexpected, though, if things go wrong on the day, you just have to take your chances. Your only advantage—*big* advantage—is that you're the one with the nasty surprise. You're the one to fear.

The dailies from the last week were piled on the floor. He was headline news, he was famous, he was the subject of a dozen theories, twenty profiles, fifty feature articles. None came anywhere near the truth; none knew his purpose. A few days back he had gone to the gym and alternated weights with aerobics for two hours without a break. In the cafeteria, afterward, he'd sat with his freshly squeezed juice and listened to a couple of fair-weather workouts at a nearby table swap ideas about him, and he had barely kept from laughing out loud.

He was everywhere. Everyone knew about him. Simply walking down a street was an act of pride, and in honor of his new status, he had decided to award himself a decoration. He couldn't have risked going to a tattoo parlor, so he had sat with a needle and Indian ink and given himself a small jailhouse tattoo on the inside of his left forearm. He'd used Drysol to stanch the bleeding and rubbing alcohol to clean the site. It looked good. It looked just like the one Silent Wolf carried in the same place.

He put on the combat pants and the high-laced boots. The broad-bladed knife went into his boot, the SIG Sauer in the square, snap-down pocket of the pants. The long, black leather coat hid the haft of the knife. He put a touch of gel to his hair and combed it back off his forehead so it hung straight and heavy to the nape of his neck. He put a small, palm-sized reel of gardening wire into his coat pocket, then picked up an A–Z from the table and took a last look. Know your ground; know the terrain.

Propped upon the table was a photo-booth four-frame picture of Aimée. They had passed a pharmacy on the walk from the Park Clinic to her flat, and she had pulled him in and thumbed coins and sat on the adjustable stool, smiling at her own reflection. Two of the snaps were against a white background and the flash had been too fierce, her face smudged white, her smile almost lost. She had pulled the blue curtain across for the remaining two, and they showed better the fact that she was pretty, that her soft brown hair could use a color-lift and a good cut, that she wore a touch too much lipstick, that there were care lines over the bridge of her nose. She was smiling hugely; smiling like a woman who, after a long time, has just remembered how it's done.

The computer carried a screen-saver image of Silent Wolf: it was the logo that announced a new game. He stood on a rooftop, looking out over the city, the skirts of his long coat belling and curling, his hair streaming in the wind.

Gideon Woolf went to the window and looked down. A tremor ran through his body, and for a moment, he leaned his forehead against the glass, letting the adrenaline surge.

If only he had known, before, that it would be this easy.

61

A bright day, but he walked in the sharp-edged shadows, he walked on the blind side. He used alleyways and side streets. The map in his head enabled him to steer clear of diversions and dead ends. It took him an hour and a half, because he wouldn't hop buses or ride the tube. If you sit still, people notice you.

He'd left time; his timing was good. In a matter like this, you worked off habit: you relied on the fact that people do pretty much the same things every day—travel, work, take a break, work, travel. Day after day, month after month, year after year, life is repetitious, then it ends. Woolf had been watching a certain man's life patterns for a couple of weeks, and they didn't vary. This man's timetable could be interrupted only by illness or death.

Woolf had paced himself to reach the street just on time: a quiet street that led to nowhere in particular. The windows of the small terraced houses reflected the sun. An old Volvo estate wagon was parked outside the fifteenth house on the west side of the road. Woolf walked past the car and checked his watch. He reckoned a minute, two at the most. At the end of the street he turned back and saw the man locking the door of his house, then turning and blipping the central locking on his car.

When he got in, Woolf got in too, though the man wasn't sure, at first, quite what had happened: some sudden weight or movement in the back, as if someone had nudged the car or pushed against it. He looked into the driver's mirror, half expecting to see a vehicle trying to pull out with too-little room, but there was nothing of that sort. He started the car and looked again in the mirror, and Woolf's face came into view.

The man gasped; his heart lurched. He turned and began to speak, then fell silent when Woolf showed him the SIG Sauer. The man started to pant as if he'd been running; his hands moved in front of his face, little half-formed defensive gestures. He looked up and down the street, but it was empty.

Woolf said, "Drive the car."

"Where to?"

"The usual place. The place you usually go to."

The man stared at Woolf, the fog of fear lifting a moment.

Woolf said, "Drive the car."

"My God," the man said.

"Drive the car."

"My God, are you who I think you are?"

Aimée watched as her husband, Peter, and her son, Ben, got ready for the game. Ben was said to be a safe pair of hands. Peter's role was to stand on the touchline and cheer. They were having a good-natured disagreement about Ben's new goal-keeping gloves, which Peter thought too large. Ben, of course, was eager to wear them. Peter gave in easily, as he always did: not because he thought he was wrong, but because he knew that, in the end, it didn't matter. It was the same in all things. He would smile and nod and agree, because conflict over such issues was a waste of time and created bad feeling. Peter was in favor of good feeling. In favor of feeling good. When they made love, Aimée felt that the need was all hers, the giving all his.

After they'd gone, she went upstairs and lay on the bed. She hoped to sleep, but sleep wouldn't come. It was hot in the room, and she took her clothes off. Being naked made her think about Woolf. She walked round the room, feeling the air on her body, feeling the way her body moved when it was unconstrained.

She lay on the bed and closed her eyes, imagining him there with her. She wet her finger with her mouth, then rolled over, her hand between her thighs. She could feel him alongside. She knelt up, head on the pillow, her hand busy, offering herself to him, feeling a flush come to her throat. She said his name out loud and shivered, as if she had felt his touch, felt him moving up behind her.

It was over too soon. She lay flat out and tried to think things through. Peter would do whatever was for the best. She would see Ben often, of course. Maybe he would even come to live with them: with herself and Woolf. It would be easy, an easy transition to make.

She slept, after a while, and had dreams that were forgotten on waking.

A side road led up to a rise in the ground; the rise fell away to a large field. Woolf drove the old Volvo up to the crest and looked down, then backed off twenty feet to where some tall shrubbery bordered a wall. Beyond the wall was a disused hospital, its windows boarded up, its brickwork covered in graffiti from the ground to a height of about eight feet, which was as far as the local pre-teens could reach.

Before driving to the field, Woolf had spent some time in the old hospital together with the other man, the pair of them there in the half-light, the dim, echoing corridors, the empty wards. There was still some equipment lying about: a gurney or two, a wheelchair, half a dozen beds. Woolf had found a small room, what had once been a side ward, perhaps. It was on the western side, and the planks that boarded the windows weren't butted up that well. Lines of hard, white light fell in straight rows on the floor.

The man had said, "What do you want? What can you possibly want with me after all this time?"

Stella was taking her one-in-seven, her rest day. Delaney was covering the last two from his Rich List: a captain of industry who never slept and a self-made man who had recently acquired a knighthood and insisted on being addressed by his title. The man's given name was Naim, and Delaney had taken delight, throughout the interview, in calling him Sirnaim. He returned to the flat to find Stella constructing a temporary white-board on one wall, complete with scene-of-crime shots, abstracts of interviews, flow charts, and a progress checker. The SOC photos brought back memories for Delaney: a street after sniper activity, stillness and blood; echoes of violence ringing in the air.

He said, "Isn't that a little obsessive?"

"I *am* obsessed. We're getting nowhere with this. Random killings; it's the worst thing. Except nothing's random, really. There's a pattern, even if it's only in the mind of the killer. If I look long enough at the parts, I might catch a glimpse of the whole."

She was adding wild cards to the known facts, a technique of her own devising. It involved swooping arrows drawn onto spreadsheets. One concerned the possible confusion between Leonard Pigeon and Neil Morgan.

Delaney saw the name and said, "An offshore bank account—maybe. It's all I could get."

Stella looked baffled for a moment. Then: "Oh, sure, secret money, big surprise." Out of nowhere, she said, "I went to see my mother."

Delaney stopped in the act of uncapping a beer. Stella had her back to him, busy with the white-board. He poured the beer, waiting for more, but nothing came. Finally, he asked, "Why did you tell me?"

"I had to tell someone."

She drew an arrow that looped down from Bryony Dean to Len Pigeon, another that looped up from Martin Turner to Bryony: death's dark connections. A skeleton map pinpointed locations and a line connected them: death's geography.

She worked systematically, annotating the board with dates, times, and circumstances, as if there might be a hidden link. Delaney drank his beer. He knew she was crying.

There was activity down on the field, but none where Woolf had parked the car, a no-man's-land between the road and the field, sunless, the patch between the bushes and the wall strewn with cans and cigarette packets. He could hear distant voices and birdsong and a plane banking to find the Heathrow approach. He opened the driver's door, then unloaded the boot. It wasn't hard work and it didn't take long. He drove the car to the top of the rise and just a fraction farther, then applied the hand brake but left the engine running while he set things up. Then he went to the passenger's side, opened the door, leaned in, and released the hand brake.

The car went over the rise and out of sight. Woolf walked away without looking back, not hurrying, making for a nearby high street, the weekend shoppers, the anonymity of crowds. There was a tiny freckling of blood on his cheek, but only someone close enough to kiss would have found it.

No one saw the Volvo coming until it was fifty feet away. Parents screamed, kids ran in all directions. The car went through at speed, missing everything and everyone, until it ran into a play area on the far side, plowing through swings and sideswiping a little wooden carousel before taking a climbing-frame full on, the engine racing for a moment, then cutting out. One of the first people to reach it was Peter the top-notch husband. He yanked open the driver's door, then stared. He just stared. Other people arrived, and they stared too. After a moment Ben arrived at his father's side and peered in through the open door.

It was a terrible accident, Ben could see that, though his father pulled him away before he could tell exactly what had happened to the driver. Peter had seen more. A man in the driver's seat, his hands wired to the steering wheel. The neck stump. The head on the passenger seat, wired in place.

What he hadn't seen was the neatly inked words across the brow of the decapitated head:

HAPPY NOW?

62

They taped off the entire field, and when Andy Greegan spotted the divot of turf the Volvo had kicked up as it went over the rise, they tracked back and found tire prints in ground that was still soft from the storm, so they taped the bushes and the wall as well.

The SOC tent covered the car and body, intact and unmoved. Fly swarm was a major problem, but there was nothing to be done: chemical sprays would have contaminated the site. The photographers had to hunker down to get shots of the head in situ. The garden wire that held it in place had cut a furrow into the forehead; a second strand went across the mouth, leaving it open in a tortured, noiseless cry. There was something bizarre about the headless torso: its rigid back, the wrists wired to the wheel in the approved ten-to-two position. Lacking a face, it seemed utilitarian: a damaged crash dummy. Only the dark red, meaty neck stump and the protruding stub of neck bone pronounced it once human.

Peter and Ben told what they could. They were questioned separately, Maxine Hewitt sitting down with the boy, Sue Chapman as backup. Pete Harriman and Frank Silano sat down with Peter. They told much the same story, except that Peter had more to tell, having had the longer look. Neither Maxine nor Harriman spent much time over the interviews. They had fifty other people to talk to.

Stella was in with Collier, who had been fielding seamlessly joined telephone calls. In order to be able to talk to her, he'd taken the phone off the hook, and its Klaxon was wailing at him.

He said, "I don't know what the fuck to do." Stella said nothing. Collier reached round, took his jacket off the back of his chair, and threw it over the phone. "Do you?" He looked at her as if she were holding out on him. "How do we nail this bastard?"

"It's the toughest crime to solve, you know that."

"I'm getting it from all directions. The press. The SIO . . ." He lit a cigarette, cupping one hand round the lighter as if he were standing in a wind.

A man who can see the end of his tether, Stella thought. To her surprise, she almost felt sorry for him: out of his depth and signaling wildly for help.

He said, "Sometimes they just don't get caught, do they? Serials. Sometimes they just stop, and that's an end to it."

"Often," Stella observed.

"Yes, often."

"Or they make a mistake." She shrugged. "Dennis Nilsen's drains. Peter Sutcliffe's false license plates."

"This guy's not making mistakes."

Stella said, "Or else he's already made one, and we haven't noticed."

The squad-room detritus covered desks and spilled from bins. Sue Chapman informed everyone that the cleaners were on strike for better conditions. It wasn't clear what sort of conditions those were, though Pete Harriman offered the opinion that they might want things to be altogether . . . well . . . *cleaner*. Sue had brought in some black bin bags.

Silano had pinned the new scene-of-crime shots to the white-board and used a magenta marker to fill in the stats. This time Stella was running the session. Collier stood a little to one side, trying to look as if he might have something to say later.

"Victim," Stella said, "George Nelms. Sixty-one, retired schoolteacher, widowed, lived alone, no police record, no bad habits that we know of, not that we expected to find any. Mr. Average. He lived quietly, he was liked by his neighbors. He employed someone to cook and clean for him. At weekends he was a volunteer helper at Green Lane Fields sports facility. He was killed by a single transverse cut to the throat. I haven't got the postmortem findings yet, but when I have them, they'll be circulated. His head was severed from his body: you'll have had all the details from the crime report by e-mail.

"There seems little doubt that this is the fourth in a series of apparently motiveless murders: the writing on the victim's forehead indicates as much." She stopped as if the bald facts were all she had to offer—which was pretty much the case. "We'll just have to proceed with this as we have with the other deaths. Talk to your contacts, just in case something's trickled down to street level. We're putting a yellow-board up by the sports field.

It'll carry Crimestoppers' number and our number"—she shrugged—"who knows?

"We're giving the press everything except the writing: so, the make, year, and number of the Volvo, the place, the exact time, victim ID, and the fact that he was decapitated. We've also said that we consider Nelms to be the most recent victim of a serial killer. This means that we'll have a press feeding frenzy to cope with, no question, and high levels of criticism, and more than the usual nutters phoning in to confess, but we've reached the stage where saturation looks like the only option. Anyway, it would be pointless to pretend. The press have been screaming 'serial' for a week or more. Okay . . . any ideas?"

The floor fan in the corner ticked. Someone's phone played its message tune. An ARV pulled out of Notting Dene, its siren picking up.

The AMIP-5 squad room declared itself an ideas-free zone.

63

Monica Hartley sat in an upright chair, her hands folded in her lap. She had applied a dab of lipstick for the occasion. A dab of lipstick, a blouse with a frill, her outdoor shoes. She said, "I went in every other day. On the days I went in, I made enough for the next day. He didn't mind eating the same thing twice, he wasn't fussy like that. They say his head was cut off. They say it was in the papers. He was in the car, but his head was off. Is it true?"

Stella said it was true.

Monica said, "I cleaned for him as well. I did two hours' cleaning and tidying and an hour cooking. I did three hours every other weekday. Does anyone know who'll get the house?"

Stella said she had no idea.

Monica said, "I think there are relatives. His wife died five years back, but I think there are relatives. I think he had cousins. First or second cousins. Where was his head, then? Where did that turn up?"

Harriman coughed, or else it was a smothered laugh. Stella said that George Nelms's head had been found in the car.

"He had his routines, you know? He was regular in his habits. I can't think that anyone disliked him. I never saw anyone go to the house. I went regular, but I never saw anyone else. He helped out at the sports ground weekends. He was a teacher before he retired. He was history and sports, I think. The thing about the house, the reason I mentioned the house, I'm wondering if he left any sort of a will."

Stella said she didn't know.

"The reason I mention a will is because I wonder about what happens if he didn't. If there isn't a will to be had. I wonder about what sort of claim I could make."

Stella wondered too. She asked about the nature of the claim Monica had in mind.

"Common-law wife," Monica explained. "I just wonder whether that gives me a right. I think it does. More than a cousin, you might say. More than a second cousin. Common *law*, isn't it? That's how it seems to me, because I used to give him sex. After his wife died, not before. I used to go in every other day, and it was what he wanted, he told me straight out. So giving him sex, giving him sex over five years, that's common-law wife in my book. Cleaning and cooking and giving sex, they're all wifely duties, no one could say any different, so who do I talk to about that?"

Harriman was looking at the floor and biting his lip. Stella said she had no advice to offer on the subject.

Monica showed them to the door. She said, "I liked him, but he never had much to say for himself."

Harriman pulled out into a box junction and sat on the grid listening to a chorus of horns.

He said, "Is that right? Is she right about that?"

"Definitely," Stella said. "A man gets laid, he loses sole ownership of his house. It's as it should be."

When the message tone had gone off during Stella's briefing, it had been a text to Harriman from Gloria: *Last night? Best fuck in history.*

"I've had a thought," Harriman told her. "I wonder whether he meant to decapitate Leonard Pigeon. The incision went right to the neck bone, I remember that."

"And he was interrupted, you think?"

"It was on the towpath, there must have been people about."

"But no one saw him."

"Maybe it was all taking too long. He panicked."

"He doesn't strike me as a panicker."

"Okay, not panicked. Just didn't have the time. What did the crime-scene analysis tell us?"

"About what?"

"About how he left the scene?"

"Behind the bench there are bushes, beyond the bushes an iron fence, then a ditch, a field, a road. That seems to have been his route."

"Right. He didn't have to walk along the towpath to get away. So maybe he did see someone coming."

"Okay, maybe. But he hanged Bryony Dean, and he shot Martin Turner."

"So is there some sort of pattern to that? A hanging, a shooting, a decapitation."

"Meaning that's what he intended, and he cut Nelms's head off because first time round, with Leonard Pigeon, it didn't go right."

"That's what I'm saying, yes."

Stella nodded. "And the pattern, if it is a pattern, tells you what?"

"No, I didn't say I had a theory about what the pattern might mean. Just a theory about the pattern."

"If it is a theory."

"Yes."

"Big step forward," Stella said.

They drove in silence for a while, Harriman shooting amber lights and overtaking on the inside. He said, "That's common law? One fuck and you're out on the street?"

Candice Morgan looked out of the window at the midrange Honda illegally parked across the driveway. She said, "Is that actually a police car, or are they trying to be undercover?"

Neil Morgan was speed-reading the press, the semiliterate tabloids and all the broadsheets, scanning them for a mention of himself. He had a secretary and a cuttings agency who also did this, but he liked to be ahead of the sort of backstabbing name-check some journalists favored. He said, "Our security services are cash-strapped. I made a speech on the subject last week."

Candice's suitcases stood in the hallway. She said, "Perhaps I shouldn't go."

"Why not?"

"If they're right. If he really meant to kill you, not Len."

Candice and the girls took a break twice a year: Paris, New York, Rome. A break from husbands and the round of tennis, lunch, gym, charity work. This time it was Madrid.

Morgan smiled. "Candice, I have visible police protection. I'm not sure what you think you might usefully add to that. Go. Have a good time. Bring me something back."

She said, "They just sit out there with their coffee and cigarettes. I could be in here chopping your head off with a meat cleaver."

"You wouldn't know where to find it."

"It's in the kitchen."

"My point exactly."

They were the sort of jokes any couple might make, though there was a drop of acid in the tone, a chip of ice in the look. Morgan's mobile rang, and he glanced at the LCD display, then let it ring.

"You're avoiding someone," Candice observed.

"A business call." He realized that sounded odd, so he added: "Unimportant business."

Candice was wearing a robe, though she was fully made-up. She had fine features and an aristocratically long face that looked better with nothing but a light tan, but she was too aware of the faint lines by her eyes and the corners of her mouth. The lapel of the robe had fallen to one side, revealing the globe of her breast, and Morgan glanced at it reflexively.

She said, "It'll be good to get away from London for a few days."

A limo was double-parked alongside the Honda. The driver, carrying Candice's suitcases, came down the steps from Morgan's house.

Candice looked into the sitting room on her way out and said good-bye. Morgan was taking a call on his mobile. He blew her a kiss. After the front door closed, he said, "Look, I did what I could. These guys seem to think I've got the say-so on this. Not true. I know people who have, but that's a different matter."

Bowman said, "They paid you."

"To do a job. I've mentioned their name. I've mentioned it several times. What more do they expect?"

"When you met with them, you were more positive, that's what I hear. That's their recollection."

"When I met them . . ." Morgan hesitated. "Things were a little different. You know how it is in politics."

"Not really."

Morgan tried to muddy the issue. "People move on, people who might have been useful, you have to take time to develop new allies."

It was a brand of bullshit Bowman had slipped up in before. He said, "Maybe I'd better come and see you."

"That wouldn't be helpful."

"We could talk this through."

"I don't think so," Morgan said. "I'm caught up in other things just now."

"The Americans are eager that we sort something out. They think it ought to be possible to formulate some sort of ongoing strategy."

"Really?" said Morgan. "The Americans think that? Look, tell the Americans to go fuck themselves."

He flipped the phone shut. It was a confident gesture, but it didn't reflect the way he felt. He opened the phone and made a call. He said, "She's gone to Madrid." Then, "No, not tonight. There's someone I have to see."

Abigail said, "Oh, well . . . Sure. Okay."

It was disappointment masquerading as indifference.

Morgan said, "I want to see you, of course. It's something I wasn't expecting. Something I ought to take care of."

Abigail picked up on the note of anxiety in his voice. "Are you all right, Neil?"

"Fine. Look, tomorrow, okay? Tomorrow, for sure."

"Yes." A pause, then she said, "I'll be here." As if it had ever been in doubt.

He made a few calls, answered a few letters, tried to settle in his study with some committee reports, but the words ran on the page. He wandered round the house. He made coffee he forgot to drink.

Finally, he called Bowman back. "Okay, let's meet. If you're worried, if the Americans are worried . . . Here's the problem: I'm under police protection. It's a precaution." He offered no explanation, so Bowman assumed terrorism. "So far as I know, they photograph anyone who calls at the house. You don't want that."

"No? Why not? We could be meeting for any number of reasons." Bowman laughed. "Offshore-investment packages, perhaps."

"I don't want it."

"Ah, well . . . that's a different issue."

"I'll try to lose them. Meet you somewhere . . ." Morgan considered for a moment, then gave Abigail's address. "Sometime after dark. So: ten o'clock?"

Bowman said, "If I get there first?"

"Someone will let you in."

"Okay," Bowman said. Then: "Is she pretty?"

Morgan called Abigail. He said, "I'll be there at ten, okay?"

"Sure." She sounded pleased. "What changed?"

"The person I have to see? We're meeting at your place. Ten o'clock."

"Okay."

"Just a brief meeting."

"Okay."

"A private meeting."

"I'll watch TV in the bedroom."

"It means I can see you after all." As if he'd arranged things to that end, as if he'd been beating his brain to think of a way.

"Yes," she said brightly. "Two birds with one stone."

People were walking their dogs in Norland Square Gardens. Woolf walked the same circuit, a man taking some exercise, a man lost in thought. Each time he passed Neil Morgan's house, he glanced toward it. He saw the Honda and knew what it meant; he saw Candice leaving for Madrid; he saw that it would be impossible to kill Morgan there, in his own house, then transport the body to some public place where all could see it. But not impossible to kill him, perhaps.

He walked head down, his nails digging into his palms. It ought to be over, but he'd made a mistake. He'd been led astray. Not the house by the river, *this* house. Not that other man, *this* man. They had been fooling someone, and they'd fooled him too. In following the car, he thought he was following the man. The meeting at the hotel, Woolf watching the man being greeted by two Americans. The house by the river—Woolf watching the man as he dismissed his driver and went indoors. Woolf seeing the night out, waking with the sun, watching as the man reemerged to take a walk by the river.

Woolf tried to remember whether the other man had looked quite so much like Morgan. He thought he had; thought he must have done. But close up? He couldn't be sure. He'd marked the man, he'd been sure of his target, he'd locked on. After that, he hadn't looked too closely.

He left the gardens, going out as he'd gone in: behind a resident with a key to the gate. In the street that ran parallel to Morgan's he found a house that was being renovated. The place had been gutted. People in that neighborhood could afford to buy a house for a million or more, then spend as much again to have things just as they wanted them. Scaffolding rose from the basement area to the roof.

Woolf counted down from the end of the street. The house was three doors from Morgan's. A sign on the scaffolding warned that it carried an alarm system.

He would wait a day or two, think things through, look at patterns. He'd seen Candice's luggage being loaded into the boot of the limo: cases, not overnight bags. Morgan would be on his own in the place for a few days, that was obvious.

Wait a day. Look at patterns. Know your terrain, your killing ground.

64

The lights were hot, but the morgue, as ever, was cool. Stella recognized the music, but couldn't identify it. A boy soprano, sweet and pure.

Sam said, "You have to get through the trachea and the thyroid cartilage. Muscle's not that easy to sever, though a strong man with a sharp knife would do the job quite quickly. He'd already have gone through the carotid sheath—through the artery and the jugular vein. Most likely, he would stand behind his victim, make the man kneel down, that way he could pull the head back by the hair and lift at the same time to expose the throat and make it taut." Sam's voice was flat and neutral. "After that, he would definitely encounter some difficulty."

"How much difficulty?"

"To decapitate his victim, he'd have to get between the cervical vertebrae—between the atlas and the axis in this case. Hacking away wouldn't do it. Well"—Sam shrugged—"no, it would eventually, of course, but you'd need time."

"Did this man hack?"

"No. He found the gap. Or, rather, he created it. He would have manipulated the head, held it two-handed and rocked it to and fro, while, at the same time, pulling upward to open a gap, maybe even partially dislocating the neck. That way, he would only be cutting connective tissue."

"He knew what he was doing."

"Possibly. Though it's easy enough to work out if you think about it."

"Yes? Who would think about it?"

George Nelms's body had been reduced to its constituents, exposed and emptied out, stripped down like a machine, but Stella still thought it looked odd without its head.

"What I *am* saying," Sam told her, "is he would have needed time."

Aimée said, "It won't be long. I won't be gone for long."

Peter was working at his computer. He said, "We'll be fine."

"Just overnight."

"It's your mother," Peter said. "Of course you must go."

Aimée's time out had been arranged before the incident at the sports field, before Ben's nightmares. She didn't know what to do. She stood in the room, dressed for work, knowing that passion would certainly overcome guilt.

"I could call in after work; before I go to—"

"I'm writing it down," Peter said. He looked up from his two-finger typing. "I thought if I wrote down what happened, I might somehow make better sense of it."

"How can you make sense of a thing like that?"

"No . . . It's like . . . it's the same as telling someone about it."

"You've told me. You've told the police."

"Writing it down is different, Aimée."

"How?"

She noticed that his hands, poised above the keyboard, were trembling slightly. He said, "I can go back to it. I can go back over it. I can change things, make it more accurate. Not details the police would want, details for me." He paused; his voice became a whisper. "Like the smell. Like the way the head looked. The face . . ."

Aimée said, "Look, I could stay, of course I could." But she knew she wouldn't.

Yellow-board feedback is random and time-consuming. You get time-wasters and glory-seekers; you get people who are simply confused; you get people who were in the right place at the wrong time. Sometimes, though, you get a piece of information that's right on the money.

A woman walking her dog had seen the Volvo parked in the grounds of the old hospital. Sue Chapman had taken the call and, yes, the woman was certain of the day and, yes, the time was right and, yes, it was a Volvo.

Stella went in the same way Woolf and George Nelms had gone in: through the front door. It had once been padlocked against vagrants and vandals, but someone had kicked the lock off long ago.

She didn't have to search. The smell told her where to go: that, and the sound, much like a distant engine: the sound of flies. Andy Greegan paced her, setting up a line of approach. They were both wearing forensic coveralls, hoods up, shoes enclosed in blue plastic wraps that were taped above the ankle, a dab of decongestant gel on their upper lip.

They reached the room, the side ward, and stood in the doorway. Greegan said, "Jesus Christ." Then he said, "Okay, I'll bring them up." He speed-dialed on his phone, but was already walking back to supervise the forensic team as they came on-site.

Blood on the walls, on the floor, on the window boards. It had puddled and soaked in. It had made long, looping patterns on the walls, thick parabolas, cascades of dribbles and droplets, a splatter painting, an abstract masterpiece.

It wasn't difficult to find it, sketched on the window boards in blood. Of course, in blood.

∧ ∧
∨

The place had been used by tramps, by lovers, by addicts. There were a couple of mattresses thrown down, tattered and stained. There were cans and condoms and syringes and feces. It was a bedroom, a lavatory, a shag pad, an abattoir. Stella closed her eyes. She could hear cries echoing in the room. A hospital. How many deaths in this place? How many lives ebbing away while relatives sat in an outer room, fearing and hoping?

And now this new death. She imagined George Nelms, down on his knees amid this foul detritus, his head yanked back, the blade at his throat. She wondered what he could possibly have done to make his killer certain that he deserved to die like that.

The forensic team arrived with their boxes and bags of gadgets. They'd seen worse.

Aimée laid him down and undressed him. She took him into her mouth. She straddled him and lowered herself, so she could look down at his face. When he reached up and touched her, a shudder ran on her flanks and a blush came to her throat.

She knew she was in love. She told him so, and he smiled at her.

They cooked a meal together, just as she had hoped they might. He was a great commis chef, chopping and stirring. He made some salad dressing to her instruction. He poured two glasses of white wine. The early summer had colored her skin very faintly, just enough to leave an almost invisible mark where her wedding ring would have been.

She was aware of being happy. The term "lighthearted" came to mind. Lighthearted or light-headed.

London streets are never quiet, never dark. The thin curtains were backed by a streetlamp's reddish glow that leached into the room and made fire patterns on the walls. Gideon Woolf lay propped on one elbow, watching Aimée's face as she slept. This business of sleep after sex was new to him; this business of waking next to her in the morning.

She was lying faceup, and the sheet was down past her waist, revealing the slight, soft swell to her belly; one breast lolled against her upper arm. She gave a little sigh, then bit her own lip, gently, and turned toward him. He felt a rush of tenderness, though he didn't know its name.

He told himself that he was with her because it was safer that way. With her so, he could control things. With her so, he could kill her.

And so he was.

65

The windows of Anne Beaumont's consulting room overlooked the park. Stella was sitting in the clients' chair, even though she no longer saw Anne for that reason. Her nightmares were still with her—the children hanging from the banister, her own child lost to her when it was barely formed—but she knew analysis was a journey and it was a journey she didn't want to take.

Anne came into the room with two glasses of wine. She said, "You sit in that chair looking out at the view, and what do you see? All the old problems."

Stella laughed. "Are you a shrink or a mind reader?"

"Same thing." Anne put down the wine and picked up a report file on the George Nelms killing. "This man," she said, "has something to prove. He displays his victims. He wants them to be seen. He takes risks by doing that: the girl in the tree, the man on the towpath . . . He could have left Martin Turner's body out of sight by the trees in his garden, but he lifted the body out and roped it to the gate. Now he kills this man, Nelms, in a deserted building; takes him there to get the job done; but then puts him in the car and rolls it into the middle of a sports ground."

"He's an exhibitionist," Stella offered.

"He is, yes, but not the kind who takes pride in his work and wants to show it off. And he's not taunting the authorities with it either—I've seen that sort of thing before, and this is different: no self-regarding letters, no threats to do it again, no 'catch me if you can.' This man is accusing his victims—the writings on the bodies—and letting the world at large know what he thinks of them; or trying to, anyway. He's exhibiting them; accusing them; and he wants the world to agree with him."

"This latest one," Stella said. " 'Happy now?' "

"It's different, isn't it? More in sorrow than in anger, perhaps."

"Oh, he was angry, all right. He cut the man's head off."

Anne nodded. "The report suggests that he might have intended to do the same to his second victim."

"It seems possible—the depth of the cut, the possibility that he was interrupted."

"So beheading is an issue."

"But the girl was hanged. Turner was shot. And the victims themselves," Stella said. "Where's the pattern there?"

"A prostitute, a researcher—"

"Possibly the wrong man," Stella reminded her.

"Okay, a prostitute, a politician, a journalist, a retired schoolteacher. Under other circumstances, I'd think they were simply random: that the killer wanted notoriety, needed to kill, took his victims where he could—there have been such cases. In one recently the man admitted that he just wanted to be famous, wanted to *be* a serial killer. But the writings . . . There's a reason for these victims being selected. They have a special significance in our man's life."

"You mean he knew them?"

"Or someone like them."

"We've looked—"

"For possible connections. I'm sure you have. That's the mystery. If this man was common to the lives of all his victims, it's likely you'd have identified him by now. He'd almost certainly be a relative or a friend." Anne took a long sip of wine. "There's some connection, though."

"We've been finding this, had you noticed?" Stella reached over and took the file from Anne, found a series of SOC shots and spread them on the table.

^ ^
V

"A calling card," Anne said. "Yes, I had noticed."

"What do you make of it?"

"In terms of his psychopathology or the thing itself?"

"Both."

"It's the hunter's mark. Trophy-taking in reverse. Some killers of this sort will take a souvenir: a lock of hair, a body part, a photo of the victim alive or dead, or first alive, then dead. Jeffrey Dahmer used to keep the heads in his fridge. This is the same thinking but in reverse: the hunter leaves something of himself at the kill, he records his presence. The same impulse gave rise to cave drawings and handprints: the sign of the prefigured kill."

"The what?"

"If you first draw your mastodon, then put your hand-mark beside it, you've already killed it in some future encounter. He's representing himself by this symbol: leaving his mark."

"And what is it, do you think?"

"What do *you* think?"

"Female torso?"

Anne peered at the photo. "You mean breasts and pubis?"

"Could be."

"I didn't see it." Anne laughed. "And what does that tell us—"

"A smiley face," Stella said. "These are offers from various police officers. DC Harriman was the tits and fanny man."

"You don't surprise me."

"Two hills and a valley. A Cheshire cat. A dog. A stealth fighter."

"Stealth and fighter being significant words."

"Yes. A clown. A tarot card—the three of swords. Darth Vader. The number sixty-six."

"How?"

"V" is the twenty-second letter of the alphabet. Three times that is sixty-six."

"One six short of the mark of the beast."

"Or you add them and get twelve. Or then add the one and the two and get three."

"Which is a magical number."

"So I'm told."

"Who came up with the numerology?"

"Maxine Hewitt."

"Did she now? Interesting psychology." Anne shrugged. "Could be any of those."

"People are thinking about it in their spare time, of which they have precious little," Stella said. "You're the shrink. I thought you'd crack it, no problem."

"All I can tell you is he wants to be noticed. The mark is authorial: it means 'I dunnit.'"

"Craving attention."

"Exactly."

"He sees himself as a victim, doesn't he?" The thought had come out of nowhere. "These people have offended him in some way." Stella paused. "Or hurt him."

"Maybe. Yes, you could be right." Anne looked at her. "What made you say that?"

"I saw my mother. She came back and we met."

For a few moments, Anne said nothing; then: "How did it feel? I won't charge you."

"She put her arms round me," Stella said. "She *embraced* me." Anne allowed a sneaky, professional silence: a prompt. "She smelled of cheap makeup and booze." Stella paused. "Same as ever . . . She's hooked up with some off-the-peg villain who sells DVDs of cage fights." Another silence. "She kissed me . . ." Stella raised a hand as if to a bruise and touched her cheek. "Just here. She kissed me as if that was the sort of thing . . . you know, the sort of usual . . . *behavior*."

Anne didn't speak. Stella leaned forward slightly in the chair, her head bowed, her hands clasped, like someone holding in a sudden pain. Tears fell straight from her eyes into her lap, salt rain, unquenchable.

Neil Morgan's car was in a residents' parking zone outside the house. The Honda was two car-lengths down. When Morgan got into the driver's seat and turned the key, two engines started simultaneously. He pulled out, watching the lights of the other car loom up in his rearview mirror.

His mobile phone rang. The voice managed to sound both accusatory and polite. It mentioned that Morgan was supposed to inform his security officers of his intended destination. He told them he was on his way to interview a new researcher: late, because the man had been in meetings. They were to meet at Soho House; it was an informal interview.

He drove slowly up Holland Park Avenue, looking for an opportunity to get through a set of lights on amber. He did it twice. Twice the Honda ran the red, staying with him. At Notting Hill Gate he signaled one way and turned another. An Imola-red BMW putting out death-dealing music cut him up and left him stranded. He dropped over the hill toward Kensington and took a couple of unnecessary back doubles. The Honda was with him all the way. He broke the speed limit on the run to Knightsbridge, by which time he was fooling no one. The Honda tailgated him and flicked its lights. He pulled over and got out. The door of the other car opened, but no one appeared for a moment, then a tall man emerged and strolled toward Morgan. He was wearing a boxy leather jacket and jeans, the latest in stakeout fashion. He looked amused. Amused and bored.

"We can't use the siren, sir. We're surveillance. So we just have to break the law, same as you."

Morgan shrugged. He said, "Look, it's a girl. A girl I know . . . you understand?"

"Of course."

"A need to be discreet . . ."

"Naturally."

"I'll be back at about midnight. Midnight or soon after."

"You're asking me to let you go alone. We go back to your house. You visit your friend."

"Is that all right?"

"No, I'm afraid not, sir. It's our job to offer you protection. Not possible to do that unless we're with you."

Morgan shook his head, irritated. "Put it this way, officer—I'm telling you to."

"Put it this way, sir—fuck off."

Morgan got into his car, made an illegal U-turn, and headed home. He overtook when he could, just for the hell of it. On his way up Kensington Church Street he passed a bus, then cut in hard, unsighting his followers, and swung into a side street, emerging at the top of Holland Park Avenue. The smile was still on his face when the Honda cruised up alongside, the man in the leather jacket wearing a smile that was broader than Morgan's and had about it a hint of malice.

Morgan's mobile rang. He let it.

Abigail and Bowman sat in her apartment and watched the clock.

"He'll call," Abigail said.

Bowman nodded. "I expect he will. In fact, that's what I'm waiting for."

"He's sometimes late. Often late. Things happen."

"I'm sure."

She didn't like him: the soft voice, the glint of ice in the eye. He switched on the TV without asking and watched a football match for ten minutes. Without looking at her he said, "Get me a drink, sweetie, will you? Scotch and water would be acceptable."

She brought him the drink and he closed his hand over hers, briefly, before taking the glass. His fingers were dry. He gave her knuckles a little squeeze and she felt a moment's pain. He continued to watch the match, which was winding down to a goalless draw. He sighed, as if that dull result was one more thing to contend with.

When the phone rang, he didn't look up. Abigail answered it, listened, then handed it to Bowman.

Morgan said, "None of this to her. She knows nothing about it—our connection, the police surveillance . . . All right?"

"Where are you?"

"I couldn't shake them. These guys are professionals."

Bowman clicked his tongue. "All this fuss. I'll come to you."

"No."

"I'll come now."

"No, listen, it's too late. They ask me about visitors. This time of night . . . it's nearly eleven. A business meeting doesn't take place this late."

"Mine do."

"Come tomorrow . . . If you must come. Look, why come at all? I know what's needed, I know what they want. I've told you, it can't be done."

"Well, that's why we need a meeting, Neil. We have to talk it through. Ideas going back and forth, time to think, a glass or two . . . Are you in tomorrow?"

"It's pointless."

"Tomorrow."

"I'm not sure. I have meetings. I might not be here."

"I'll come late," Bowman said. His voice was even softer. "Be there." He hung up the phone and walked toward the door, then paused, as if struck by an afterthought. He went to Abigail and put his hand under her chin, squeezing slightly, lifting slightly, enough to give a little pain, enough to bring her up onto her toes.

He said, "Tell him to be there."

66

People waking with people . . .

Pete Harriman opened his eyes and knew he felt happy, but couldn't remember why. Then he remembered Gloria, sleeping next to him, and the happiness was colored by the merest touch of anxiety. Suppose he always felt this way? God knows what that might lead to. He resolved to make a call as soon as he could; he hadn't seen another woman for more than a fortnight. Gloria was becoming a pattern; a fixture.

He went to the kitchen and made coffee, then took it into the bedroom. Gloria was sitting up in bed and looking at him, a smile on her face that made his head swim.

The window partly open, the curtain drifting and sending swathes of sunlight round the walls, a traffic hum from Ladbroke Grove, someone shouting in the street outside.

Aimée watched the movement of light for a while, half asleep, flooded by his warmth. She took his hand and slipped it between her legs. He stirred and turned, eyes opening, then closing again.

She whispered, "I love you," and he nodded, smiling. She shrugged the covers away and reached for him, the breeze cool on her back, the clean line of his limbs, her lips on his, his hands moving, her hands moving, the sunlight on the walls, life going on outside.

She thought she would sacrifice anything for this.

Delaney was sleeping facedown. Stella slid across him, letting her body rest on his a moment, then nipping the skin by his neck with her teeth before moving away. His arm came round to catch her, but she'd gone.

She stood in front of the homemade white-board and tried to find a pattern, as if a mind still fuzzy with sleep might be a better receptor. Shreds of dream came back to her: an encounter with her mother who somehow became Monica Hartley . . . Delaney on the ship again, shouting words into the wind . . . voices echoing in the disused hospital. The white-board's deaths—details of deaths, depictions of deaths—added up to nothing. Separately, they were tragedies; collectively, a riddle.

Delaney appeared and opened the fridge. He said, "My morning starts with orange juice and snapshots of the dead."

"It helps me think."

"And you're thinking of . . . ?"

"Him. The killer. Waking up, drinking orange juice, thinking of dead people, people he's killed."

"People he's going to kill."

"Exactly."

"Got a picture of him? In your head, I mean."

"Oh, yes . . . You wouldn't pick him out in a crowd. Someone like you, someone like me."

The Beamer boys were out cold. They were KO'd. They were in the substrata. A night of booze, dope, and clubbing will do it to you every time. They didn't live together, but they often woke up together after such a night when they'd been too bombed to make a move.

They were in a flat in Kilburn that belonged to a girl who thought of herself as the girlfriend of one of them, and so she was. Nominally. Loosely speaking. More or less. Her name was Toni.

Toni woke up, drank a pint of water, threw up, had a flash-memory of last night's activities, got dressed, and went out to buy the morning-after pill. In Kilburn High Road exhaust gases rose in columns of murky sunlight.

Harriman and Stella met by chance in Coffee Republic: a two-shot Americano for her, an espresso for him. They walked past Notting Dene nick, sipping, Stella doing all the talking.

Harriman said, "I've got a problem."

"A woman."

"Yes."

Stella laughed. "What's new?" Then: "She's pregnant?"

"No."

"She's possessive."

"No."

"So you tell me."

"I think about her when she's not around. I miss her. I'm missing her now."

Stella stopped in her tracks and looked at him. She said, "You're in trouble."

Delaney made himself some eggs he didn't really want. He walked round the apartment as if he were looking for something. He sat at the keyboard and couldn't think of a thing to say. He switched on the TV—war and rumors of war.

He made a phone call. Martin Turner wasn't the only editor he'd worked with.

67

Sekker called early. He had the sun at his back when Tina Mooney answered the door, and she shielded her eyes to see who it was. A bad start to the day. He was carrying a Grolsch six-pack, the dew from the chill cabinet still on it. He looked past Tina to where Ricardo was standing a little farther down the hall.

Entering, he nudged Tina aside. He said, "I expect you've got things to do."

They sat either side of a Formica table in the sunless kitchen and talked things through. Sekker reminded Ricardo of his obligations.

He said, "We don't really need your connections, we don't want to put you out of business. Just this: whoever you're dealing with, whatever you're doing, you're doing it for us. It's a takeover. So we need to see throughput, and we need to see a paper trail. No freelance anymore, okay? Nothing on the side, nothing under the wire, because we'll get to hear about it. You can have the action on Harefield, except anything over a hundred K you hand over to us. Smaller amounts go sixty-forty in our favor. In return for this—and as long as you don't try to deal on the side—you keep your fingers, your nose, and your ears. When can we expect the first payments?"

Ricardo was looking at the table, a small chip in the Formica, a food stain, a loose section of edging. He said, "It takes time. Your man will know. He'll understand. The money has to move."

"Sure. So, when?"

"I haven't got anything running. People have to come to me . . ."

"We know you've been busy, Ricardo, there's no shortage. Jonah was putting work your way, so here's your chance to cut out the middle man. Put yourself about a bit. Talk to the dealers. It's where the money comes from, yeah?" Ricardo nodded. "There's gear being sold on this estate every hour of every fucking day, Ricardo. There's a whassname . . ." Sekker made a gesture: everything in one place.

"Clearinghouse," Ricardo offered.

"Yeah. And the people that run it haven't got a fuck of a lot of leeway. They have to be careful about money. We know that, you know that. They can't walk into Barclays with a bin liner full of used notes, now can they? You probably know that Jonah's out of commission; he's not well. He used to deal through us. Now it's you dealing through us, except we're leaving the arrangements up to you." Sekker smiled and cracked his third can. "Since you're so fucking good at it." He took a long pull. "So all that money—all that *dirty* money—is sitting around the place making people nervous. I don't think you'll have any trouble drumming up a bit of business. Give it a couple of days, yeah? To get something moving. To get something *in train.*"

He stood up, taking his beer with him. Ricardo hadn't touched a drop.

Woolf sat in his operator's chair in the scorched room and played the *Silent Wolf* game. The streets were dark. White lines slashing the screen were rainfall. The Wolf's enemies were shadows flickering in alleyways, in doorways, on rooftops. They came at him, and he killed them.

While he played the game, he heard only rain, saw only shadows. When the last antagonist was dead, Woolf looked up and saw sunlight streaming in through the closed window, refracted onto the ceiling, splashing the walls. He drew the curtains and lay on the bed. The TV was on, as always, but soundless: a 24/7 news channel showing flame bursts and pillars of smoke in hill country, attack helicopters tilting, tail up.

He closed his eyes, but the image stayed as if the screen was in his head. It changed as he drifted along the edge of sleep, the colors brighter, the sounds leaking in.

A road, white under a layer of dust. A patrol: five men. They seem alert but relaxed, because they've done this before. Although this is a designated combat zone, things have been quiet for a while, and the men are wearing berets, not helmets. Their weapons are held low, fingers along the trigger guard. The houses in the street show signs of shell damage: some have burned and look ready to fall; others seem virtually untouched. A dog barking in one of the back streets. Radio music.

A girl is walking up the street. She seems to be moving in slow motion.

Although she's a way off, Woolf can hear her talking, and he knows she's talking to him. He also knows that this is an image from sleep's border-land, because she was never there, not at that time.

A flicker of light at the corner of his vision is neither the sun reflecting off glass nor a trick of the heat haze, though in the instant he takes it to be one or the other. Then he hears the shot and, with the shot, the cry.

He is in a room with the girl, and now he knows he is dreaming. These events are shuffling like a pack of cards. She is loading a bong with raw opium, and he is smiling, because, pretty soon, he'll forget about what lies outside the room: the conflict and chaos and fear.

After a while the images blur. It seems she is naked. It seems they are making love. He feels good; he no longer feels afraid. They lie together and talk. He answers all her questions.

The men walking in single file, the road white, no sound save for the radio music, a long melodic line that lifts and curls like a blown scarf.

The girl walking toward him. The gun flash.

He came to, his face damp with sweat: with sweat or tears. He stripped and stood under a lukewarm shower. He knew the dream was really a jumbled memory. He thought about the girl. He thought about the girl he'd killed. He thought about Aimée and the way her look struck through him. He thought about Neil Morgan, who would be the next to die.

He sat in the operator's chair and played the *Silent Wolf* game from the beginning. He was waiting for the night.

Maxine Hewitt felt a weird sense of unease. She and Frank Silano were walking through school corridors toward the headmaster's office. She said, "I feel threatened. I know it's stupid."

"Going to the headmaster's office," Silano suggested.

"School. Just school."

"You weren't happy. Bad girl, bad reports—"

"Fuck off. I had great reports."

"So your problem was . . . ?"

"I'm gay, Frank."

He shrugged. "I know that."

"I was gay then."

"People knew?"

"People suspected."

"Which meant?"

"Taunts, kicks, graffiti on the wall. Maxine Hewitt eats pussy."

"Kids can be cruel," Silano observed.

"Kids?"

"Okay, people."

"Which is why school makes me shivery."

They were almost there. Richard Forester was standing at his office door to greet them. He looked every inch a headmaster.

Silano asked, "How is it now?"

Maxine smiled. She said, "Think of it this way—I used to be hated for it. Now there's a law against hating someone for it. And I'm a law officer."

Forester put them in chairs that faced his desk. The chairs were small with tweedy seats and had narrow wooden arms. His chair was large and leather and swiveled authoritatively. He said, "I can't believe it. I can't believe it's happened. I mean, I knew him."

"The reason we're here," Maxine explained, "is to ask you whether you can think of any reason why George Nelms might have been killed. Any connection that occurs to you, any odd occurrence, anything from the past."

"Nothing," Forester said. "There's nothing. I can't think of anything. I don't suppose anyone could. George Nelms . . . it's so improbable."

His desk carried a calendar, a digital clock, an appointments book, a telephone, a pen rack. They were all aligned perfectly, positioned for size and bulk and confined to the top left-hand corner.

He smiled. "There are some people you might think of as having a secret life, but George wasn't one of them."

Both Maxine and Silano had read the report containing Stella's notes on Monica Hartley.

"The problem is . . . our problem . . ." Silano told him, "it seems clear that Mr. Nelms knew his killer—or was known to him; it's not quite the same thing."

"I can't imagine he did." Forester shook his head.

"We're not saying they were close friends. Just that Mr. Nelms had some connection with the man who murdered him. And we wonder what that connection might have been."

"You're not suggesting it was through the school, surely?"

"We'll need to talk to members of staff," Maxine said.

Forester looked startled. "Yes. Yes, all right."

"Enemies," Silano said. "Did he have any enemies that you know of?"

"Here at school? No, certainly not. He was very popular."

They talked more but learned nothing. The recently retired George Nelms, it seemed, was spotless of character and had only friends and admirers. As they were leaving, Maxine asked, "What was his subject?"

"He was our sports teacher," Forester said. "Sometimes he might fill in if a teacher was unavailable but just in a supervisory role."

"Just sports?" Silano asked.

"Yes." Forester added, "And the cadet corps. He was very generous with his time."

The Beamer boys were cruising. They had topped up with a few pills and a can or two, and they were feeling fine. Toni had gone with them, and the car was a little crowded, but they could handle it. The sound system made their nerve ends rattle. Toni was lying full length across the boys in the backseat, her head in her boyfriend's lap. The boy was thinking, idly, that in a while he might put that head to work.

The Toyota came up out of nowhere on a cut-through road between the Strip and Notting Hill Gate. The boy driving the BMW caught it in his wing mirror and had just enough time to yell and slap the accelerator, but the other car was alongside already and there was no time to find a turnoff. He drove a mazy line, weaving back and forth on the crown of the road, but it was too little, too late.

The gunshot was loud and authentic. Beamer boy swung the wheel instinctively, hitting the curb, bouncing, clipping a roadside tree, then finding the road again and changing down a gear to get traction. His passengers were yelling and swearing and falling about all over the car. In the middle of it all there was a scream. When the boy looked again, the Toyota was nowhere.

Toni was facedown on the floor. She was sobbing. She said, "They shot me, they shot me, they fucking shot me, Jesus Christ, they shot me."

The seat of her jeans was red and wet.

68

The money has to move.

Ricardo knew his business. Even though his deals were small time, they linked with bigger deals; the money amalgamated, it coalesced, you could think of it as tributaries flowing into a river; a river of money, and no saying where it had come from or where it was going.

The best way to launder money is to own a bank, or have a friend who owns a bank, or have some kind of hold over someone who owns a bank. Whichever it is, there's a fair chance that the bank, or the banker, will be Russian.

You start with "placement": the cash is paid into your bank, or your friend's bank. Then comes the "layering" stage: when the money takes flight and winds up in other banks. You'd want to make this stage as complicated as possible—multilayering—with a complex network of transfers in your home country and worldwide but, eventually, it will all wind up overseas. Finally, "integration": the money is defrayed, it buys houses, it buys businesses, it buys prime-location holiday homes with golfing facilities. The income feeds back to the depositors, or else the homes and businesses are sold after a while.

There are other ways and many of them. You can use cyber-payments and trade in digital money. You can use no-limit value cards like Mondex and make telephone transfers to a trickle-down system. Money markets are open twenty-four hours a day, three hundred sixty-five days a year, so the money never stops moving. You can use trust systems like Chop or Hawallah, when your receipt will be a torn playing card or a laundry ticket, and money never crosses a border or registers on an electronic system. You can use the futures market, buying and selling the same commodity under a broker's anonymity, paying the commission, maybe even taking a small loss. You can buy antiques or jewelry. You can team up with someone who owns a casino, buy chips, play the tables, win a little, lose a little, then cash in.

You can bring your money back through any one of a hundred offshore facilities whose owners are a mystery. There are Caribbean islands with a population of a few thousand and better than five hundred banks that are owned by the Nothing Corporation whose board members are John Doe, Mickey Blank, and Jack Noname.

Drugs aside, money laundering is the biggest illegal international business. The sums are astronomical: hundreds of billions of dollars, for sure. Ricardo just wanted a fraction of this. A fraction of a fraction. He'd worked hard to secure his minuscule corner of the market, and he was seriously unhappy about being muscled out, though he remembered Jonah nailed to his chair and accepted that London was a bust.

He'd gone out to buy a newspaper, cigarettes, a lottery ticket. He took his usual read from the rack, then stopped short. There were a dozen or so different papers on display, and one of them carried a picture above the title advertising a feature article in that day's issue: Delaney's article on Stanley Bowman. It wasn't a name Ricardo recognized, but he'd seen the face before. He'd seen it in a rearview mirror.

He opened the paper and started to read. As he read, he smiled.

Toni was tired of hearing how lucky she'd been. She didn't feel lucky; she felt unhappy and angry and sore. The boys had dropped her a block from the hospital and she had limped down to A & E, shouting with pain, her hand clutching her ass. By the time she got there, the left leg of her jeans was sopping.

The boys had explained that it wouldn't be wise for them to go with her (though of course they wanted to). There would be too many questions to answer (and they really didn't have the answers). The police would be called, for sure (which might well prove embarrassing).

So maybe she could say she was out for a walk when . . . Or was lying on the grass in the park when . . . Or she couldn't remember quite what . . . Toni asked them exactly what it was that someone shot in the ass wouldn't quite remember, but by this time they were dumping her on the pavement. On her ass on the pavement.

It must have been because she'd been lying full length in the car that the bullet had gone through the fat of her backside, clipped the passenger seat, and deflected into the dashboard. The boys looked at the hole in the dash and cursed. The boy in the passenger seat had wanted everyone to know that he'd come that close.

That motherfucking close, dude.

Toni had wailed, trying to look round at the damage, and her more-or-less boyfriend had told her, yeah, they'd get her somewhere first, go looking for the Toyota team later. He'd made it sound like a concession.

Now she was on her hands and knees, ass up, while a doctor stitched the exit wound, then applied a dressing as a cop, with a poor sense of timing, asked her questions. The cop was a woman who liked a joke, but she wasn't ready to allow that Toni had been walking when she was shot, because the angle of the wound was wrong, or lying in the park, because the same applied, or that she was confused about the incident, because somehow that didn't strike true.

Toni decided to hold to the amnesia story. She'd heard about injury trauma, and it sounded like a good idea. She could shrug and shake her head and speak about walking and lying in the park as false memories.

The cop was skeptical. Toni told the cop to kiss her ass.

Gideon Woolf was dressing to go out, this time, in black. Silent Wolf wore black at night and became a shadow . . . no, less than a shadow. The long coat wasn't right for climbing. Instead, he put on a roll-neck, a hooded top with zipper pockets, 501s, sneakers. The knife went into his waistband under the hoodie; the gun into one zipper pocket; into the other, a homemade grappler—a thin rope the end of which had been unraveled and self-lashed to a heavy glass paperweight.

The sky was darkening by the minute, a heavy blue dusk. He felt good. He felt that necessary buzz along with a tightness in the throat, a tightness in the gut. His fingertips tingled. On TV there were scenes of conflict, then a politician invoking God, then men spilling from the back of a truck in windblown rain.

A voice said, *The infantry, going forward as one.*

Woolf experienced a sudden flashback to his waking dream.

Men walking in single file, the road white, no sound . . . A flicker of light at the corner of his vision . . . Then a shot, a cry . . .

Coward. You filthy fucking coward.

It seems they are making love . . . pretty soon, he'll forget about the conflict and chaos and fear. They lie together and talk. He answers all her questions.

Dirty girl. Oh, you dirty bitch.

The images staggered him, and he put out a hand, steadying himself against the doorjamb. He squeezed his eyes tight shut. Aimée's face swam up behind his closed eyelids, her smile, her lips moving: *I love you.*

What can I do? Aimée . . . what can I do now but kill you?

He sat in his operator's chair for a moment or two, breathing deeply, channeling his thoughts to the task in hand. Silent Wolf stalking the alleyways, moving unseen over rooftops. A street glow from the Strip played on the ceiling, pink and green neon; car horns sounded; engines revved; voices shouted threats or invitations. He was ready. He left the scorched room, his step light as he went downstairs.

On TV, the politician was still talking about God.

69

Stanley Bowman thought he had better things to do. There was money to be moved, some clean, some slightly soiled, some distinctly grimy. There was a deal to be closed, perfectly legit, and another where the names had been changed to protect the limitlessly guilty. There were several aboveboard companies to be looked after, some of which carried government contracts and could name members of Parliament among their directors.

A long time ago Bowman had learned that high-profile respectable businesses with high-profile respectable connections were great camouflage for certain less public activities. Working both sides of that divide took time, but it also brought rewards: the dirty work trebled your profits, the open-book businesses brought status and position—people wanted to write feature articles about you.

He wasn't happy about playing go-between, but the Americans had both influence and amazing connections. Their business was worldwide, highly profitable, and wholly legitimate: a growth industry that showed no sign of falling off. It depended on war, and there were wars round the globe, wars 24/7, wars that had been going on for decades, wars that had only just begun, territorial wars, religious wars, racial wars, drug wars, doctrinal wars, wars that depended on old grudges, on new antagonisms, wars for political gain, wars for democracy, wars for domination, wars that were being fought out of habit, out of hatred, out of ignorance.

Wars require weapons, and Bowman was very anxious for a piece of that particular action. It was in his interests to help crack a market where he could be broker. Like Bowman, Morgan had taken American money; he couldn't expect simply to shrug and say, "I tried."

Bowman parked and walked past the Honda without really noticing it. When Morgan let him in, he noticed the glance that went over his shoulder and laughed.

"Are they out there—your minders?"

"I told you."

Bowman could hear yells and explosions from a farther room. Morgan had been watching TV. They went down a long hallway to the back of the house, and Morgan poured drinks before bothering to switch off the movie.

"Now," Bowman said, "we need some sort of a game plan. These people with influence . . . Who's got secrets? Who's in debt? Who's ambitious?" He smiled. "Who's got something to lose?"

Woolf looked ahead; he looked back down the street. People searching for a restaurant, people strolling. He walked past the house, to the end of the street, then started back. The restaurant door opened and closed; the strollers turned the corner. Woolf dropped down into the basement area of the house with scaffolding.

There was an alarm warning clamped to one of the scaffolding poles. From his vantage point below, Woolf looked up and saw the passive infrared detectors on the first level of the scaffolding. He went back to the street. A car went by, then a pizza-delivery bike, its wasp-whine fading. Woolf threw the grappler, lobbing it underarm. The weight rose and arced perfectly, dropping over a pole on the third level. He fed the rope out until the weighted end came to hand, then tied a running knot and pulled on the rope again, sending it back.

The next part was tricky: he had to clear the first level and the infrared. He held the rope in his teeth and climbed onto the railings that bordered the basement area, his feet placed carefully between the spikes, then wound the rope round his right hand and launched himself, pulling hard and lifting his body in order to rise feet first, like a pole vaulter. His heels smacked the scaffolding, then his back, leaving him breathless for a moment. He crooked his knees and got first his lower legs, then his thighs, onto a scaffolding plank and hauled himself upright.

He climbed the poles to the top of the house, pulled aside the flap of a tarpaulin, and stepped into the roof space. From there he went down to the basement kitchen and from there into the walled garden. When he hoisted himself up, he could see Neil Morgan's garden.

Bowman was beginning to form the opinion that Morgan was a smart operator: smarter, anyway, than he'd seemed. What this guy wanted was more money. What made Bowman suspect that? Well, the fact that Morgan kept insisting that money had nothing to do with it, money didn't come into it, money wasn't the issue. He thought it might be time to make a call to the Americans to find out what they could offer to sweeten the pot.

The bathroom was his excuse for getting time alone: no point in making a phone call with Morgan in the background trying to keep up the pretense that he'd done all he could no matter what the kickback. You had to have the promise of cash on the table; you had to be able to say, "So how does a hundred K sound?"

But before the call, a little something, a lift, a treat. He used a shaving mirror to cut three lines and rolled a twenty-pound note. It was a good hit. He gave the first line time to soak in, then dipped his head for the next. He could hear that, downstairs, Morgan had switched the TV back on.

Woolf had crossed the gardens that separated him from Morgan's house and tried the basement door. If he was unlucky he could tap out a pane of glass and reach through to the key, or pop a window, or remove a door panel, but he hadn't really expected to meet a problem. In the game, Silent Wolf moved swiftly and easily from place to place, frame to frame, moment to moment; it was how things worked.

He'd tried the door and it was unlocked, of course. People like Morgan just didn't feel that vulnerable.

As he climbed the stairs from the basement, he could hear Morgan and Bowman talking. One of the men laughed. A door opened. Woolf saw Bowman going upstairs. It was a complication, and he knew he probably ought to regroup and rethink, but he also knew that Morgan's wife would return, that the security would continue, that this might be his only chance.

He moved quickly and quietly down the hallway to the room, taking out the gun, glancing toward the stairs in case the other man returned. The door was partly open, and Woolf could see Neil Morgan standing by the fireplace on the far side of the room and drinking whiskey. When Woolf walked in holding the gun, Morgan was motionless for a moment, then he picked up a fire iron and backed off.

Woolf said, "You filthy coward."

He walked toward the man, the gun high and pointing at his face, though he had no intention of firing it. A shot would be heard, and in any case, he wanted to use the knife.

Woolf said, "You! You filthy fucking coward."

Morgan gave a yell. His gaze was fixed on Woolf, but at the same time, he was reaching blindly with his left hand, two fingers extended. Woolf looked for the panic alarm, its double red buttons, and spotted it mounted on the wall close to the door. He moved to herd his man away from it. Morgan yelled again, calling for help. Woolf rushed him, anticipating the swing of the fire iron, left to right, and blocking it with his arm. He kicked on the turn, straight-legged, taking Morgan just below the sternum, and the man went down, dropping the fire iron, retching air.

Woolf yelled at him, "You coward! You! Filthy coward!"

He picked up the iron and clipped Morgan on the side of the head: enough to pacify him. Morgan's eyes clouded, but maybe he saw Woolf draw the knife, maybe he suddenly knew who this man was, because he found enough strength to get onto all fours and go hands-and-knees for the panic alarm. Woolf lifted the iron and hit him again, the blow sending the man forward. He found the buttons, fingers forked, and Woolf hit him a third time.

That third blow wrecked something in Morgan: it broke a link somewhere deep in the man. He convulsed, gagging, his limbs flipping wildly. Woolf got behind him with the knife, wanting to steady his man for the cut, but it was impossible. Morgan was on the move, bucking and rolling. The blade cut his head, his arm, his shoulder.

In his mind's eye, Woolf saw one man walking downstairs, two more running across the road to the front door. He lashed out once more with the knife, cutting Morgan across the face, then ran.

It wasn't the TV Bowman heard, it was Morgan's cries, Woolf's shouts. The coke had sharpened him up, but also made him slightly detached. He'd snorted the third line, then made his call, getting the answer he'd hoped for, though not at first and not without difficulty.

The American said, "This guy already owes us. Tell him that."

"He needs a sweetener."

"He's got expensive habits or what?"

"It's the way forward," Bowman said. "I'm sure of it." He added, "You have to realize too that I'm putting in a lot of work here."

The American sighed. "Morgan's not the only one in need of a sweetener."

"Time's money," Bowman said. "I can only do so much on a limited budget."

"What are we talking here?"

Bowman settled into a negotiation. It was what he did best. To some people, negotiating was a tiresome necessity: claims and counterclaims, white lies, chopped logic, ground gained and ground lost. Bowman knew it to be his true language, the language of his country, the language of his tribe.

They agreed on two sums, one for Morgan, one for Bowman. They had come with a threat on the side.

Woolf was at the end of the hall and starting down to the basement when Bowman walked downstairs to make his offer, smiling a cool coke smile and not noticing the sudden silence. He'd had just enough time to get into the room and be standing over Morgan's body when the Honda men came through the door.

Morgan's convulsions had dwindled to a series of shudders and tremors. He lay splashing in his own blood like a landed fish. Then he lay still.

70

It was late by the time Stella and Harriman sat down with Bowman. He said, "It was a business meeting. I went upstairs. When I came down—" He spread his hands expressively.

Stella said, "You didn't see anyone? Hear anyone?"

"No, but there must have been someone . . ."

"There was no sign of forced entry," Stella observed, "though forensics are still at the house."

"Why would I kill him?" Bowman asked. "Why?"

"I'm asking questions," Stella told him, "that's all. You were at the scene when his security officers came in. You're all we've got. You can wait until your solicitor arrives—do you want to do that?"

"Yes," Bowman said. Then, "No, no, it doesn't matter."

"What kind of business?" Harriman asked.

"Business advice." Bowman was busking.

"What kind of business advice?"

"Money matters."

"Keep going," Stella said.

"Where best to invest it." Speaking softly, slowly, the mild Scottish accent soothing the vowel sounds.

Stella raised her eyebrows. "You're not a broker, are you?"

"I can be if the occasion demands." Bowman passed a hand over his face; he might have been distressed, Stella thought, or irritated. He said, "There are people who know me. People who will vouch for me."

"Will they vouch for your cocaine habit?" Harriman asked.

"You want to talk about that?" Bowman laughed. "A man's been murdered."

"No," Stella said, "he's not dead."

"Oh . . ." Bowman almost shrugged. "Oh, well, that's good."

"He's unconscious. He might die yet."

"Ah . . ." As if he'd forgotten he'd mentioned it, Bowman said, "People who know who I am. Who know I wouldn't—"

Harriman said, "We know who you are."

Bowman nodded. He said, "Good. Okay, then . . ." No one spoke for a moment, so he said it again: "That's good."

They were using an interview room at Notting Dene. Stella and Harriman stood in the corridor, each holding a carton of vending-machine coffee, thin and bitter. They could hear the noise from the front desk: drunks, victims, people with nowhere to go.

Harriman said, "He's a face. Big-shit businessman."

"You think that makes a difference?" Stella sipped and grimaced. "Really?"

"No, but he didn't do it."

"No, he didn't. Not unless he changed his suit and swallowed the knife in the time it took the security people to get there."

"It's our guy," Harriman said, "isn't that what you're thinking? This time he gets the right man, gets Morgan, but his timing's off. The knife cuts—he meant to decapitate him, but Morgan fought back."

"Yes," Stella said, "I think it's our guy."

"Bowman?"

"Let him go."

"His solicitor's on his way."

"And so?"

"I was thinking of the cocaine."

Stella laughed. "Flash business dude snorts coke. There's one for the record books."

"We'd hand him over if he was panhandling the subways, boss."

"He's our only witness."

"Near-witness."

"Yes, near-witness. He was there."

"And saw nothing."

"Maybe he'll remember something. At the very least we need him for purposes of elimination: fingerprints, DNA . . . Let's keep him on our side."

"Maybe he'll be good for some investment tips."

"Investment?" Stella laughed.

"Bit of inside information," Harriman said, "a nod and a wink. Impoverished copper one day, rich bastard the next."

"Tell him he can go," Stella said. "Thank him for his time and cooperation, tell him we'll need to speak to him again, give him the leaflet on counseling services."

"Why do you think he was there?" Harriman asked. "Him and Morgan . . . what's the connection?"

"God knows," Stella said. "Wheelers and dealers, movers and shakers; they're all up to it."

The sky was growing light when Harriman got back to his flat. He undressed in the hall and went into the bedroom, which was empty and shouldn't have been. He walked through to the kitchen and found Gloria making coffee. She looked him up and down as he stood butt-naked in the doorway.

"You cut right to the chase, don't you?"

He grimaced. "I have to be up in a couple of hours."

"Why wait till then?"

He put on a robe, and they sat at the breakfast bar with their coffee. Gloria made some eggs. Birds started up: London birds, they never sleep either. Harriman kissed her. He said, "No point in going back to sleep now."

"But going back to bed?"

"Different thing."

Gloria was tall and full-breasted and slender-hipped and had flawless skin to go with her Latin looks, but that wasn't the reason why Harriman was starting to think he'd like her to be around all the time.

Wasn't the only reason.

Stella made some notes, sent some e-mails, drank a couple of vodkas. She found the paper with Delaney's piece on Bowman and was momentarily confused, as if the man were somehow out of context. She read it and found out just what a hotshot Stanley Bowman was. The piece was accompanied by a portrait of the man that made him seem younger and better-looking than Stella remembered, his goatee, his gunslinger's mustache.

She took a pair of kitchen scissors and cut the photo out, then pinned it to the white-board along with the SOC photos, the living face-to-face with the dead.

71

Acting DI Brian Collier stood in the doorway listening as Stella briefed the team. He looked like a man with a dismal two-day hangover that just won't lift. In the doorway was where Mike Sorley had usually stood: not in deference, simply allowing his officers to do what they did best. Collier's retreat from center to periphery had been noticed by everyone, though some thought it had come a little late.

Stella said, "Traces of blood in the hallway, on the stairs to the basement, disturbance to plants in the next-door garden . . . It's as much as this man has left of himself. Forensic tests are being made, but we're pretty certain he gained access to the empty house and crossed gardens to get to Neil Morgan's."

"He's athletic," Frank Silano observed. "Upper-body strength."

"We're getting CCTV from the area, as many tapes as we can for the square and the surrounding streets. That includes the street where we think he must have gained entry to the empty house."

"If he bypassed the alarm," Andy Greegan said, "he must have known where to look."

"Okay," Stella said, "who do we talk to?"

"The builders and the scaffolders," Greegan said.

"Scaffolders," reflected Harriman, "the pit bulls of the construction industry."

"What about MO?" Maxine was scanning the SOC report. "Did he write anything on Morgan or leave that triple-vee sign?"

Stella shook her head. "No."

"In too much of a hurry," Harriman suggested.

"But we're sure it's him?"

"Let's hope DNA will tell us. Until we know differently—it's him." Stella paused. "Here's our problem. We don't know how long his list is or who else might be on it. If it wasn't for the writing—the notion of some purpose or another—the victims would look completely random. We can't second-guess what's coming next."

As the briefing broke up, Collier walked away. Stella found him in his office, the desk he had so meticulously cleared now piled high. He said, "It could have been a nice black-on-black or some bag-bride getting done for her stash, but no, I walk straight into a fucking serial, I draw some mental bastard who runs round my patch topping people like the wrath of fucking God."

Stella placed some files on his desk: a drop in the ocean. She said, "It's lousy luck."

Collier looked at her. "Are you enjoying this, Stella?"

"No, boss, I'm not enjoying it. People are dying."

"What's the pattern here? He'll stop or he'll make a mistake and get caught: isn't that what we're relying on? A mistake."

"A mistake would help."

"Or else he's never caught. He just becomes history." Collier lit a cigarette. "Like me."

Candice Morgan had flown back from her girls-only funtime break and was sitting in the relatives' room wondering if her husband was going to come back to her from the operating theater dead or alive. She had asked the question a number of times, and no one seemed eager to give her a straightforward answer.

Morgan had been on the table for five hours while surgeons removed a hematoma cluster from his brain. The knife wounds had been cleaned and stitched with little attention to cosmetic effect; surgery took precedence. The cut to his face went from the left point of the jaw, across the mouth and nose, up the right-hand cheek, to snag the corner of the eye and then into the hairline. Given that the surgeons had scalped Morgan and trepanned him, it seemed less a disfigurement than a grace note.

A nurse looked in to let Candice know that the operation was still in progress. Candice asked, "Is he going to die?" Half an hour later a different face asked if she would like a drink. Candice asked, "Is he going to die?" When the surgeons were finally done with Morgan, a consultant came to see Candice to let her know that the operation had, so far as they could tell, been successful and that her husband was not dead. "Yes," Candice said, "but is he *going* to die?"

When Ricardo had realized that the face he'd seen in the rearview mirror that night close by Wormwood Scrubs was Bowman's, his thoughts first turned to blackmail.

You want a large piece of my action, you bastard? No, I'll have a large piece of yours.

The problem with this idea, and Ricardo knew it, was that it would require nerve that he suspected he didn't have; it might also require muscle he *knew* he didn't have. He thought of Sekker and people like Sekker: he'd met such people before; they were a special breed; they lacked qualities that most people took for granted—a conscience, for example, or regret, or pity. Most of all they lacked imagination. They were people who could nail a man's hands to a chair and chat to him through his screams. He decided to cut his losses and move on. Harefield was rich pickings, but the world was full of people who knew how to steal without knowing what to do next, people in need of a middle man, a matchmaker.

It was early afternoon, and the view from the eleventh floor of Block B was of a flawless blue sky warped by rolling scarves of pollution. A flock of gulls cruised by on their way to the garbage dump. Ricardo sat with Tina over a Pat's Pizza and made plans; he'd heard that there were some unlikely areas opening up. The Midlands. Nottingham, he told her, was a real frontier town.

Tina put the TV on and watched a love story in which things kept going wrong. Ricardo lay back in his chair, eyes closed, but he wasn't sleeping; he was planning. He might not have the balls to front Bowman, he thought, but there were other ways to make the man's life complicated.

In his mind's eye Ricardo could see a little bomb with a very long fuse.

Maxine Hewitt and Sue Chapman were sitting in a dimly lit room watching CCTV footage. They had the lights down because the tape quality was poor. They watched citizens going about their business, observed, recorded, unaware.

All those lives, Maxine thought, all those connections.

"It's crap," Sue observed. "You couldn't ID anyone from this. Kids in hoodies steaming a shop, you're looking at a blur with something blurry inside it."

People walking their dogs, people shopping, couples hand in hand, *Big Issue* hawkers, Gideon Woolf crossing the road at a run, his long hair flying, the tails of his long coat flying, just beating a black Freelander as it switched lanes.

Ricardo said, "Don't tell Stella where we're going."

"I can get in touch, though?"

"Oh, yeah. Yeah, I want you to get in touch. Definitely."

"It was a long time. I hadn't seen Stell for a long time."

"The thing is," Ricardo said, "I'm going to fuck him up."

"Sekker?"

"Sekker's boss."

"Okay," Tina said. "Good. How?"

"It's complicated."

Tina nodded. "Okay." A thought occurred to her. "Will he know it was you?"

"No. This is a long-range thing. It's a hands-off thing. We'll be gone."

"To Nottingham."

"Somewhere."

"Nottingham sounds good."

The movie was on its way to a happy ending, bad luck reversed, all obstacles overcome, the lovers steadily but surely advancing to limitless joy.

"Stella's part of it," Ricardo said. "Some information I need to give her. Maybe you could do that."

"Okay. I'll tell her. What is it?"

"Later," Ricardo said. "I haven't got it all straight yet."

Delaney said, "What's Stanley Bowman doing on your crime-board?"

Stella told him. She said, "Neil Morgan and Stanley Bowman—two off your Rich List, am I right?"

"Two of fifty."

"But these two are connected."

Delaney laughed. "They're all connected. Money connects them. Influence connects them. Friends in high places connects them. They're connections themselves."

"So what is it, exactly, that connects Bowman and Morgan?"

"Who knows?"

"Not me," Stella said, "but I'd like to," and she looked at him.

"I can try."

He was opening a bottle of white wine. She fetched some glasses and put olives in a dish: olives and wine, the evening sacrament. The first long sip tasted wonderful, cold and crisp, the aftertaste of gooseberry.

He said, "So what do you think?" as if the question had only just been asked, as if it were fresh in both their minds.

Which it was.

Stella put down her glass and crossed to him. She held his hands to her breasts, as if she were swearing an oath. "I have to sell Vigo Street first."

"No, you don't. We'll sell this, buy somewhere, the money from Vigo Street can come along later."

Stella nodded. She said, "Yes. Okay. When?"

"Whenever you like."

They kissed. They clinked glasses. She felt elated and completely lost.

Candice Morgan sat at her husband's bedside and watched the heart monitor throw its little loops. She had spent some time with the consultant after Morgan had returned from theater; she had asked whether he was going to die. The consultant had said he thought not. In fact, he was pretty sure of it.

The pay-to-view TV was showing a news broadcast in which chaos played side by side with disaster. Candice watched without watching, her mind elsewhere. She was thinking, *Don't die. Please don't die.*

The room was warm, and Candice dozed for a while. The TV threw flicker-frames on the wall, and the sound of sirens floated up from the street. After ten minutes or so, she woke and looked across at the bed. Morgan lay on his back, utterly still, the monitor ticking and blipping. Candice stared at him, nothing in her face of softness or concern.

Don't die, *you bastard.*

72

Silent Wolf in the rain-lashed alleyways, in the dark dead ends. His principal adversary was Ironjaw, a cyborg made almost invincible by radical surgery. Research had shown that Ironjaw was almost as popular as Silent Wolf with the kids who played the game, and the game-makers were already developing an Ironjaw spin-off.

James and Stevie Turner sat side by side on their grandparents' sofa and took Silent Wolf through another adventure. The swirl of his coat, his snarl, the glint of a streetlamp on the blade of his knife . . . Desperadoes and lowlifes came at him out of the shadows and were sent straight to hell. James was well on the way to Level 8, where Silent Wolf stood on the edge of Ironjaw's Badlands Abyss, his death toll in the upper hundreds.

Their grandparents hated the game for its indiscriminate violence, and they hated the fact that James and Stevie played it in every spare moment. They tried confiscating it, but the boys became badly upset; they almost seemed to be suffering withdrawal symptoms, and Stevie's nightmares became more frequent and more distressing. It was difficult enough, trying to cope with their own grief and their daughter's limitless depression, without also having to deal with two boys who rarely spoke, who seemed to have retreated into the game-world and violent streets of an unnamed city.

"What is it?" the grandfather asked. "Why do you like this game so much?"

"It's him," James said. "It's Silent Wolf."

The grandfather played the game when the boys had gone to bed, but the technology was too fast and too subtle for him. Next day he asked James to coach him, thinking, maybe, that if he could be part of it, he could break into their world, get close to his grandsons and help them.

James talked him through the rules and the moves. Silent Wolf stalked the streets; the weather worsened; the skies darkened; red-eyed killers came at him from every doorway.

Stevie said, "And he killed Daddy. Why was that?"

Later, the grandparents talked. They could see what was happening, they could see why the boys were so addicted to the game. It was a necessary fantasy. Because if a cartoon character had killed their father, then, obviously, their father couldn't really be dead.

That night, the grandfather put the game into the player again. He didn't get far, so he canceled it and watched the title trailer: slanting rain, a distant lightning strike, Silent Wolf slipping through the crowds on Mean Street, taking an alleyway shortcut. A man emerged from hiding, a cleaver in his hand. Silent Wolf high-kicked; his knife glittered in the light from a barroom window; the man went down.

It repeated endlessly, balletic and bloody. The grandfather backhanded a tear from his cheek.

The bleachers were up in Byrite, the cage in place, the fighters standing by the gate. Going into that space was like entering a tunnel in a windowless train. Voices swarmed on the walls and crowned over the cage like a firestorm. The fighters jogged on the spot, looking away from each other, looking at the floor. One of them was a white guy with dreadlocks: a Wigger, thick in the chest, his shoulders and biceps a little rockfall that went all the way to his bunched fists. He curled a gobbet of spit on his tongue and blew it down between his feet.

Ricardo was making a book. He and Tina would be gone soon, but there are cage fights all over, and he expected to find this sideline wherever they happened to wind up. Ban cockfighting, ban badger-baiting, ban dog-fights, ban fox-hunting, and the next blood sport will be man on man in a seven-foot-high cage with no way out. Cage-fighting was covering the map. It was almost respectable: Mike Tyson had flown in to MC some Manchester fights.

There were few rules: no biting, no head-butting, no eye-gouging; that aside, it was go anywhere, do anything. The only other thing banned was avoiding trouble—no pussies in cages. The fighters wore thin leather gloves, so you knew that blood would be drawn, bones would be broken, damage would be done, and deaths were a distinct possibility. For Ricardo, it had all the potential of a growth industry. Set up the contest, charge an entrance fee, take bets on the fights, pay someone with a Super-8 camera to film each bout, then distribute the DVDs through your CAGE FIGHT KILLERS Web site.

The fighters went into the cage along with the referee. The baying from the crowd grew; Ricardo raced up and down between the bleachers taking bets, all of which were going on the Wigger, which wasn't too surprising, since his opponent was slighter, his torso sloping down to a narrow waist. Worst of all, he was a good-looking guy. How could a pretty boy win a cage fight? With a two-man contest, though, you could only come second, and there was money in the purse for the loser.

Ricardo took a bet from Sekker, who was sitting on a ground-level seat close to the door. Sekker grinned. "It's an execution, this."

Ricardo nodded. "The Wigger."

"He'll kill him, won't he?"

"Looks like it."

They were shouting into each other's faces to make themselves heard.

"So I bet on the other guy, right? Because dreadlocks looks a winner, so he'll go down, won't he?" A pause. *"Won't he?"*

Sekker was asking a question that required an answer Ricardo couldn't supply.

"It's not a fix. Best man wins."

"Not a fix?" Sekker looked confused.

"No. Straight fight."

Sekker smiled, then he laughed. The laugh couldn't be heard above the din, but it looked infinitely threatening.

He said, "Don't shit a shitter," and handed Ricardo two hundred in low notes. "On Pretty Boy." He added, "Catch you later, right?" Ricardo hesitated. *"Right?"*

Sekker had turned his attention to the cage before Ricardo had the chance to nod agreement. Pretty Boy stood in the middle waiting for the Wigger, who was making a tour of the cage, smashing his hand against the links, staring his opponent down. A Klaxon sounded, and the Wigger charged in, slugging. Pretty Boy turned like a matador, taking a punch on the arm, clubbing down on the Wigger's neck as he went by, making the man stagger. Instead of following up, he stood back like an artist admiring his work.

The Wigger turned and paused. It took him a moment to assess what had happened: to assess it and log it and make an adjustment. So this guy was tricky, okay, but he wouldn't look so smart with his nose all over his pretty face. The Wigger shuffled forward, fists held high, elbows over his midriff. He flicked out a left. If you want to box, we'll box. Think I don't know how to do that?

Pretty Boy feinted to the head, and the Wigger swayed. Pretty Boy came the other way, getting in a hook to the heart that rocked the Wigger just a little. He bored in, using his shoulders and head, his weight taking Pretty Boy back to the chain link. The Wigger put in two solid punches to the ribs and heard his man grunt.

Okay, you skinny shit, you're meat. You're *my* meat.

73

Crack, scag, brown, E, ganja, benz, speed, dex, angel, oxy, reds, black whack, diesel, barb, Nazi crank, blow, skunk. The whores were doing some midday backseat business, some alley-wall business, even some back-room business where the guy had the time and the price. The shebeens and the basement casinos were running two-way traffic. An Imola-red BMW was cruising the side streets, on the prowl, the boys just a little juiced on some of the Strip's low-budget products.

They found Donna as she was leaving Store24 with a few things she'd bought and a few things she'd lifted. It could have been any one of a dozen girls who liked to hang with the Toyota team, but Donna was there, and Donna would do just fine. When the Beamer passed her, then came to a stop, she turned to run, but two of the Beamer boys had got out a little way back and were right behind her, smiling broad smiles. As they hustled her to the car, she screamed, and one of the boys slapped her hard in the face; then she was in, a boy on each side of her, the driver shifting down a gear, the tires whinnying.

Toni's maybe-boyfriend looked Donna up and down: micro-skirt, crop-top, spaghetti straps, deep cleavage, ebony skin, a dewdrop of blood under her nose from the slap.

He said, "They shot my girlfriend in the ass." Donna had nothing to say on the subject. "So there has to be payback, yeah? Some kind of ass thing. Something we can do to your ass. Any ideas?" On ass-work, Donna was mute. The boyfriend laughed. He said, "We'll think of something."

Three five-minute rounds and it had become pretty clear, with one to go, that the fight was an even match: the Wigger's punching power and stam-ina, sure, but also the Pretty Boy's skill and cage-craft. The Wigger did damage whenever he got close. It was likely that Pretty Boy had a rack of cracked ribs; he'd also taken a few to the face, and both his eyes had cuts, leaving broad tributaries of blood on his cheeks and neck. The Wigger wasn't marked in that way, but Pretty Boy had landed a lot of punches from the side and the back, most of them taking the Wigger on the neck or high on the skull and the man had a foggy look about him: his face vacant, sometimes, as he turned to find his opponent.

The men stood at either side of the cage, their backs to the mesh, Pretty Boy breathing hard, his hands at his sides, the Wigger holding his fists up as if he'd forgotten to drop them and eyeballing the crowd as if to say, *Don't doubt me.*

Ricardo was still collecting bets, though he was giving evens now. People who'd bet the Wigger were howling at him to finish the job: he could do it, the guy was out on his feet, blinded by blood, easy pickings. Sekker was looking smug: a man in the know. When the fighters came out for the last, the Wigger seemed to have been listening to ringside advice, because he went in hard and fast, hooking to the head. Pretty Boy took one and seemed to soak it up, then went down on one knee. The Wigger leaned in, still punching, but his opponent had his arms up, crossed at the wrist, deflecting.

When the Wigger shifted position to find kicking range, Pretty Boy rolled and got to his feet, backpedaling fast, knowing the other man would be hunting him down.

74

Street cops have contacts, and Brian Collier hadn't been Acting DI for so long that he'd lost touch. Sitting behind his desk with its files and folders and downloads, he could feel his bones calcifying and his blood thickening. His trip to Stonebridge to see a chis had been pretty fruitless, all in all—a chis would have contacts too, and some of them would be men more than happy to kill, but they killed to a purpose: intimidation, revenge, profit. They might even enjoy their work, but their work wasn't random. Criminal businesses have their killers just as corporate businesses have their lawyers.

He threw the Freelander across two lanes, getting a horn blast from a trucker, and settled down on the outside lane, knowing he would have to cut back at the next set of lights. The Freelander was big and pushy, which was why he liked it. Carbon footprint? What carbon footprint?

When he made the switch, the car to his left was anticipating it and slipped down a gear, outpacing him. He glanced sideways—boys out for a ride, out for trouble, their sound system loud enough to ripple the windscreen. As he watched, a girl in the backseat signaled him, her mouth wide open, before a boy on her left put a hand to her head, pushing her sideways and out of sight.

The Beamer made a turn off the main road into the web of housing that surrounds the Strip. Collier followed. He could see the girl's arm, raised, as if to protect her face, the boy leaning in, his hand also raised.

Sekker was looking at Ricardo, Ricardo was looking at his feet, everyone else was looking at the cage, where Pretty Boy was on his knees and taking hefty kicks. There was a minute left on the clock. The Wigger shifted position to take the man under the heart and that would have ended things, but he somehow missed his kick. You couldn't see how it had happened, though the slightly vacant look on his face was a clue. He fell back and rolled over. Pretty Boy got into a crouch and stayed there for a moment, then straightened up; he seemed just too tired to get to his opponent.

The Wigger was close to the cage-side. He spread his fingers and got a hold on the mesh, then pulled himself partly upright; a second handhold got him to his feet. He looked across to where his opponent was standing at the center of the cage, his face a blood-mask, blood dripping from his jawline to his chest, a red web, a map of pain. Pretty Boy took a step forward and grimaced, as if his cracked ribs might suddenly collapse like spillikins. You could hear him wheeze. The Wigger bounced on his toes; he did a little jig.

The jig said, *Hey, I'm fine. I'm in great shape. And look at you: like you were in a car crash, like you were in a head-on. So I'm gonna dance over there and pound the living shit outta you. Get ready, sucker, because here I come.*

The ringside judge stopped the clock as it came up to the fifth minute. One other rule in cage-fighting—no ties.

Maybe the boys in the Beamer hadn't noticed the Freelander follow, or maybe they'd seen it but didn't care. Collier had put in a call for backup, but he hadn't expected the Imola-red car to stop quite so soon. He made another fast call, giving the street name and postcode. A voice told him that an ARV was five minutes away. Five, maybe a little more. Donna was being hauled out of the car. The micro-skirt had gone. She stood in the street in her crop-top and heels and panties, the boys circling, laughing, herding her toward a house with a faded red door. The windows in the street were blank, as if no eye had ever looked through them.

If the boys had been having less fun, Collier might have been seen earlier. He shouted, *"Hey!"* He was holding his warrant card up and out, as if it might make a difference. The boys turned to look at him.

One of them produced the Brocock ME38.

When it comes to strength, when it comes to energy, when it comes to lactic acid and oxygen depletion, there's a limit to how far you can reach inside yourself. These are physical attributes, and everyone has limited resources. When they've run out, though, there's another reserve that you can draw on. People think it's courage, but that's only likely to keep you going until you're completely drained. The thing most likely to get you out of trouble is intelligence.

Pretty Boy looked across to where the Wigger was dancing and ducking, his fists pummeling the air, and knew that the man had about an ounce left, maybe a gram. On the other hand, Pretty Boy could feel something closing in on him, like being on the edge of sleep; on the edge of death. He thought that a single movement might tip him over.

He looked at the Wigger, smiling through blood, and spoke to him. He couldn't be heard over the howling from the bleachers, but the words were readable to everyone.

Pussy. You fucking pussy.

The Wigger stumbled slightly in his jig. He righted himself and took a step forward. The punters bayed and screamed. Blood wasn't enough; blood and bone weren't enough; blood *money*—that was the issue. Their man crossed toward the middle of the cage, looking to be light on his feet, shedding energy he didn't have. When he was a little more than an arm's length off, he made a rush.

Pretty Boy sidestepped and swung wildly, using his arm as if it were nailed on, taking the Wigger a little below the waistline of his shorts, making him check, as if he'd stopped to think. The next blow came from the side, two-handed, ill-aimed, but deflecting off the boss of the Wigger's shoulder and connecting with his throat.

The Wigger took a step back, then another, knees bending, arms out as if looking for support. He sat down hard and bowed low, his head falling toward his knees.

He stayed like that. The ringside judge rang the bell.

Collier saw the gun, but there was nowhere to go. He was out in the middle of the street walking fast toward them, no cover either side, his own car more than twenty feet behind him. Nowhere to go but on. Donna was looking at him as if he were Mister Too-little-too-late. The boys were laughing.

Collier said, "Shoot me. You'd better shoot me, you little bastard, because if I get over there I'm going to fucking kill you." He knew that the closer he got, the more unmissable he became. "Put the gun down, put the girl down, and that'll do for now."

Donna took half a step toward Collier, and the boyfriend pulled her back. Just for a moment the boy with the gun turned the weapon toward Donna, as if he might threaten Collier by threatening her. In that moment Collier reckoned he had something of a chance. He thought, *This guy's thinking of alternatives; he doesn't want to shoot a copper.*

He kept walking. He was fifteen feet away when the boy with the Brocock lined up on Collier and fired.

75

Sekker and Ricardo were in the living room of 1169, Block B. Tina was in the bedroom, being invisible.

Sekker said, "You're full of shit, you know that? Straight fight?" He laughed. "Listen, they made a good job of it. That good-looker?—he knows how to take punishment."

Ricardo had seen the fighter afterward, and he wasn't so pretty anymore: eyes so swollen he could hardly see, front teeth gone, a cheekbone broken, his nose Z-shaped. He was just a Harefield regular, no connections to crime, with a wife and family to care for. It had been three years since he'd had work, and the fight purse of five grand was more money than he'd ever seen in one place in his life. The gate had grossed eight grand, the book three, and the DVD would make a couple of thousand without the download money: all Ricardo's.

Sekker was drinking the six-pack he'd brought with him. He said, "So, a good day about to get better. You've got something for me."

Ricardo handed him a sheet of paper. Written on it were a code word, a telephone number, a bank account number, and a man's name: Vanechka. It was a laundry line.

Sekker looked at it. "This all?"

"He'll know. Make the call, give the code word, ask for the money to be deposited in that account."

"This name—Vanechka . . ." He got the stress wrong: Vanech-*kah*.

"The money travels, okay? It goes on holiday, takes things easy for a while. Then it has to start work. The question is: What does it do? Earn interest? Buy property? Invest itself? There's another question: How soon does your man want it to come back to him? He'll know all this. After a while, he'll get a phone call—which way to go? He'll be talking to this man, Vanechka. Or he should be. Tell him to make sure."

Sekker took his beer with him when he left. Ricardo went into the bedroom. Tina had been packing; she closed the lid on the last case and zipped it up.

Ricardo said, "You can write that letter to Stella. I'll tell you what to say."

Collier felt as if someone had nudged him. Next moment he reached the boy with the Brocock and hit him, all his weight behind the punch. Something broke under his fist and the boy went down. The gun skittered along the road.

Collier took Donna by the arm and pulled her toward him. The boyfriend hadn't let go, so Collier hit him too: a couple of short-arm blows that came straight out of the training manual. He pushed Donna toward the Freelander and she kept going, looking over her shoulder, half expecting one of the boys to come after her, but they were more interested in Collier, who had gone in the opposite direction and collected the gun. The boy who'd had the gun was on his feet now and standing next to the boyfriend.

Collier couldn't work out why they had neither attacked nor run. He waved the gun in their general direction and said, "Who's next?"

When he put a round through the windscreen of the Beamer, the boys decided it was time. They piled into the car. The driver knocked out the shattered windscreen glass, and they reversed hard, whacking the side of the Freelander, then coming round on the handbrake. They cleared the junction and hit the main road as the ARV arrived. The driver paused long enough to get an okay from Collier, then kept going, the Imola-red Beamer just in sight.

Donna was standing in the road, high heels and panties. She seemed to be putting out an arm, as if needing assistance, and Collier went toward her, his own arm extended, then he saw the look on her face and realized she was not reaching but pointing. Pointing at him.

He looked down and saw his shirt, a blue shirt, red from armpit to waist. That explained things: the boys had been waiting for him to drop.

James and Stevie went to their grandfather with a shopping list: it was short, just two items. James had noted them in a neat upright hand.

Silent Wolf: Urban Legend.

Silent Wolf: Urban Warrior.

James said, "We might have the wrong one."

Stevie said, "Silent Wolf, the avenger. Silent Wolf, death dealer. Silent Woolf cleans filth from the streets in the city that never sleeps."

76

Dear Stell

You know that Ricardo and I have got to move now. Trouble with his business, I think it is, but this is not to bother you with that. I am sending it to your work at Notting Dene addressed to you as personal as I never got told were you are living or what's happening in your life now. Well I know you must be busy but I wish we had seen more of each other during my brief time on Harefield, which was more brief than I ever thought it would be, but life is like that as they say. It was peculiar being back there after such a time as you might think and it brought back the old days.

I expect you remember the times we used to have. It was hard at times as we both know but I like to think of them as good times, the two of us together, and I hope you have nice memories of those times as I know I do. Perhaps you remember trying to get a dog and being told it wasn't aloud, then we got some mice and they ran out, it was hysterical. Can you remember my friend Eric who was with us for a short time and he didn't like them at all and went out with us laughing at him I seem to remember. Well Stella those times are gone and we have all moved on and changed but perhaps we will hook up again some time soon and we can talk about those times. It was tough, but we looked after each other didn't we? I was so proud of you with school and your degree and those things and being in the police though that was an odd thing in some ways wasn't it seeing were we came from. You were always good with your homework and I know they thought that at school too. I think back and there we are in the flat, block c at the top, you and me, not that we didn't have problems with money etc some times what with your father going off but we were always there for each other I do know that. Anyway, Stell, I have to close now because Ricardo has found us a place to be. I don't know were exactly yet but we have to get out of here tomorrow Nottingham I think it is. Ricardo has had some sort of problem with a man called Stanley Bowman who was in the paper and he asked me to tell you this and say that if you look for money going in and out of his bank this Bowman and were it came from you will find it interesting as will customs, or tap his phone, or ask for his accounts, and it will be a large deposit from abroad.

Well I must stop now Stell as there are things to do when you move. I have been writing this on Ricardo's computer and it is slow work for me with two fingers and spell-check bringing me up short. I hope you are happy and expect you must be but I didn't have a chance to ask. Much love from, Your loving mother, Tina. xxx

Stella was holding the letter with her fingertips, as if it might unexpectedly ignite. She slipped it into one of the lockable drawers in her desk, then looked around like a prisoner searching for an escape route.

Harriman came by and said, "Ten minutes, boss, car park—all right?"

She said, "Yes," or thought she did.

She couldn't go to the women's room, because anyone might come in there, but she sure as hell couldn't stay at her desk, so she walked out of the squad room and out of the building and got into her car, but she couldn't stay in the car park either, with people coming and going, so she started the car and drove without thinking where she might go, and soon realized she couldn't drive much farther because she wasn't able to see all that well, and she was getting horn blasts from either side, so she turned into the car wash just off Shepherd's Bush Green.

She sat in the wash-tunnel, hedged on both sides by the rag-rollers, yellow rinse-rollers front and rear, windscreen slathered in foam, everything dim, the roar of machinery, the rollers' clatter and slap, and howled and beat the dashboard with her hands and cried so hard, so *hard*, that she thought something inside might break.

Little Stella Mooney, all alone, tears like stones.

Harriman said, "Sorry, where did you go?"

"Don't be sorry. I had some calls to make."

Stella had fronted the car-wash men with her makeup a tide line round her jaw and her tearstains plain to see, but she'd parked in a side street and carried out a wet-wipe repair job before driving back to the squad room. Now she felt fine. She felt steady. Apart from anything else, the bitch was leaving. Nottingham—far enough to be out of mind.

Harriman said, "You remember the problem I mentioned . . ."

"The girl you unaccountably miss."

"I'm seeing another girl tonight. Different girl."

"And this is your solution to the problem."

"This different girl is a very hot girl."

"Sounds to me like your troubles are over."

"Yeah," Harriman said, "that's what I think."

He was looking out of the window, his eyes slitted against the head-on sun, though he might have been frowning.

Stella sat down with James and Stevie and got some pretty straightforward answers to her questions. A cartoon character called Silent Wolf had killed their father.

Were they sure?

Yes.

Had they seen him do it?

Yes.

Where did this happen?

At home.

What did he look like?

Like this.

Stella took the game that James handed her. There was Silent Wolf, his long coat, his mane of hair, his yellow eyes. His kick had skied one attacker, another was arching back, the impact-star from the Wolf's fist nailed to his chin. The city skyline was a dark silhouette.

She flipped the disc over to read the blurb, and there was the emblem his enemies had come to fear: the mark of the wolf.

Λ Λ
V

77

The AMIP-5 team spoke to the manufacturer, were briefed on the game's market profile, interviewed the team of nerds who had created Silent Wolf. The nerds were freaky obsessives all right but not killers. Harriman and Greegan went over the SOC stills and videos; they put up new cordons and arranged to revisit the scenes in case there were other symbols, other pointers, that they might have missed. Frank Silano spoke to the design company who'd packaged the game: their designers were checked out and found to be solid citizens with wives, children, and only minor coke habits.

Maxine Hewitt and Anne Beaumont sat down with James and Stevie and their Game Boy, all of them taking a walk with Silent Wolf as he freelanced out along the razor's edge. Maxine had obtained the full set of Wolf games, and the boys were heads down, silent, following every move, racking up a score.

Between games they talked about the time Silent Wolf had killed their father.

Stella and Anne found an office that wasn't in use. It contained seven chairs, a white-board and easel, and a photocopier with an OUT OF ORDER note tacked to it. They pulled two chairs round to face each other, a mini-conference.

"What's the profile now?" Stella asked. "I mean, crazy, sure, but—?"

"I need time to look at the games." Anne was flirting with a cup of squad-room coffee. "Follow the narrative."

"The narrative? Easy: he kills people."

"Yes, but look, there's the business of motive. How did he get started? Is he killing out of revenge or is it a warped sort of altruism? He thinks he's ridding the world of evil, remember that. In a way, he's on the side of right. It's rough justice—he's judge, jury, and executioner—but he's not an indiscriminate killer, and he doesn't kill for pleasure."

"No?"

"Well, all right, sure, he's good at it, he has preparation rituals, he assumes he has the moral high ground, and he feels no remorse—all of that. But his victims are deliberately chosen and clearly tagged as bad guys. Silent Wolf's a vigilante."

"You think our man sees himself that way? Tell me how his victims *qualify* as bad guys."

"If I knew that," Anne said, "I'd know almost everything. A similar sort of question is: Why does he identify so strongly with this character? There are hundreds of superheroes and shoot-'em-up games."

"You think the game influenced him?"

"No balanced individual ever became a killer after watching screen violence, or reading a book, or reading an account in a newspaper."

"There are copycat crimes—well documented."

"Sure, I said *balanced* individual. Obviously that doesn't describe our man . . . all the same, I think this game has some sort of special significance for him."

"Because the hero's victims aren't random and aren't innocent."

"Could be." Anne sipped her coffee and immediately set it aside. "One thing seems sure: he's adopted the persona of Silent Wolf. From what the boys said, he looks just like him."

"Which is why they're so fixated on the game," Stella said. She frowned, remembering something. "The grandfather . . . something he said. Yes, one of the boys told him they were worried they'd got the wrong one—the wrong Silent Wolf adventure, I suppose. Did you or DC Hewitt ask them about that?"

Anne nodded. "Yes; but I already knew what the answer would be. These kids live in a screen culture. They see violence of this sort in a game, and it's fiction; they see it on TV, and it's the news; how do they distinguish one from the other? How do they tell the difference between a target centering, a missile firing, and a house exploding when on one occasion it's game graphics, on another it's a real missile and a real house with real people in it? The images are identical."

"So . . . when they asked whether they'd got the right one?"

"They were looking for a certain scene and wondered if it would be in another game, because they couldn't find it in the one they'd got. What they had seen in life, they expected also to see on screen."

Stella felt a chill. "They were looking for the scene where their father is killed by Silent Wolf."

Anne nodded. "Maybe they thought . . ." She paused, because the idea had only just come to her. "Maybe they thought they could put it on rewind; maybe they thought they could hit the stop button and make everything all right."

Stella took her notes into DI Collier, who reached for them with a stiff, awkward gesture like a man with a pulled muscle. The dailies, with their scare-'em headlines, had been thrown on the floor along with files, reports, memos: MONSTER . . . SIEGE . . . CRAZED KILLER . . . FEAR . . . STRIKE AGAIN . . .

She asked, "What did they say at the hospital?"

"That it looked worse than it was. He clipped me just back of the ribs. It would have missed a thinner man, so they told me, which was fucking wonderful to hear. Lot of blood, only two stitches."

"The ARV caught up with them . . ."

Collier smiled. "They ran their car into a fence; bones were broken."

"That must have made you feel better."

Collier shrugged, then regretted it. "I was slow. Desk jobs make you rusty."

"You saved her," Stella said, "and you got shot doing it. Good job, boss." Collier looked at her: both of them taken by surprise. As she was leaving, he said, as if to no one in particular, "I'm crap at this. I'm a street cop. I'm out of my fucking depth with all this paper."

Harriman and Greegan were walking through the Strip. Their trip round the scenes of crime had resulted in nothing new, though there were a few changes. The tree was now in full leaf, and the old hospital had bred a thousand species of crawling and flying insects.

It was neither afternoon nor evening, that depressing, headachy time of day when body-sugar levels dip and everything slows down. The whores, the shebeens, the casinos, the cafés, were idling and the lunchtime drunks weren't yet seeking a freshener. Smells of fast food and gasoline and spilled booze rode the city breeze. Harriman stopped for a moment, looking at a man on the opposite side of the road; the man looked back, smiling and yanking his crotch. It was Costea.

"Friend or acquaintance?" Greegan asked.

"We raided a casino down here . . ."

Greegan remembered. "The guy with the razor. You had to go across the rooftops to nab him."

"I'm not good at heights."

"What's he doing up here?"

Harriman shook his head. "Some smart brief got him bail by the look of it. I expect I abused his human fucking rights in some way."

Greegan looked across to where Costea was leaning against a black four-track Merc. The man waved a cheery finger. Greegan said, "Does he look like that all the time, do you think, or only when he's on the job?"

Harriman cast a glance at Costea. "What?"

"No, not him. Our silent wolfman. Does he get into costume when he gets up in the morning, or—"

"Who knows . . . Why?"

"Because now we have a description," Greegan observed. "Now we know what he looks like."

They'd left the car at the bottom of the Strip and walked to the SOC, because a lorry had spilled its load up on the rise. Greegan fished in his pocket for the keys, then checked his watch. "I'm heading home," he said. "You?"

"Definitely. Hot date."

Greegan sighed and sang a couple of lines of "Memory." They got into the car and drove the fifty yards to the end of the Strip, where the traffic backed up.

Gideon Woolf was walking in the opposite direction, masked from them by a high-sided van, thinking of a letter he had to write.

78

Stella was adding a picture to the white-board in their flat—Silent Wolf, his desert camouflage combat pants, his long coat, his ruff of hair. Delaney was watching the news, reading through an article, opening wine.

Stella asked, "Stanley Bowman, Neil Morgan—"

"I asked around," Delaney said. "The only connection anyone could come up with was that Bowman had fingers in many business pies and Morgan has influence with various committees."

"They were talking business—if that's what it was—very late at night."

"So off the record, you think?"

"I do, yes. Money matters, Bowman said. Where to invest."

"You know"—Delaney poured the wine—"politics and business are much the same thing these days. They all swim in the same sea. Sea of Sleaze. Is that him?"

He was pointing at the artist's impression of Silent Wolf.

"We think so."

"The fashion for combat fatigues," Delaney observed; "it says 'I'm hard,' but it's also something to do with belonging, don't you think? I'm a soldier, I'm combat fit, and I'm ready. The paramilitaries in Bosnia used to wear them as if they conveyed authority. You'd get pulled over at a checkpoint by some illiterate kid with a bad-attitude problem and a liking for violence. He'd be wearing combats and a New York Mets baseball cap. So far as he was concerned, he was the law. You might live or die on his say-so."

"They were militia?" Stella asked.

"Nationalists is what they called themselves. Arkan's Tigers, for instance: nothing more than a bunch of homicidal thugs. Patriotism's a repulsive thing."

He looked shaky for a moment, and Stella reflected on what he must have seen but would never speak about.

Harriman's date was called Miriam, and she was definitely hot. She was catwalk hot, drop-dead hot, perfect-in-all-departments hot. One of the departments in question was bed, which is where she and Harriman were doing everything you could possibly do without throwing your back out or pulling a hamstring.

Afterward, Harriman took a shower: an unusual event; why wash that scent away? Miriam's bathroom had everything, just like Miriam, but he felt uncomfortable there, and when he emerged to find that she had unpacked lobster from the fridge and put a bottle of champagne on ice, he felt his appetite wane.

They ate the food and drank the champagne. Miriam talked, but Harriman didn't have a hell of a lot to say. An hour later he left, telling her that he would call her. He'd call her soon.

Miriam knew what that meant.

When he got back to his own apartment, Gloria was on the answer phone.

Hi, whassup? You still working late? Hmm . . . You know what? I've got a funny feeling about you. Not so funny, really. Not funny at all. Want to talk about that?

He could still smell Miriam, so he got into the shower and stood with his face raised to the jets, gasping, like a man drowning.

Delaney was at the checkpoint. The boy in combats and baseball cap had just unslung his gun. One minute Nathan Prior was standing at Delaney's shoulder, the next he was on the other side of the checkpoint, beckoning and smiling. Delaney started to shout at Prior, but the words were a mouse-squeak. The boy lifted the gun to Delaney's head, except now it was a pistol, and Delaney and the boy were making that iconic image of execution from the Vietnam War: the prisoner shot on camera.

Delaney was yelling, but only he could hear. Prior beckoned, smiling. The gun made a mechanical sound, like tumblers falling, and the bullet started along the barrel.

Stella lay beside him as he muttered and twitched his way through the dream. She thought she knew what all these combat-zone dreams meant.

That morning an estate agent had called to tell her that they'd had an offer on the Vigo Street flat. The buyer was offering the asking price. She put a hand on Delaney's arm and he half woke, staring at her.

"You were having a bad dream."

"Okay," he said, and closed his eyes. "Okay," as if he'd expected nothing else.

79

I am the one in the papers, but it's over now. I have no more calls to make. The ones who died deserved what they got, and there is nothing left to say. To let you know this is genuine, I can tell you this one thing that hasn't appeared in the papers, I wrote on them about their offense. Leonard Pigeon was a mistake and I am sorry for that.

Gideon Woolf at the computer in his room high above the heat and lights of the Strip . . . A thin charcoal dust from the scorched beams sifted down onto the keyboard as he inserted the game and waited for the logo to arrive on the screen, for the low, slow notes of the music, for the first graphic of yellow eyes on a black screen, then the skyline of the city fading in below a rose-colored sky.

Silent Wolf walked him down unlit alleys and round blind corners; they were the street-sweepers; where they walked, enemies fell; they were invincible.

It's over now . . .

But there was still Aimée.

80

The letter was in Brian Collier's mail. He opened it and read the first couple of lines before realizing what it was. Stella picked up his call as she was leaving Coffee Republic, and by the time she reached the squad room a forensic officer was already on the way. She read the letter hands-free.

"It's him."

"Could it have leaked—the writing on all the bodies?"

"I don't see how. Anyway"—she was remembering that, yes, she had told Delaney—"it hasn't been in the press, and that's the only way a crank would have known about it." She hunkered down to get an eye-level view of the envelope that was lying on Collier's desk, next to the letter. "This doesn't look like a self-seal. If he licked it—plenty of isolated DNA. That'll tell us for sure."

"I wonder if he means it," Collier said.

"That he's finished?"

"Yes."

"He's nuts," Stella said. "Who knows what he means?"

"He means he's killed his chosen victims, the ones he set out to kill."

Stella sat in Anne Beaumont's basement kitchen and watched as Anne chopped vegetables. A large pan of water was simmering on the stove.

"This is a man who thinks he's Silent Wolf, enemy of Ironjaw, for Christ's sake." Stella leaned back in her chair and closed her eyes for a moment. "What makes you think he's working off some sort of logical game plan?"

"Depends what you mean by logical. Remember Leopold and Loeb? They killed because they felt like it."

"He even dresses like Silent Wolf."

"Well, we think he does. James and Stevie might have projected that. But, yes, it's a fair bet. How mad does that make him? We all imitate styles of dress in order to belong or impress. Mods, greasers, punks, hippies, politicians in gray suits, the bare-midriff look, hoodies. You, for instance, have obviously been strongly influenced by Parisian haute couture."

"Fuck off."

Anne laughed. "He's playing a role, because he believes he has a role to play. There's a key to this lock, and it's something to do with the cartoon hero's brand of frontier justice. He's paying back; he's settling a score; he's demonstrating his worth . . . I don't know. Somewhere along the way, there's a major trauma."

"You're cooking," Stella said, as if the oddity of that had only just struck her.

"I am, yes."

"We unwrap . . . sometimes we defrost." After a moment, Stella added: "Delaney's having nightmares: bombs and battles."

"You suspect he's going to find himself a war . . ."

"I do."

"And what do you think about that?"

"I think he might well get himself killed. I think he's a selfish bastard. I think trying to stop him would be a bad move."

"I think you're right."

"Here's another thing. I had a letter from my mother."

"Why?"

"She's leaving. Or else she's left."

"What did it say?"

"She was passing on a message from her boyfriend, whose links with the criminal world seem pretty well established . . . no surprises there."

"A message?"

"A tip-off, really. I've also passed it on."

Anne took a chicken carcass from the fridge, broke it, put it into the pan, and added the vegetables.

"What is that?"

"Stock. For soup?" Stella nodded as if it was something she did every day. "What else did she say?" Anne asked.

"She made reference to my happy childhood, our precious time together, the way we'd always been there for one another, the laughter we'd shared, the evenings when she'd read to me as I sat in bed sipping my Ovaltine."

Anne shook her head. "My God, she's in trouble."

"*She's* in trouble?" Stella's laugh bore no trace of humor.

"Yes," Anne said, "that's right. She needs help. Can't you see that?"

Stella sat in silence for five minutes, while Anne stirred and flavored. Finally she said, "Yes, I can." Then: "But fuck her, okay? Fuck *her*!"

"You owe me some money. It hasn't arrived." Bowman's tone of voice was genial, which was what made it threatening.

The American sighed. "Is he going to get better?"

"No one seems to know. For now? Count him out."

They were talking about Neil Morgan, who showed no sign of being able to check out of ITC. Candice had set up camp, with a director's chair, coffee flask, health snacks, and a makeup bag. She watched his monitors, the slow rise and fall of his chest, his face wiped clean of all expression.

Don't die, you bastard!

The American said, "So get me someone else."

"I'm working on it."

"Work harder."

"Happy to. I expect the money's on its way."

"This is a long-term thing," the American observed. "It's a market thing, a worldwide thing. Just now? I've got two deals in train. I've got a coup on the move. Big order for small arms. The new government will need to keep the population on side. I've got antipersonnel mines and mortars going out to a civil-war situation—protection of territory, or religion, or whatever. This is all good; this is all fine. What I really need is throughput, I need volume, I need your market and for that I need help."

"And the money's about to arrive," Bowman said, "have I got that right?"

"Yeah, yeah . . . for Christ's sake."

"Good," Bowman said, "because that'll be a great incentive."

"What happened?" the American asked. "It was, like, a break-in? Morgan got in the way?"

"Looks like it."

"Hey, the world's a dangerous place."

Bowman sat behind his vast desk in his vast office in his vast house and watched the tiny, bright jot of a mile-high aircraft tow white plumes across the sky.

He didn't think about landmines, or the field-workers and children who would tread on them. He didn't wonder about the civil war and who was worshipping the wrong god. He did think about coming downstairs and finding Neil Morgan, though, and remembered the damage the man had undergone, the knife slashes, the fault line on the skull where the fire iron had struck, the broad spillage of blood.

Bowman would need another politician, someone who liked money, someone who thought of politics as a high-risk, high-rewards game, someone who knew that the meek would never inherit the earth.

He didn't expect to have to look far.

81

Frank Silano had posted an abstract of the killings.

Bryony Dean—hanged
Leonard Pigeon—decapitation attempt
Martin Turner—shot
George Nelms—decapitated
Neil Morgan—decapitation attempt

"Okay," Stella said, "if we take Pigeon out of it, if we work on the assumption that the killer was really after Neil Morgan, then we can also assume that the intended method was decapitation, so we've got a hanging, a shooting, and two decapitations. Why?"

"Silent Wolf carries a knife," Maxine observed. "Weapon of choice."

"He sometimes carries a gun," Silano said.

"And karate-kicks the shit out of people," Harriman added; "he's a multitalented man."

The *Silent Wolf* game was now a squad-room feature. Harriman had racked a good score and so had Silano, but no one had come close to Sue Chapman, who, among her colleagues, had earned herself the title of Silent Wolf Bitch.

Stella said, "Silent Wolf never hanged anyone."

"So this is his pattern, the killer's."

"That's what the profiler says, and it seems right to me."

"Hang, chop, shoot, chop, chop," Maxine offered.

"We're taking Pigeon out of it," Silano reminded her, "so it's hang, shoot, chop, chop."

"No," Harriman said. "The guy thought Pigeon was Morgan, so it's really hang, chop, shoot, chop in that order." He looked at Stella. "We're looking for the reason for that particular pattern, that particular order?"

"It's one of the things we're looking for."

Tom Davison's cubicle office sported a large poster of Rembrandt's painting *The Anatomy Lesson of Dr. Deyman.* The head on the eviscerated body had been replaced with that of a Hollywood actress, and a speech bubble read: *Don't meddle with what don't concern ya.*

Davison was showing Stella a photograph of a partial boot print. He said, "The blood is Morgan's, of course. The boot is one of those calf-length, lace-up combat-style boots. You can get them pretty much anywhere. Same print in the garden by the empty house, same again in the house itself."

"DNA at the scene?"

"Sure. It's sorting one lot from another. Which we are."

"Fingerprints?"

"Same thing. However"—Davison shuffled some papers and found a lab report—"it looks as if he did leave prints this time, prints we can probably isolate, anyway; two sets on the fire iron and what looks like a matching partial on a door frame."

"Anything on the letter?" Stella asked.

"We haven't had it long enough."

"It's a priority."

"We know that."

He smiled at her, and she remembered the smile or, at least, its sleepier, sexier version.

What is it about me that I'm drawn to men who deal with the dead or the dying, with people who kill?

What is it about them that they're drawn to you?

Stella was having a two-way conversation with herself as she nudged her car out into the tailback, then played yellow-box chicken with a black cab. London driving was all about attrition.

It's not so much that he's planning to go to dangerous places; it's that he hasn't told me.

Ask yourself why.

Okay . . .

Stella cut up a Volvo to make a lane switch, found herself blocked by a parked truck and switched back, cutting up the Volvo again: horn blasts and the flashing of headlights.

He doesn't want my opinion on the matter.

Maybe. Or he just doesn't want it to be an issue.

Why not?

He isn't used to it?

Because he's not used to having to take anyone else's opinion into account.

That's right.

But he was the one who suggested we move in together, buy a house even, thereby ipso facto involving another person.

Which means he's taking a risk.

Is ipso facto right?

Fuck knows.

You mean living with me at all is a compromise?

One he's prepared to make.

Oh, well, big fucking deal.

Says you. But turn it around.

How would I feel if I wanted to do something but worried about someone else disapproving?

Yes.

Hmm . . . Okay.

Not so good, huh? Don't like being corraled.

Not much.

So here's a guy who can see the downside of involving someone else in his life on a permanent basis—a buying-a-house-together basis—but goes ahead and makes the suggestion anyway.

He's a good man, and I'm lucky to have him.

Was there a note of cynicism in that?

I don't like being nagged at.

My point exactly.

Sorley came through on her mobile. Her Bluetooth was somewhere, anywhere, so she drove one-handed and let go of the wheel entirely to change gear.

"He's a cartoon, he's loony tunes." Sorley sounded like a sketched-in version of his old self.

"I hope you're not letting Karen know where those report folders came from."

"Karen doesn't see them. I keep them under the bed."

"Got anything else under there, boss?"

"Don't you start."

Sorley had nothing much to do but watch TV and not smoke. In fact, he was a heavy nonsmoker; his nonsmoking activities were world class.

"He says he's going to stop killing—that he *has* stopped. You saw that?" Stella said.

"I saw it. And if he means it—"

"We might never catch him. Right."

"Like he was a man on a mission, and now it's come to an end."

"What are they saying about you?"

"They're saying I have to lose weight, take exercise, moderate my drinking—"

"You can drink?"

"Not yet. When I start drinking again, then it has to be moderate."

"What's that?"

"What?"

"Moderate."

"Well, they've given me a units card. Tells you how many in a single Scotch, small glass of wine, half of bitter, you know . . ."

"Single this, small that, half of something else. Sounds mealymouthed."

"The thing is," Sorley said, "if you can have, say, three units a day—"

"Is that the allowance?"

"For a man. Less for a woman."

"Oh, good . . ."

"That would be twenty-one units a week. So I mean, can you drink the twenty-one on Monday and go on the wagon for the rest of the week?"

"Oh, yeah," Stella said, "I don't see why not." Then she said, "He's loony tunes, all right, but there's an X-factor."

"Like I say, man with a mission."

"Get well soon, boss."

"I am well."

"Get better than well."

"Stella . . ."

She knew what was coming and she told him not to say it, but he said it anyway. "Karen told me. You saved my life."

"It wasn't intentional."

He laughed, which was what she'd expected, then asked: "How's acting DI Collier?"

"Acting up."

"You turned down too many promotion boards."

"I know. Look, he's finding it difficult. I almost feel sorry for him."

Her arm was cramping, so she switched hands, drifted, and overcorrected. A patrol car cruised alongside for a moment, then dropped back to tail her.

"I'm going to have to go, boss. I'm about to get arrested."

She dropped the phone, took a left turn without signaling, changed down, accelerated hard, made another turn, and parked. In her mirror, she saw the patrol car pass the junction, bucking as it hit a speed bump.

She picked up the phone and dialed. When she gave her name, the estate agent said, "You're accepting their offer?"

"They'll go a few grand more," Stella said, "otherwise why would they agree to the asking price?"

"I'm not sure."

"Push them," Stella said. "Gentle push."

"If they say no?"

"Push again."

She got back into traffic, the sun low now and glossing her windscreen.

You're delaying. You're backing off.

I know what I'm doing.

You're going to have to make a decision, sooner or later.

Fuck off.

Remember you used to have these dice—you used to make choices by throwing dice?

Not really.

You did.

A couple of times. It was Anne Beaumont's idea, not mine.

Why not throw the dice?

I don't know where they are. I lost them.

Throw them in your mind.
In my mind?
Because that's where the decision gets made anyway. Five and below,
don't sell. Six and above, go for it.
Is that any way to choose the future?
Good as any . . . Okay, thrown yet?
Yep.
What was it?
I don't know. The sun's in my eyes.

Gideon and Aimée out for a stroll, hand in hand, a couple in love, she in a short skirt and an emerald crossover top that showed some cleavage and deepened the color of her eyes, he in jeans and a T-shirt, just like any other guy.

She paused, reaching up to kiss him. She wondered whether it would ever fade, this constant sexual need of him. She could feel a flush spreading down from her throat, and her nipples hardened. She thought it must have something to do with his being the perfect match, the *one*.

They spoke about going away and agreed it would be soon. They decided on a place: it was by the sea. They decided on a day. They would go by train; he wanted that, and it seemed a wonderful idea. They would meet at the station. They chose a specific meeting place; they chose a time of day. In her mind's eye, Aimée saw them sitting on the train as it slid away from the platform. Then she was in the train beside him, the view from the window a blur, like her old life. She closed her eyes and lifted her face to the sun.

A walk in the park. It was hot, and they'd been out for a while, so they rested in the shade of a tree.

The mark of his triple-vee high on the trunk.

82

Three A.M. and London's false neon dawn a spreading blush in the sky. A blackbird ran through its repertoire in a plane tree close to the window of Stanley Bowman's study.

The American money was through, and Bowman was in the process of making it invisible. It had come by a circuitous route to a host account, but Bowman wasn't content to let it stay there long. He had several methods, all of which involved the money taking flight, but he was worried about the frequency with which they'd been used recently; in an electronic age there is always the danger of a stalker.

He called the American to confirm delivery: it took three seconds; then he dialed the number that Ricardo had given to Sekker. A recorded voice offered a prompt, and Bowman gave the code word. The line went dead, and Bowman hung up. It was all as it should be. Ten minutes later he received a return call. A voice asked him to nominate a bank account. Bowman gave the number. There is, in all such transactions, an issue of trust. The voice asked Bowman for a designated sum, and Bowman gave the information. The bank would be identified, a John Doe account opened, and Bowman given code-word access to the account. Half the money would be deposited and a commission taken. Then Bowman would send the second half of the money. After that it would travel for a while—a few red routes, a few cash highways. It might even divide and redivide in the interests of faster movement. Flight capital is like a jet stream: you know it's high and swift, but you can't see it. Finally, Vanechka would be in touch to talk about defraying an investment.

Bowman had the TV on with the sound down. While he made his phone calls, he was accessing Teletext share prices but also, from time to time, channel-hopping. The late-night movies were all-action affairs, blood-baths, fire-fests, robowars. Cops advanced the cause of law and order, and the bad guys went down. In an urban killing field, the incoming took out house walls; smart bombs found cellars and dugouts. Foot soldiers sprinted from cover to cover, yelling instructions, putting down a field of fire as they ran.

Bowman gave himself a Scotch that was either the last of the night or first of the day. He watched the movie for a few moments, then switched to Poker Nite. The phone rang, and a voice let him know that his money was well on the way to becoming anonymous.

In an urban killing field, the incoming took out house walls; smart bombs found cellars and dugouts. Foot soldiers sprinted from cover to cover, yelling instructions, putting down a field of fire as they ran.

Stella was watching a roundup of the day's news, because she was too tired to read but too wakeful to go back to bed. As she watched, a soldier fell as if his strings had been pulled. A building mushroomed, its walls bellying out as black smoke enveloped it.

Is this what you want, Delaney? Is this where you plan to be?

She almost obeyed an urge to wake him and ask for an answer, but it would be too close to asking for commitment. Some things have to be freely given. She spent a few minutes staring at the white-board, as if an answer to everything might suddenly appear there: her killer, her lover, her life . . .

On TV an embedded reporter spoke of kidnaps and executions. The war-zone sky was lit by flares and burning buildings.

Aimée had been woken by the sound of her own voice. She might have shouted his name, she couldn't be sure. Peter and Ben were sleeping. She hoped their dreams were good.

The kitchen still held the heat of the day. She made tea, then switched on the TV with the sound low, looking for a distraction: she didn't want to have to think about the letter she was planning to write. A letter because she intended to be gone before Peter knew; she wouldn't be able to listen to his pleas, or to Ben's, or to look at their faces.

She glanced at the TV without really seeing it. In an urban killing field, the incoming took out house walls; smart bombs found cellars and dugouts. Foot soldiers sprinted from cover to cover, yelling instructions, putting down a field of fire as they ran. An embedded reporter spoke of kidnaps and executions. The war-zone sky was lit by flares and burning buildings.

If it hadn't been her own voice that woke her, it might have been a memory of his voice as he spoke her name. She pictured herself lying beside him in whatever bed they would find in whatever place they would come to on her first real night of freedom; it was where she most wanted to be.

Gideon.

She thought she would stay up and see the dawn in, because then she would feel a day nearer to that moment at the train station, their meeting, their departure, the new life.

The incoming, smoke, rubble in the streets . . .

Stella turned from the white-board to the TV and back again. Men running from cover to cover. Silent Wolf, dressed to kill.

There was something she recognized in all this but couldn't isolate; something nagging, like a word on the tip of the tongue or some memory half brought back by a certain smell. It came and went, sometimes almost in focus, then becoming foggier. She closed her eyes, searching for it, and other thoughts crowded in—spoilers—her mother's face, made sluttish by drink; the book floating down from eighteen stories; Delaney in the TV war zone.

Suddenly she felt exhausted, as if something deep inside had been tapped and drawn off. She lay down on the sofa, a cushion under her head, and started to drift into sleep immediately. The TV was still playing softly: soft gunfire, soft explosions. The pictures on the white-board seemed to warp and move, as if the TV images had become transposed.

Delaney running up the white road. The incoming . . . smoke . . . Men in desert-combat camouflage. A house mushrooming. Silent Wolf looking down on the scene, his yellow eyes, his yellow hair.

She sat up, her mind clearing, the images coming together to make a little narrative, a little story. The killer's story. Now she remembered: Delaney's encounter with the border guards in combat fatigues. Davison with the photo of a print left by a combat boot. Sorley speaking of a man on a mission.

She made a call.

Gloria clambered sleepily across Harriman, picked up his mobile, and put it next to him on the pillow. Without opening his eyes, Harriman said his name.

"He's a soldier," Stella said. "He's a soldier or else he used to be."

83

The white road, the five men. A radio playing music.

A daylight patrol and nothing much to worry about, because this is more of a goodwill mission, this is a meet-and-greet, no need for helmets, weapons at standby, well inside the safety zone. Call it a presence. The locals are friendly: already persuaded. No one expecting to see action, no one expecting to be tested, and Gideon Woolf is glad of that, because he thinks he's probably had enough. Enough of being under fire, enough of close calls, enough of close-combat standoffs.

There's a shake in his hands and a sick feeling in his gut, this day and every day. He's ashamed of his fear, but he can't fight it. Only one person in the world knows about this.

The girl's name is Camilla, or so he thinks. Kah-mila, she said. He's not the only man with a local girl, but he might be the only man with a girl like this: one who listens to his fear, helps him forget, holds him against her body until the shakes stop.

When he'd relaxed, when the opium had taken the edge off, when he'd had enough of her body, she would ask him when she might be seeing him again, where he would be next day or the day after, where she might find him. She would stroke his feverish head while their whispers went to and fro, her questions, his answers.

The men walking in single file, music from the radio, the gun flash. A man goes down, and suddenly the street is no place to be. The three men leading the patrol return fire, while Gideon Woolf finds cover. He knows he should use his weapon, he knows he should engage, but to do that would be to give away his position. He is pressed back in a doorway, hearing the screams and the gunfire. He can see the legs of the man who was shot.

Woolf's chest is constricted, it hurts, and he can't get his breath. Some detached, some disgusted part of himself registers that he is pissing his pants.

The other three men should be dead, but it seems the idea is not to kill them. Their attackers want hostages, they want captives. As the men are hustled toward a jeep, Woolf steps out of cover: just a couple of feet or so. He has a clear line of fire and the element of surprise. The attackers number ten, maybe twelve. He could bring some down, scatter the rest. He could draw fire: that would be the tactical thing to do. Maybe his comrades would die, maybe not; maybe he would die; but the opportunity is there.

One of his comrades sees him and shouts his name. Shouts an order. Even from that distance, it's easy to see that the man's eyes are wide with fear. He shouts again, pleading. Woolf's hands shake, and a gobbet of puke floods his mouth. Things blur, as if he were about to faint, and there's a noise in his head like white water.

A moment later . . . it seems like an hour later . . . he's still standing in the street. The jeep has gone. Twenty feet away, a man lies dead. Of his other comrades, no sign.

The radio is still playing music.

84

Maxine Hewitt was a good detective, and one of the attributes of a good detective is an eye for detail and a reliable memory. She went back to her notes from the meeting between herself, Frank Silano, and George Nelms's former headmaster, Richard Forester. She found this:

MH: What subject?

RF: Sports teacher.

FS: Only that?

RF: Cadet corps.

Stella took the interview with Pete Harriman. In the headmaster's office they asked questions that they hoped would get them what they wanted without revealing exactly what that was.

Stella began: "Mr. Nelms was in charge of the cadet corps . . ."

"He felt that some boys were well suited," Forester said, then gave a half smile. "Some boys well suited, some good for little else."

"He encouraged them to join up?"

"Certainly. Look"—Forester couldn't see where the line of questioning was going, but he had an uneasy feeling about it—"it wasn't just a case of dumping the no-hopers. There were boys who showed particular aptitude."

"What for?"

"The army. Armed services."

"In what way?" Stella asked.

Forester paused fractionally. "Leaders of men."

Stella noticed the hesitation. Was that it, she wondered, or do you mean an aptitude for violence?

Harriman said, "Did you keep a record?"

"Of what?"

"Boys who were in the cadet corps."

"Of course."

"Could we see it?"

"How far back do you want to go?"

Stella made a quick calculation. "Ten years?"

Forester pressed an intercom button on his phone and asked for the file. He said, "There's no news?"

"The investigation is ongoing," Harriman said, as if he normally spoke like that.

"And you're asking about the cadet force because—"

"All of Mr. Nelms's activities are important to us," Stella told him. "We might not know what we're looking for until we find it."

Forester looked away, and his mouth trembled very slightly. "It's been a terrible shock. The way he died—what happened to him; the stuff of nightmares."

Your nightmares, Stella thought.

A secretary brought in the file and Stella flipped the names. She said, "Could I have a photocopy of this? For reference."

Harriman saw her expression change, just fleetingly, the way someone looks when they see, in a crowd, a suddenly familiar face. When they got into the car, she handed him the list, folded back to the last page.

Woolf, Gideon.

She said, "There are coincidences in the world, but this isn't one of them."

It was like hauling something up from deep water: the closer it got to the surface, the quicker it came. From having nothing, Stella suddenly had almost everything. All a matter of record; Sue Chapman's work made easy. Name, onetime address, age, family history, explanations . . . even a photograph.

It was a head-and-shoulders portrait of a young man with a brutal haircut, a beret raked just so, a dress uniform. The man supplying the photo and the history was a lieutenant-colonel whose edginess was apparent.

"It was an unpleasant episode," he said. "He would have been court-martialed had any of the witnesses survived, but the facts were clear enough. A good deal of it came from him, in point of fact; a confession of sorts. Anyway, it was clear that the man couldn't continue. His breakdown was genuine enough, or so I'm led to believe." The lieutenant-colonel allowed a touch of skepticism into his voice.

"Not helped by the tabloid press reports," Stella guessed.

"That was a leak—shouldn't have happened, but there were people who wanted him exposed."

Sue Chapman had already sourced the front pages: COWARD! GUTLESS! A SOLDIER'S SHAME! BASTARD! and the unanswerable HOW WILL YOU LIVE WITH YOURSELF?

"Who told them?" Stella asked.

"Look . . ." The lieutenant-colonel's edginess took on a tinge of aggression. "It was a dreadful thing to do. Four men died, three of whom might possibly have been saved if the man had acted as he should. He was a pariah. I don't approve of the leak—we prefer to keep army business to ourselves—but I can understand why some people wanted him pilloried."

"Especially since he wasn't being court-martialed."

"If you like. It wasn't just a matter of cowardice in action. It's likely that collaboration was an issue—if inadvertent."

"How so?"

"Some sort of an involvement with a local woman. It's by no means clear how the kidnappers knew they'd meet little resistance—that it was a small patrol on a routine exercise. It's entirely possible that pillow talk was involved."

"You think this relationship, this involvement, was sexual?"

"I expect so. Isn't that the usual method for extracting information—a honeytrap?"

Dirty Girl.

Stella said, "One of the newspaper reports claims that Woolf was hospitalized for a short while after the event."

"Yes, he was said to be having a breakdown. I mentioned that."

"Was that before or after the newspapers got the story?"

"He was a coward. His comrades were murdered. Those are the facts that concern me."

"The point is," Stella insisted, "that the hospital in question wasn't for psychiatric patients. One of my colleagues contacted the paper that ran the story, then the hospital. Their patient had sustained some physical injuries. He'd been beaten up."

"Yes, I know about that. It's not at all clear where the incident took place. It's under investigation." The lieutenant-colonel decided to try a switch-tactic. "You say he's needed to help you in the course of certain investigations."

"That's right."

"Investigations concerning what exactly?"

"Like you," Stella said, "there are certain things we have to keep to ourselves." As if it didn't matter much, she asked, "One man was shot during the attack, the others were taken."

"Yes."

"How did they die?"

The lieutenant-colonel sighed. "One was hanged, more or less on the spot. The other two were decapitated."

Shoot, hang, chop, chop.

The wrong order, she thought. As if it made a difference to the dead.

On her way back she took a call from Tom Davison.

"The Morgan crime scene. The envelope flap. Did you ever have any doubt?"

"Never," Stella told him.

"Me neither. And we were both right. He attacked Morgan, he wrote the letter." A pause, then Davison said, "Are you any closer?"

"Yes and no. He's a soldier, or used to be." Something occurred to her. "How come his DNA wasn't on the database?"

"You're talking about the police database, which is for bad people," Davison said. "There is an army database, but it's not amalgamated with ours: it's just for soldiers, who are not, de facto, bad people. I know they shoot people, but they do it for Queen and country. What else have you got?"

"We know his name, we sort of know what he looks like, we know where he used to live, we know his mother is dead, that his father sold up and is living in a care-home. We know why he did what he did, we know all sorts of things. But we think he's stopped; and people can disappear."

"You know what he looks like?"

"General description." Stella didn't want to talk about Silent Wolf the games hero.

"So post a compufit."

"You know what that does—it lets the guy know we know, and he goes underground."

"Okay," Davison said, "revert to Plan A."

"We don't have a Plan A."

"Yeah, I guessed."

85

A man falls facedown on the road, the road white with dust, his combats messed and bloody, blood on his hands where he clutched his chest, a broad seep-age of blood coming from beneath his body and puddling by his head, flies already beginning to feast on it, one leg jerking and drumming the ground.

Gideon Woolf has found cover. He can hear the rattle of gunfire, the cries for help. He stays back, he stays out of sight.

The man on the ground is unmoving now. There's an inertness about him that lets you know he's dead: as if he had fallen from a great height and the dust had settled, his heart had settled, to stillness. Engines rev and roar; there are two jeeps, maybe three. As they drive off, there are bursts of gunfire aimed only at the sky: a celebration.

A minute goes by, five minutes. Gideon Woolf moves out of cover. There are people emerging from houses, some of them are applauding. Gideon is aware of the wet stain on the crotch of his combats. He throws down his weapon and starts up the street. A kid of about ten picks up the gun and trains it on Gideon's back. He makes a hacking noise like automatic *gunfire. In the distance, but coming in fast, you can hear the clatter of heli-copter blades.*

Gideon keeps walking, as if he were following the jeep tracks. Two streets away he finds another man hanging from a street sign. The sign had been hit by mortar fire and only the pole-framework was left, a perfect gibbet. The man's hands are tied behind his back, and his feet are tied, and there is a piece of paper tacked to his chest, a sign telling the world that the soldier hanging there is dirt from a dirty country of dirty people.

The helicopter lands in an uprush of dust. Men run toward Gideon, shouting reassurances. They think he is a survivor-hero. Later, they will come to know him better as a filthy coward.

The images are a little blurry, a little grainy, because the video equipment isn't state of the art, but it's easy enough to see what's going on.

Two men in orange jumpsuits sit on the floor, their hands bound, a five-day stubble on their cheeks. Behind them stand three men who call themselves warriors. They are posed, their automatic weapons held at an angle. The hostages have signs pinned to their chests that let the world know that they are no less dirty than the man who was hanged. They are dirty bastards. They are dirty lying bastards.

The Internet sends these pictures to the global village, and Gideon Woolf is watching on his computer. He has seen the sequence twenty times before. The first time he watched, he cried, but now his face is like stone.

One of the warriors steps forward, drawing a long, curved knife from his belt. He grabs the hair of one of the soldiers and yanks the man's head back, putting strain on the tendons of the neck. He makes a flourish with the knife and calls on his God, then slits the soldier's throat. The man hops and writhes. A gusher of blood arcs up; it splashes on the other soldier, who knows he will be the next to die. He is sobbing, his head bowed, his shoulders heaving. The warrior keeps cutting until he reaches the neck bone, then twists and wrenches to tear the ligaments and get his blade be-tween the vertebrae.

He holds the head aloft in the name of God.

Gideon watches again, then breaks the Internet connection. He puts into the computer a game he has just bought. The hero carries Gideon's name into the world like a banner, and Gideon is pledged to do the same, pledged to prove himself.

He buys a pair of plain glasses with a pale yellow tint, he dyes his hair corn-blond, he buys army-surplus desert fatigues and a long, cotton duster-coat. The game becomes an obsession; it becomes a way of life.

From the vantage point of the scorched room he looks down on the city, his combat zone, his killing ground.

86

Sue Chapman had been working to tie Woolf's victims to the words written on them, the accusations, and events in that street white with dust.

Once she knew what she was looking for, the task was easy enough and, in Bryony's case, needed no research at all. She was a hooker and that had been enough to make her a stand-in for the honeytrap. Nelms was simple too: the man who had put Gideon Woolf through his cadet training and, probably, encouraged him to join the army. Turner and Morgan didn't take a lot more work. Turner's editorials said yes to war in a loud voice; his paper had been noted for it. Morgan had taken the same view: Sue's desk was littered with transcripts of radio and TV shows, interviews, articles, all of which carried the same message: send in the troops, do it now, stay till the job's done.

Bryony and Nelms were personal. Turner and Morgan were public and unignorable.

Now the squad-room white-board had been stripped of all material except the names of the victims.

Leonard Pigeon's name was at the top and in brackets: dispensed with; a mistake. The words on Pigeon's arms had been meant for Morgan, that was clear. The other names all carried a rider.

Bryony Dean: "DIRTY GIRL"—GW's involvement with local woman.
Martin Turner: "LYING BASTARD"—editorials/press reports.
George Nelms: "HAPPY NOW?"—persuaded GW to join army.
Neil Morgan: "FILTHY COWARD"—pro-war MP.

Anne Beaumont was at the briefing, because Stella wanted everyone to hear what Anne had to say.

"It's to do with effacement—of his actions and of himself. The one depends on the other. It also has to do with self-worth and with a very unpleasant system of equivalents. Okay? Men died because he was afraid, so he needs to prove himself fearless. To do this he performs the very act he was incapable of: he kills. Not only that, he kills people who seem, to him, blameworthy, just as he was blameworthy. He kills a prostitute, because a prostitute betrayed him. Or if not a prostitute, a woman who traded sex for information. He kills the man who talked him into becoming a soldier. He kills a journalist and an MP, both of whom were high-profile supporters of the conflict.

"He's trading one death for another: canceling them out, and what's more, he thinks they deserve it, so that's all right. He's also reinventing himself: no longer the despised coward, no longer the man who left his comrades to die, he's a killer, he's fearless, he brings justice to an unjust world."

Anne paused and smiled a rueful smile. "Think of the moment when he found the vehicle for this—someone with his own name, a games hero, someone who doesn't really exist until Gideon Woolf becomes Silent Wolf, someone who's without fear and also free of doubt, someone whose killings exist only in game-world. It must have been like finding himself, a remade self, someone who could be the new him."

Silano asked, "He says he's stopped."

"Four deaths," Anne said, "or at least four attempts. That balances the deaths he has on his conscience, it proves he's no coward, it removes four sinners from the world: sinners in his terms, anyway. So, yes, maybe he will stop."

"Okay," Silano said. "Let's say he's stopped. Who is he now?"

"You mean is he the disgraced Gideon Woolf or is he Silent Wolf, the avenger . . ."

"Yes."

Anne nodded. "That's a very good question." After a moment she added, "I wonder if he knows."

The squad was chasing leads, though there were few.

Friends: none could be found. Other men from the regiment, yes, but no one who knew much about him. People said he was a loner, he was quiet, he didn't complain.

Teachers: they had him as an average student; no, a little better than average. He was quiet, he wasn't a problem.

People from his old neighborhood: he seemed like a nice enough boy, a quiet boy. Look, who knows? He kept himself to himself.

Anne Beaumont picked on the words "quiet" and "loner." "A secret life," she said. "A strong fantasy world is a protection against things. Ask another question: he was quiet, yes, and he seemed nice enough, but ask whether he was liked. Ask whether he was *likable*."

"Because?" Stella asked.

"Because I suspect 'quiet' will become 'surly' and 'loner' become 'loser.'" Anne sighed. "On the one hand, you have to wonder why there might be damaged and disturbed people in the army; on the other, it's not a puzzle at all."

Maxine Hewitt and Frank Silano visited the home-from-home that Gideon Woolf's father had picked out for himself. A care-worker took them to a room where twelve elderly people sat round the walls in chairs and slept while the television played to their dreaming heads.

Gideon's father was woken, and all four of them went to a side room. The old man informed them that they wouldn't be able to speak to Gideon, because he had been killed in action. Maxine glanced at Silano, wondering what to say next.

Silano said, "We heard he was alive after all . . ." Maxine admired the "after all." "We wondered whether he'd been to see you."

"He's dead," the old man insisted. "He died out there."

"Who told you he was dead?"

"We weren't supposed to have children. Too old. She died, then he died, and that leaves me."

"Did Gideon ever come here to see you?" Maxine asked.

The care-worker caught Maxine's eye and shook her head.

Maxine tried again. "When was the last time you saw him?"

"Gideon's dead. He's dead, he died in battle, that's for sure, I know that for sure."

The sun high and bright, the care-home lawn dotted with chairs where residents dozed away what was left of their lives.

The care-worker asked, "Has he got a son? We've never seen anyone. No visits, no letters . . ."

"You thought he might have made it up—someone who died in action?"

"We wondered. So many of them invent things. He's not so old, and he's not incapable. More than anything, he seems to have just given up."

"On what?" Silano asked.

"On himself."

"He has a son," Maxine said, "somewhere."

In the car, Silano said, "They have to—have to make up the past."

"Yeah?" Maxine was lowering a visor against the sun. "Why?"

"They forget the truth of it."

"How do you know that?"

Silano just shrugged. Maxine realized that she didn't know a hell of a lot about Frank Silano.

Gideon Woolf's father went back to the TV room and sat in his usual chair. He wanted to sleep but couldn't. On screen was a wide shot of a young couple standing on a hilltop and looking out at a green valley with a river running through. The man had his arm round the woman's shoulders, and as they stood there, you could tell they had overcome some troubles, made some right choices, and had a good life ahead of them.

The old man looked round the room at the faces shuttered by sleep. He said, "Well, he's dead to me."

87

Because Anne was in the squad room, Stella showed her Tina's letter, which Anne read without comment. Later they went to Coffee Republic, because Anne had declared AMIP coffee a contravention of her human rights. On their way, Stella bought a paper that had somehow tied Woolf's killings to the phases of the moon, a method that enabled them to tell the police when he would kill again.

"Which is the big question," Stella said. "Will he?"

"His psychopathology is likely to have been modified by recent experience," Anne said. Stella looked at her. "Depends what killing people did to his head. How unstable he's become."

"He's killed several people," Stella said. "Becoming unstable isn't the issue—he *is* unstable."

"Depends what you mean."

"It does?"

"Think about it," Anne said. "The army considered him unstable because he *didn't* kill people."

The text tone on Stella's mobile rang. She read the text and sent a quick reply. When she looked up, Anne was smiling at her. "I thought I'd leave it to you to mention the letter."

"I sometimes wonder," Stella said, "whether I'm misremembering everything—she's right and I'm wrong. Maybe it really was like that, tough but happy, a mother who did her best. Maybe she did read me bedtime stories."

"People often reinvent the past," Anne told her, "if it's too painful to remember."

The text had been from Andy Greegan, letting Stella know that the compufit she had ordered was on her desk. The image was a compilation of Woolf's army mug shot and the Silent Wolf logo, stranded somewhere between man and graphic, Silent Wolf's dorky human half brother. Alongside it was a reproduction of the games hero and a note to say that the killer's appearance might resemble that image. Finally, it gave his name.

Stella and Brian Collier looked at it together. She said, "It's a risk. He goes to ground, or he changes his appearance—and if he really looks like this, that would be easy enough to do. There's a good chance he's already changed his name."

"I know." Collier shrugged. "But if he's really backing off, we have to go after him."

"Press release?" Stella asked.

"Everything . . . everywhere . . . Especially the tabloids, they'll love it."

An odd silence settles over hospitals at night, not a dead silence but a silence that certainly has something to do with death: as if there were a stealthy presence in the empty corridors, as if sleep might be just a step from oblivion.

In the midst of that silence, Neil Morgan woke up. He lay open-eyed for a while, the instruments around him registering the sudden metabolic change, then he raised an arm like a man waving to a friend. He tried to sit up, and the motion triggered a sensor that set off an alarm. A staff nurse rushed to the door of the side ward; another put in a call to the duty doctor.

Morgan smiled at the nurse, though he didn't know he was smiling. He spoke to her, though he didn't know what he was saying.

Aimée lay awake listening to the patter of her heartbeat. Peter slept at her side, unmoving. It had been another hot day, and the roof beams creaked as the house cooled.

The room was dimly lit by a low-wattage bulb on the landing and Aimée could see her clothes stored on a dressmaker's rail beyond the bed. She would take almost nothing with her, she had already decided on that, just a small bag of clothes and the few things that mattered to her. It was a new life and she wanted to start fresh. It would be wrong to put photographs about the place, wear the clothes she had always worn, behave as she'd always behaved. She wanted a new way of seeing the world.

She supposed she should feel guilty or afraid or both, but she didn't. Just tomorrow to get through, then everything would change. Her heart fluttered like a bird in a cage trying its wings.

Candice sat with a doctor in an office not far from the side ward. A few initial tests had been made, but at this time of night, it wasn't possible to explore Morgan's new waking state comprehensively. More tests would be arranged for the morning.

The doctor had good news and bad news. The good was obvious: Morgan had emerged from the coma. The bad was less easy to see at first, though it was there in the glazed look in his eyes and the randomness of his speech. The doctor spoke of neurological damage. He spoke for a while, using the terms of his trade, but the short and comprehensible version was that Neil Morgan was away with the fairies.

"Can he understand me?" Candice asked.

"It seems very unlikely."

"Can he respond to questions?"

"Well . . . no. Not in the way you mean."

"In what way, then?"

"We know so little about conditions of this sort. It's possible that he has his own method for interpreting the world and some sort of codified means of communicating with it, but in real terms—terms that you and I recognize—he's lost contact. His understanding of what's going on round him appears to be severely impaired, he can make sounds but not form words, and he's lost the ability to monitor and control his own actions."

"Will he recover?"

"People do."

"Will *he*?"

"It's impossible to say."

Candice managed to shout without raising her voice. "Make a guess."

The doctor shrugged. "All right. My guess is that he won't."

Candice returned to Morgan's bedside. He was propped up by a bed-back. He turned his head to look at her, then seemed to lose interest; he uttered a long, involved sentence that made no sense at all; when she leaned in close he recoiled slightly, then gave a little, wet laugh. Watching from her desk, the nurse thought Candice had leaned in to kiss her husband. This wasn't true. She was cursing him.

Candice knew that Morgan had numbered bank accounts offshore. She knew that only he knew those numbers. She knew that the accounts contained millions. They'd had conversations about that money. What if something should happen to you? What if you suddenly dropped dead?

Morgan's response had always been the same: "It's better that you don't know." Candice understood this to mean that the money wasn't strictly legal. It irked her to be kept in the dark, but she assumed that though she didn't know, someone would: the family solicitor, it had to be.

When Morgan was comatose and likely to die, she had got in touch with the solicitor and asked about the money. He had no knowledge of any such accounts. She told him that was impossible—he must have been told. He assured her that he had not. There were, of course, certain instructions in the case of death or impairment, but none of these made mention of off-shore accounts.

Which is why Candice had sat so long at Morgan's bedside, waiting, saying over and over like a prayer, *Don't die, you bastard.* Which is why she now leaned close to him, her lips at his ear, and cursed his soul to hell.

88

Two days later Costea Radu walked into the front office at Notting Dene and asked to speak to DS Stella Mooney. Costea the Pimp was wearing a three-quarter-length black leather coat, a black T-shirt, and a sunny smile. Stella called Frank Silano in to sit with them.

Costea said, "I got something you want."

Stella gave date and time to the tape, repeated what the man had said, and asked him to agree that he had, indeed, said it.

"Something you want."

"Which is?"

"Yeah, first I need something back—guarantee." He gave Stella a little knowing grin. "I got bail. You fix this. Good. This time, better deal, okay? This time I walk."

I didn't fix your bail, you creep, but I'm glad you think I did.

She said, "Difficult for me to give something in return for something you haven't yet given me."

Costea had to think this through. When the process was complete, he took the folded front page of a tabloid newspaper from his pocket. "This was yesterday. I know this guy."

"You do?"

"Not *know* him, not like that. I see him."

"Where?"

"Places . . ." Stella waited. "Places, around, I see him sometimes." The tape recorded Silano's cough, then silence. "I can tell you where is he, but there must be something for me."

"Tell me what you have in mind."

"Soon I am in court, yes?"

"And?"

"I give, you give."

Stella chose her words carefully. "I'm not able to offer any undertaking to you concerning the charges against you, or the outcome of your trial.

However, if any information you give to us does assist us in our inquiries, I'm prepared to let this be known to the court. DS Mooney ending the interview with Mr. Costea Radu."

She signed off with a time check. Costea looked at her, still smiling. He said, "And now?"

"Reduced sentence."

"Discharge."

"Oh, for Christ's sake . . ."

"Community service."

"You're facing kidnap and malicious wounding, bottom line."

"How bad you want this guy?"

"It's an offense to withhold information."

"Okay, I tell you I see this guy on tube, that help? I see him at airport, I see him in big car next to Queen Elizabeth."

"Where did you see him?" Stella asked. "Community service, a hundred hours. Last offer."

It made no difference to Costea whether it was a hundred hours or five thousand, because he wasn't planning to be the person doing it. He said, "Up on the Strip. Big house on the rise, he live there. Come with me and I show you."

Stella said, "Stay put. This officer will wait with you."

She ran to Collier's office. She said, "We might have a location. I think we have. I need authorization for sidearms issue, Hatton gun, extra bodies."

In the interview room Costea smiled at Silano, who smiled back. Costea's smile meant, *I know police. There's always a deal.* Silano's meant, *She was lying. You're going down.*

Gideon Woolf was walking the streets. He looked different now. The compu-fit was bad, had only appeared in two tabloids and didn't look much like him, but the picture of Silent Wolf made him particularly edgy: the clothes, the hair. He had worn a beanie to go out and buy a home dye, then taken his hair back to its natural brown. Black 501s and a loose shirt had taken the place of the combats and the long coat. He felt weakened; he felt insignificant.

How did they know about Silent Wolf?

Aimée had given him a mobile phone number in case of problems. He called her and listened carefully for any sign that she might have seen the papers. She sounded fine, excited, a woman in love. She repeated their meeting time to him and he said, yes, that was right, that was when the new life would begin.

He walked for an hour, circling, his head bowed. Silent Wolf stalked his footsteps. Their shadows collided and merged. He thought of his new life as Silent Wolf and his new life with Aimée and knew he had to choose.

She knows me. She knows who I am. She knows my name, and they know my name. Safer if she's dead.

As he walked, he thought of what the new life might have been. The image that came to him was of a couple standing on a hilltop and looking out over a placid valley where a river cut a silver seam, the man's arm round his lover's shoulders. He thought he'd seen it in a movie on the TV in the scorched room, the TV that was never switched off.

Gideon paused, as if he could see that scene in front of him; then Silent Wolf's shadow blotted it out.

Safer if she's dead—and soon . . .

He didn't know if the voice in his ear was his own or that of the hero.

Aimée had written a letter to Peter and Ben. It said many things, but mostly it said no way back. Ben had an after-school club, so he and Peter would both be home at about six o'clock, by which time Aimée would be clear and gone, on the train, somewhere else. She had thought she might feel something drawing her back—the child, perhaps—but all her thoughts lay in the future.

She packed a bag, taking, as she had promised herself, nothing of the past. The house was oppressive to her, the rooms stifling. She thought of Gideon and ached for him.

89

Stella Mooney in the scorched room, the TV on, the computer showing its yellow-eyed screen-saver.

Forensics had turned up the gun, the knife, the combats, the long coat. They had done their preliminary work and were now going through the rest of the house, though it was clear they had got what they wanted: the room was thick with traces. Stella was dressed in SOC whites, the hood up, her shoes covered. The sun was flooding the window and the burned smell scratched her sinuses.

Harriman came in looking rueful. "He picked the right time to be out."

Stella nodded. "Either he left in a hurry and won't be back, or he'll see the door off its hinges and police vehicles in the street."

"Why would he have left?"

"The pimp brought us here, but he could equally well have tipped Woolf off, just for fun. He thinks he's doing himself a favor, not us."

"Put the door back," Harriman suggested, "send forensics away, then sit and wait."

"News travels fast on the Strip."

"Sure, but—"

"If you like," Stella said. "Sounds reasonable. You fix it."

She sat in the operator's chair, brought up the Internet connection, and went to Bookmarks. Two men in orange jumpsuits and behind them the self-styled warriors. One of the warriors stepped forward, drawing a long knife.

Stella in top-to-toe white, a ghost in the scorched room.

Aimée had been to the supermarket: the last time she would drive that car, the last time she would make that round-trip. She brought the shopping indoors and packed it away in the fridge. It was food Peter could cook, food he and Ben particularly liked.

The last time she would be the good wife.

She put the letter on the mantelpiece where it could be seen. She went out, slamming the door and giving it a little shove, to ensure it was properly shut, the way she always did.

He didn't know where he was or how he'd got there. There was a band of pain behind his eyes and his legs felt weak, as if the battle of shadows had been a real contest and himself the loser.

Must I kill her?

He walked on, hearing only one answer to his question. The sun seemed to be bearing down on him and the roadside slipstream was a toxic mist. He turned away, finding a gate between railings, and then, suddenly, he was somewhere he knew, somewhere he recognized.

Aimée had known she would be early, but then why not? She was living the new life, she was stealing a little of their future before he came to claim his part.

She sat at their chosen bar in the station concourse with a glass of cold white wine and watched the travelers. Everyone with a purpose, everyone with a destination, everyone—Aimée included—brightened by the sun.

She checked her watch. She couldn't decide whether to look for him—to catch him coming across the concourse toward her, smiling as she rose to greet him—or to lose herself in her thoughts and allow herself to be surprised when he was suddenly there at her side.

I love you. I love you. I love you.

She was anonymous until he arrived and happy to be so. The sun struck rainbows from the bevel of her glass.

They had set up as Harriman suggested—door restored, vehicles cleared, officers waiting in the room, others deployed in the street to give warning. Activity on the Strip slowed to a near-halt, except for the curb-crawlers, who speeded up. It would be a semaphore to Woolf, and Stella knew it. She walked down the Strip and found Costea in a cubicle bar; when she walked in, the silence was cymbals and drums.

Costea pointed to the street. When they were outside, he said, "You come here, you find me, you do this to fuck me up?"

"To talk, that's all. He's not there."

"This is my problem?"

"Where else might he be?"

"Did I say this guy is my brother? I know where he live and I show you, what else you want me to do?" He glanced over his shoulder. "Fuck sake, these guys see me talking to you . . ."

"Would anybody else know? Did he use any of the girls?"

"No. Never fuck, never score, I didn't know him from that. Just see him going up and down. All I do—watch Strip, watch punters, watch girls. Watch out for me."

"Okay," Stella said. She looked up and down the street. "Everything's gone quiet."

"Yeah. Fuck, Mrs. Mooney, you are bad for business."

She headed back up to the rise, but then kept walking, as if she knew where she was going.

And, after a while, she did.

Aimée went to the station entrance, although they had arranged to meet at the bar. Then she went back. He wasn't outside, so she tried the barroom. Going from sunlight to the bar's dim interior made her half-blind, so she visited each table in turn, peering at people, barely noticing their indignant stares. He wasn't there.

She ran across the concourse to the platform where the train waited, their destination announced on the red LCD display, the digital clock ticking the time away. Then she made a tour of the shops, the newsagents, the cafés, before going back to the bar, back to the concourse, back to the platform. She was crying, though she hadn't noticed it.

But he'll come. There's time. He'll be here.

People were hurrying toward the gate that led to the train, hurrying in case they might miss it. Aimée thought that if she looked away, then back, he would be there, running, held up somehow but here now, and they would sprint for the train and get aboard just as it moved away, breathing hard, falling into each other's arms, and that moment, the moment when they nearly missed the train, would be a part of their new life, something they would laugh about sometimes, a story to tell their new friends.

She looked away, then looked back. He was nowhere.

90

Not chance: it wasn't anything remotely like that, and certainly not guesswork or de- duction. What had led Stella to her destination was a certain kind of knowledge that arrives unbidden: infallible, irresistible. It rose from the kind of certainty that brings to you, in a crowded street, the person you have just been thinking of.

•

The park was full of people but he was the only one Stella could see. He was sitting on a bench quite close to the tree where he had hanged Bryony; so much tension in him, so much grief, that it seemed to radiate. He didn't look much like himself, but as she got closer, Stella could see the indistinct lines of the Indian-ink homemade tattoo on the inside of his left forearm. Closer still, she saw it clearly, though she had known what it would be.

∧ ∧
∨

The procedure was keep your distance, observe, follow if necessary, don't approach, call for backup. She took out her phone, turned to face away from him, pressed a speed-dial number, spoke two sentences, then turned back. He was still there, sitting quietly, his hands in his lap, his forearms upturned as if to catch the sun. As she walked toward him, he leaned back on the bench, looking up at the tree, and Stella followed his eye line to where a breeze shifted the leaves and the leaves scattered sunlight.

She sat down next to him. She said, "I know who you are."

The train pulled out.

Aimée watched it until it was out of sight. The platform was empty, but if she looked hard enough, if she refused to look away, there was a ghost train with two ghost passengers, the only two aboard, sitting in a window seat and watching her as she watched them leave. She raised a hand to wave, but the image wouldn't hold.

Something kept him. Something prevented him. Something not his fault.

She knew it wasn't so.

She went through the concourse at a dead run, howling. She teetered in a wild arc, her arms outstretched, her mouth wide open, as the other travelers, the ones with somewhere to go and someone to go with, moved away, amazed.

There was no one near her as she ran, spinning, arms out, a mad woman, shouting his name, over and over, as if he might hear her, as if, even now, he might come.

Stella Mooney and Gideon Woolf, side by side on the bench.

She spoke to him in a voice that was both soft and low, and he nodded, listening carefully, because she seemed to know all sorts of things, and understand them too. His life seemed clearer to him when she talked about it, his needs more obvious, his reasons more credible.

After a while, it was his turn to speak, his voice barely more than a whisper, letting her in on secrets, sharing hopes, answering all her questions, his newfound friend, his patient confidante.

91

Gideon Woolf sat in a holding cell at Notting Dene. It was daylight outside, but dark in the cell and a light high on the wall threw a pale shadow. His shadow. His own.

He stood up and extended his arms and the shadow flew. He smiled because things had turned out well.

Now he wouldn't have to kill Aimée, which was good.

Now the world would know him for himself, which was good.

Now there would be no more talk of cowardice or betrayal.

He would tell them everything. He had already made a start with the woman who had sat with him on the bench. When the others arrived and had driven him to this place, he had continued to talk. He was anxious to let them know who he was and what he was capable of, because the more he explained the more he understood.

The only thing he would keep from them was the moment when Silent Wolf stood on the prison wall, searchlights scanning the towers, the siren blaring, guards with rifles running this way and that, the Wolf's silhouette stark and clear for just a moment before he swung down into the city streets and was lost to sight.

It was as if the house had exhausted most of its oxygen.

Aimée's breath came short and shallow. There were tiny silver spangles flickering at the corner of her vision, and she felt as if each step might pitch her forward onto her face. She took the note from the mantelpiece and opened it, going line by line, as if she were reading it for the first time. Then she burned it.

It was ten to six. She sat on a kitchen stool and looked round—everything just as she'd left it, everything as it should be—and wondered how it could be possible that she was there in that utterly strange place.

Somewhere the hiss and rumble of a high-speed train.

Somewhere a landscape beyond a window.

Two people looking out, side by side, lovers in love.

When Peter came through the door ten minutes later, Aimée was preparing dinner. There were days when he brought her flowers, and this was one of them.

A day like any other.

92

Rain came in from the west.

It rained for three days without stopping, which slowed the city down. The tailbacks were longer, tempers were shorter. The AMIP-5 squad wrote reports and signed off, one by one, the job done. Brian Collier was a happy man. There was still the catch-up paperwork, of course, but he'd already vowed "never again."

Stella hadn't ever taken a liking to Collier, but a corner had been turned when he'd got shot saving Donna from a certain gang rape. And at least he hadn't been hitting on her, a fact she shared with Maxine Hewitt.

"No," Maxine said, "he's been hitting on me. He tells me he's blessed with a gigantic cock."

"I can't vouch for it," Stella said. "Did you tell him you're gay?"

"Oh, sure."

"He didn't believe you."

"Apparently, I need a gigantic cock to change my life. Is our man still talking?"

"As if he'll never stop. His life is one big adventure in which the bad guys go down and justice is served."

"His brief will go for post-traumatic stress disorder."

"All this could have been avoided," Stella observed, "if he had simply done his job."

"His job?"

"Killing people."

Stanley Bowman didn't really notice the rain, he was too busy dealing and playing, playing and dealing. Just now he was in a West End casino looking at ace/king of diamonds in the hole and two diamonds in the flop.

He had received the call from Vanechka and given the code word. The call had proceeded just as Bowman had expected, but what he didn't know was that the code word had sent a little shock wave down the line. It was the word he'd been given by Ricardo, but it was a bad word: not the wrong word, but a word that meant, *Deal this guy out and fast*; that meant, *This money is tainted, this money is cutting a pathway that will take you straight to jail.*

He caught a high diamond on the river and went all in. At just the same moment his dirty money was traveling at terrific speed back up the laundry line and making a noise like a lit fuse. The people who had received Stella's tip-off would see it and know what it meant. They would intercept the money and reroute it, just to keep things flowing, just to keep Bowman sweet. When they'd got everything, *everything*, then they'd make their move.

A player with three jacks thought he saw a bluff and matched the bet. Bowman flipped up his ace/king. He smiled the smile of a man who expected to win.

A Rich List smile.

Lawyers had asked questions and doctors had given the answers: they didn't expect Neil Morgan to recover his faculties. Candice wondered what unbelievably, unspeakably, unchangeably shitty luck had brought her to this. She sat at his bedside and asked him for the numbers of the offshore accounts; he responded with a wet grin. She asked him again; he grinned again. She was surprised to find just how deep hatred could go.

The lawyers had taken note of a clause in Morgan's papers that read "if I die or become incapable of managing my affairs." The instruction concerned a woman named Abigail Gray, and the file contained a letter that should be delivered to her. There were clear instructions to the lawyers that all this should be dealt with as a matter of the strictest confidence. When Abigail opened the letter, which she would three weeks later when clearances had been secured, she would find the names of several banks, each with an account number beside it. The number alone was authorization for withdrawal of funds.

Beyond the rain-streaked window, planes were dropping out of the cloud cover, one every half minute. Candice thought Barbados would be nice. For Neil, a day nurse and a night nurse; for herself, sea, sand, and sex. She would take the flight a week later, sharing business class with Sekker and his girl, who were beating the hurricane season, just as they'd planned.

Stella touched base with Mike Sorley and got him on his mobile. He was taking a walk by the river, and Stella could hear the sound of rain rattling his umbrella.

"Should you be out in this?"

"Light exercise is what the doctors said."

"You got my report?"

"They'll go for post-traumatic stress disorder."

"That's what DC Hewitt said."

"What was it with the MP—Morgan?"

"Pro-war, like Martin Turner, but we now know that he was mixed up with a company that deals arms, a nonexecutive director."

"A fixer."

"That would be it, yes. And recipient of a fat backhander."

"You think Woolf knew?"

"It's doubtful, boss. Any idea of when you'll be fit for work?"

"Soon. Definitely. A week or so. I heard DI Collier hasn't enjoyed his time behind a desk."

"You heard right."

"But did he do a good job?"

"Ask the SIO," Stella said, "but, look, it's a piece of piss, isn't it—shuffling a few files around, issuing memos."

Sorley sat on a bench under his umbrella and watched the rain dimpling the water. He lit a cigarette and inhaled deeply.

Just this one.

93

When the rain stopped, the summer came back in: clear skies, a hot sun. Everything dried off and London moved back outdoors. In the square by Machado's restaurant, tables had been set out and strings of white lights hung in the trees.

Stella and John Delaney were drinking champagne and sharing a seafood platter. The champagne was because Delaney had signed off on his Rich List. Editorial tact had removed Neil Morgan from the series.

Stella said, "Any of them you liked?"

"No. Well, Bowman, classy sort of guy, you know . . . cool operator."

"Not a job you enjoyed."

"It paid well."

"Yeah, sure."

"It wrote easily."

"You hated it."

Delaney laughed. "Okay, I hated it." He poured champagne, then up-turned the empty bottle in the ice bucket and signaled for more.

Stella tapped the back of his hand. It meant "listen." She said, "I know what you're thinking and I know why you're not sharing it with me."

"Think so?"

"You're thinking of a war zone."

He looked genuinely surprised. "Shit-hot Detective Mooney."

"You're thinking of the old life, and you're thinking that feature articles are for has-beens." He was silent. She asked, "Seen anyone yet?"

"A couple of people." He didn't mention Martin Turner; it seemed un-necessarily complicated. "Look, Stella—"

"Any takers?"

He shrugged. Then: "Well, yes . . ."

"Will you go?"

He drank the last of his champagne. The swifts were back, circling and banking, their cries lacing the night air.